BRYANT & MAY
London Bridge Is Falling Down

CHRISTOPHER FOWLER

PENGUIN BOOKS

TRANSWORLD PUBLISHERS

Penguin Random House, One Embassy Gardens,
8 Viaduct Gardens, London SW11 7BW
www.penguin.co.uk

Transworld is part of the Penguin Random House group of companies
whose addresses can be found at global.penguinrandomhouse.com

Penguin
Random House
UK

First published in Great Britain in 2021 by Doubleday
an imprint of Transworld Publishers
Penguin paperback edition published 2022

A CIP catalogue record for this book
is available from the British Library.

ISBN 9781529176674

Offset in Sabon by Jouve (UK), Milton Keynes.
Printed and bound in Great Britain by Clays Ltd, Elcograf S.p.A.

The authorized representative in the EEA is Penguin Random House Ireland,
Morrison Chambers, 32 Nassau Street, Dublin D02 YH68.

Penguin Random House is committed to a sustainable
future for our business, our readers and our planet. This book
is made from Forest Stewardship Council® certified paper.

For Pete, for all of it

PART ONE

London exists because of London Bridge.

Peter Jackson

I

THE GIRL ON THE CROSSING

May in Regent's Park could put a spring in the step of a corpse.

Crimson and saffron flowerbeds, enamelled lawns, fountains glittering beneath an azure sky. Twelve thousand roses in Queen Mary's Garden, blossoming in a riotous display of colour that was positively vulgar. The month brought forth scented air and warmth to the back of the neck.

Sammi Jansome's hand hurt. She had spent the previous afternoon slicing lemons and her knife had slipped. The lemon juice had got under the dressing and made her wince every time she lifted a tray. She'd had to stop and buy some waterproof plasters in Boots but there'd been a queue and now she was running later than usual. Usually she wore her black Adidas trainers and changed in the staff dressing room, but this morning she had snapped a lace while retying it on the tube and had been forced to don her pumps.

She cut through the park from its lower corner near Baker Street, heading for her shift at the US ambassador's residence. Winfield House stood behind fifteen-foot-high black iron gates that appeared decorative but could withstand a missile attack.

The bland chocolate box of a building on the north-west side of the park had been commissioned by the Woolworth heiress Barbara Hutton, who had lived there with her husband, Cary Grant. Once it had provided hunting grounds for boar and deer. Now its marquees held smug receptions and charity fundraisers in the vast manicured garden.

Sammi was the toastmistress responsible for charging glasses. There were rarely fewer than two hundred guests in the watery green garden room. The champagne glasses had to be half filled before the room was opened, then topped up as they were handed out.

Right now the sergeant-at-arms would be ensuring that the same geometric volume of glassware was available on every table. Someone else would set out individual chocolates, spacing them equally across the tables. The treats were decorated with Belgian fondant, each dressed with a tiny red satin sash like Christmas tree ornaments. They hid the fact that no expensive savoury canapés were being served this afternoon. The Grade I tuna had been set aside for tomorrow's event with the Japanese ambassador.

Her task was simple and exact, and slotted in with a hundred small tasks performed by other employees to form a seamless whole. The ambassador's residence had too many staff and too much protocol. Its laws were as rigid and inviolable as those at a Tudor court.

Sammi couldn't wait to leave her job, but at least it made up for the chaos of her home life. Having to stash her daughter in a dilapidated Bayswater hotel room while she waited for new accommodation was tough on both of them. She always warned Doto to stay in her room because some of the residents looked untrustworthy, especially the badly shaved men who hung around the lobby.

Sammi saw that she was four minutes behind schedule and quickened her step, heading towards the barrier of clipped hedges that marked the park's Outer Circle. A sudden breeze swept over the parklands in a twisting undertow that ruffled the feathers of swans and ducks, fluttering the new foliage on the trees.

The park's curving road was among the quietest and most beautiful in the capital. Sammi wondered if she would be able to escape today's event by eight. She needed to press her uniform, get Doto's dinner, pay off all of her outstanding bills. Time out of work needed to be minutely planned.

The black and grey Daimler was a dinosaur of a vehicle, its heavy polished panels fronted with an immense chrome radiator grille and six lamps. It was travelling at surprising speed around the park's outer perimeter.

Larry Cranston had a naturally bad-tempered outlook coupled with the twitchy impatience of someone in a long queue. Although he thought a lot, very little came of it, and right now his mind was far away.

He needed to make some big money fast, before his debts were called in. There were some people you could delay paying back, like your tailor or your vintner, and others you simply could not mess around. He ran through a list of names, trying to recall how his credibility stood with each of them. The importer from Guangzhou had seemed amenable but could turn nasty. He knew some very unpleasant people. What was his name?

Cranston failed to see the crossing because he was trying to remember how much interest he owed the importer. If he had looked up he would have seen a small woman in a hurry, a flash of red sweater, short black hair, a blue nylon backpack. His nearside headlamp caught a jeaned leg and snagged the material, spinning something under the front wheel of the car so that one moment she was on the crossing and the next gone.

The Daimler slammed to a stop, as much as it could.

Cranston clambered out and looked about himself. There was no one around to see what had happened. He began to doubt that he had even glimpsed someone on the crossing.

When he dropped to his knees and peered under the nearside tyre he saw what looked like a bundle of clothes. Cranston's whisky-fogged brain began to reconstruct what had just happened.

The body was dark and tiny, trapped beneath the Daimler's rear nearside wheel and its arch. It looked terribly smashed up, the ribs quite flattened, but he could see no blood. He peered closer: a slender hand, a twisted shoe, a split bag. There was obviously nothing he could do for her.

He couldn't simply drive off. Although the road was utterly deserted there were cameras everywhere protecting the embassies and residences. He could be seen from a dozen different angles.

Cranston put his hand to his mouth. His breath was rank with alcohol. He needed to get to a pub and down a brandy or two, then say he'd needed a drink to steady his nerves after the accident. Because it *was* an accident, her suddenly jumping out like that without any warning. Actually, it was her fault for not looking properly.

He heard a groan from beneath the car. Was she still alive or was it the metal settling? He bent down. He was sure that an eye was fixing him accusingly.

'Listen, don't try to move, OK? You've had a bit of a nasty tumble. I'm sorry if you feel I was going too fast. I'm off to get help.'

Making his way over to the Windsor Castle, he entered the deserted bar and ordered himself a large Rémy Martin, downing it with shaking hands. Then he called the police.

As Deputy Chief Constable Dean Marshall cruised the park's Outer Circle he spotted the Daimler, angled and distanced from the kerb. The driver was missing and the engine was switched off.

Lying flat on the ground, he prepared himself. The body was tangled under one of the rear wheels, badly mangled, twisted about itself. It looked as if she had been snagged and dragged, then tumbled beneath the braking vehicle. The plastic swipe card around her neck gave him an ID. Sammi Jansome, a Latvian national and staff member of the US ambassador's residence.

He reached under to touch her wrist and was about to test for a pulse.

'It's OK, we're on it,' said a young woman behind him. The ambulance had arrived in swift silence and the EMT leader in military-green fatigues was looking down at him, gloving up. 'We'll get her out.'

'I think she's dead,' Marshall said, rising and standing back as the team went to work. He walked around the Daimler and saw that it had *Corps diplomatique* plates. Embassy officials considered themselves above the law.

The Daimler's brakes had been applied about seventy feet from its stopping point. The speedometer was an old analogue one but by calculating the vehicle's momentum from its mass and velocity Marshall could tell that the driver had been hitting thirty in a twenty-mile-an-hour zone. The ground was dry and smooth, but the front tyres had failed to scorch the tarmac.

All of which was likely to place the girl legitimately on or very near the zebra crossing. Marshall stuck his head through the open window of the Daimler. The interior stank of alcohol – whisky by the smell of it. When he stood up he saw a sweaty, overweight businessman in his early thirties with slicked-back hair, dressed in an expensive suit two sizes too small. He was moving towards him like a drunk whose life depended on not tripping over. Marshall had limited experience of such people, but he didn't look much like a diplomat.

'Hello, I'm Larry Cranston. I'm rather afraid I was driving.' The voice was British and upper-class, ludicrously so. He stuck out his hand in introduction. Marshall stared at it.

'Where have you been, sir?' he asked.

'Awful thing. I was shaken up. I needed a drink to steady myself so I went over there.' He pointed in the direction of the Windsor Castle pub, although it could not be seen from the main road. He might just have emerged from a Turkish bath, he was sweating so much. 'I couldn't get a signal on my phone and needed to call in the accident, but when I got there it started working.'

'So you called the ambulance here.' Marshall walked back to his car and took out a Breathalyser kit.

Cranston saw the kit and backed off. It was the last thing he wanted to see. 'I don't need that. I just had a brandy to buck me up.'

'The car smells of alcohol, sir.'

'Well, there were people in it last night who had been drinking. Obviously not the driver.'

Marshall handed him the kit. 'Please just follow the instructions.'

Cranston's faltering bonhomie vanished altogether when he registered two and a half times over the legal alcohol limit. A second test confirmed the excess.

'I need to make a couple of calls,' he said, digging for his phone.

'You can do that when we get to the station.'

'Can't I call now?'

'You can but anything you say in the car will be recorded and can be used against you. It would be better to wait.'

Mr Cranston seemed amazed, as if he had committed a minor traffic offence and had not expected there to be any consequences.

'Do you feel unwell, sir?'

'Well, I have a bit of a headache—'

'You do realize you hit a pedestrian, don't you?'

'Yes, I suppose so. I thought it was just a bump.'

'A young woman.'

'Oh. Is she all right?'

'No, sir, she is under there.' He pointed to the medics man-oeuvring a steel tray beneath the girl's legs. 'You didn't see her?'

Cranston slicked his hair back in place. 'Funny thing, she must have just stepped out of nowhere.'

'On the clearly marked zebra crossing.' Marshall pointed to the Belisha beacons at either end.

Cranston shook with denial. 'No, no, I don't think she could have been. If that had been the case I would most cer-tainly have seen her.'

'Let's get your statement down while my lads take a look at the car. They'll be able to reconstruct an accurate sequence of events even if you can't.'

Cranston glanced back at the Daimler crossly. 'Is this going to take very long?'

'You're under arrest, sir, so it'll be as long as it takes.'

Cranston looked at his wrists. 'Are you going to handcuff me?'

'That won't be necessary.'

A light flickered in Cranston's dazed eyes. 'I know I sound English but I'm actually an American citizen. I've lived there most of my life.'

'Don't worry, I'm not going to kneel on your throat.' Mar-shall lowered Cranston's head as he guided him into the back seat of the police BMW.

'I think you'll find I'm exempt from British law,' Cranston called from within the vehicle.

'Let's get the paperwork done first,' suggested DCC Marshall.

2

THE END

'You can't say those things,' Simon Sartorius whispered.

'I can say whatever I like about my life,' replied Arthur Bryant. 'It was me who lived it.'

The editor imperceptibly narrowed his eyes. 'You know you could be cancelled over some of your opinions.'

'Oh, I do hate these neologisms. Trains and newspapers get cancelled, not people. The book contains my opinions, and opinions are not facts. To what specifically are you objecting?'

The publisher breathed out and thought of the dog-eared, grubby-edged manuscript with which he had been presented. 'Well, all of it really.'

The old man beside him leaned closer, exhaling sherbet lemon fumes. 'But of all the investigations I've allowed you to render into print this is the most essential. *Cela explique tout!* It's the key to understanding our working methods and explains how we finally came to such a ghastly, ignominious end.'

Sartorius was unconvinced.

Bryant attempted to plead his case. 'These are the definitive memoirs of our unit, Simon. I didn't make any of it up; it all happened, sort of. The police need to win the hearts and minds of the public, and when my readers get to this final volume they'll see why we acted the way we did. It's a key, like King Lear confiding to the audience that he's had blinding head-aches lately, a useful explanatory footnote that Shakespeare never got around to adding. Fair play, the Bard banged out some crackers in his time but he could have explained what he was on about a bit more. Why not have Ophelia admit she was brassed off before going down to the river?'

Oh Lord, he's comparing himself to Shakespeare now, thought Sartorius. 'Perhaps you could tighten up the narra-tive,' he suggested. 'It's rather confusing.'

'Ah yes, sorry about that. I accidentally included some pages from *The Comparative Linear Densities of Fibres*, a fasci-nating reference work in its own right but not one which elucidates the present page-turner.'

Sartorius sat back and studied the scrofulous old gentleman at his side. In the background the song 'A View To A Kill' played on, rescored for a Hammond organ. Its melody was strangulated and painful, like an escape of trapped wind dur-ing prayers.

What can I do? Simon worried. *Tell the old boy we're end-ing his contract? His previous volumes of memoirs had a slightly higher batting average than expected but he can't have many more games left in him.*

'The manuscript needs a bit of knocking in,' he began cau-tiously. 'If I were to take this on, would you agree to some changes?'

The editor's cricketing terminology passed Arthur Bryant by. He was engaged in laboriously unwrapping a boiled sweet. 'I've finished the sherbet lemons. Do you want a rhubarb & custard? What sort of changes?'

'Well, we might have to whack the ending into the long grass. It's a bit over the top.'

'It's exactly how I remember it.'

'That's what worries me. Perhaps you could make it less . . . fanciful.'

'I'm not sure that will please my readers. Mind you, they're a fickle bunch. They're bound to post rude remarks on Amazon saying it's not as good as the last one. I have to trust them to see through the more exuberant sections to the inner truths beneath. After all, what is truth?'

'Well, it's the facts about something rather than what's imagined or invented.'

'And if I add some more of these little "truths" of yours, do we have a deal for the next volume?'

Sartorius considered the idea. 'Tentatively,' he whispered, and then immediately hated himself.

'Well, if it's time to pad up and head out on to the pitch once more I think this calls for a celebration. Shall we have a magnum of something shamefully decadent?'

'Mr Bryant, we're in a crematorium.'

Sartorius looked back at the handful of black-clad mourners in attendance. Before them, red velvet curtains were draped on either side of a spotlit coffin. The pre-recorded organ music switched to the theme from *Titanic*. It sounded as if it was being strained through a sock.

'Oh, but death is a celebration of life, don't you think?' said Bryant rather too loudly. ' "In my father's house are many mansions." If death is a room it would be the grand ballroom, and I'm already in the vestibule peeping through the door.'

Several mourners shushed him. He leaned on his malacca walking stick and rose to his feet. 'Let's get out of here. This music's giving me the pip. "My Heart Will Go On"? It seems unlikely, seeing as his has just been burned to a crisp.'

The woman in black beside him started crying as Bryant pushed past, the editor helplessly following his lead.

'Why do people make such a fuss about living and dying?'

he asked, leading the way through the ice-pack of chairs. 'All it takes to get through life is a spirit of resigned amusement. Anyway, three weeks is too long to wait for a funeral. If he was a chicken Kiev they'd have had to throw him away by now.'

The ex-wife of the deceased proffered a white-gloved hand. 'Thank you for coming, Arthur. I'm sure you must find Herbert's death upsetting.'

'Not half as upsetting as when he was alive, I assure you.' He pressed her glove and moved on.

Mr Arthur Bryant was a living legend only in the sense that he tended to come across as a fanciful conceit built up around a kernel of truth. Ageless, graceless, penniless, ineluctable and occasionally insensible, a champion of underdogs, an enemy of overlords, a beacon of bewilderment in uncertain times. Also London's longest-serving detective. Beloved by staff, detested by bureaucrats, he was perhaps not the best ambassador for modern policing methods but by crikey he knew how to track down a murderer.

With his snowy tonsure, crinkled features and alarming false teeth, his stout barrel body and rolling sailor gait, Bryant cut an odd figure crossing the emerald lawn of Golders Green Crematorium, ignoring the 'Keep Off the Grass' signs. Like any very senior senior he had his good and bad days, but today was so good that Simon Sartorius had to raise his pace to stay abreast of him.

'Actually, I shall miss Herbert, or "Spotty" as we used to call him,' Bryant exclaimed, 'a brilliant biochemist and the last of the gentleman confidence tricksters. He once sold a friend of mine her own house. What a card. I suppose there's a chance he's not even dead. I said that to his widow. One tries to give hope wherever one can.'

'Do you go to the funerals of all your informants?' asked Sartorius.

'Only the ones with indiscreet relatives. That's how I found out about the Warren Street kipper scandal. They were hiding cocaine in their fillets.'

'About your manuscript: I will need to run it past our legal team,' Sartorius warned. 'There could be serious implications both for the unit and for you personally.'

'Oh, don't worry about that.' Bryant waved the thought aside and tramped between the brass memorial plates set in the grass like museum descriptions. 'The Peculiar Crimes Unit has gone. Rain stopped play, as you'd say.'

The editor was surprised. 'Oh, I didn't realize. That must have come as a shock to you.'

'Not at all. We'd long been expecting it.'

'You'll be able to enjoy your retirement then.'

'There are some things to do first. I have to stop us from being killed.'

'Us?' A look of alarm swept across his editor's face.

'Don't look so worried.' He clapped Sartorius on the arm. 'I've got it all worked out. It may seem an utter shambles but everything ties up very neatly at the end. You wait and see.'

Sartorius watched as the odd little man examined the memorial plots, deadheading the bouquets that failed to meet his approval with the end of his walking stick.

3

THE MEMO

PECULIAR CRIMES UNIT
A Metropolitan Police special unit founded in 1944 with a remit to prevent or cause to cease any acts of public affright or violent disorder committed in the municipal and communal areas of the city of London.

The Old Warehouse
231 Caledonian Road
London N1 9RB

STAFF ROSTER, MONDAY 10 JUNE

Raymond Land, Unit Chief
Arthur Bryant, Detective Chief Inspector
John May, Detective Chief Inspector
Janice Longbright, Detective Inspector
Dan Banbury, Crime Scene/Forensics
Meera Mangeshkar, Detective Sergeant
Colin Bimsley, Detective Sergeant

Sidney Hargreaves, Intern or something
Giles Kershaw, Forensic Pathologist (off-site)
Strangeways, office cat

PRIVATE & CONFIDENTIAL MEMO
FROM: RAYMOND LAND
TO: ALL PCU STAFF

I have something very exciting to say to you all.
  Goodbye.
  This is the last email I will ever have to send out. It's going-home time. As your unit head I'm required to give three months' notice. When I suggested leaving early the Home Office was most enthusiastic. As I look around this office for the last time, from the one-legged pigeon that stares at me through the window to the weird green patches on the ceiling and the disappearing floorboards, I know I'm doing the right thing.

  Our counterparts at the Met used to arrest drug-dealers by counting the Ferraris on council estates. Now they're seizing rapid-fire weapons from gang bosses using encrypted comms. We're in North London, not Iraq.

  Nobody's job gets easier. Look at us. We had to work without support and even do our own building repairs, which would have been simpler if the two Daves hadn't sent Janice's belt sander out of the window. I've seen memos accusing me of incompetence. I was copied in on them. I admit it upsets me. I'm not like Mr Bryant, who's reached the point where he doesn't care what anyone thinks of him.

  I like to think I made a difference. I brought in new legislation to prevent the playing of Christmas songs in police vehicles and implemented health and safety rules after our last fire. My loyalty has been beyond question. When charges were made against you lot I always intended to give you support. I held the line against the unit's closure. It's a different world out there now.

Our unit took the cases the Serious Crime Command wouldn't touch with sterilized forceps. There was more than enough work to keep us busy. And why? Because we still went out on the streets. Most local officers are deskbound. God knows what they do all day but they're not trying to make drunks stand upright while their mates throw kebabs at them.

If you've been to Paris you'll know that areas around stations are meant to be disgusting, but this neighbourhood of ours has been transformed into an overpriced millennial wonderland. The sex clubs have been turned into salad bars. Even the brothel on Belgrove Street has become a gluten-free macaroon parlour. If it wasn't for the amusement arcade on the corner there wouldn't even be any rent boys. Male prostitution has always been a traditional trade around here, like blacksmithing.

Our remit is as out of date as Mr Bryant's trousers. We've joined the list of things nobody wants any more, like desk calendars and Nigel Farage. This morning the Home Office is finally making good on its long-standing promise to close the unit. They've asked me to help improve their efficiency by not being here and I'm happy to comply with their wishes. I've emptied my desk and will be catching the 2.30 p.m. from London Bridge. I'm heading back in time to the Isle of Wight. That's the last you'll see of me. I leave behind my Harry and Meghan commemorative tea mug and an unused set of office dumbbells.

Before I go let me give you a word of advice.

As you know, our last investigation was our last investigation. You may have noticed that the Met officers came in and took their equipment back, leaving only your personal laptops and effects, Mr Bryant's 'medicinal' herbs and

Strangeways. The furniture in the operations room has to be returned to the various places you stole it from. Mr Bryant's Black Museum of criminal artefacts, his unstable petri dish experiments and his collection of Mexican novelty pencil sharpeners, which are not only impractical but anatomically inaccurate, would have been confiscated if the lock on his door hadn't been electrified.

'It wasn't a very high voltage,' said Bryant indignantly. 'It worked better than that tear-gas thing we rigged up last year.'

If anyone else has anything dodgy left in their lockers, now's the time to get rid of it. I'm handing out investigation disclosure forms. The Home Office needs to confirm that you have no ongoing cases on the books before they can proceed. Please return them to me within the next hour, and don't add vulgar drawings, Colin. After officially releasing you from duty today you will be required to vacate the building immediately, and not hang around outside like a bunch of benefit scroungers waiting for the next iPhone to come out.

When the dust has settled and this place has been turned into a vegan fondue bistro, perhaps we can meet up for a meat-free sausage or something. In the meantime, my advice for dealing with the Home Office is: answer their questions politely, agree to everything and under no circumstances tell them why the operations room smells funny. We do not want them taking the floorboards up. I think you all remember why.

I know you don't believe me but I'll miss this chamber of horrors. It's full of – well, I wouldn't say wonderful memories, more like things that still make me jump when I wake up in the night. Mr Bryant accusing complete strangers of murder; Colin falling out of the window in a witness interrogation; Dan setting fire to his jumper with a taser during his Safety First presentation; me getting strangled. And the happier moments, of which I'm sure there were one or two.

You know the drill for being shut down, you've been threatened with it at least twenty times in the past. Unfortunately, this time there'll be no last-minute reprieve. When the unit was founded in the 1940s, it was, I'm told, immediately placed on the at-risk list and has remained there ever since. We were never accorded any respect, and I think I know why. We're too smart for our own good. This is England; nobody likes a clever dick. We prefer plodding all-rounders with common sense.

When I see Colin eating microwave noodles over the bin because they're too hot not to fall out of his mouth but he can't wait for them to cool down, I don't think of him as an impartial custodian of British democracy. But clearly somebody fears what we know, because my every attempt to put us on a more respectable footing has been met with contempt and dismissal. The interconnected cyberworld of modern policing is no place for a unit that still puts tinsel round its windows at Christmas, so let's give them their pyrrhic victory and move on.

On a personal note, I shall miss the police cake bake-offs and the PCU Film Club nights, despite those Hungarian films about shepherds Mr Bryant made us sit through. There was always a sense of camaraderie when we were together, even if we were just trying to revive Strangeways or listening to one of Dan's incomprehensible talks on webcam cables.

Last month I had the great satisfaction of turning down my ex-wife Leanne's attempt to get back with me after she decided that life in a caravan with a penniless Welsh flamenco instructor was not to her liking. Perhaps it's time for us all to fly away and be free. Bearing this in mind, I've narrowed down my options to travelling the Samarkand Silk Road or building a loft extension. I'm opening the doors of your cages, sending you into the world. Get the flock out of here.

I'm sure you will all find other jobs. I'm told the hospitality and service sectors are 'where it's at' these days. Amazon has positions open for anyone interested in heavy lifting. Do whatever your heart dictates. Just don't join the Met as a number-cruncher. You don't have the discipline for it.

If you can't find alternative employment I'll try to arrange compensation from the Home Office. I probably have some pull there after meeting their head of HR at a speed-dating night in Dartford. She came out with some pretty embarrassing revelations after her second bottle of Prosecco, I can tell you. I still feel guilty about putting her on the wrong train home. And never calling her.

As for our senior detectives, they're due a well-earned rest. There will be no more rewriting witness statements to improve the syntax, no more embarrassing social faux pas at awards dinners. I still cringe at the thought of Mr Bryant asking the leader of Camden Council if she'd had Botox or a stroke.

'How was I to know?' Bryant complained. 'No wonder she poured custard over me.'

'And cut our funding,' replied May.

Obviously I'm disappointed with the way things turned out. I thought that one day we might be recognized in the field. Instead I'm afraid we might be recognized in the street.

I never asked for much in life and I never got it. I feel sorry for those of you who are now stuck with time to kill before your expiry dates. I'm sure you'll think of something to do. It only remains for me to wish you the best of luck in the future and to remember that not everything was my fault.

Let's not say goodbye, but *au revoir*.

On second thoughts, let's say goodbye.

4

THE GET OUT OF JAIL CARD

The city's copper light shone on the low cloud ceiling.

The neon spears of its office buildings dissolved halfway but their glowing windows continued upward into the murk so that they appeared to shine suspended in the sky. Grey mist condensed in the streets, stripping away the clues of time, but there could be absolutely no mistaking the familiar skyline that rose by the banks of the great river.

New York City.

Paige Henderson pulled off her woollen Kangol cap and slid on to the red leatherette bench seat opposite her former mentor. She looked about the diner, took in the red walls, red tables, red meat. She hated this place. It was like having a meal inside a human body.

She had agreed to meet Benjamin Alvarez in one of the last unironic, old-fashioned diners left in TriBeCa. 'I'm running late. My hotel had no broadband tonight, how is that possible?'

'You're in Columbus Circle?'

'How do you know?'

'That was us,' Alvarez admitted. 'There was a security breach earlier and we had to kill some comms. We traced it back to a British hacker who'd "accidentally" found his way into the system.'

Alvarez beckoned her into the place setting laid out beside him. 'We get a lot of random attacks from incels with grievances. There's no network, no organization, just a bunch of low-spectrum guys eager to be a pain in the ass. If we had to, we could run this city without communications technology. Crash the network and it would still function.'

'How do you figure that?'

Alvarez looked at her as if she was stupid. 'It's an island, Paige. Shut the bridges and you could control things from here with a team of foot messengers. Most of the people who really matter know each other. Actually, I'd prefer that. No traceability.' He looked around for a waiter. 'How's jolly old London?'

'More like here than you'd expect. The same population but twice the size. It really shouldn't work but kind of does.'

Alvarez caught the waiter's eye and ordered for both of them, two Scotch rocks and two chilli burgers, just like the old days. 'You're a closet European, Paige. I don't know why we still trust you.'

'I'd stay on if my husband wasn't buying the fixer-upper in Woodstock. It has no electricity. It's not a fixer-upper, it's a tearer-downer but city ordinance, what can you do? Looks like the end of my plans for a longer posting.'

Alvarez shrugged. 'I don't know how you lasted so long. You can't buy Velveeta, Cheez-Its or ranch dressing in England. Call that civilized?'

'Believe it or not, Europe doesn't think a balanced meal is a hamburger in each hand.' Paige accepted a tumbler of Scotch from the waiter and set it down with her hands flat on the checked tablecloth, as if waiting for a starting pistol.

'Deborah keeps saying we should try for San Diego. She

tells me it has sea and sunshine and outdoor activities, like she's trying to get a five-year-old to eat vegetables.'

'So you'll be heading west just when I get back to the East Coast.' Paige lifted her hands and took up the tumbler, touching it to Alvarez's.

Alvarez swigged his whisky almost as if it was mouthwash. 'I heard you've been doing great things without my help.'

This was how it had always been between them, teacher and pupil. They were ex-MIT, both statisticians and social scientists at heart, but Ben had not moved on. Whenever Paige was back in his circle he reminded her that he had taught her everything. But she had proved herself since then. After four years in London she wasn't his pupil any more. He was still in the same position while she had been talent-spotted and fast-tracked. She didn't like his boss or want his job. When she returned, she would be above his pay grade.

The pair had met ten years earlier in the Dominican Republic at a CIA centre that didn't exist. The site had been covertly established to assist teams stationed near Guantánamo Bay. Alvarez had an apartment in Brooklyn Heights but ran between there and Washington, although his wife was Californian so he and his family mostly headed west for vacations. Paige spent little time in NYC and never for pleasure.

When their schedules collided, they met down at Dan's Diner near Chambers Street Station. Why Ben insisted on dragging her to this particular joint every time they met was a mystery – the meat tasted pre-chewed – but Paige suspected there was someone in his vast immigrant family who had lived in the neighbourhood before the rents quintupled. Those ties were hard to break.

'Ben, I have something I need to talk to you about.'

He narrowed one eye at her. *Is this gonna cost me?* The spot where their two organizations overlapped was a fog zone nobody wanted to spend too much time in. 'I guess it's off the record.'

'It could cause a disproportionate amount of trouble.'

'Is this another one of your global doomsday scenarios? Have they still got you crunching numbers on those things?' He probably didn't mean to sound belittling but that was how it came out.

Paige didn't take offence. 'You don't think this feels like a slow-motion apocalypse?'

'Every generation fears it may be the last one, Paige. End of empire is the hardest thing to take.' He sat back while the waiter set down their plates. 'Read about the Romans, the Persians, the Caliphate. None of them ended happily. I disapprove of our alliance with the Russians—'

'Agreed.' She pulled a Stars and Stripes cocktail stick out of her burger. 'A shrinking population of jumped-up farmhands ruled by illiterate robber barons. I have something that could play right into their hands.'

Ben was intrigued. 'Tell me.'

'London,' said Paige. 'You know the deal. It's a complicated set-up. A network of defence units with the territorial forces at one end, MI5 and MI6 at the other. Somewhere in the middle of the system there's an information hole. A major security breach. I'm dealing with mid-level MI5 staffers liaising between the Home Office and the London Metropolitan Police. They gave us a couple of names.'

She threatened her fries with an upturned ketchup bottle. 'There's a former FBI guy called Larry Cranston, moved out here from London after his post-grad, got married, became a US citizen, the kind of loser most sane people go out of their way to avoid. Ever come across him?'

'Not in my circle.'

'He was posted back home and wrecked everything he touched. Thanks to his old school contacts he failed upwards and found himself working for the US ambassador. His wife got sick of being embarrassed at public events and sued for divorce.

'He'd been flagged up as someone who was sniffing around, looking for a fast track back. Last month he screwed up big time. He was driving around Regent's Park and killed a young migrant worker on a crossing. Her daughter was taken into care and her family want their questions answered. Cranston was DUI, so he got the bright idea of claiming diplomatic immunity because he's technically a diplomat and was in a vehicle with CD plates. As soon as he got out of the police station he tried to jump the next flight here but got turned back at Heathrow.

'The Brits expect him to stand trial, so his lawyer tried to work a loophole. The woman who died was employed in the catering staff at the US ambassador's residence, but they'd let her work permit lapse. In the lawyer's eyes it's a no-brainer, an embassy-protected former FBI agent versus an illegal alien. Someone in the Home Office asked me to step in because I knew the guy. My instinct was to send him back here before he could do any more damage.'

Paige cut her burger into tidy quarters. Alvarez had picked up his with both hands. 'What was he doing in London?'

'What bureaucrats like Cranston always do,' said Paige, 'upsetting the locals and leaving someone else to clear up the mess. He was closing one of the Bureau's dead-letter departments. It was the kind of safe job even he couldn't wreck. After his arrest he decided to play his Get Out of Jail card. He thought I'd be interested in "something useful", quote-unquote, that he could hand over. When I asked him for proof of purchase he backed off.'

'Was he bluffing?'

'I guess he thought I'd take whatever he had to sell, then throw him to the wolves. I know Cranston's old boss and I wouldn't eat dinner with the guy unless someone tasted my food first. So we now have a situation of mutual distrust.'

'What do you want me to do?'

'Ask around. See if someone here would be happy to take his intel in exchange for a flight home and no risk of extradition.'

'Paige, why would we consider accepting something you turned down?'

'Because I want to get rid of him but you may find him valuable. Cranston needs to deliver his package and will do anything to seal the deal.' She raised her eyebrows at him. *Your call.*

'We'd only touch the intel if there are no bloody prints on it.'

'Clearly, times have changed.'

'We're trying to keep our noses clean in London at the moment.'

'We can hold off the prosecution while you check out the goods. I've known you longer than anyone, Ben. I can work with you. Either Cranston is bluffing and just trying to keep his ass out of jail, or what he has is so important that he's thinking about the highest bidder. There's a name I stumbled over when I talked to the local police. This guy.'

She pulled a photograph from her jacket and placed it between them. It showed an old man with an unruly white tonsure and a face like a 1950s newspaper found under floorboards. He was dressed in a baggy tweed suit and a stained waistcoat, with several yards of pink scarf looped loosely about him in a way that could invite an Isadora Duncan-style accident. He was leaning against a Belisha beacon, engaged in scraping something disgusting off the sole of his boot with a lolly stick.

Alvarez considered the photograph with distaste. 'He looks like a bum.'

'His name is Arthur St John Aloysius Montmorency Bryant. He's based in . . .' She turned over the photograph and read the reverse. '. . . King's Cross, London.'

27

Ben turned his tumbler, thinking. 'I haven't heard that name for years. He's on our side, theoretically. Headed up some kind of below-the-radar outfit. Once caused us a lot of trouble. But it couldn't be the same person. He can't still be alive.'

'If it is him, he's still working. What did he do to you?'

He gave a mirthless laugh. 'He released a group of around a hundred undocumented migrants into the UK without Home Office permission and we were hit with the fallout. There were unverified stories about him tampering with evidence in Crown cases. He burned his unit down more than once. It's insane – he looks like he couldn't tie his own shoelaces without assistance. You'd think you could handle him without raising your pulse.'

Paige waited while the waiter took their plates. 'I'm just flagging a possible problem. As soon as he sees "CIA Directive" on his emails he'll fall in line. His unit's just been pulled out from under him, but that won't necessarily stop him from causing trouble. It's worth you checking out whatever Cranston is sitting on.'

'And you just happened to think of me.'

'Your loyalty is beyond question and I can trust you. If Cranston's little surprise gift puts people at risk we have to take it away from him.'

'You need to make your own decisions, Paige. But I'll back you. Don't let anyone else get suspicious, especially the British Home Office. And keep that crazy old guy in the local unit out of the picture.'

'I have a handle on it,' Paige assured him. 'Cranston is dangerous because he's desperate. If he starts making noise he'll attract sharks. I need to keep him out of the British press. Once he's delivered I'll buy you the time to get the goods checked out.'

'Paige, it's always a pleasure seeing you.'

'At least you don't have to pay for the burgers here,' she said, rising. 'Doesn't your family still own this joint?'

'That depends on which family you're talking about. I'll go with you on this so long as nobody important gets hurt.'

'You don't have to worry about that,' said Paige. 'It's only the outsiders who need to be afraid.'

The photograph of Arthur Bryant was left on the table between them. A spatter of ketchup that looked like blood had obscured his innocent face.

5

EAU DE DEAD PERSON

Most of London's background goes unnoticed, from its Aberdeen granite kerbstones to the walls made of soft yellow bricks that chink and split neatly when you hit them with the edge of a trowel. But there's one unusual architectural feature everyone sees and nobody notices.

It is everywhere, hidden in plain sight. A typical example can be found on King's Cross Road, a two-minute walk from the front door of the now doomed Peculiar Crimes Unit. Here the houses are built upon terraces of stone and have shops attached to them like shoeboxes. Despite filling the metropolis with factory chimneys, the Victorians believed that life was improved by nature, so each plot included a front and rear garden. A nation of shopkeepers found a new opportunity to display their wares by building stores in the front gardens, keeping the rear ones sacrosanct. Those are London's ancient grounds, lower and older than the rubble-filled roads. What you choose to do with your slice of greenery is nobody else's business.

However, the back garden of number 58 Cruikshank Street was causing concern.

It was Mrs Ormond at number 60 next door who called the police. 'Report anything unusual,' they said, so she did. She called them for every little thing, from the 'unsavoury' conversation she'd heard outside her front door to the smartly dressed young man who used her gutter as a urinal every Saturday night after the pubs turned out. Besides, she had a soft spot for the local constables, especially PC Shamar. He'd have made a dreadful dance partner – he was as tall as a Dutchman – but he had a cheeky smile.

'I've dealt with her before. She's a right pain in the arse,' warned PC Richards as she dragged a blue plastic milk crate across the alley and stood on it. 'You know she's got us on speed-dial.'

'Is she the one who called up to complain about fireworks being let off on Guy Fawkes Night?' asked PC Shamar. 'I've been round here before. I don't know why we have to listen to her. She keeps giving me funny looks.'

'Maybe she fancies you.' With a grunt Richards stood on tiptoe and peered over the fence. 'She swears there's a rough sleeper in the gardens. And she says she's had rats coming over from the kebab shop.'

'It's good to see you getting some exercise,' PC Shamar remarked.

'Everyone pops on a few pounds when they break up with someone.'

'I thought they lost weight.'

'You should be doing this, you've got the legs for it.' PC Richards hoicked herself further up. The fence creaked ominously.

'What can you see? I'm guessing nobody's been out there with a strimmer lately.'

'Are you kidding? It makes Beirut look like Kew Gardens. There's something moving under that pile of rubbish.'

PC Richards could see that the garden to number 58 had not

been touched in months. Its central path had vanished beneath a fecundity of nettles and white trumpet vines. A stubborn species of buddleia native to canalside King's Cross had taken root and grown into a sturdy-trunked bush of fairy-tale proportions. Mounds of foliage had rotted and formed hummocks that made the garden impassable. A bamboo fence was bowing under pressure and looked ready to explode on to next door's lawn.

'That's the trouble, all that bamboo. They want to be careful, they'll get pandas in and you can never get rid of 'em,' said PC Shamar, peering over without need of a box.

'While we're here, let's go round the other side and give 'em the knock.' PC Richards had no sense of humour. She climbed down and dusted her hands.

The pair headed to the front of the house and tried number 58's doorbell. They had already spoken to the occupier of the ground floor, more by accident than design. He leased the café with the unpronounceable name at the front and lived on the first floor above it, but explained that the lady at the top had sole use of the garden. He had been especially concerned about the sighting of rats as he was already on a hygiene warning from the health inspectors.

'No answer.' PC Shamar stood back and looked up at the top floor's dusty windows. 'I don't want to talk to Mrs Ormond again. Let's try the other neighbours.'

The other neighbours turned out to be two stoned Italian students who spoke no English, an elderly woman from the Philippines who spoke English in a form they could not decipher and a paralysingly shy middle-aged man who anxiously stressed that he never spoke to anyone unless he absolutely had to because you couldn't trust anyone around here, they were all prepared to murder you for loose change, not that anyone used coins any more because of germs.

Finally they tried the neighbour whose garden abutted Mrs

Ormond's from the street behind, his boundary line being the end brick wall shared by both gardens. 'She is an elderly lady,' the dark-eyed Mr Hatterjee told them, 'here long before me, *yaar*, and here I have been for twenty years. I'm always seeing her outside, keeping the flowerbeds immaculate. She looked in very good health.'

PC Richards shot her partner a look. *Past tense*. 'When was the last time you saw her?'

'It must have been over a year ago.'

'Is that when the garden started getting messy?'

'I suppose I'm not noticing for a while, but it could have been around that time.'

'You didn't mention it to anyone?'

'In what *chakkar* would I get myself into? It's not my business, is it?' The neighbour was indignant. 'People come and go on a daily basis. You do not ask what they are doing.'

'So what do we do now?' asked PC Shamar once they were back on the street.

PC Richards thought for a moment. 'Borrow the keys to the main door of 58 from the kebab man,' she decided.

'He won't like you calling him that,' said PC Shamar. 'He's trying to go upmarket.'

'How do you know that?'

'He's got a sign up saying "No Tramps".'

Upstairs they stood outside the second-floor flat and rang, but there was still no answer. The hallway was beige, dingy and airless. It smelled of damp carpet and fried food.

'She could be away,' said PC Shamar.

'She could be dead.' PC Richards dropped to the floor and tried to see under the door. A white paper corner protruded. She fished it back out. It was a two-week-old electricity bill. There was a dust bunny attached to its edge.

'The guy downstairs brings up her mail. I'd say it's reasonable cause for concern. I'll take responsibility.' PC Richards rose and placed her formidable shoulder against the door's stile, just above the lock.

'You won't do it like that,' said PC Shamar. 'Let me.'

He tapped one of the four door panels and listened. 'See, this style of door, it's pukka, came with the house, old and heavy, quality wood. When they get replaced, the new ones are cheaper and lighter. The best way to tell the difference is by tapping the centre panels. And this one's a replacement.'

He booted the bottom panel hard and it popped out unbroken. Removing the batten, he reached in and unlocked the door from the inside. 'There you go, minimal damage, two ticks to replace.'

'I'll give you a shout the next time there's something I want kicked in,' said PC Richards.

The air inside was dead. The rooms beyond the hall were perfectly neat. In the kitchen, a chequered tea towel had been carefully folded and hung over a drawer handle. The draining board looked as if it had been polished. There was a plate in the sink rack. A dried-out mug of tea had a bag still hanging inside it.

PC Richards tried the light switch. The electricity was working, so she went around the flat putting all the lights on. She hated those cop shows where investigators crept about in the dark with torches.

'You can't smell that?' asked PC Shamar, rubbing a hand across his nose.

'I can't smell anything,' said PC Richards. 'I fell off a trampoline when I was a nipper.'

'OK, I'm getting an uncooked-leg-of-lamb-left-out-of-the-fridge-for-a-month smell with top notes of pear drops. Eau de Dead Person.'

'You good with smells, then?'

'I've got a *parfumier*'s nose, me. Flats with renters smell of nothing but skunk, but the one I really hate is "Olds who never go out". They give off a biscuity smell like an unwashed duvet. I bet she's in front of the telly.'

They found her at the centre of the sofa inside a crocheted blanket, but there was no television before her. She was tiny; her feet would not have touched the floor. Her grey hair was tied back in a neat bun. Her eyes were closed. A partially exposed right arm showed signs of desiccation; the central heating had dried her out.

'Make sure she's dead,' said PC Shamar.

'Of course she's bloody dead.'

'Just check for breath. I was talking to this doctor who reckons that really small women can last in comas without any food for over a week.'

PC Richards put her hand next to the old lady's mouth but felt nothing.

PC Shamar went to the living-room window and opened it a few inches. 'Nobody should die alone like this,' he muttered, visibly upset. 'Let's call it in.'

'Maybe you shouldn't touch anything else in case they need to do forensics,' said PC Richards.

'She was an old dear whose grown-up kids couldn't be arsed to visit her any more,' Shamar replied. 'What's to investigate?'

'If your old mum died like this you'd want someone to check into it.'

Shamar looked back at the body and shrugged. 'My mum's thirty-seven,' he said.

6

THE SPONTANEOUS APPEARANCE
OF A CRIME

Two minutes after Raymond Land sent out his staff email, doors opened along the first-floor corridor of the Peculiar Crimes Unit and wary heads poked out. Everyone was waiting for a signal. When the end of Arthur Bryant's walking stick protruded from the doorway of his office like a Martian tentacle they all knew where to go.

It was just as well the unit chief was no longer at his desk, as there was still no door on his office and he would have seen them creeping past like saboteurs on a night mission.

The staff members shut the door of the operations room quietly behind them and assembled around their whiteboard, one of the few office items they still possessed. The room had darkened with the threat of rain. Banbury tried the lights but only three of them came on. A fourth flickered neurotically. Strangeways toppled into his litter tray and began to strain. Sidney Hargreaves, the newest and youngest member of the team, looked around the room and tried to work out why she had chosen law enforcement as a profession, despite having seen what it had done to every member of her family.

As everyone looked for somewhere to sit, Arthur Bryant took control, surveying the motley group assembled before him. They looked lost and embarrassed, employees waiting to be given details of an unfavourable redundancy package.

'I've identified a flaw in the system that could be useful to us,' Bryant told them. 'The Home Office isn't simply allowed to reassign ongoing homicide cases to other divisions. If there's an inquiry still in progress they can't shut us down.' He looked from one confused face to the next. 'That's why Raymond needs us to sign the investigation disclosure forms.'

'We cleared our desks before they were taken away,' said Janice Longbright. 'The only thing going through this place at the moment is the draught from that broken window in the lavatory.'

'Then I suggest we find a case fast and, you know . . .' He prestidigitated his fingers. '. . . backdate it.'

'That's illegal,' said Dan Banbury.

'So are many of the best things in life,' Bryant ventured. 'Chasing the ducks in St James's Park. Popping behind the bar after closing time. Slapping the French.' He peered myopically at his phone. 'The Home Office team will be here in, oh, it's going to rain in ten minutes.'

John May helped him out. 'You're in your weather app. Three-quarters of an hour.'

'A crime isn't just going to spontaneously appear.' Meera Mangeshkar scowled even more angrily than usual. 'Why don't I just go out on the street and arrest someone for looking shifty?'

'You're not with the Met,' said May. 'Besides, unless you're going to kill him it won't cut the mustard. What about digging up an unsolved case and leaving it open? That would be legitimate.'

'Oh, *legitimate*, you're so boring.' Bryant blew impatiently. 'Let's make something up.'

Janice Longbright considered pointing out the impropriety of such an action but changed her mind. The PCU had long ago been forced to cut through thickets of red tape by adopting a more flexible approach to policing. Besides, the Home Office treated them in such a cowardly and underhanded fashion that it was time they pushed back.

Dan Banbury opened a file of historical cases on his laptop. 'Plenty of these are unsolved, so they're technically open. Would they do?'

Janice stood by him for a look. 'They date back to the first half of the last century, Dan. Everyone involved in them is probably dead.'

'Mind my grief,' said Bryant indignantly.

'No disrespect intended. We can't just alter the dates.'

'Use the most recent open case. Leslie Faraday never reads documents. I'm not sure anybody at the Home Office does. What about the Kensington Strangler?'

'We've used him before,' said May. 'It's not possible to do what you're asking. Everything leaves an electronic trail.'

Bryant rang Giles Kershaw at the St Pancras Coroner's Office. 'Hello, Giles, have you got anything interesting in your drawers? Very droll. Your cadaver drawers. Deaths by misadventure, unknown causes, anything we can legitimately claim to take an interest in. Spontaneous combustion would be good, or an appalling accident. What about that drunk who climbed over the St Pancras Church railings and got a gilded spear up the jacksie? Oh, he pulled through. What a pity. Just fax over your admission reports. What do you mean, you haven't got a fax machine? When did they go? Oh. All right, send them by phone, but no morgue photos. I accidentally forwarded the last one to the priest at St Aloysius and frightened him out of his chasuble. Don't ask questions, Giles, just do it now. Thank you so very much.' He turned to the others. 'We're in luck, it's been a busy month, he's got more inert bodies than the House of Lords.'

The painter William Frederick Yeames never enjoyed critical acclaim.

He was shunned by the more prestigious art galleries, but the public loved him. Yeames specialized in so-called 'problem' pictures, narratives that depicted unresolved dilemmas, and his 1878 painting *And When Did You Last See Your Father?* became his most celebrated work.

It depicts the Parliamentarian usurpers of a Royalist household questioning a child during the English Civil War. The figures are placed in a rectilinear and very gloomy wood-panelled room, yet are seen clearly from the side in such a way that each member of the group can tell their own story.

Arthur Bryant was reminded of the painting as he looked around the operations room. The staff members waited anxiously beneath the half-light of missing ceiling panels, surrounded by blue plastic crates and layabout sheets of hardboard.

On the far right of the picture the unit's IT guru Dan Banbury sat hunched over his laptop in a pose that could have been used in a medical dictionary as an example of bad posture. The task of plugging and patching the unit's colander-like online security consumed him to the point where he got home late, ate badly and exercised not at all. He had been intending to find a local job that would allow him more time with his family, but pride in his work prevented him from leaving until he had located all of his HDMI cables.

Behind him Meera Mangeshkar stood tensed and musket-straight. At school she had been asked to name her best quality. Her answer, 'an extremely suspicious nature', had not been well received but had opened a career in law enforcement. She had yet to inform her fearsome mother that she was intending to marry a fellow officer, and it was the only thing in the world that broke her out in a sweat. She was prepared to stand up for the unit because she believed in justice and fair play, and because she got to share an office with her future husband, where she could accurately record the number of trips he made to the fridge.

Colin Bimsley provided the central joist to the tableau, and was cheerfully unaware that anyone might be thinking about him. He was by nature as simple as a cat and as strong as a vault, but only a fool would underestimate his character. He stayed on through the unit's difficulties because he came from an old East End family where you were either a cop, a tailor or a thief, and if you abandoned your post you might as well shoot yourself.

Janice Longbright felt the same way. Gladys and Harris, her parents, had worked at the unit and in the Met respectively, and had raised their daughter to respect the law above all else, so it had been a surprise to them when she chose to become a Soho nightclub hostess. They failed to see that her choice gave her control, and when she finally moved to the unit she brought with her all she had learned, along with her penchant for vintage glamour fashions. She had recently been excited to find a Playtex Cross-Your-Heart bra in its original 1960s packaging, and filmed herself unboxing it on TikTok.

In the corner sat Janice's daughter, Sidney Hargreaves. Born into the twenty-first century and unable to conceive of a world before iPhones, she was graduating from intern to detective constable. Her resilience was born of youth, fearlessness and not knowing better. Reaction to her arrival had been mixed; while everyone welcomed new blood, they also felt decrepit standing anywhere near her.

At the left of the picture were John May and his partner Arthur Bryant, the oldest serving detectives in London. Like avant-garde musicians and science fiction writers, they were only understood by those in the know. The unit's rebellious spirit existed because they had instilled it. May was a bedrock of sound sense, elegance *in extremis*, a mitigating conscience and a cool temperament to counter his partner's more lurid behaviour. Silver-haired, divorced, unlucky with the women he loved so much, even the one who had recently shot him, he could not leave the unit because his penance was to be the guardian angel of his partner.

And what could be said of Arthur Bryant that had not already been uttered in anger, disbelief or devotion? His brain was as young as his body was old, his manner was rude, his behaviour unpredictable, but his eyes showed kindness and curiosity. He had a creased, comfortable face, boisterous dentures and the physical elegance of a bin bag. How was it possible, everyone wondered, for him to remain so resolutely optimistic in the winter of his life? Bryant knew that the world belonged to those who did not do as they were told, so he never did. He took the view that evil would triumph if good people did nothing, so he always did something. He was a disruption, a glitch, an anomaly.

Enough introspection – let's have actions, not orations.

Bryant examined the sheets Banbury had just laboriously printed out for him. 'Our coroner is technically seconded to this unit so there's no reason why one of his corpses can't be ours. The Home Office is required to keep this building open until our duties have been fully discharged. That should buy us some time.'

'For what?' said Sidney, looking up from her tablet.

'What do you mean?'

'They'll expect results.'

'And that's what we'll give them.' Bryant ran his eye down the list. A fatal heart attack outside the Skinner's Arms; an old lady found dead of natural causes in Cruikshank Street; a high court judge who got stabbed during a performance of

When Can I Have a Banana Again at the Ration Book Follies of 1950. That last one was possibly too far back. He passed the pages to his partner.

'What happened to the Drummond Street attacks?' asked May.

Bryant checked the list. 'When was that?'

'Two years ago. Around twenty Asian teenagers were delivering takeaways and drugs in the Drummond Street area. The gang leaders urged their crews to eliminate the competition and then vanished, leaving their foot soldiers to take the blame.'

'We were told to regard each homicide as separate until gang links could be proven, which couldn't happen because the gangs had already dispersed. We need something simpler. Leslie Faraday can be fooled with a stuffed mouse on a stick. It just needs to appear legitimate.'

Appear legitimate, Sidney wrote on her iPad. Every day at the unit brought another bump in the learning curve.

The Home Office liaison officer turned up expecting to be handed the keys to the building but found everyone still on-site. It was obvious that Leslie Faraday needed someone to share his disbelief, an accomplice who would roll their eyes and tut along with him, but today he only had Fatima Hamadani, a young Mancunian administrator who dealt with her boss by placing her thoughts elsewhere whenever he spoke.

'Well, that's a bit of a stumbling block.' The Home Office liaison officer shook his head with some violence. 'Why is this the first time I'm hearing about the case?'

'We only just remembered it,' Bryant explained. 'Like when you go to the shops and only remember what you went for hours later.'

Faraday gave him a sour look and lowered himself into the nearest chair with a delicacy that suggested a colonic problem, leaving them to stare at the folds of his vast stomach. 'I hesitate to call these case notes,' he said, holding up a single crumpled page. 'It doesn't seem as if there's anything to investigate.'

Bryant had little respect for the portly civil servant, whose incompetence could be triangulated from space. He decided not to mention that the case was in the hands of the Met, who would discreetly subject it to Death by Paperwork. Faraday stared at this shred of information as if trying to discern a hidden message. Although he was incapable of absorbing data, his impersonation of someone understanding typed sentences was relatively plausible.

'And you say it's an ongoing investigation?'

'Oh yes,' said Bryant innocently. 'We had a team around there just this morning.'

'How long will it take to conclude?'

'It's hard to be accurate.' Bryant's eye was agleam with mischief. 'I'd say a minimum of a fortnight.'

May gave his partner an imperceptible headshake of disbelief.

'Mr Faraday,' Ms Hamadani began, 'it would be advisable—'

Faraday raised a prohibitive hand. 'I'm thinking, Fatima.'

Bryant knew exactly what he was taking into consideration: the stinging humiliation of his last clash with the unit and his desire to exact revenge. Faraday craved order and simplicity and empty inboxes. His work consisted of turning down anything that was expensive or confusing. He glanced at the evidence Bryant had placed before him. It was mostly gibberish but he picked out the odd worrying phrase. He was especially bothered by 'inconclusive evidence would require further investigation'.

'I'm more than happy to go through the case with you in far greater detail,' Bryant offered cheerfully.

Dear God, no, thought Faraday, *we'll be here all morning.*

He was anxious to have the PCU building sold off as quickly, as possible but as usual Bryant stood in his way. His nemesis still had a few well-placed friends, and the last thing Faraday needed was anyone asking questions about his own department's disastrous performance. As much as it pained him, he realized he would have to hold off for a few more days.

'I can't let you requisition any equipment,' he warned. 'You'll have to make do with what you have. And no using any of these unregistered so-called "informants". The unit is closed but for the clearing up of this one case, is that understood?'

Bryant caught Hamadani's eye and she held his glance. There was something private going on between them but Faraday could not fathom the meeting's undercurrents. He wanted to wrap things up because the unit's tea was too strong – why they couldn't use bags was beyond him – and he wanted to get to the fishmonger near his office before they ran out of haddock.

'Leslie, I know the closure is taking longer than planned.'

About thirty years longer, thought Faraday bitterly. Bryant's pudgy smiling face made him want to snap pencils in half. 'You can help us by dealing with this as quickly as possible,' he snapped. 'Fatima, Uber – now, please.'

'Well, thank you so much for coming. Are you sure you won't stay for dinner?' Bryant gave him an unctuous smile. 'Only it can be dangerous for lonely travellers up on the moors at this time of night, when the hound is out.'

'He's mad,' muttered Faraday as he all but pushed Fatima out of the door, 'utterly mad.'

'I don't know why you're worrying so much,' Bryant told the others after the civil servants had left the building. 'We've bought ourselves a few more days.'

Meera threw down her pen. 'What's the bloody point? Why stage some grubby little deception just to stave off the inevitable?'

'Because it's not inevitable, Miss Mangeshkar,' said Bryant with passion. 'I am going to keep the unit open even if I have to kill someone myself. I have a plan.'

'Then why don't you share it with us?'

'I'm not a sharer. You don't see me taking pictures of my dinner and posting them online.'

'Faraday thinks you're barking.'

'I get that a lot.'

Janice Longbright gathered up the contents of the folder Faraday had left behind. 'What case did you tell him we were still working on?'

Bryant looked over her shoulder and pointed at a page. 'This one, the old lady who died of natural causes in her flat. Obviously I phrased the circumstances more obscurely. Like this bit: "Death most likely due to *Montani semper liberi*." '

'What's that?'

'The state motto of West Virginia. Faraday didn't even bother to take my case notes with him. You do know why he's so easy to bamboozle? He's lazy. He relies on Fatima to brief him. Where did the old lady live – Cruikshank Street? That's a five-minute walk from here. Miss Hargreaves, someone can show you how to pull up the Met files—'

'I've already done it.' Sidney turned her phone around.

'My God, someone who's technologically literate,' said Banbury. 'Welcome, fellow traveller.'

'Go and take a look at the flat, just so that we can say we've done our homework,' Bryant suggested. 'You'll need someone with you.'

'I'll do it,' said Janice.

Sidney put her foot down. 'No mother–daughter stuff. You promised me.'

Meera grabbed her jacket from the desk. 'Come on, then. Let's get you out into the mean streets of London Town.'

'I don't understand,' said May. 'Why look into a death that isn't even flagged for investigation?'

'Because I need something to hold them off a little longer,' Bryant told him.

'Then what?'

May waited for an answer until he realized that none would be forthcoming. 'You can't get a murder case out of someone who died from natural causes.'

'You don't think so?' Bryant replied. 'Watch me.'

7

THE FIRST VISIT

Sidney cast a furtive glance at a cadaverous young Ethiopian who was trying to put his right foot into the same trouser leg as his left. She could not imagine why he was getting dressed in the street.

'I didn't think King's Cross would be such a . . .'

'A cosmopolitan melting pot?' Meera suggested.

'. . . a shithole.'

Sidney looked across the station forecourt. An elderly man was feeding pigeons chocolate biscuits. A smartly dressed African woman held a Bible high above her head, ranting at the sky, the last to be saved. A drunk lay asleep in a pool of dirty rainwater. Two girls dressed as insects were handing out breakfast bars to passers-by.

'I admit it's not Chelsea,' Meera conceded. 'You should have seen it a few years ago. The local crooks met passengers from the North as they came off the trains. We placed bets on who would reach the end of the street with their wallets.'

They were standing in front of King's Cross Station, on a concourse palisaded with shiny steel bollards that marked the boundary line of railway property. Police jurisdiction changed at the line, which was why so many of the city's more socially challenged citizens remained on one side like zombies waiting for fresh brains.

Sidney had only recently returned to London, and had yet to find vestiges of the metropolis she had last seen at the age of five, before her father had taken her off to Europe. It felt as if she was looking upon it for the first time. She tried not to let her amazement show. The thoroughfare before her was a patchwork quilt, as if no planner had ever stopped to think, *How should this look?* Only in the backstreets were any two blocks alike. Even though it was summer, moss grew between every pavement slab and every join where wood met brick. She could not make sense of it.

When Meera Mangeshkar strode off along the pavement and headed straight into the traffic as if failing to notice that vehicles were roaring all about her like panicked wildebeest, Sidney froze; then she realized that her life might depend on keeping up.

They weaved their way between buses across the Euston Road, courier cycles darting between trucks like silverfish. It seemed to Sidney that whichever direction they picked sent them upstream against the flow of life. The kaleidoscopic mismatch of people, hurled together like piles of old clothes in the wash, overwhelmed her. The streets were impossible to contain or define. It would be best, she decided, to let everything move around and over her, and concentrate solely on the task at hand. Stay focused, keep listening and learning. Everything was new, everything was contradictory, but she had no intention of allowing anyone to note her surprise.

They were standing opposite a curving row of houses. The brickwork of the scruffy Victorian terrace still bore the faint markings of a painted advertisement for pre-war weighing machines. At street level, bright new shops marked the resurgence of the once run-down neighbourhood. Faux-natural coffee bars had replaced the transport cafés of previous decades. A few exhausted trees had been punched into the pavement like fenceposts, their brush-stroke branches barely able to retain foliage, like weary strippers clinging to dignity.

Meera spoke to Constantin Yavuz, the owner of the Almaqahaa Alkabir Lilmahata restaurant beneath Mrs Hoffman's flat. Its name translated as 'the Grand Café of the Station', although everyone called it Al's. It made the cantina in *Star Wars* look like Marks & Spencer. Constantin went off and returned with a set of keys for her.

'You do know that's an unpronounceable name for a café, don't you?' she told Yavuz, pointing to his sign.

'Only if you're from here,' said Yavuz.

Meera unlocked the narrow front door at the side of Mr Yavuz's café. 'The old lady lived on the top floor. They've taken her to Giles for a cause of death. He's the nearest coroner. I don't know what it's like inside.'

'I'm not squeamish.' Sidney followed her up the stairs.

Meera studied the kicked-in door. 'That's the Met for you. They could have gone and asked for the key. It's a case for the welfare services, not us.'

'We saw dead bodies at the college,' said Sidney, as if to reassure herself. 'They didn't bother me.'

'You'll see some sights on this job that will. The first dead child will stay with you forever. Women handle it better. Colin's hopeless.' Meera unclipped the yellow police seal from the second-floor doorway, pushed the door wide and turned the lights on.

The kitchen looked as if it had last been decorated in the 1980s but was bare and clean. Spices and herbs were arranged in pots along an open shelf. Two red mugs hung from a wooden stand. A single blue plate sat in the dish rack. The only dirty item was the tea mug and its dehydrated bag.

'I hate where I'm living,' said Meera. 'I wonder if the rental agent would give me dibs.'

Sidney leaned over a plastic card index box on the kitchen counter. 'Can I touch anything?'

'Her death's not suspicious but you'd better not without gloves.'

'So we're *pretending* to investigate?'

'Just while the old man's trying to get us off the hook.'

Sidney peered inside the box. 'She alphabetized her recipe cards. Neat writing.'

'Old people always have great handwriting. Except Mr Bryant. His notes look like worm casts.'

'The recipes are cross-indexed. Look at this: "Lamb Casserole, see Stews". How old was she?'

'Ninety-one, I think.' Meera dropped on one knee and looked in the lower cupboards. A regiment of cleaning materials faced out, orderly and ready for inspection. 'This is more than just tidy. Everything's been cleaned. It's OCD or something.' She looked in the fridge. 'There's not a scrap of food in the place. She doesn't have a freezer. Every shelf is labelled. The fridge has no smell. Weird.'

Sidney reached up and opened a door. 'There's a cupboard labelled for tinned goods but it's empty. Any food anywhere?'

'Hang on.' Meera had to stand on the tips of her boots to reach the top cupboards. 'Nothing. This one's labelled "Rice and Grains" but it's empty as well.'

Sidney tried another cupboard and took out an enormous pile of flattened soap wrappers, riffling through them like a pack of cards. 'What's carbolic?'

'No idea.'

'She got through a lot of the stuff. And cat food. No cat though. How did they find her?'

'The woman next door complained about the garden and a couple of plods popped round.'

'There's a collapsible NHS wheelchair in the hall. But all those stairs.'

'So she couldn't go out without help.' Meera tried to open the wheelchair but the arms would not unlock.

'What did she die of?' Sidney asked.

'Don't know. Old age?'

'There still has to be a cause of death.' She walked back into the kitchen and opened the pedal bin. 'It's not right.'

'Of course it's not. Happens all the time in big cities.'

'No. I mean something's not right in here. Look.' Sidney took a clear plastic sack out of the bin. 'She recycled. Who recycles at ninety-one? She doesn't have any food. This is all just waste paper.' She let the bin bag rotate.

'I should have spotted that, considering the number of bins I've dived into. You should try it sometime.'

'I won't learn anything rooting around in a skip,' said Sidney.

'You'd be surprised at what people throw way. They chuck homicide evidence into bin bags. We found a drug-dealer's hands in a DHL Jiffy bag once. And in Chinatown we came across a geezer buried in a bin full of noodles coated in sweet and sour sauce. He was bright orange. The undertaker couldn't scrub it off. They didn't mention stuff like that on your course, did they?'

Meera tried the kitchen taps, and then disappeared into the hall. 'The water's off,' she called.

'Maybe she didn't pay her bill,' said Sidney.

'It's the stopcock by the boiler. It's been turned off.' She grunted. 'Hang on. Now try.'

Sidney lifted the cold-tap handle. After a sputter of air, water poured from the spout.

'She couldn't have done that,' Meera said. 'Not without a very long reach and a strong grip.'

They went to the living room where, according to the Met

constables, the body had been found. Three framed mono-chrome photographs were arranged on a wall, but they were just faces lost in shadows and smoke. Magazines stood squared off in a 1950s red wire rack. The most recent issue was three months old. TV guides had been arranged by date.

'There's no telly,' said Meera. Where a television might have been placed was a large painting of London Bridge at sunset, seen from the north bank of the Thames.

In the centre of the room was a grey three-piece suite. The sofa cushions still held the secretions and indentations of Mrs Hoffman's body. A crocheted blanket had been tightly rolled up and set to one side, much as a bivouacked soldier would roll a sleeping bag. A side table held a Scrabble board and a book of crossword puzzles, none filled in.

'Does this feel like an old lady's flat to you?' Meera asked.

'I've never been in an old lady's flat,' said Sidney.

'Well, it doesn't. My auntie Prisha kept everything neat. She had thirty little china poodles lined up along her shelves. Her flat was warm and cosy. This is like a stationer's office or something.'

Further along the hall was a large light-filled bedroom that overlooked the back of the terrace. The bed was carefully made, its side table holding a small chrome tray and a single framed photograph. A crocheted sunflower cushion lay on the coverlet. There was a smell of violets and naphthalene, the chemical in mothballs.

'Why did she stay on the sofa instead of in here?' Meera wondered.

'Maybe it was warmer.'

'Why is there no food in the kitchen at all? *Everybody* has something non-perishable in their cupboards.'

'Unless she'd eaten it all and was starving and couldn't get out to the shops,' said Sidney gloomily.

'OK.' Meera clapped her hands briskly. 'It's not for us to

sort out, we're just arse-covering here. Next stop, knock on the neighbours, check health and phone records, find her nearest relatives and get her carer's number. Trace, interview, eliminate: shouldn't take more than a couple of hours.' She held open the front door. 'First let's go and talk to Giles Kershaw.'

Rosa Lysandrou came to the door of the absurd Victorian gingerbread cottage that housed the St Pancras Coroner's unit and peered between the pair of them. The housekeeper pulled a heavy black cardigan around her shoulders and stepped out into the little garden, turning it into a corner of England that would be forever winter.

'Where is he?' she demanded to know.

Meera looked behind herself. 'Where is who?'

'That horrible godless old man.'

'Oh, you mean Mr Bryant.'

'The last time he was here he left his teeth in the chapel.'

'Yes, he asked me to get those back,' said Meera. 'He says he took them out because pizza gets under his dental plate. They're his second-best spare pair.'

'He shouldn't have been eating pizza in front of Our Lord. It's disrespectful.'

'Jesus broke bread,' said Sidney.

Rosa folded her arms in her patented not-to-be-messed-with mode. 'Pizza is Italian and therefore Catholic. And I don't know who you are, young man.'

'Whatever,' said Sidney.

'Mr Bryant says—' Meera began.

Rosa lost her remaining thread of civility. Bunching her fingertips together, she shook her hand at Meera. 'How do you work for this man? How? Mr Bryant comes in here with his insults and jokes, the home of the dead! He told me he used to be a lumberjack and when I asked him for proof he said he hadn't kept a log. Why is he like this? One day he will pass beyond the vale of tears and there will be no more jokes.'

'Mr Bryant thinks the world is God's joke on him.' Meera grew impatient. 'Can we see Giles now?'

'He is Mr Kershaw to you.'

'For heaven's sake, let them in, Rosa,' bellowed Giles, striding over with an outstretched hand. 'You must be Janice's daughter. Good Lord, you have her eyes. Perhaps we can persuade you to leave them to us when you go. Corneas like that are too good to waste. I'm delighted to hear you've joined our happy band, but I'm afraid you're too late this morning. Meera, hi.' He led them into the building.

'What's happened?' Meera asked, following him.

'Two porters from University College Hospital came and took most of my outstanding cases away. Someone's on to you.'

'Why would they have done that?'

'I think old Bryant tried to convince the Home Office that anything here legitimately fell under his jurisdiction. They left me the only cases I had no doubts about, an alcoholic, a drug addict and an old lady.'

'The old lady,' Meera repeated, looking at Sidney.

Giles checked the page in his hand. 'Mrs Amelia Hoffman, 58 Cruikshank Street.'

'That's the one.'

'Come to my office.'

Giles pulled the plastic grip from his hair and shook it out. To Sidney's eyes he didn't look like a man used to inserting plastic tubes into dead bodies. He had an impossibly plummy voice and looked like a Nordic tennis star.

The coroner led them to a walnut-panelled room with leaded windows facing the cemetery and ushered them to seats. 'This is the only remaining room with its original fittings,' he said. 'It helps me to think in here. When I look

54

through those trees I fancy the ghosts of Mary Shelley and Thomas Hardy still walk here.'

'Can we get back to this century?' Meera snapped.

'You might show a little more respect for the spirits of the past, Miss Mangeshkar; we're on consecrated ground here.'

'Point taken,' Meera conceded.

'You want to know what happened to her. There aren't any real surprises. I can tell you what will be in my report to Mr Bryant. Mrs Hoffman suffered a care failure. Her body shows all the classic signs of neglect.'

'What are they?' asked Sidney.

'Malnutrition, dehydration, poor condition of the skin, eyes and hair, untreated sores. Somebody should have spotted what was happening and protected her. Unfortunately, nobody seems to have done so.'

'You're saying her death was avoidable.'

'I don't know whether it was avoidable or not. I examine the dead; you have to sort out the living. Of course it's depressing that one still gets cases like this but it's hardly surprising when families are socio-economically fragmented. Perhaps she'd simply had enough of life and stopped eating. We see it more in elderly men whose wives have died. They don't know how to take care of themselves. Microwaves have been a boon there. Mrs Hoffman was malnourished.'

'Was that what killed her?'

'Dehydration and partial collapse of her left lung compounded the problems. She had a bronchial blockage composed of uncleared body fluids. Obviously a heavy smoker in the past. I imagine she had respiratory difficulties.'

'There was no medication in her flat.' Sidney looked from one to the other. 'No apparatus, not so much as a tissue.'

'That's something you should look into. From the way her body was curled up I'd say she passed away in some pain. She wouldn't have been thinking clearly enough to take care of herself.'

'The place was spotless. As if someone had been in and tidied.'

'I'm a scientist, not a psychologist. I know nothing about her state of mind.' The truth dawned on Giles. 'Your boss is not going to be able to build a PCU case out of this. You can tell him from me that the verdict will be neglect with the compounding factor of emphysema.'

'How long do you think she was dead?' Meera asked.

'Over two weeks.' Giles slipped his paperwork into a folder. 'There'll be the usual squawking from Social Services and the press: "Why this shameful tragedy must not be allowed to happen again." We start and end our lives in helplessness. Tell Mr Bryant I need a forensic entomologist to check her bacterial growth and see if there's been any arthropod action, if he has a way of paying for it. Here.' He gave a copy of the notes to Meera. 'This is as far as I can take it right now. I heard they came to close down the unit this morning. Why is Bryant still fighting them?'

'The unit is his life.' Meera tucked the paperwork away. 'It's all our lives.'

They headed back out into the hall. Giles beamed at Sidney, his natural sunniness lightening the gloom. 'Miss Hargreaves, do you want a tour of the facilities?'

'Not really,' said Sidney, 'unless it's different to others.'

'What would you like, a latte station and beanbags, a bowling alley?'

Sidney turned to leave but stopped. 'She had a microwave. Did she starve to death?'

'Lack of adequate nutrition was a contributory factor. She hadn't had a proper meal in several days. In cases of neglect, we sometimes have to ask ourselves how much we can do for people if they don't want our help.'

'How do you know she didn't want help?'

Giles thought for a moment. 'There's something . . . I don't know. Her hips were necrotic but she should have had some short-distance mobility. It's not my job to understand what was going through her mind.' He was about to say something more but Sidney had already headed off down the steps. Giles's blond eyebrows furrowed. 'I can't believe she's Janice's daughter. She's nothing like her mother.'

'She doesn't take any nonsense.' Meera shrugged. 'And she's getting on well with Mr Bryant. I think they're learning from each other.'

Giles rolled his eyes. 'Heaven help us.'

'It might do him some good.'

'I was thinking about her,' replied the coroner with a sigh.

8

THE MYSTERIES OF HUMAN BEHAVIOUR

Bert the chimney sweep may well have thought that the roof-tops of London were a sight to behold, but he'd have spat out his beer upon seeing how the view across the metropolis had changed. The first thing he'd spot would be the shining silver spear of the Shard, somewhere between an outsized church steeple and an elongated pyramid, another hub around which the great wheel of London could revolve.

Arthur Bryant stretched his creaking back and turned his binoculars to the most easterly spoke of that wheel, where the braggart buildings of the financial district swaggered up against each other. Below them stood boxes of cloud-coloured concrete and chromatic rainbow glass, like a parade of psychedelic seaside chalets. Lower still were the serrated slate roofs of Edwardian terraces.

To Bryant's mind the view had gained fresh layers of intrigue. Take him to the countryside and he'd be checking his watch in under twenty minutes, but put him here, on the pigeon-soiled roof of the PCU, and he was in his grubby element. He had grown up with rain-damp bricks and soot, the metal tang of rolling stock, the perfumed balm of pipe tobacco, the thunder of road drills and whooping of sirens. Somewhere within earshot there was always yelling: not in pain or anger, just a need to bellow across the street.

He panned his binoculars along the peculiarities of the horizon. A Victorian school with a rooftop playground. A bar bedecked with coloured light bulbs. Chimneypot windmills. A wire-mesh fence knotted with rainbow ribbons. A baroque clock tower unattached to any building.

'How did you get up here so quickly?' May emerged from the attic stairs and leaned against a chimney stack, patting dust from the sleeves of his smart grey suit.

'Bannisters,' said Bryant. 'A friend to the elderly.'

May caught his breath. 'I'm not as young as I thought I was.'

'You should try being me for a while. When I go to bed I have to dismantle myself. But I'm still here. I don't moan every time something changes colour and drops off. I get on with my work.' He looked up at a cliff of dark cloud. 'Filthy weather coming in.'

May followed his eyeline. 'Are you sure?'

'Oh yes. South cones have been hoisted.'

'What does that mean?'

'I have absolutely no idea. Weathermen used to say it. Oh dear. You know you're getting old when you find yourself using past tenses a lot.'

'What are all these?' May touched the toecap of his brogue against a stack of six tea chests.

Bryant patted his pockets for matches. 'I got Colin and Meera to shift them up here before the removal van arrived. No one must know about them. I need somewhere to keep them safe and dry.'

May shooed an inquisitive pigeon away from his foot. 'Why, what's in them?'

'Evidence files, memorabilia, all the clutter I've accumulated over the years. They were at the back of the attic. The oldest box hasn't been opened for decades. I haven't the faintest idea what's in half of them. I didn't want the Home Office getting their hands on our history.'

May lifted the lid of one chest and removed a rhinoceros-hide shield. Underneath it a green ceramic gorgon's head stared up at him. 'Is there anything worth keeping?'

'I'm not really sure. I kept a catalogue of contents written in code, but lost the code key. Then I lost the catalogue.'

May dug deeper and produced a stuffed bat on a stick.

'Oh, that lights up.'

May put it back. 'I'll get a tarpaulin put over them, but we won't have access up here for much longer.'

'Perhaps you could shift the chests next door. No one would think of looking there.' Bryant pointed across to the chimneypotted roof of the Ladykillers Café. 'I'll come up with you and Janice one night and the three of us can go through it all.'

The gorgon's stare was giving May the creeps. His bullet wound had started to throb. He quickly replaced the lid on the chest. 'Yes, why don't we do that? I look forward to sitting here at midnight sifting through Santeria fetish tokens and looking for scraps of paper written in Aramaic.'

Bryant thrust his hands into his trouser pockets and set his jaw into its predisposed Churchillian position. 'We are not leaving this unit, John.'

'How can you be so sure?'

'I told you, I have a plan. I was going to discuss it with you before you were inconsiderate enough to get yourself shot.'

His partner had undergone surgery just after Christmas, and was still moving with less speed and more care than usual.

'I've had some meetings and will fill you in as soon as I get the rest of the information I need.' Bryant picked up a fallen book entitled *Mortality & Mentalism* and gently replaced it in a crate.

May studied the boxes with apprehension. 'Do you know how far the world has moved on since you collected all this stuff? CCTV and electronic tracking were just the start. You need to learn about predictive policing, following patterns of criminal behaviour through algorithms.'

'I've been thinking along those lines for years.' Bryant pulled a rectangular leather case from one of the boxes and wiped the dirt from it. 'My informants have been helping me.'

Unzipping the case, he revealed a pack of A2 sheets clipped together along their left edge. The tracing layers showed homicide patterns from 1899 to 1999. A complex multi-coloured key code ran along the opposite side.

'It's a bellwether, an evolving map of London crime psychology across the decades,' Bryant explained, unfolding the pages lovingly. A pigeon landed on the chimneypot behind him and gave them an insolent stare.

May leaned the charts against the stack and studied them. 'Why have I never seen these before?'

'It started as a hobby. I was trying to combine criminal patterns, geography, psychopathology, class, age, income, quality of life and so on, to understand where we might be heading next. This isn't the only one.'

'What do you mean?'

'I have sixteen further volumes at home in the airing cupboard, all with accompanying notes. I could have produced more but Alma wouldn't let me dismantle her towel rack.'

'Have you come to any conclusions?'

'About the mysteries of human behaviour? That's a little hard to say.' Bryant held his pudgy hands outstretched across the rooftops, a strange gleam in his eyes. He looked a bit mad. 'There are connections that can't be discerned without the help of specialists.' His hand roved above the distant grey buildings of Shoreditch. 'That's why I rely on my informants. They see what I can't.'

John looked out across the rooftops. 'What do you think they see?'

'An emotional map. A phantom network stretching in every direction, through every building, into every family, more pervasive than your "internet". There's a shadow city where unconscionable choices are made and unacceptable deals are brokered. My outliers know this. They're here among us, blinking like beacons, showing us the way.' He gave May a friendly pat on the shoulder. 'Time's running out. Don't worry, I'm putting everything in place. It's going to be interesting.'

An eerie wail arose from his trousers. He took out his phone. 'Sorry, new ring tone, the theme from *Forbidden Planet*.' After listening for a moment he wandered off to the edge of the roof and produced his pipe, a sign that he wanted to be alone.

May longed to know what his partner was thinking, but it was like trying to map the shape of the universe.

9

SLIPPING THROUGH THE CRACKS

Bloody sodding hell. Larry Cranston stood in the doorway and wiped raindrops from his suit jacket. It was too small for him now and refused to button up. He wasn't dressed for the sudden change in the weather. Most of his wardrobe was in Somerset. Everything else was in Belgravia.

Water was dripping down his neck. He checked his phone again. He'd called his old boss at the FBI but had been fobbed off by some brisk youngster who said she would pass the message on when she clearly had no intention of doing so. What was he supposed to do now?

His court date had been postponed and he was in limbo, his lawyer awaiting the introduction of a 'special circum-stances' plea that would bail him out. His only other friend at the FBI was also avoiding him, the police were still gathering evidence and he had not yet been able to lay his hands on the only bargaining chip that would save him from jail.

Worse, any minute now the investigation team would realize that he was not entitled to claim diplomatic immunity any more. His ex-wife would be more than happy to explain why.

Criminal immunity could be afforded to the dependants of staff at London's consular missions, but Larry was no longer linked to his wife. Their divorce had been finalized four months ago. He would act dumb and they would press charges, unless the one card he had left to play paid off.

So now he waited.

He hadn't thought he would have to start all over again, but here he was back on the street. The old woman wasn't hard to follow. She was dressed in a baggy floral sack that made her look like a giant seed packet. For the briefest moment it crossed his mind that she might be expecting him to turn up and somehow disguised her appearance, but he dismissed the thought as paranoia. He wondered how he could make her acquaintance and gain her confidence without raising suspicion.

He was not someone strangers took to, he knew that. He found small talk unnatural and had never lost his social awkwardness. People tended to move away from him at cocktail parties. After taking him to a handful of embassy events, his ex-wife had tactfully suggested that he should remain at home in the future. All he had done was talk to a couple of the guests about investment opportunities. Olivia had told him that such importuning was unacceptable, but how else was business done? Her disillusionment had settled over their marriage like a shroud.

The woman in front of him suddenly turned, looking in his direction almost as if she was making sure he was there, but he realized she was just getting ready to cross the street.

She stepped into the shop opposite and was now buying cigarettes. At her age she must have decided that there was no point in giving up.

What the hell am I doing here? he asked himself. If he'd been wrong about Amelia Hoffman, what made him think that this one would be any more useful? Annie Wynn-Jones was about fifteen years younger than Hoffman by the look of it, probably in her mid-seventies. She reminded him of a great-aunt who used to power around the countryside on a quad bike berating farm workers. She had finally died with fierce reluctance at the age of 102.

Wynn-Jones was still in the shop, on her phone by the look of it. What could he gain by following another old lady about? It was bloody undignified. He had backed himself into a dead end this time, but had to go on. What alternative was there? Killing himself was the coward's way out. His father would never forgive him.

He concentrated on the woman in the shop.

'Is there anything else?'

'No. No, thank you.'

Annie Wynn-Jones paid for her packet of mints and drew behind the scratch card display to watch the man who had been inexpertly following her for the past hour. She could hardly have missed him, overnourished, underdressed, in a rather unforgiving blue suit with wet shoulders.

He looks like a more dissolute Hugh Grant, she thought, *if one can imagine such a thing. I could outrun him even with my hip.*

When she peered closer, she realized he was younger than she'd first assumed. His clothes were expensive but old-fashioned in a bad way, and he was terribly out of shape. Now he was hovering uncertainly outside the bakery opposite. He couldn't have been more obvious if he was wearing a sandwich board.

Annie had dressed older than her natural look; it helped her to disappear. Waiting until his attention drifted (and it only took a noisy van driver to distract him) she stepped out of the newsagent's and dropped into the darkened doorway of the bankrupt restaurant next door, the better to watch his next move.

Like a child, he was so amazed by her disappearance that he might have been watching an adult repeatedly pull off their thumb. He rushed away in pursuit of whichever notion had now surfaced in his head and she set off in the direction of Highbury Corner, where she was due to meet the other member of their group.

The operations room of the PCU had become a Battersea Dogs Home for unlovely desks, multi-coloured chairs and benches, most of them filched from Caledonian Road Junior School. It looked like a cross between a student squat and a McDonald's play area. When John May entered, the others came to attention. He belonged to an elite group of staff members who had been unsuccessfully murdered on the premises, and therefore commanded greater respect.

'Mrs Hoffman's case isn't strong enough to build an investigation around but we need to keep you on it until my partner reveals his incredible master plan for saving us all,' he said. 'What have we got?'

Janice was wedged behind a tubular steel desk built for twelve-year-olds. 'From what we can ascertain so far, Mrs Hoffman refused to be attended by healthcare services and was competent enough to convince them that she didn't need any help. She spoke to them in person and was quite adamant. She'd stopped going out and was turning away home deliveries because the bloke downstairs had arranged to bring packaged meals up to her once a week.'

'I met the Bubble,' said Meera.

'Racist,' said Sidney without looking up.

'Bubble and squeak? How can that be racist? You do know he's Greek?'

'Defining him by nationality.'

'Yeah, 'cause he's actually Greek.'

'Actually he's Turkish.'

'Yeah, but Cypriot, so he's almost Greek. If you're not prepared to make sweeping generalizations you're not going to
enjoy being out on the street. Anyway, he didn't look like the
kind of guy who'd do anyone a favour.'

'Mr Yavuz has just finished a one-month jail sentence for
assault,' said Colin. 'He reckons he paid a member of staff to
take over Mrs Hoffman's deliveries in his absence. The guy did
a runner with the shop takings and nobody thought to check
on the old lady. She had a mobile and an emergency beeper but
wasn't in the habit of using either of them.'

'Dan, what are you doing down there?' asked May.

Banbury was crawling across the floor with cables bunched
in his hand, despairing at the state of the floor sockets. The
only time he was truly happy was when he was rewiring the
office. 'You'll all have to share plugs until I can get some of
these working again. I can't believe someone's had all my
High-Speed HDMI 1080p cables.'

'When was Mrs Hoffman last seen out and about, anyone
know?' asked May.

'She was still attending her local health clinic in March,'
said Janice. 'I can't find anyone who saw her after that.'

'Didn't the clinic check up to see if she was OK?'

'She was passed on to Social Services with an "At Risk"
flag and was sent some government flyers, but nobody visited
her. A charity called Euston Seniors periodically checked in
but her carer was dismissed just after Christmas.'

'It sounds like there was a lot of miscommunication and
she fell through the cracks in the system,' said Janice. 'She
was probably too proud to call anyone, tried to look after
herself and failed.'

'This is a bit odd.' Colin was staring at his phone. 'The
carer texted me back, but only to say that she doesn't want to
talk about it. Let's pay her a surprise visit.'

*

Thunderous clouds blossomed over the city like black ink dropped into water. Colin and Meera took the Ginger Line to Peckham Rye, emerging from the station just as it began to rain. After the renovated streets of King's Cross, the scarred landscape of South London came as a shock.

The high street looked almost derelict. Having been knocked about for over a century the terraces appeared to have been soaked in dirty mop-water, but the shops beneath them housed primary-coloured bars and cafés. The juxtaposition of scruffy and smart exemplified a certain kind of London neighbour-hood, cheerfully louche in sunlight while trouble killed time, waiting for the evening shadows.

They found Jacey Shaw folding tea towels into a '3 for £5' display in a chaotic charity shop called the House of Every-thing. The heaviness in her movements suggested a life survived instead of enjoyed, but there was kindness enough in her face.

'I'm sorry, I didn't want to talk about Mrs Hoffman on the phone because there were other people around.'

She led them outside beneath the shop's awning, where there was enough cover for her to have a cigarette. She nearly took her eyebrows off with the lighter and quickly turned the flame down. 'Amelia was one of my favourite ladies. I went in to see her a couple of times a week. There was never much to do in the flat – she wouldn't have a telly, said it killed the art of conversation – so we played word games. She had to teach me; I didn't know any.'

'Did she have any friends?' asked Meera.

'She said she didn't want friends. She didn't trust them.' She directed smoke away from them.

'What happened to her family?'

'Her brothers and sisters all died long ago. Amelia said she'd lived too long. Her husband popped his clogs back in the eight-ies. She has a daughter who works somewhere in Wimbledon and there's a grandson.'

Meera remembered the wheelchair in Mrs Hoffman's hallway. 'Was there anyone else close to her?'

'Not really. She didn't talk to the other ladies at Euston Seniors, said they were all gaga. Social Services outsource patients to us. It's not fair, a charity having to do the government's work. Amelia had earned the right to be looked after in her old age. But I loved the job. All my ladies were lovely, and she was a dear old thing. A bit wobbly but very sharp-witted. Well educated. I got the feeling she'd come down in life. She took no nonsense from anyone.'

'Why did she stop coming into the centre?' asked Colin.

'Her legs were giving her trouble, so I started going to her.'

'But you're not with Euston Seniors now. Why did you leave?'

Jacey's features clouded. 'They said I stole some money.'

'From Mrs Hoffman?'

'No, from one of the other ladies at the centre. I didn't. She was paranoid, always accusing people of taking her stuff; everyone knew that. She didn't have any money to lose, poor thing. I stood my ground. It was a matter of principle. But they were worried about their reputation and I lost my job over it.'

'Who took over Mrs Hoffman's care from you?'

'That's just it, nobody did. We lost some staff in the cutbacks. I was told not to continue visiting because they couldn't vouch for me any more. But it's not just a job. You form proper friendships. I said, "I didn't just care for her, I care about her, I've got every right," but they said no. I went round there a few times but there was never any answer.'

'You didn't report it?'

'No, because the café owner downstairs told me he delivered food to her and she was fine. And I heard there were a couple of old girls who sometimes came and took her out. People she used to work with.'

'Do you know their names?'

'She didn't tell me who they were. She never talked that much about herself. Besides, I had troubles of my own to deal with. I feel terrible now, knowing she died all alone like that.'

'It sounds like you knew her better than most,' said Colin. 'What do you think happened?'

'I reckon maybe she had a fall and couldn't use her call button for some reason. I can't believe nobody checked up on her. Usually there's a care avatar appointed, someone to make sure the ladies aren't left without support. You should talk to Sherry Evesham at the centre.'

The Euston Seniors Day Centre was a glass-fronted box covered in children's drawings of rainbows and sunflowers. It sat between a Sichuan restaurant and a bookmaker's on Chalton Street, just off Euston Road. The charity was just a few hundred yards from one of the busiest thoroughfares in London but there were few cars or pedestrians. Noise was muffled by the mature plane trees that lined the broad pavements.

Sherry Evesham took them to the coffee point, away from the communal room where most of the elderly visitors sat reading or watching a cookery programme.

'They're all women,' Meera said, looking around.

'It's always the way.' Sherry picked up a fallen walking stick and handed it back to a resident. She did not see the need to lower her voice and let them follow her on her rounds, putting chocolates back in tins and refolding cardigans. 'The men have all the fun and drop dead when they're done; the women live on for another couple of decades. Our ladies are often rather startled to find themselves here.'

'They must be,' said Colin. 'Realizing they're going to be stuck in front of daytime TV for the rest of their lives.'

'We haven't got the resources to find different activities for them all. We were supposed to offer a range of therapies but then the cuts hit us. The number of elderly people who need our help increases every month.'

'Who kept an eye on Amelia Hoffman?' asked Meera.

'After her helper left Mrs Hoffman stopped coming in. It's often what happens.' She unthinkingly wiped a smear of jam from a table with the J-cloth she kept tucked in her sleeve like a handkerchief. 'Our ladies can get very attached. They don't want to switch to a new face.'

'Did you check up on Mrs Hoffman afterwards?'

'We didn't need to. A social worker called.'

'When was this?'

'I want to say mid-March but it might have been a bit later. I can send you a copy of her file.'

Meera was not satisfied. 'What did the social worker report?'

'Just that Mrs Hoffman was going to be looked after by a relation. There was a letter from her. There were a few bits and bobs in her locker so I sent them on.'

'What did she leave behind?'

'Nothing much: a jumper and a book. She'd used a lovely photo as a bookmark. She was in her flat smiling and hugging a big sunflower cushion. She looked very happy.'

'Do you have contact details for the social worker?'

'We didn't meet. It was just a phone call.'

An imperious-looking woman in a striped robe suddenly joined them and waved her hand in front of Sherry's face. 'I've been calling to you and you've been deliberately ignoring me. Somebody has taken my vowel.'

'Excuse me a moment.' Sherry turned to her visitor. 'You don't have a towel, Lily. You had a wash at home.'

'I want to report it stolen again.' She noticed Meera for the first time. 'And you – you have a magnificent problem.' She turned smartly and left.

'Sorry, Lily's been having trouble with words since her

stroke,' Sherry explained, 'but she's well taken care of. Social workers visit from Camden Council. They have more information on the day guests than we do.'

'Did nobody run a background check on Mrs Hoffman's relative? Am I being thick or something?' Meera looked at Colin. 'You allowed a total stranger to end Mrs Hoffman's visits?'

'You don't understand.' A tone of defensiveness came into Sherry's voice. 'This isn't a high-security prison, it's a place where seniors sit in comfortable armchairs for the afternoon. To get on to our list you need a code issued by the council. We offer non-medicinal palliative care. We're *meant* to be offering meditation, yoga, stretch classes, music and movement, but that's all gone out the window. People come to us from inside the care system, recommended by their GP.'

Colin looked up at the corners of the room. 'I don't see any cameras.'

Sherry folded her arms against him. 'That's because there aren't any.'

Meera felt herself becoming more annoyed. 'Do you know how this "close relation" was related to Mrs Hoffman?'

'I'm afraid not.'

'Did *anyone* make contact again?'

'If they did it would have been Mrs Makarov's job.'

'Can we talk to Mrs Makarov?'

'She went back to Lithuania. Our best worker and she wasn't allowed to stay here. I don't have any contact details for her. This is volunteer work; people come and go all the time. Do you know how overstretched we are? Most of us have no formal training. Mrs Hoffman wasn't even coming into the centre any more.'

'I guess it was just one more name off the books for you.' Meera tapped Colin on the shoulder and hiked her thumb at the door. 'Please send Mrs Hoffman's file to my phone.'

'That'll have to be approved, so you won't get it until tomorrow. I can give you her letter.' She opened her folder and removed its pathetic contents.

Meera took it from her and seethed all the way back to the PCU.

'We wouldn't have even picked up the bloody case if the old man wasn't trying to con the Home Office. There's nothing to indicate that anyone looked after her. How often does this happen across the country? How many people slip through the system? And why do we have to get involved in this?'

'It's an admin problem for the council,' Colin agreed. 'Let Mr Bryant see the letter and that'll be the end of it.'

But that was not the end of it, only the very beginning.

10

THE SECOND VISIT

Early on Tuesday morning Colin and Meera found the detectives restocking their desks and returning dust-fattened books to shelves. It looked as if they were settling in permanently.

'Have you seen my copy of *Lost Zoroastrian Architecture* or *Sexton's Necromantic Theosophies*, the lipogrammatic edition?' Bryant was asking his partner, who had chosen to ignore him.

'Are those your old desks?' asked Meera, amazed.

'The two Daves very kindly took them apart for us and stored them on the roof,' said Bryant. 'Along with my books. Although I seem to be missing a fascinating volume on competitive owl posturing. But do come in.' He waggled his Spitfire at them. 'My esteemed *compadre* has allowed me a pipe.'

'Won't it set off the smoke alarm?' asked Colin.

Bryant pointed to a jagged hole in the ceiling that looked as if it had been made with a crowbar. 'Sadly the alarm suffered an accident. What can we do for you?'

'This may be nothing . . .' She glanced uncertainly at Colin.

'I just sent you a file from a woman called Sherry Evesham who works at a day-care centre.'

'I'll never find it. Just tell me.' Bryant blew fragrant blue smoke over his books.

'I googled Mrs Hoffman's former home address: 82 Stanley Road, Cheltenham. She trained at something called the CSO, Oakley Road, within walking distance of her home. She was employed there as some kind of statistician.'

'The Composite Signals Organisation. They came out of Bletchley.'

'What do you mean?'

'Cipher breakers and information gatherers. Government security. It must have been a long time ago.'

'She was in King's Cross for a long time.'

'It doesn't mean much by itself. What do you think, John?'

May instantly grasped the implication. There was only one place to work if you were a statistician – at Britain's most famous intelligence and security site. 'Employment at GCHQ is a red flag no matter how long ago it was,' he replied.

Colin looked confused. 'Losing you a bit here, Mr May.'

'It means she was one of us, Colin. She'd have trained at the Government Code and Cypher School and would have automatically gone into GCHQ.'

'You mean she was a spy or something?'

'They got through a lot of very bright secretaries and some of their senior intelligence officers were female,' said Bryant. 'Women scored highly at intercepting and translating signals. Devious minds. We need more details.'

'There's something else,' said Meera. 'A social worker said Mrs Hoffman would be cared for by a relative but it doesn't look like anyone else went to her flat.'

'That's . . . interesting.'

'I know what you're thinking, Arthur,' May told his partner.

'Not everything's a conspiracy. I can't imagine that at ninety-one she posed much of a threat to anyone.'

'Why not?' said Bryant. 'Information is intelligence. You can withhold what you know at any age, whether you're fifteen or a hundred. It's when you decide to release it that you become dangerous. If she was at GCHQ, details of her work would be time-sensitive, depending on the importance of her position. Did she have security clearance?' Bryant jabbed his pipe in his partner's direction. 'You won't get the answer from her employers. GCHQ deported the journalist who first revealed their existence in Cheltenham. It would be better to go after her friends. She must have had some at the day-care centre.'

'How could an old lady die of neglect and starvation in the most crowded part of London?' Colin asked. 'Why didn't anyone check on her? She wasn't living in a Welsh farmhouse; she was just off the busiest road in the whole city.'

'No signal,' said Sidney, stopping in the detectives' doorway.

'I'm sorry, Miss Hargreaves, were you addressing one of us?' asked Bryant with exaggerated politeness.

'I overheard.'

'Ah, I didn't realize you were attending this meeting from the corridor. Please do continue.'

'Hoffman had no way of communicating with the outside world,' said Sidney. 'I checked her phone records. From the end of February until the time she died she made no phone calls.'

'You can't get a signal in her flat,' said Meera. 'I tried. And if she had a computer it's not there now.' She handed the detectives the letter. 'Sherry Evesham received this at the day centre.'

Bryant was less interested in what it said than how it looked. 'Sunflower notepaper. Not new. It's been kept in a drawer for a while, and before that it was left out on a table or counter.' He pointed to the worn creases and a corner that had discoloured in sunlight.

'She had a thing for sunflowers,' Meera said. 'Apparently there was a photo that showed her hugging a sunflower cushion. It got returned to her so it should be in her flat.'

Dan Banbury knelt in the middle of the living-room floor and peered underneath the sofa. 'I can't believe they didn't check under here.'

'Meera and Sidney only stuck their heads around the door.' Bryant wandered into the living room with a litre can of pink paint in one hand. 'I have a feeling there's something more going on.'

'A feeling.'

'Yes, a feeling. Sometimes one has to look beyond the facts.' He and Banbury had come to number 58 Cruikshank Street to conduct a more thorough examination of the premises, although the CSM felt they were wasting their time.

'You can usually expect to find Mars bar wrappers, empty peanut packets and fruit-juice bottles.' Dan reached in deeper and searched, but found nothing. 'Making meals becomes an effort, so they start hiding snacks within reach.'

'No one wants to admit that they can't cope,' said Bryant. 'Spending too much time alone isn't good for you. First you're independent, then you're stubborn, then you become strange.'

'Speaking of which' – Dan indicated the can – 'what's the paint for?'

'I found it in a cupboard. "Peach Bellini" Dulux gloss, oil-based. I thought it looked more like "Hot Pink Blush" myself. About a third empty, but there's none on the walls. An anomaly.' Bryant dropped himself sideways into a floral arm-chair and dug out a stick of liquorice. 'A pity the room can't tell us if she was distressed or in trouble.'

Dan fished an empty bottle of paracetamol from the side of the sofa. 'These aren't much use for serious pain manage-ment. There's no medication in her bathroom cabinet. I can't believe she reached that age without taking regular doses of medication. I'm already on three a day.'

'You have children so you're ageing faster. According to her GP she's supposed to have been on an entire regimen of tablets.'

Dan rose and stretched his back. 'As you so rudely point out, I am a family man. I can't imagine what it's like to be alone. To be honest, it would make a nice change. I don't suppose you were ever alone in Whitechapel.'

'Fat chance. There were three generations living in one tiny terraced house.' Bryant conducted the conversation with his liquorice stick. 'Grandparents in the first-floor back room, Mum and Dad in the front, me downstairs behind the scullery, my poor brother and the budgie in the middle back, the dog and the tortoise in the yard, the mynah bird in the kitchen, the neighbours on the doorstep and at the garden fence, everyone talking at once. Living like that is a thing of the past.'

'So are larders, polio and outside toilets.' Dan placed the painkiller bottle in a plastic bag. 'It doesn't look as if anyone else has set foot in here. Seems clear-cut to me. She was too proud to ask for help; the neighbours thought the carers were handling it and vice versa.'

Bryant chewed thoughtfully. 'No fingerprints or footprints other than hers?'

'Nothing. I don't see how you're going to get any further on this one.'

'Someone had Mrs Hoffman's support removed,' said Bryant, wrapping the remains of his liquorice in a paper bag.

'Then you must have found something I've missed, Mr B. I've taken swabs from the kitchen counter, the fridge and the door handles.'

'There's this.' Bryant produced an opened packet of spearmint gum. 'It was under the cushion. Mrs Hoffman had a dental plate. What was she doing with sticks of chewing gum?'

Heaving himself to his feet, he wandered off into the bedroom.

Banbury heard a thud and a grunt, and went to look. Bryant had climbed on to a small set of aluminium folding steps and was reaching up unsteadily. 'Old people always stash stuff on top of their wardrobes. They're the only people who still *have* free-standing wardrobes.'

He pulled a shoebox forward but started to lose his balance. Dan managed to keep him upright. 'You shouldn't be doing this at your age.'

'I shouldn't be doing anything at my age. Waking up each morning comes as a delightful surprise. Take this.' He passed down the dust-thick box.

They opened it on the dining-room table. Bryant had been hoping to find the kind of documents everyone keeps: a birth certificate, school reports and awards, but there were only photographic prints, eighteen of them in all, some taken many years earlier.

'What are you looking for?' asked Dan.

'Recurring faces, the daughter, the grandchild, friends, anything that reveals her life.' He laid a selection on the table and prodded one photograph with a thick forefinger. 'This woman is in eight of the pictures and there's a third friend in six of them.'

They were looking at a sturdy woman with cropped grey hair, about fifteen years younger than Amelia Hoffman, and another, blonde with intense deep-set eyes, in her early to mid sixties. 'Can we find out who these two are?'

'That's your job, Mr B. You're the detective. What do you detect?'

Bryant fanned the photos across the table, then dug about in his old leather satchel and produced a rectangular magnifying glass with a built-in LED light. 'Do you remember this, Dan? You bought it for my birthday. I was going to regift it to someone I didn't like but it's turned out to be quite useful.'

He examined the photographs again. 'These two, the grey-haired woman and Mrs Hoffman. They've known each other for a long time, at least thirty years. The younger annoyed-looking one is a vegetarian living in central London, comfortably off, intelligent, likes a drink and a show. Very patriotic. They probably all worked together at some point. When Mrs Hoffman ran out of money the other two topped her up. Old friends then, but their ages are a decade apart at least, which means they didn't meet at college. Mrs Hoffman was religious and once worked in a circus.'

Dan looked doubtful. 'Where do you get all that from, Sheer-Luck Holmes?'

Bryant held up one of the photographs. 'I use my eyes, Dan, something you should try instead of staring at your walkie-screen all day. This photograph was taken in Mildred's vegetarian restaurant just after it started out in Soho, when the area still had an edge. You can see Greek Street through the window behind them. This was back in a time when nobody ate vegetarian food just because it was fashionable. They went to Mildred's because it was virtually the only veggie place in town apart from that Indian on the Strand. Judging by the cars outside it's the late 1980s, which fits because Mildred's opened in 1988.'

He tapped another shot. 'In two of the photos there's part of a brochure showing, in this one on the table, in the other on the seat next to Mrs Hoffman.'

'Theatre programmes,' said Dan.

'It looks like the three of them were theatre buddies.' He could tell that the plays they'd seen were Michael Frayn's *Copenhagen*, which had run at the National Theatre in 1998, and *Wolf Hall*, which had played in 2013. 'From the backgrounds, both of these shots were taken at Joe Allen's, obviously their post-theatre restaurant of choice. It means that by the time they headed home it was close to midnight, so Mrs

Hoffman's friends must live within easy reach of the theatre district. The red wine on the table is definitely from that part of the menu where the prices start to climb. A birthday celebration? Red wine rather than a glass of bubbly, so probably not. Weeknights, too – I can't quite make out the date on the daily menu but no other day has as many letters, so it has to be a Wednesday.'

He moved on to the next photograph. 'Then there's this shot of Mrs Hoffman and the grey-haired friend in Piccadilly Circus. The Cinzano and Gordon's Gin signs are still there, but the building on the left has a "To Let" board over it, which makes it 1974.'

Dan was unimpressed. 'I don't see how you could possibly know that.'

'You don't recognize the building behind it? That's our company doctor's office. Dr Gillespie sits right behind where that sign used to be. There are only a handful of shots with all three women together, in restaurants again because before selfies you had to ask the waiter to take the picture. In this one someone's bought Mrs Hoffman a watch, which I saw a few minutes ago in her bedroom. But if you look at the photograph again you can see a second gift, an envelope under the watch, just inside the wrapping paper. What's that sticking out? Not a card but banknotes. Mrs Hoffman didn't put the money straight into her purse. She was uncomfortable about taking it. Look at her face. The cross around her neck suggests piety. The shoes are her best going-out ones, but they're badly worn. They realize she's broke and want her to take the cash.'

'And the part about her joining the circus?'

'I put that in to see if you were paying attention. I'd have an Ayrton Senna each way on the rest. The question is, how do we find the other two ladies? The answer may be here.'

He held up a photo of Mrs Hoffman and the grey-haired

woman seated in a spring garden. In the corner was a small triangular shadow. 'This is the most recent one. Mrs Hoffman is clearly older. That shadow is an elbow, so it was taken by a third person. Our other old lady?'

Dan looked closer. The grey-haired woman had a blue plastic splint on her right arm. 'It was taken a year ago,' Bryant said, 'warm enough to eat outdoors. See the daffodil-yellow sign behind them? An Easter gastropub menu with a date at the bottom. The architecture of the houses behind suggests it's somewhere in central London again but there aren't many pubs with gardens like that. Could be Hampstead, Golders Green, Neasden? They'd probably go north, not south, and not too far. It looks as if the friend has sprained or broken her wrist. So we have an event tied to a date, and an injury. Let's start calling around.'

'What about the third woman?' asked Banbury, setting down the restaurant shots beside each other.

'Not much to go on except she's Scottish – the tartan scarf.'

'Lots of people wear tartan.'

'With a matching skirt in the same clan? That's loyalty, not fashion. The pin looks unusual. Can you get more detail out of this?'

'It's not pixels, Mr B., just ink on paper. I could use different filters to bring out the shadows and create a 3D image. Anything more will start costing us money.'

'Forget it. Hang on, what's that?' He dug out his trifocals and touched his snub nose to the photograph. 'The propelling pencil on the pub table, flat sides, crosshatched silver, quite old. Does it look familiar to you?'

Banbury tipped the photograph to the light. 'No, should it?'

Bryant opened his jacket and set something down on the table. When he removed his hand, Banbury saw that it was a similar style of pencil.

'They were always used by scientists and academics, I've

no idea why. A 1930s design.' Bryant turned the silver pencil over. 'I inherited this one from my predecessor.'

'What are you talking about?' Dan's brow furrowed. 'You founded the unit. You don't have a predecessor.'

'No I didn't. And yes I do.'

'Wait.' Dan pressed his eyes shut. 'Explain yourself.'

Bryant picked the pencil back up again. 'I have a feeling Amelia Hoffman was not just a secretary at GCHQ. She was in a more elevated position, and so were her friends.'

'What she did when she was younger is irrelevant, isn't it? There's nothing out of the ordinary here.'

'Except the chewing gum,' said Bryant. 'Did you look in the wardrobe?'

'Yes. Everything's neatly put away.'

'She didn't own much in the way of fashion. You don't when you get older. I've had this waistcoat since Churchill's funeral. The death of vanity leads to the birth of maturity. But there are no shoes. All she had were the slippers she died in. She must have owned some. I think someone took them away to prevent her from leaving the flat.'

'No shoes at all?' Banbury scratched at the back of his neck.

'No shoes.' He tapped the end of the propelling pencil against his false teeth, thinking. 'I want you to come back here with all the equipment you can find and dismantle the place. Get me proof that someone else was here, manipulating her, pouring poison in her ears.'

'I don't think there was any sign of a toxic—'

'*Hamlet*. Is it possible to fake a death like this?'

'You're fighting the obvious, Mr B. It's a demise by natural causes exacerbated by neglect, not a concealed murder. I know it's not what you want to hear, but you can't manufacture a case without something to support it.'

'Then you'll have to trust my instincts,' said Bryant stubbornly.

'I'll have to pull in some favours to get the equipment I need.'

Bryant placed a hand on his old friend's back. 'Dan, it may not be a murder case but something is definitely wrong here. I can feel it in my bladder.'

'If you don't mind my saying so, Mr B., your bladder is a far from reliable indicator.'

'Tell me about it. I have another reason for going further with this. I think there's a link between me and Mrs Hoffman.'

Dan gave him a look. 'What do you mean?'

Bryant leaned forward confidentially. 'Do you remember my Tibetan skull and how I got poisoned? It left me with little cognitive lapses. Random memories have disappeared from my brain but I remember this. Before she went to GCHQ I think Amelia Hoffman might have worked at our own unit.'

11

A SERIES OF PERMANENTLY LOCKED DOORS

Raymond Land stood outside the office with his hand held hesitantly above the door handle.

If he opened the door there was a good chance he would expose himself to ridicule for the way he had handled the Home Office, but he urgently needed to speak to his detectives. He had missed his train home last night, of course, and had been forced to stay in a King's Cross Travelodge. He saw his refuge on the Isle of Wight retreating but was in two minds about it.

Land was in two minds about everything, which probably made him weak, although he wasn't entirely sure about that either. The past few months had taken their toll. Being held at knife-point during an investigation had left him with an interesting array of phobias, including a new-found queasiness about darkened rooms. Victims of crime were visited by family liaison officers, and in any other part of the force he would have at least been offered counselling. Instead his staff slapped him on the back, took him to the pub, made off-colour jokes about his traumatic experience and stuck him with the drinks bill.

The door creaked eerily as he opened it. He peered around the jamb and was astounded to find himself in a half-finished recreation of the detectives' former office. Dave Two was painting the last wall in a graceful shade of teal.

'How did you—?' he began, amazed.

'Come in,' said John May, in his usual position, looking as if he had not been shot, suspended and rehired at all, but had possibly been sitting there the whole time. 'He's not here, you're safe. What's happened?'

'Fatima Hamadani just rang to warn me that Faraday isn't going to accept the validity of your so-called case.'

'That should please you,' said May. 'It'll get you back to your garden in time to devastate the rest of your spring planting.'

'I don't know what you— How do you know about that?'

'I saw the footage.' The local police had sent a drone over Land's house and filmed him ineptly hacking at his flowerbeds. 'What's the matter? You don't look very happy about it.'

'That's the thing. I feel awful – can I sit down?' He glanced longingly at Bryant's comfortable crimson velvet armchair.

'Not there, that's Arthur's thinking chair. Use the stool.'

Raymond perched himself with his hands between his thighs. 'There's something else. The Home Office wants to go after the informants Bryant used on past investigations on the grounds that they were unqualified personnel.'

For decades, the PCU had relied upon knowledgeable amateurs to provide them with intelligence. 'Arthur couldn't work without them,' said May. 'They're his secret weapon. They provide information in good faith.'

'Anything they provided was technically inadmissible in court, you know that. What are you going to do? You can't just hang around here hoping Faraday will change his mind.'

'Arthur's found something.' May tapped his laptop key-board and turned the screen around. 'When we look at old people we see them as they are now. We don't consider how different their lives might once have been. Amelia Hoffman had a past. She was employed at GCHQ.' The monochrome photograph on his screen showed a pretty young woman lean-ing on a desk next to a man in a lab coat. 'Arthur thinks there's something odd about her death.'

'What do you mean, odd?'

'Someone posed as a relative and deliberately cut off her social care. They stopped anyone from coming to the flat, prevented her from getting out and turned off her water.'

'You mean they left her to die? Do you have any proof?'

'We're looking for it right now.'

Raymond bit a nail. 'Faraday's gone into a series of meet-ings but he'll start chasing me again tomorrow. I'll delay him as long as possible but you have to show me something concrete.'

May was puzzled. 'I thought you wanted to retire to the Isle of Wight with Leanne and weed your flowerbeds.'

'It turns out I haven't got green fingers,' said Land. 'Tomorrow, proof, on my desk, first thing.'

The Cork & Bottle wine bar in Leicester Square was a Lon-don institution. Its orange-tiled décor appeared not to have been touched in fifty years. Hidden beneath the teeming street, it had turned its dingy subterranean unfashionability into a badge of honour.

Rosemary Milton was seated awkwardly on one of the counter stools like a broad boat perched on a slender slipway. Time and feeding had expanded her once lithe form. She had ordered a bottle of red and the third of it she had already downed had brought a ruddy glow to her face, as if she was lit from within.

Bryant was only five minutes late. He remembered now that Rosemary was a bit of a lush.

'Darling, I was beginning to think I'd have to finish this by myself, how *are* you?' She turned a cheek as plump as a factory chicken. Bryant mimed kissing it and demummified himself from scarf, overcoat and jacket before clambering on to the opposing stool. His Oxford toecaps did not touch the ground. 'Rosemary, it's been a while, you're looking very . . .' He searched for a word and gave up.

'I glammed up for you,' she said coquettishly, pouring him a drink. 'Do you like my hair?'

He glanced at her orange head and failed to hide his shock. 'Oh, I thought it was a hat.'

'You know I'm the very soul of discretion.' She swallowed an enormous mouthful of Merlot. 'Even though I'm not at GCHQ any more, I'm under a lifetime data restriction and it's been worse since the Tempora programme hack. You do *not* want to know about pressure from the NSA, let me tell you.'

In the absence of ale, Bryant ordered a glass of water and some nuts. 'You said you would ask around for me. Did you have any luck?'

'It's a bit of a funny one this, because it's all so long ago.' She heaved a shiny black bag on to her knees and unclasped it. 'Amelia Hoffman stayed at GCHQ for more than a decade. I think I may have met her but one met so many people back then.'

'What was her department?'

'Something called diplomatic cryptosystems. I don't know what they did exactly but I'm sure you can hazard a guess. GCHQ kept a very low profile until *Time Out*'s investigative journalists exposed them in 1976, back when it was a serious magazine.'

'I guess she left to get married. Her daughter was born in

1974, which seems a bit late. Do you know what she did after that?'

'Not a clue, lovey. The rest of her career might have been redacted.' She drained her glass and refilled it. 'I can tell you what she did before, though. Her application is on public file.' She tapped at her phone and showed him the screen.

'Employed by Mr Bentley Trusspot,' Bryant read.

'You don't forget a name like that. Sure you won't have a glass?'

The Cork & Bottle had apparently become a place of pilgrimage, because a young couple who had clearly not been alive in the seventies came in behind them dressed in perfect period attire. The man wore a purple kipper tie known as a 'chest warmer'. His girlfriend was largely crocheted. Rosemary smiled indulgently at them. 'They have no idea, do they?'

'What do you mean?'

'How we lived back then. They've got the clothes but will never understand how different the world was. To think that we elected a prime minister because he won a yacht race. That's the trouble with the past – you can never truly return to it.'

'Bentley,' Bryant repeated, turning back to Rosemary. 'That was his middle name. His first name was Edward.'

She set down her glass and focused. 'You knew him?'

'He was my mentor. I was very young and impressionable, probably no older than sixteen. I'd never met anyone like him. He was intellectual, impassioned and rather otherworldly. Never quite in the room with you.'

'So he took you under his wing. Is that where all this came from?'

'All what?'

She waved her hand around his head. 'Unfettered thinking. What happened to him?'

Bryant knew exactly what had happened to his superior, but decided not to tell Rosemary. There were certain details he was happier keeping in limited circulation.

Rosemary stared into her rapidly emptying glass. 'Amelia Hoffman must have left traces somewhere. Trouble is, I don't know anyone on the inside who could grant you access. After staff die their records are still protected. When it comes to government secrets, you find yourself facing a series of permanently locked doors.'

Rosemary's department had been closed down and she was bereft without her old job. A barfly with a grievance does not make a good confidante. Bryant decided not to tell her why he was looking into Hoffman's background. He wasn't entirely sure himself.

'You know about these people, Rosemary. Do you think there's any likelihood that she could have had access to classified information?'

'It's doubtful.' She tipped the last of the bottle into her glass, including the sediment. 'We were the mushroom ladies, fed manure and kept in the dark. She'd have had knowledge commensurate with her position. Besides, her information would be half a century out of date by now.'

'Perhaps she knew something that could still affect people today,' Bryant murmured.

Rosemary ran a finger around the rim of her empty glass, calling attention to it. 'In all my time there I never knew what effect my work had on anyone outside. It left plenty of scars though. My marriage collapsed. My family stopped speaking to me. I couldn't tell anyone what I was doing, and the worst part is that I will never be allowed to. They put the burden of responsibility on us at a young age but never told us how to deal with it. Your indoctrination stays with you, stamped through you like a stick of rock. Even now, when I hear whistle-blowers explaining end-to-end encryption or international data abuses I still can't help thinking of them as traitors. Shall I get us another bottle?'

'I have to go.' Bryant was already wrapping himself in his favourite green scarf. 'Thanks for the information, Rosemary. They pay for my drinks here. Knock yourself out.'

She asked for the wine list. By the time she looked back to thank her old friend, he had gone.

Bryant paced before the unlit fireplace. 'Bentley Trusspot was my first boss.'

'You mean here?' asked May, confused.

'He was my predecessor, the real founder of the Peculiar Crimes Unit, employed by none other than Winston Churchill himself.' He patted his pockets but found no sweets. 'By the time I arrived at the unit he was on his way out. He'd blotted his copybook rather badly and was forcibly removed. It broke him. He went to GCHQ but never adjusted. A couple of years later he was released from his contract, and soon after he killed himself. He injected grapes with Nembutal, a pernicious drug thankfully banned now. Bentley was highly respected in the security community. I imagine GCHQ took Mrs Hoffman on at his recommendation.'

'Are you sure you never bumped into her?' May asked.

Bryant studied the damp patch on the ceiling, thinking. 'Did I tell you how I got this job?'

'Yes.'

'Which version do you know? When I had my interview with the PCU – we didn't have first, second and third interviews in those days, just a twenty-minute chat – Bentley was still running it. I do remember a young lady taking notes. I can't be absolutely sure but it might have been her. I thought the interview went well but Bentley didn't come back to me for several weeks. When I finally received a letter and was called in, he and the young lady had both gone. On my desk

I found a training manual with a note welcoming me to the unit, a silver propelling pencil and my own tea mug.'

'It was a bit more rock and roll in those days.'

'You may scoff but in a strange way it was. There were no managers and very few meetings. We had to stand by our own decisions. The sense of responsibility, that every day you could make a difference, was tremendous. Of course, we were one of a dozen covert units created by Churchill during the war, and apparently Winston never believed in standing on ceremony. He invented the onesie so that he wouldn't have to waste time choosing what to wear at work. He could never get adequate funding and was forced to keep most of his sabotage planners hidden.'

'Why, if they were getting results?'

Bryant rested himself on the edge of the desk. 'The armed forces felt that employing people in subterfuge units was underhand. They were staffed by non-military personnel, many of them not only female but amateur. They didn't follow the rules of engagement. Churchill argued that it was better to mount an exercise that could remove a single key opponent rather than carpet-bombing civilians to achieve the same ends, but he was shouted down. Several units achieved an astonishing level of success and changed the course of the war, but their staff only received grudging thanks from the generals.'

'What happened to them all?' asked May, looking through one of Bryant's books, entitled *The Pictorial Encyclopaedia of Spies.*

'In peacetime there was nothing for them to do. Some went to MI6. Hoffman might really have known where the bodies were buried.'

'It's a big jump from there to the present, Arthur.'

'You're right. I can't think of any reason why someone would suddenly pay attention to her after all this time.'

'If her GCHQ work is embargoed, what about her work here? What happened to everything after the unit moved from Bow Street? Surely you must have kept the important stuff?'

'We did.' Bryant's aqueous blue eyes rolled up at the ceiling. 'It's in those tea chests up on the roof.'

12

THE THIRD VISIT

On Wednesday morning Londoners woke up to the usual litany of metropolitan horrors: cancelled trains, violent crimes, political betrayals and the story of a frail, lonely old lady who had been left to die in the centre of a crowded uncaring city. A journalist had picked it up from somewhere and had interviewed the café owner, Constantin Yavuz. Breakfast show pundits expressed disgust. Social workers blamed councils. Councils blamed government funding and MPs blamed pundits, closing the circle.

At number 58 Cruikshank Street, Amelia Hoffman's flat was being meticulously taken apart. Banbury had dismantled the sofa, which was now arranged around the floor like parts of a model aircraft kit. Arthur Bryant decided to look in on his way to work and was already annoying his CSM by standing in the wrong places dropping bits of bacon roll on the carpet.

'GCHQ would have taught her to be secretive,' Bryant pointed out, licking his fingers. 'She could have hidden something here.'

'Mr B., it was decades ago. Can you stop *touching* things, please? Why would anyone care what some old granny did?'

'You've no imagination, have you?' Bryant wiped his hands on a tissue and sought refuge in an armchair. 'The post-war units were staffed by lateral thinkers and non-conformists. Did you know the War Office hired thousands of amateur radio enthusiasts to listen for enemy Morse code signals? They employed the kind of men who tinkered in sheds and women who instinctively kept diaries.'

'And you love all that, don't you,' Dan muttered, undoing a hexagonal nut on a sofa arm.

'Yes, I do. It shows initiative. No idea was considered too ridiculous; they hid microdots under postage stamps and messed up German radar signals by dropping clouds of tin foil over cities. They developed exploding paint and fake trees made of steel, hid codes in church bells and reduced the names on railway station platforms to three inches high. They were so successful in hiding the country from enemies that taxi drivers had to use the corporation names on manhole covers to find out where they were going.'

'Your kind of people, in other words.'

'Absolutely.' He balled his sandwich bag and tossed it into Banbury's forensic box. 'Our unit was created by the same backroom breed who'd been employed to think their way out of a war. They had no social skills, bad diets and poor hygiene. They lived in a world of abstracts. Their presence was kept secret even from parts of the War Office. They had no equipment and were left alone to come up with results.'

'Just like us.'

'Nobody wanted anything to do with them or to acknowledge how effective they were. One secret unit managed to steal the entire archives of the German navy without them noticing – thirty tons of documents.'

Banbury knelt to detach a cushion cover and peer inside it.

'I bet you're sorry you missed out on that part. I'm finding nothing inconsistent with the idea of a widowed elderly woman living and dying alone.'

'I don't get it.' Bryant picked up the stack of shoebox photographs and flicked through them again. 'After a long career, marriage, motherhood and friendships, all that's left is this? The place has been wiped clean.'

'Maybe she didn't like to remember the past. Not everyone does.'

'Then why keep photos of her colleagues?'

'Perhaps she was happiest then. Some people prefer to work than be with their families.'

Bryant stopped at one photo of a bald man in a lab coat. 'Hang on, I know this fellow. Herbert Constantine. An outspoken scientist and convicted fraudster. Lovely chap. How did she come to know him?'

'It always amazes me how people know each other. My wife knows my old PE teacher. It's a good job I've not got a suspicious nature.'

The most faded photo in Bryant's hand showed the interior of a gloomy, cluttered office with Amelia at her desk, impossibly young, her fair hair tied back, looking up at the camera and smiling. She was poised over the keys of an enormous black metal typewriter, a cigarette between the fingers of her right hand.

'She loved her job enough to keep an absolutely terrible photograph of her office. She liked data, order, science. The flat tells you that. There's nothing sentimental or frivolous here, no family mementoes, nothing out of place. There wasn't much money in her current account but she seemed happy enough.'

'What happened, then?'

'Someone came into her life. Her contact with the world was cut off. Social Services, the charity carers, her food supply, even her water. The only ones who could help her were warned off. It could have been a tragic cascade of missed opportunities and connections. She certainly wasn't conned out of her savings. And look at the books on the shelf behind you. They're all high-level scientific and mathematical works. *Digital Encryption: Communication and Conscience* was only published two years ago and looks well-thumbed. At ninety-one she was still keeping up with developments in her industry. She catalogued her recipes and alphabetized her magazines. She knew where everything was, but there are things missing. Look at this.'

He dragged Banbury over to a window ledge and ran his forefinger along the surface. 'She regularly sprayed it with polish, except here – there's a rectangular shape where the shine is thinner. What used to stand here for so many years that it left a silhouette? Why did she get rid of it? If she was in trouble why didn't she try to get help?'

'Maybe she wasn't thinking clearly.' Banbury's brow furrowed in frustration. 'She was old and frail, probably a bit cranky.'

'That's it, is it? We put everything down to senility?' Bryant unlocked the catch on the living-room window and opened the casement. 'Perhaps you'll get divorced and reach her age one day. Tell me you're absolutely sure that her death was misadventure.' He squinted down at the overgrown garden and swung the window shut.

'Then do something useful,' Banbury snapped back. 'You found the photos. Find me something more to work with.'

It was, Bryant decided, a reasonable request. Where else was Mrs Hoffman likely to store documents? He opened the sideboard door and found himself looking at a bundle of letters tied together with parcel string. The correspondence dated from the mid-1980s, handwritten in green and red inks. It didn't look promising – dry summaries of office life, peppered with acronyms and nicknames. Beneath them were gas bills and bank statements. He was about to set them down when one of the numbers on the top statement caught his eye. Thumbing back through the loose leaves, he made a note of how many times the same number appeared.

In the drawer of her bedside table was a book of brittle press clippings. 'You have to remember that the saboteur units constituted a closed world,' he called back, folding the photographs and statements into his coat and heading for the hallway.

'Is that it?' asked Dan. 'You didn't find anything else?'

'There's nothing else to find. She wasn't—' He mentally bit his tongue. *Don't voice your theories before you've had a chance to prove them.*

'Then I have something for you.' Banbury held up a small clear bag containing what appeared to be diamonds.

Bryant halted and squinted. 'What's that?'

'Ground glass. I took it from the U-bend of her kitchen sink.'

'Do you always take the U-bend off when you're checking out a crime scene?'

'We still don't know if it is a crime scene. And yes, I like to be thorough.'

'So she broke a glass.'

'It wouldn't have created residue this fine. I checked her kitchen cupboards and found a mortar and pestle. The pestle had been washed but there were one or two matching granules of glass on it.'

'We need to get the autopsy report from Giles. I'll let you finish up here. There's something I have to do.'

'Why would someone have gone to the effort of killing her with ground glass?' Banbury turned the bag by its knot. 'Giles would have spotted an internal haemorrhage immediately. It would have been easier simply to push her over.'

He glanced up but Bryant had already gone.

The back garden of number 58 Cruikshank Street was accessed from the rear of the ground floor. Bryant stepped down into it and counted out several paces. He stopped and looked around his boots. The dusty begonias and hydrangeas had been crowded out by lavender and drain-fed buddleia weeds that sprang from the bricks with branches as tough as pipework.

Leaning on his stick, he bent down and spread his hand in the weeds. It was exactly where he thought it would be, lying on top of the dark London clay. Picking it up, he blew the loose soil from it.

The pewter model was cheaply made and out of proportion. London Bridge had suffered many indignities in its lifetime but being made into a paperweight was one of the worst. Shoving it into his voluminous pocket, he clambered out of the garden.

At 11.35 a.m., Janice Longbright took a call from an incensed Sherry Evesham at the Euston Seniors Day Centre.

'What did you lot tell them?' Sherry demanded to know. 'I've had the press on the phone all morning, accusing us of neglecting Mrs Hoffman; people calling up and shouting abuse at us. Several regulars have already rung to say they're cancelling their accounts. We rely on donations to keep this place running. I already told you what happened. Who else did those officers talk to?'

'Our investigations are confidential, Mrs Evesham. We don't allow the press to access communications but we have limited control over journalists. Talk to Mr Yavuz. He's the owner of the café below Mrs Hoffman's flat.'

'He had no right to talk about such matters.'

Longbright tried to be diplomatic. After crimes were committed, blame was a medicine ball thrown from one player to the next. 'Mr Yavuz can say what he likes. I suggest you release a statement setting out your position. We've been through the file you gave us. The letter from Mrs Hoffman is a fake.'

There was a small aghast silence on the other end of the line. 'What do you mean?'

'It's not her handwriting.'

'Did you check with Social Services? Did the same thing happen with them?'

'They went through a change of personnel during the reorganization of their departments, and somehow Mrs Hoffman's file was misnumbered and lost. The new employee didn't know of her existence.' Longbright could tell the care manager's confidence had collapsed. 'Bad decisions, bad timing. It's not always possible to assign blame.'

When she heard the buzzer to the street entrance, she rang off and looked out of her office door. Arthur Bryant was making his way up the staircase as if climbing the north face of the Eiger.

'I need you to take a look at Mrs Hoffman's bank account.' He handed her his walking stick, the top of which had a silver cobra with a mongoose in its mouth. He turned so that she could help him off with his overcoat, which was three sizes too big and had a houndstooth check that made him look like a greyhound trainer.

As she struggled with his coat, bag and stick, he forced the loose statements on her. 'They came from her flat. Look at the account number. That's us, isn't it? I don't mean the main account, something older, see if you can find out when.'

'How much older? How could you have remembered that?' Longbright tried to catch the pages as they dispersed from his fists. 'I didn't know they still printed out these things.'

'How else would you get your bank statement?' He dared her to answer. 'She was paid on the last day of each quarter, a pittance, which is presumably why no one's ever picked it up. It looks like the amount never changed.'

'I'm sorry, Arthur, I have no idea what you're talking about,' Longbright admitted.

'You wouldn't believe how many people tell me that. Mrs Hoffman was on our bloody payroll.' He raised the page in front of his face. 'She was one of our employees and we didn't even know it.'

13

SYRINGES AND BISCUITS

Stumpy the one-legged pigeon hopped back and forth on his windowsill, lasciviously eyeing the ham sandwich on the other side of the pane of glass. Last week Dan Banbury had attached a pair of wires to a plate of thin sheet steel and sprinkled some seed on it before placing it out on the sill, thinking to scare the bird away by shoving a couple of hundred volts up its beak. So far Stumpy had studiously avoided the trap. Suddenly a pale sad face loomed out at him, shook its head and vanished.

Raymond Land had decided to change his password and now found himself shut out of his mail server. He stabbed ineffectually at the keyboard, much as a nervous passenger might randomly punch buttons in a stalled lift. It didn't help that the sodding pigeon was staring at him again.

No matter how hard Land tried to escape this building it seemed to draw him back in. He feared that one day he would be found lying under his desk as the staff argued about how long he'd been there. Once again his indecision had created an impossible situation. He had tacitly supported an outright lie designed to keep the unit open under false pretences, one last doomed play from his misguided team that could only end in tears. It was time for him to put his foot down.

Bryant's entrance was broadly pantomimic and timed to make him jump. He was wearing a shirt that looked suspiciously like a pyjama top beneath his partially unravelled green sweater. He slapped a page on to Land's desk and pinned it with a fat thumb.

'She worked here, Raymondo. Look at the salary amounts and dates.'

'What? Who? Mrs Hoffman? How is that possible?' Land took the statement from him and searched out the matching numbers. 'We were paying her? How far back do the payments go?'

'She was here before our first director Bentley Trusspot offered her a job at GCHQ. Mrs Hoffman, *née* Amelia Gerwitz, was plucked from the smart set at Cambridge, probably by one of Trusspot's gimlet-eyed finders, and put to work at the unit. She left to set up a cryptanalysis department.'

'I have no idea what that is.'

'From the Greek *kryptós*, meaning "hidden", and *analýein*, meaning "to loosen" or "to untie". It seems she worked for us before and possibly during her time at GCHQ. It would explain why there's no record of her name on the books. The payments appear to have been set up to be paid in perpetuity.'

'Why would this bloke Trusspot have wanted to keep her salaried forever?'

Bryant gave his boss a meaningful look. 'To keep her mouth shut.'

Land was lost. 'Who knows what went on at the unit in those days? It was before my time, before everyone's except yours and you can't remember our door number.'

Bryant wasn't listening. 'I need to talk to someone who

remembers Trusspot. Luckily I know a chap who's still around and lives nearby.'

'I know you're in there, I can see you behind the curtain.'

Bryant pushed the tip of his malacca cane against the doorbell again, then took a step back and looked up. A shadowy figure peeked through the window and vanished once more.

'This is ridiculous,' Bryant called. 'I can stay out here all day.' *If I had a chair*, he thought, looking about.

'I can't let you in without a mask,' Dr Rees called down.

'Then chuck me one and open the door.' As he did not own a watch, Bryant checked his wrist with flamboyant impatience. Dr Rochester Rees was a security expert specializing in epidemiological events, and, despite being daily convinced that he was in the final stages of some malignant undiagnosed disease, he remained completely healthy in his eighties. The bony little academic eventually opened his door and reluctantly admitted his caller.

Rees was wearing a sky-blue NHS paper mask and oven mitts. He was as thin and fragile as a denuded sparrow, with bulging mauve-lidded eyes and a sharp little nose. 'I can't find my sterile gloves,' he said, leading Bryant upstairs. 'Are you clean?'

'Clean living, more's the pity.'

Bryant stepped into a white-tiled living room with a gleaming steel-surfaced counter running down its centre. Dozens of plastic syringes stood on their ends like bullet cases waiting to be filled. The doctor had built a home-made laboratory that sat within the shell of his apartment. There was a strong smell of burned magnesium in the air.

'Does the landlord know you've done this?' Bryant asked. 'What are you up to? I thought you'd retired.'

'Old scientists never retire, we just get written out of the equation, so to speak.' Rees placed a batch of plastic pots in a mini-fridge and removed his mitts. 'Leave your coat in the hall and sit over there at the kitchen counter. Try not to get germs over everything. I suppose you'd like some tea. Let me sterilize some mugs.'

He brought beverages to the counter. Bryant scalded himself touching the side of the mug. 'What are you working on?'

'You know better than to ask that.' Rees twitched at the imposition of the question. 'Most projects are open-ended. We come aboard in the middle and leave with the work still unfinished. You can add to the aggregate knowledge but you rarely get the satisfaction of closure.'

'I didn't think you'd still be working.' Bryant settled his homburg on his knee. 'Didn't your unit lose its funding?'

After his wife died Rees had been arrested for releasing hundreds of diseased laboratory mice in the Hammersmith Palais ballroom during a dance contest. Although his purpose had been to highlight animal-testing conditions it hadn't done much for his reputation as a serious scientist and it certainly hadn't been appreciated by the finalists for the bossa nova.

'Some of us stayed in touch. We try to stay abreast of the latest developments but we can't afford to conduct any research of our own. It's little more than a hobby now.' The doctor's protuberant eyes had inner fire. 'It's an exciting time for epidemiologists. Someone outside the mainstream needs to peer-review the data. We submit quarterly conclusions. It's up to others to act on them.'

'You know they won't listen to a bunch of retired scientists.'

'Then they'll miss the next big pandemic. Ebola and measles. It's highly likely they'll combine and sweep the world.'

'You can't have a disease called Ebeasles. Besides, don't they spend billions tracking this sort of thing in huge laboratories now?' Bryant studied the Muji sample trays lined up across the counter.

'Gigantic systems fail because of tiny mistakes,' Rees said, folding his legs and rocking back on his stool, 'and someone needs to point them out. In medieval hospitals midwives noticed that their patients were more likely to survive if they washed their hands. But when the uneducated are swamped by forces they don't understand they succumb to superstition. The surviving mothers were called witches and the midwives stopped washing, setting obstetrics back a century. When the Black Death killed sixty per cent of Europe, the Flagellants' Movement took root in Germany. White-robed men whipping themselves to bloody shreds in atonement for God's wrath. We punish ourselves for the manifestation of original sin. To find a remedy you have to go to the root, and historically it's never where you think it will be.'

Talk of sin and death had perked Rees up no end. Their conversation always headed in the same direction, but this time Bryant had a peculiar sensation that it was somehow important. 'You knew my first boss well, didn't you?'

'It was a long time ago but yes, Bentley Trusspot was a good man. He was always on the cadge, forever trying to pinch an extra bit of budget, but he fought on our side. He's been dead for decades.'

'Did he leave any record, write his memoirs, anything like that?'

'Of course not. You can retire but you remain under contract forever.' Rees risked a sip of his tea. 'We worked side by side for seven years, hardly ever went home before midnight and I still never learned anything about him.'

Bryant thought back to his first impressions of the Peculiar Crimes Unit: the cluttered sepia rooms with sloping floors, the overflowing ashtrays and green glass lamps that threw cones of light against the curtains. Shadowy figures moving between desks covered with folders and bulldog clips, endless pots of stewed tea, murmuring and muttering, sums added up inside heads, pencil stubs behind ears, scrawled-on scraps, sketches pinned to walls, half-eaten sandwiches left on chairs.

'Do you remember someone called Amelia Hoffman? Or Gerwitz?'

Rees scratched at his beak, thinking. 'That depends. There was a pretty little thing, very bright, we all fancied her. I was in awe of them all back then, of course.'

'What would she have known about your work? I heard she was a secretary.'

'Don't you believe it. That might have been her job description but the girls were more than that. Most units had den mothers looking after the staff. Scientists can't be trusted to tie their own shoelaces. Women like Amelia kept their schedules, supplied their equipment, paid their salaries and acted as go-betweens for their superiors. They kept us on track. We tended to fall apart without them.'

'Could she have known anything that would put her life at risk?'

'They were administrators, not scientists. She'd have been privy to a lot of sensitive information but would never have known what to do with it.'

'What if she had been approached by the other side, the Russians perhaps?'

Rees gave him an old-fashioned look. 'Those women were ferociously loyal to the State. We all were, although we were prone to creating poisons and explosives without imagining what anyone might do with them. We spent months replicating *Yersinia pestis*, the Black Death, then one of us left a vial of it on the Piccadilly Line. Luckily it was unstable and would have become inert, not that we ever found it. After the old units were disbanded everyone dispersed. Women like Amelia found work in America, where the idea of a secret unit was less controversial.'

'The unit I joined wasn't dealing with government secrets,

just criminal cases,' Bryant reminded him, but he knew what Rees was getting at. The divulgence of intelligence was a treasonable act. 'Someone went to the effort of making it look like she died of natural causes. It was important not to draw attention to her.'

'And yet you noticed,' said Rees, scrubbing the spot where he had touched the counter with an antiseptic wipe. 'If she still had something to confess about her old career, who would be left to listen to her?'

'There's no time limit on some secrets,' Bryant replied. 'Would she have stayed in touch with Trusspot after leaving?'

'I wouldn't be surprised. He went from your unit to GCHQ but he still liked to use his regulars. He knew he could trust them.'

'Someone didn't trust Amelia Hoffman.'

Dr Rees's mauve-lidded eyes blinked furiously. 'Mr Bryant, I'm more comfortable with global diseases, although I must acknowledge a correlation between viruses and crime. Physical contamination is traced back to moral corruption, so we burn out the source, bleed the organs and purge the mind, and just as we congratulate ourselves it pops up in an unexpected form somewhere else. There's a nice traditional feel to the way diseases circle the earth. Information has the same spread pattern. It expands outwards from a central starting point, burning through the crowded hotspots, bypassing those in isolation, forwarded by super-spreaders.'

'Crikey, you might have hit on something there.' Bryant took up his homburg and jammed it on his head. 'What if Amelia is the source of the contamination? Suppose you and your pals reach a conclusion others don't want to hear, what happens then?'

'Then the others will ignore it,' Rees replied sanguinely. 'They know no one important is listening to us.'

'Amelia Hoffman wasn't ignored,' said Bryant to himself.

'Somebody paid close attention. I must go. Is there anything I can get you?'

'I don't suppose you've got a clearance pass for the retroviral replication laboratory at the Francis Crick Institute?'

'Sadly not,' Bryant admitted.

'Then just some epithelial syringes the next time you're passing,' said Rees hopefully. 'And perhaps a packet of ginger nuts. The ones covered in chocolate. Terribly bad for you. But then so is *Yersinia pestis*.'

14

THERE ARE NO BESTSELLERS ABOUT EMBEZZLEMENT

From his window, Raymond Land had watched Bryant returning and now waited for him to clump slowly up the stairs. He knew the detective would head straight for his office.

'Did you learn something?'

'Of course. I always learn from my informants.' Bryant attempted to extricate himself from his scarf.

'Well?'

'Well what?'

'What did you learn?'

'Oh, that Amelia Hoffman is Patient Zero and Ebeasles is going to try and kill us all.'

Land raised his hands. 'Wait. Wait. Can we just pause the crazy for a moment? Are you trying to build a conspiracy theory out of one old dear's death? Because it's in incredibly poor taste if you're planning to use her as a way of keeping the unit going.'

'Oh, Raymondo,' cried Bryant, 'surely when – I mean, if – you're found dead in some grim little single person's bedsit above a kebab shop in Shepherd's Bush, you'd want us to do some digging and find out why you ended up there all alone and friendless and dying some sad awful lonely preventable little death, wouldn't you?'

Land's stare was sharp enough to de-stone a mango.

Bryant ticked the points off on his stubby fingers. 'After Hoffman moved to GCHQ either someone here made an accounting error and never cancelled her salary payments or we paid her for a service that she continued to provide clandestinely, right up until the time she died.'

'She was a bit long in the tooth to be Mata Hari. What kind of service could she possibly have been providing?'

Bryant pulled his scarf over his ears but caught it in the fishing hooks that were sewn into his hat to prevent theft. 'After Trusspot's reign all sorts of unsuitable bosses came through here with their own agendas, each more hopeless than the last until finally you joined,' said Bryant. 'I thought you looked after our accounts.'

'I just sign off on them, I don't go through them in detail,' said Land. 'Ingrid does the bookkeeping.'

'Ingrid?' asked Bryant. 'Why have you never mentioned her before?'

'Ingrid Krause, she's freelance, only sends me a note if I've done something stupid.'

'You must have built up quite a correspondence. Mayhap you could ask her about these aberrant remunerations.' He waved the page in Land's face.

'It's probably for photocopying or something,' said Land wearily. 'Mayhap? Why can't you talk normally? I don't see how a bookkeeping problem is going to turn Mrs Hoffman's death into anything other than an unfortunate failure of the healthcare system. This won't be a case for your memoirs. Your readers want blood and guts. There are no bestsellers about embezzlement.'

'I'll prove to you that everything is related.'

'Why are you so driven by this?'

Bryant rolled his eyes theatrically. 'Because I want to know the truth.'

'Which is what?' Land felt as if he was walking into another of Bryant's casually laid traps.

'Amelia Hoffman was targeted because of something that happened when GCHQ employed her.'

'You want to go up against the government's security services?' Land felt the chill breeze of trouble ahead.

Bryant rummaged in his coat pocket and set the highly unattractive pewter model of London Bridge down on Land's desk.

Land leaned closer. 'What on earth is that?'

'A souvenir.' He pointed to its baseplate, which read: 'Greetings from Lake Havasu City'. 'London Bridge. Purchased for the grand sum of ten dollars.'

'Dollars?'

'In 1967 a chainsaw magnate bought the nineteenth-century London Bridge from the City of London. He had all the pieces numbered and shipped them to Arizona, where it was rebuilt. Everyone said he was mad, but the man who had helped to create Disneyland turned it into a successful theme park. One of Mrs Hoffman's friends bought this for her. Why? She liked bridges. In her living room there's a painting of the same bridge when it was still in place over the Thames with its original lamps, cast from Napoleon's melted-down cannons after the Battle of Waterloo. The picture occupies the spot where you would normally put a television, so it's clearly of some significance to her. This souvenir stood on her window ledge for years, then vanished.'

'And you just happened to find it.'

'I thought to myself, what would you do if you were housebound and needed to alert someone? She threw it from her living-room window. John and I need to go to Wimbledon.'

'Wimbledon.'

'Victor needs a run.' Victor was Bryant's rusted canary-yellow Mini Minor. 'It's where Mrs Hoffman's daughter works. I need John to come with me as my brakeman. Victor tends to creep forward at the lights.'

'Fine,' said Land, 'do whatever you need to do, just don't infect the rest of us with your madness.' He tried to stare Bryant out of the door. 'Well, don't just stand there. Go, go before I tell someone what you're up to.'

Wimbledon does not feel like a village, but nor does it quite feel like London. At night the side streets quickly tail off into darkness. Houses are set back from the road behind trim front gardens. There is a surfeit of bay trees. Towns at London's edge are quieter and cosier. Wimbledon had tennis and horses and a fine theatre of gold and crimson, with stained-glass screens and baroque fittings.

Ellen Hoffman had not kept her ex-husband's name. She was waiting for them inside the Wimbledon Theatre, at the head of the stalls. As their eyes adjusted to the low light the detectives saw that she was in a wheelchair. She raised a hand in greeting. She was in fluent control of her mobility. Her motorized chair was plastered with showbiz decals and moved as fleetly as a limb.

'Thank you for seeing us,' said Bryant. 'This is DCI John May. We're looking into your mother's case.'

'Oh?' Ellen glanced from one detective to the other. 'I wasn't aware that it had become a "case".'

'There are some questions about her final days. We're trying to fill in the gaps.'

The wheelchair whirred and turned. 'She never came all the way out here.'

'It's a beautiful building,' said Bryant appreciatively.

'One of the largest theatres in London. There used to be Turkish baths in the basement, can you imagine?'

'I saw the statue of Laetitia on the roof. The Roman goddess of gaiety, if memory serves. Why did your mother never visit?'

'Amelia had no time for the theatre. She couldn't see the point of it. My mother was not given to imagination.'

Bryant had seen the theatre programmes in Amelia's flat and knew this wasn't so. When it came to families, emotions clouded the truth. Perhaps she simply didn't have much respect for her daughter.

'She didn't really understand people at all. Pictures, words, numbers, but not people. I only ever saw one play with her, Joe Orton's *What the Butler Saw*. God knows what she made of that. We were perfectly civil to one another, but we didn't get on. Nobody says you have to understand your family, do they?'

'Tell me a little more about your mother,' Bryant suggested.

'She was rather high-born. Her father was a British army general and had married into Viennese aristocracy. A lot was expected of Amelia but she didn't conform to their standards. I liked her for that. Later her work took precedence over everything.'

'How often did you see her?' asked May.

'I didn't neglect her, if that's what you mean. But I didn't see her.'

Bryant was surprised. 'Not even as she got older?'

'She didn't want me visiting. We would never have known what to say to each other.'

'When was the last time you contacted her?'

'Just before Christmas. I wrote because she liked receiving letters. She was recovering from a cold. I asked her if she'd seen a doctor and she told me she had.'

Bryant knew that Mrs Hoffman had not seen a doctor.

'She was not a natural sharer. I never saw much of her even as a child. When I damaged my spine in a car accident the first question she asked me was whether I had been drinking. She was worried that I would be charged with an offence; thought it might affect her security clearance. She wasn't allowed to talk about her work so there was just a gap there. I knew better than to ask her.'

'Do you know what your mother did?'

'Not really. Some kind of counter-intelligence work, checking for subversives, encrypting sensitive information. It was before I was born.'

'What did she do after she left GCHQ?'

'She freelanced for security companies until retiring. I suppose she would have gone on – she loved the work – but she wanted to move back into London. She didn't like my husband and never spent any time with our son so we kept a respectful distance. Even so, she could have contacted me if there was a real problem. It was a sort of unspoken rule between us.'

'Did you ever think of her as vulnerable?' asked May.

Ellen gave a little laugh. 'Not for a second. She was tough as nails. Got it from her mother. Her memory was failing a little. She used to know all these mathematical equations and codes by heart.'

'After she retired, how did she spend her time?'

'That was the problem, of course. She had no idea of what to do with herself. She hated television. Thought it was vulgar. She didn't take holidays even when Dad was alive. I tried to help her from a distance.'

'In what way?'

'I arranged for a meal-delivery service but she didn't like the menu and cancelled it, preferred to make her own arrangements.' She tapped her rings against the wheelchair arm impatiently. 'I offered to take her shopping. She found the idea absurd.'

I'm with her there, thought Bryant. 'She had some friends of her own age, didn't she?'

'A couple, but she didn't see them very often. If somebody doesn't want your help you can only do so much for them. I've already had the press on to me this morning, asking me how I feel knowing my mother died alone in a squalid flat. I'm sure that flat was immaculate.'

'I would advise you not to speak to the press,' said May. 'Did your husband talk with her?'

'Oh, darling, he left years ago. He couldn't cope with this.' She gripped the arms of her chair. 'I wasn't in it when we met.'

'What about your son?'

She grew more dismissive. 'Why don't you ask him, if you can find him. I have no idea where he is but he should be easy enough to track down.'

'Why?'

'He has a police record for assault and battery,' Ellen explained. 'If you're looking for someone with anger management issues, you might want to start with him.'

Larry Cranston was still trying to understand how he had got himself into this situation.

He had been minding his own business, tootling back from lunch, driving a little carelessly perhaps but there had been hardly anyone about. He wouldn't have been drinking if he hadn't been feeling so stressed about his debts. So he'd had his usual bottle, red and heavy; you couldn't eat a steak with just a glass of water. And now, thanks to the stupid girl jumping out on the zebra crossing in Regent's Park, here he was still waiting, still without a plan for getting himself out of the country.

A woman called Paige Henderson was supposed to be his 'extraction facilitator', which made it sound as if she was going to pull his teeth out, but she'd also said to think of her as a friend, and what were friends for if not to help you out in a crisis? She had agreed to help only on the condition that he first delivered what he had promised, but now that the delivery was delayed she had stopped returning his calls.

Some police superintendent had already asked him to speak to the girl's parents in Riga and explain what happened to their favourite daughter. He had refused to do so, fearing that his own words would incriminate him. Who knew what further indignities he would be subjected to?

Now he was stuck in the claustrophobic mews house off Belgrave Square that his father had purchased for his mistress. After being trapped there for eighteen months waiting to be intermittently landed upon by a man with gout and leaky heart valves she had vanished overnight, taking only what was hers and never contacting him again.

He couldn't even head back to the family seat. Most of his decent shirts were in Somerset. Belgravia was as silent as a cemetery, its buildings like giant white headstones. Nobody lived there any more. It was hopeless trying to buy decent plonk anywhere, and as for cigarettes, one had to walk almost into Pimlico to find a tobacconist.

He had foolishly mentioned his other bolt-hole to Amelia, the hidden East End flat he had bought to rent out. He would probably have to go there next, even though it was in a basement and full of the most ghastly cheap furniture because it had been intended for tenants, not him. It was all such a bloody, *bloody* mess.

Paige Henderson had said they would speak again once he was ready for the exchange. She would arrange a time and place where they could meet, and the very next day he would be in the first-class departure lounge at Heathrow heading for New York.

Wonderful, he'd said. Perfect.

Except he still didn't have what they wanted. He wondered how long he could delay their meeting before Henderson gave up on him and walked away, withdrawing his only escape ladder. It was time to stop being so patient and *English* and start making things happen, even if more people got hurt in the process.

His journey had started the month before on King's Cross Road, quite the most revolting street he had ever had the misfortune to set foot upon. Most of the people there were in some sort of leisurewear, wandering around clutching cans and aluminium trays of noodles, trainers blindingly white, teeth flashing as they laughed and shoved at one another. In Los Angeles or Melbourne one expected people to be badly dressed but, really, London? Why she lived there was a mystery. It was the last place anyone would want to—

Ah.

Amelia Hoffman had hidden herself in plain sight. Given her background in subterfuge, it made sense. He had located the flat, situated above some kind of cafeteria selling rancid foreign meat. The smell had made him bilious.

When she opened the front door with the brass chain carefully attached, he saw through the gap a patient, steady eye. He should have taken that as a warning.

'I'm sorry to intrude upon your privacy.' He had adopted his most chiselled pronunciation, what he called his Olivier RP. 'It's about your bookkeeper, Ingrid Krause. May I come in?'

The implacable eye remained in place. 'What about her?'

'Mrs Hoffman, I know she handles both of our accounts and . . . well, it's a rather delicate matter.'

Still she did not move. Given she lived in this disgusting neighbourhood, he couldn't blame her for not flinging the front door wide and welcoming him in.

He made a show of glancing behind him, as if he was expecting to be followed. 'It's possibly not something that should be discussed in public. My card.' He passed it through the gap. It had the address of the ambassador's residence embossed in black. 'Perhaps if we could talk somewhere a little more secure?'

Secure. In hindsight this turned out to be the key word.

He heard the chain rattle.

Moments later, he was inside.

PART TWO

London Bridge was made for wise men to go over and fools to go under.

Old London proverb

15

SOMEONE TO RESPECT

The sky over Greenwich was determined to be interesting. There were bruised blue cumulonimbi above the red-ball pinnacle of the Royal Observatory, white cotton balls over the masts of the *Cutty Sark*, ripples of grey cirrus beyond the Isle of Dogs and patches of sunshine scudding across the sloping grasslands of the park. Nobody looked up. Changeable British weather was not news.

Ellen Hoffman's son was currently on a home detention curfew in a large-windowed flat on the elegant Georgian side of the old naval town. It was a world away from the shabby Edwardian terraces along Trafalgar Road, where even the name of the town was pronounced differently.

Although Edgar's flat was freshly decorated there was no disguising its limited space, something that must have become quickly apparent to him now that he was trapped here. The grey plastic dome on his ankle showed beneath his jeans as he restlessly prowled about his narrow living room.

Janice had brought her daughter with her; it was important

to get Sidney used to physical confrontations with Persons of Interest. Edgar sat down before them, impatient to start.

Let him wait, thought Janice, looking around. She breathed him in. The air was stale, too long without a window open. The living room was geared around an expensive-looking gaming console. An iridescent blue fly lay dead on a glass coffee table. Why didn't he sweep it away?

She had met Edgar's type too many times to be interested. Smart but unfocused and lazy, attractive in a late-night way, mystified by his own unpopularity. Detention had made him fractious, but he was not about to spoil things by losing his temper.

'Who gets your food?' asked Sidney.

Edgar noticed her for the first time. 'My HDC officer drops it off.' He mouthed at her. '*Home Detention Curfew*. You're too pretty to be a cop.'

'She's my daughter,' said Janice. 'How long have you been wearing the tag?'

He looked down as if noticing it for the first time. 'I don't know, three weeks, four.'

'So you have another eight weeks.'

'You've got my charge sheet; you already know the answer. Why don't you speak to my keeper?' He pointed at Sidney. 'She's not old enough to be doing this job. You're embarrassing me.'

'Did your mother tell you how your grandmother died?'

'I saw it online. Neglect. That's a weird one.'

'Why?'

He concentrated on picking at a nail like a recalcitrant schoolboy. 'We weren't allowed to see her. My mother said Amelia didn't want anything to do with us.'

'Mrs Hoffman was malnourished and dehydrated when she died. You think that's what she wanted?'

'The Social was supposed to take care of her needs. It's

their job.' Edgar thrust his hands into the pockets of his grey hoodie and flopped back in his chair.

'You could say it's your job, as family.' Officers were not meant to express their own opinions, so she trod carefully.

'I haven't any money, I couldn't even get over there, and now she's gone and I'm stuck here. She and my mother – long story. Ellen is what they like to call "highly strung". The wheelchair was the best thing that ever happened to her. It gave her a prop so she could turn everything into a drama.' He pulled at the sock caught beneath his ankle band. 'Can you have a word with someone and get this off me early?'

'And when did you last see your grandmother?'

'About five years ago. I was going to a party and looked in on the way. I just stayed a few minutes. She seemed all right then.'

'What makes you think she was all right?'

He shrugged. 'She didn't have to live alone in that flat. She told me she was still doing a bit of work.'

'What kind of work?'

'She said she was taking care of some people. She seemed happy.'

'How did she look?'

'OK, I suppose. I mean, old people all look the same, don't they?'

'Did you ever ask her about her job?'

'No, why would I?'

'Curiosity.'

Edgar looked down again at his ankle bracelet. 'So can you help me with this?'

'No, why would I?' Janice rose to leave. 'The crime you committed isn't the crime we're investigating.'

Edgar grew agitated. 'Wait, I saw her once more, a couple of years ago. Bumped into her on the street and met one of her friends. They used to work together.'

'What was her name?'

'I don't know, Annie something – a double-barrelled name, but Amelia called her Auntie Annie. This woman was living by herself in Covent Garden.'

'Leave it out. Nobody lives in Covent Garden any more.'

'It was a street just off the old market, I swear. That's why I remember. They'd just been to some old-school heavy-food restaurant. Maybe Long Acre, somewhere like that. Amelia pointed and said something like, "That's where my friend lives."'

'What was the name of the restaurant they ate at?'

'I don't know.'

'When was this exactly?'

'I – don't know.'

'You're a regular mine of information, Edgar.' Janice rose to leave. 'I know where to find you.'

They searched among the neon ice-cream parlours and doughnut shops for the tucked-away entrance to Greenwich tube station. 'That was a waste of time,' Sidney said, digging for her travel pass.

'Maybe not. There are dozens of fancy restaurants around Covent Garden Market but there can't be that many old ladies still living alone opposite them. It'll take us a few goes but we'll get her.'

'It'll be faster to run an online search.' Sidney reached for her phone.

'We can go there right now and ring doorbells,' said Janice.

Sidney's phone had no connectivity. She moved it around but finally gave up. 'It's been doing this ever since I let Mr Bryant use it.'

'That was your first mistake. Let's try it the old-fashioned way today.' Janice gave her a conciliatory pat on the back and steered her towards the platforms.

*

Constantin Yavuz was second-generation Turkish, born in Duckett's Green, North London, raised in the gaudy family restaurants that stood between the Christ Exulted Church and the Salisbury pub. With a loan from his father he had opened a kebab shop in King's Cross, reinventing it according to the area's ever-changing tastes. It was currently masquerading as a sort of vegetarian café, although being Turkish he had made sure there were lamb options.

Working in King's Cross turned everyone into an expert on human behaviour, and Mr Yavuz fancied himself more of an expert than most. He had watched as the porn cinema opposite became a nail bar and the pub turned into a mosque, and judged each new customer within minutes of meeting them. He liked the Islamic guys because they didn't drink, even though his wife complained that they just sat around with glasses of mint tea while their women slaved and their kids ran wild. He worked hard, sweated by the grill and tried to keep the place hygienic, no easy task around here.

When police officers came to his place he knew there would be trouble, and right now he regarded Colin Bimsley and Meera Mangeshkar as an obstacle to be removed before they scared off customers.

'I already bloody told you what happened,' Constantin berated the officers, setting a falafel tray on the glass counter. 'Take one of these while they're hot.'

Colin rolled the scalding chickpea ball from one palm to the other, then bit into it. 'Did you hear from your employee, the one who scarpered without bothering to feed the old lady?'

'Why would I hear from Ali again? He emptied out the bloody till when he left. I reported him to the other cops, the real ones, innit.'

Meera was irked. 'You mean the Met officer who takes care of this stretch, a porky Nigerian bloke with a slashed ear?'

'That's the one, PC Maduka, he said he'd look into it, never heard from him again.'

'You wouldn't have. What's Ali's last name?'

'No idea. His name wasn't Ali, either. We call everyone Ali because it's easier. He might have been Syrian. This is a crazy corner, people come off the train and walk into the first place they see, either ask for a job or steal anything that's not nailed down. You have to keep an eye on everyone. I have four kids, all girls, they call me all the bloody time. Dad, can I have my eyebrows done; Dad, can you drive us to Nando's. No one in London has time to listen.'

He brandished a kebab skewer at the doorway. 'These people on the street, they all thinking about who is there and who isn't there and what the next thing is, they don't notice anything but I notice – I see them all. I try to be nice guy, give money to the girl on the corner who cries all the time; when guys come in here too pissed to order I give them all the trimmings and don't rip them off.'

He razored a slice from an immense plug of amber-coloured lamb and handed it over the counter to Colin. 'Tell me that isn't bloody gorgeous. Know why? High turnover, everything keeps fresh.' He leaned on the counter, avuncular and smelling of warm meat. 'I feel bad about what happened. The lady – she was a nice old thing but I didn't know her. She wasn't one for small talk. Open the door, say thank you, close the door. A posh lady, someone to respect. When she stopped coming downstairs a friend of hers came in and asked if I would leave her meals, just in case.'

'What kind of friend?'

'A senior lady, same sort of posh voice, grey-haired, old but what do I know with Botox and filler now. She was very businesslike, paid cash in hand for three months.'

'You could have mentioned that earlier,' said Meera.

'You didn't ask.'

'Didn't you find that a bit odd?'

'I guess Mrs Hoffman asked her to do it. I thought my sentence would be suspended, especially 'cause it was just over a bloody tax bill that got lost in the post, but I got a bloody month. It wasn't a real jail, more like a detention centre. It happened a bit quick. I had to call in some favours to keep the café running, which is why the old lady didn't get her deliveries.'

'This friend who paid you cash for the meals Mrs Hoffman didn't get, we need to find her,' said Meera. 'I don't suppose you put it through the books?'

Constantin decided to take offence. 'Of course I bloody did, you think I'm stupid or something?' He went to the folder beside his till and ran back through the slips. 'There you go. Miss Angela Carey, 72 Moon Street, Islington N1. Like I told you, posh.'

Meera took the slip and folded it into her pocket. 'Did you ever see anyone hanging around Mrs Hoffman's place?'

'Lady, when I'm working I don't see nobody except the person standing in front of me wanting extra hummus for the same price. Him, usually.' He waggled his thumb at Colin. 'Or them other detectives of yours, the two Daves.'

'They're not detectives, they're builders,' Meera told him. 'Did anyone else ask for Mrs Hoffman other than this grey-haired lady?'

'Let me ask around.' He headed off into the kitchen and returned a minute later. 'Some geezer about thirty-five, slick hair, smart but a bit fat, another posh, acted like he owned the place. Came in to ask who lived upstairs.'

'Where did you get all that from?' asked Colin, amazed.

'Anita, the dishwasher.' Constantin looked back proudly. 'She's OCD, innit. Remembers everything.'

'Call us if Ali comes back.'

Meera left a PCU card on the counter while Colin called

the detectives. They were running late for a meeting at the unit. As they turned into the Cally Road and crossed through the waiting traffic, Colin unthinkingly took Meera's hand.

She pulled it away sharply. 'You cannot hold my hand in public, Colin! It undermines my authority.'

'It would be nice if you told someone I'd proposed to you,' he muttered.

'Let's wait until the time is right.' She stopped before a restaurant window and straightened her jacket. 'You have to get past my mother first.'

He blew a raspberry. 'Mate, I'll breeze that.'

'We'll see. You're meeting her for tea.'

'But I've got boxing!'

'I haven't told you when yet.'

'Well, whenever it is. I'm dead busy. It'd be better towards the end of summer.'

'You don't get to choose when. She's summoned you and will ask a lot of questions, so you'd better do some homework.'

'She'll be all right after I bung her a bottle of fizz and a bunch of garage carnations.'

'She doesn't drink and she has hay fever. And she's got a very clear picture of who she wants me to marry.'

Colin grinned. 'What's this picture like?'

Meera turned and considered him. 'Let's just say you're not in it.'

'I feel like a woodcutter having to pass a test before winning the hand of the princess. I can't change, Meera. If I lie she'll see through me.'

'Don't worry, you'll have inside help,' Meera assured him. 'I'd rather be a woodcutter than a princess anyway.'

16

ALL ABOARD THE SS *LOONY BIN*

John May tried to squeeze around the tea chest that stood in the middle of his cluttered office. 'Does this thing have to be here? Couldn't you have got the two Daves to put it somewhere else?'

'Good Lord, no, we don't know what's in it yet.' Bryant looked horrified by the idea. 'What if Raymondo saw inside? You know I'm always hiding things from him.'

'What sort of things?'

Bryant waved his hand airily. 'Oh, marijuana, explosives, the goat, Madame Blavatsky.'

May vaguely recalled seeing a threadbare stuffed goat on its hind legs and a wax effigy of the phony spiritualist. It was bad enough that his partner's 'Brown Bess' flintlock musket had been precariously propped in a corner once more. 'I don't know why you hold on to all these things.'

'They're more than just mementoes. Everything in this box is from an unsolved case. After I've gone they may be the only proof that a crime was committed.'

'But keeping everything – you remember how Raymond was after he found bees in his office?'

Bryant had briefly kept a hive in one of the spare rooms without the chief noticing. Unfortunately, the bees had got out through a broken ventilation pipe and followed the scent of a honey-coated power bar that lay uneaten inside Land's desk, where they remained bottled up and vibrating with fury until he opened his drawer the following morning.

Bryant pulled a crowbar from beneath his chair and attempted to lever the lid off the chest. 'I knew I'd find a use for this one day. It belonged to Coatsleeve Charlie, one of the finest burglars I ever arrested.' With a grunt he sprayed splinters of wood about the room. 'I've noticed people have started to say "burglarize" instead of using the more concise verb "to burgle". I suppose a "burglary" will soon become a "burglarization". I started to despair for the English language when I saw the word "quadrilogy" in print.'

'Why don't you let me do that?' May tried to take the crowbar from him. He already suspected it had been used on the smoke alarm.

'I numbered all the boxes. If Trusspot left any files behind they should be at the bottom of this one. Give me a hand, will you?'

May lent his weight to the crowbar and several steel staples popped out as the lid came off. The yellowed blocks of paper had been marred by mildew, water damage and mice. Most were filled with type hammered out on ancient Remingtons. Bryant lifted out a desiccated rodent corpse with two fingers and unfolded a packet of forms.

'Listen to this. "Ontological non-partisan documentation was ordered by restricted-information dispersal group expeditors." That's how governments cover their tracks.'

Rooting deeper he pulled out a reeking gas mask, followed by a lethal-looking knife with a notched blade. 'Gosh, Home

Guard equipment. It was a different world then.' He tugged the mask over his face and struck a pose with the weapon.

'What on earth are you doing?' Raymond Land stood in the doorway looking horrified.

'What do you want?' Bryant asked. 'Can't you see we're working?' No one could understand what he was saying so he dragged the gas mask off. 'Raymondo, do begone. You're not allowed in here.'

'Where did you get that? Why aren't I?'

'You said you were leaving so we cancelled your security access to the room.'

'I don't need a pass to enter my own offices.'

'Of course you do: this is a separate area of the building.' Bryant flung an arm around the walls. 'Think of it like Monaco, a principality with its own borders. We can issue you with a temporary code while we process your renewal application.'

'For God's sake put that knife down, you look like Hannibal Lecter's grandfather.'

'All we need is a deposit on your annual subscription fee as a sign of good faith. A purely nominal amount. You're already getting a staff discount.' Bryant appeared to be using X-ray vision to search for his boss's wallet.

Land started to reach inside his jacket. 'All right, how much?'

'Call it a bullseye.'

'What's that?'

'Fifty smackers. Cash only.'

He was halfway to handing over the notes when he came to his senses. He withheld the wad. 'You're supposed to be finding out what happened to the old lady.'

'As indeed we have been, my old grumbletonian.* We've launched a murder investigation.'

---

* Constant complainer, 1710.

'What are you talking about? You can't do that without going through me.'

'My dear fellow, we do everything without going through you. It's faster and easier. We're looking for a male, Caucasian, well spoken, mid-thirties, with an air of authority, overweight, dark-haired, spotted asking questions at the café underneath Mrs Hoffman's flat, the Almaqahaa Alkabir Lilmahata. You try saying that with a dental plate. I suspect he instructed Mr Yavuz's employee to stop delivering Mrs Hoffman's meals. Having cut off her care visits and her food supply, he stood over her and withheld everything she needed to stay alive, patiently waiting while she died of what appeared to be natural causes. I can't think of a more perfect murder.'

'That's horrible,' said Land. 'What on earth put this idea into your head?'

'A book of unsullied crossword puzzles. I noticed there were no writing implements anywhere in the flat. There were notepads in the kitchen and living room but no pens. Her jailer took them away because he didn't want her to write, in case she tried to leave anyone a message. She managed to throw the hideous pewter souvenir from her window, so I asked Dan to check and see if there was anything else. Oh!' Bryant clutched at the breast pocket of his coat.

'Are you having a heart attack?' Land asked, concerned.

'I just remembered.' Bryant fished inside his coat and pulled out a creased sheet of writing paper. 'No pens but I found this among the bills in her sideboard.'

He carefully flattened it out on the desk. A simple line drawing appeared to have been made in haste. It showed an extended triangle overlaid on a circle and a cross, possibly forming a sceptre.

'Have you ever seen something like this before?' May asked.

'It looks familiar.' Bryant narrowed his eyes and held it up to the light. 'It reminds me of something you'd find on street furniture. Like the symbols on London lamp-posts.'

'What symbols?'

Bryant waved his hand lightly. 'Oh, you know, Coco Chanel. If you look at any Westminster lamp-post you'll find a squiggle on one side with three loops, raised gold out of black, forming an elaborate W. On the other side are the linked backward Cs of the Coco Chanel logo. The story goes that the Duke of Westminster was infatuated with Chanel but she turned him down, saying, "There have been many Duchesses of Westminster, but only one Coco Chanel." So he put her on the lamp-posts.'

Land rose and plucked at his trousers after sitting on the stool, which he now realized had some kind of glue on it. 'I'm sorry, I am not climbing aboard the SS *Loony Bin* for another trip to the London That Never Was.'

'The story's not true anyway,' said May. 'The W and the Cs stand for Westminster City Council.'

'You spoilsport,' Bryant complained. 'I prefer my apocryphal version.'

'If Mrs Hoffman needed assistance, why not chuck the paperweight through the windowpane and make a noise?' Land asked.

'And have him silence her before help arrived? Besides, a symbol can convey as much as a sentence. In our everyday lives we are surrounded by hidden codes. Take Toblerones.'

Land groaned. Bryant ignored him.

'The Toblerone logo of the Matterhorn hides a bear from the coat of arms of Bern, where the chocolate is made, and the word "BERN" can be found hidden inside the brand name. That's just a chocolate bar. Who knows what this symbol holds?' Bryant rerolled the scrap of paper and returned it to his sweet-filled pocket. 'Hoffman knew her property fell under our jurisdiction. She also knew that the PCU has a very specific mindset. She had it and we have it because it came from her generation. You're the only one who doesn't have it, Raymondo, but that's not your fault, because you weren't always in the force, were you? What were you again, a postman?'

Land was indignant. 'No, I was an integrated communication systems manager.'

Bryant nodded sagely. 'So, basically a postman.'

'It was a bloody rewarding job, unlike this one,' Land pointed out in indignation. 'I've been in the force for over twenty years. It feels like three hundred. Where do you think you're going?'

Bryant was knotting the belt on his voluminous tweedy tent. His clothes tended to look as if they had been used for something else first.

'My partner and I have an interview to conduct. John, you're coming with me. We can finish the office later.' He framed his hands before him. 'I'm thinking heliotrope for the end wall.'

17

CHOSEN FOR MINDS, NOT LEGS

While the detectives headed up City Road towards Islington to see Miss Angela Carey, Janice and Sidney were working their way through Covent Garden, searching for another retiree.

In almost five centuries Long Acre had hardly changed. It was still filled with expensive trading posts. The ground floor of every house remained a fussy knick-knack shop or an Instagrammable restaurant. Sidney climbed some iron-railed steps and checked out a brass-boxed menu. 'This is going to take forever.'

Janice beckoned to her. 'Ellen Hoffman's son said they went to "some old-school heavy-food" restaurant. These are all chains – burgers and burritos. The fancier ones are lower down.'

Halfway along Maiden Lane the student queues for noodle cafés ceased and the shops became more expensive and reticent. Sidney stopped before a pair of red-canopied windows inscribed with gilt art nouveau lettering.

Rules – Founded 1798

Cupping her hands, she pressed her face against the glass and saw rich autumnal colours, polished dark wood, a profusion of red velvet, gleaming brass and copper, yellow walls filled with oil paintings, a glass *coupole* decorated with baroque flourishes.

'Their steak and kidney pudding is legendary,' said Janice. 'Have you eaten there?'

'No, but your father once had dinner there with the police commissioner and brought me back some sticky toffee pudding in a napkin.' She sighed at the memory. 'There was some kind of hospital the next street over.'

Sidney had already found it on her tablet. 'St Peter's, Grade II listed, opened by Prince Leopold, Duke of Albany, 1882, closed 1948. Says here it was built so that the wards could be changed into flats after it was decommissioned. Henrietta Street. An apartment building.'

'It sounds like Edgar misremembered where his grandmother ate. It's worth a try.'

They located the entrance to the apartments and pulled at the great brass handles on the front door.

'I guess we're going to have to ring all the doorbells,' said Janice.

The flats on the ground floor yielded no responses. A young American man in a red baseball cap and shorts came bounding down the stairs.

'It sounds like you're looking for Miss Wynn-Jones,' he told them. 'She's in the apartment above me, third floor.'

'Blimey, it feels like an old film in here,' muttered Longbright as she looked up at the curved copper lampshades in the hallway. 'Like *Dead of Night* or something.'

'What, zombies?' They avoided the lethal-looking trellis lift and set off up the stairs.

'Not zombies, you naïf. A British film made in 1945,' said Longbright. 'Five people meet in an old house, but they've met before in their dreams. It's very disturbing, especially the tale about the ventriloquist's dummy.'

'Oh. A black and white film.'

'You're living with me so you'd better get used to seeing a lot of them. I won't be able to relax until you know the difference between Rita Hayworth and Rosalind Russell.' She stopped before a door and rang the bell.

They waited. Sidney sighed and leaned against the marbled wall.

'Long hall,' Janice mouthed at her.

Annie Wynn-Jones opened the door. She smiled up from beneath a pudding basin of neat grey hair, looking from one to the other. There was an air of strength and stillness about her, a calm expectancy that suggested she'd been waiting for them. She appeared kindly. It was a calculated impression.

'Miss Wynn-Jones?' Janice unfolded her unit ID. 'Can we speak to you about Amelia Hoffman?'

'I was wondering when you would arrive.' She held the door wide. 'Call me Annie. Please come in.'

The flat was awash with light, opening into a great room running the width of the building. On one side a minstrel gallery was filled with design books. They made their way between steel and stone sculptures, potted palms and early-twentieth-century art. A fiery abstract panel suggestive of the Thames at sunset formed the centrepiece and was surrounded by paintings of 1951's Festival of Britain, sumptuous blocks of crimson, sharp blues and yellows.

They seated themselves in Eames chairs, rich black leather and chrome. The windows opposite looked out on to the mature trees in St Paul's churchyard. For a moment Janice wondered who was going to be interviewed.

'There are still a few corners where it's possible to forget you're in the city,' said Annie. 'When I bought the flat Covent Garden was still just a place to get cheap vegetables. Let's talk about Amelia, shall we? I don't know how I can be of use to you.'

'Anything you can tell us will help.'

Miss Wynn-Jones straightened a magazine on the coffee table between them. Longbright noted that its headline read: *Neural Evolution Special Issue.*

'I met her in 1965 when she became my supervisor at GCHQ. She married my fiancé. A long story, not terribly interesting. It didn't affect our friendship because I never really liked him. I can't abide poor behaviour. He died anyway. I left GCHQ at the end of the sixties, but Amelia and I stayed friends on and off over the years. We shared the same interests.'

'What kind of interests?'

'I suppose you know what she did for a living.' She tapped out a cigarette and fitted it into an amber filter. Sidney gave her a stony look.

'I'm smoking because it's my home. I shouldn't in front of Federico.' She pointed to a motionless emerald-feathered African parrot on a perch by the fireplace. 'I've always had pets. As a child I had a tiger cub, when it was the fashion to keep them. Amelia and I were both from Foreign Office families posted overseas: Calcutta, Mombasa, Hong Kong. We were politically committed but we were most fascinated by what had been happening at Bletchley. I'd missed out on the war years, so of course the codebreakers thrilled me. Why is it that we always want to be a part of something we've just missed? The cipher experts were a special breed. They didn't think like normal people.'

'How do you mean?' asked Longbright.

'Most of us look at a street sign and just see a name. They had a sixth sense that would let them see anagrams and signifiers, hidden pathways. We wanted to be like them, but we also wanted to serve our country. When you go to a dance and listen to a boy whispering nonsense in your ear you soon realize how unimportant sex is compared to good work.'

'What did you actually do for GCHQ?'

She waved smoke away from the parrot. Federico slowly raised a black claw as if putting a curse on her. 'We weren't decoders; our task was less definable. We looked beyond letter substitutions to the behaviour patterns of the senders. Cryptography had been simpler in the early days. At the start of the war the Germans cracked our code by looking for repeats of the letters GNOM, because telegraphers had a habit of signing off with "Good Night Old Man". All those figures and symbols translated into lives lost and saved. We had no contact with the general public. The psychological aspect of national security was a new field study. Our bosses felt it was peculiarly suited to women.'

'So you worked together,' said Longbright.

'For different bosses, on different teams and at different times, but yes, we knew each other and were like-minded. After the Cold War there was plenty of freelance work to be had.' She studied the end of her cigarette. 'Our task was to subvert and deceive. If a diplomat had the ear of someone powerful, we put words in his mouth. If he had an untrustworthy adviser, we poisoned his reputation. We became the queens of disinformation, Amelia and I.'

'And you remained in touch over the years.'

'Not as closely as before. Friends are like untethered boats, kept together by the tide of time but tending to drift apart. We were both too independent-minded to be close. There were often arguments, but I understood her.' Behind her, the parrot gave a very realistic cough.

'But there's a third friend, isn't there?' said Sidney. 'The three of you? Who's the other one?'

Seasoned officers followed their instincts in interviews, and Janice knew Sidney had misjudged the moment, pushing forward when she should have stayed silent. Wynn-Jones's smile remained in place but her manner cooled. 'I think you're mistaken. There were really just the two of us.'

'But I've seen photographs – a third woman, all of you sitting together in a restaurant.'

Annie turned to her with all the condescension of the experienced. 'Getting old is a process of learning how to detach yourself from people, dear. We had a great many friends, most of whom have passed.'

'I saw her.' Sidney was not about to give up. 'She's very intense-looking with blonde hair. Slimmer and younger. You were together for a birthday party.'

'Perhaps I've overstated our positions. We knew very little about each other and only did what our bosses told us to do.' Her voice had a harder edge now. 'The rest of the field was dominated by men. In our department women got a fair chance. We were chosen for our minds, not our legs.'

'Did you visit Mrs Hoffman in the days before she died?' Janice asked.

'No, she had asked me to respect her privacy and I did so. She sent me a letter telling me that she wanted to be left alone. She said she would never go to a hospital. "Nobody should die surrounded by strangers," she told me. We both assumed she had years left in her, but one never knows how these things go. Life loses its certainty and the old become scared. Illness is by its nature a surprise. But we were never scared. Our work had empowered us.'

'Do you still have her letter?'

Annie dismissed the thought with a wave of her hand. 'I hold no truck with sentiment. I threw it away. The end of life is uninteresting and funerals are only enjoyed by the maudlin. I said my farewell to her in private. To do otherwise would be to go against everything we believed.'

'Wasn't that rather premature?'

'I understood the reason for her letter. She was telling me we would not be in contact again.'

Longbright studied her. 'And Miss Carey, are you still friends with her?'

There was a tremor in an eyelid, nothing more.

'You do remember the name? Angela Carey?'

'We speak on the telephone.'

'We're interviewing her today.'

'I can't imagine why.'

'Did you know that someone posing as Mrs Hoffman's carer stopped anyone from getting near her?'

Wynn-Jones maintained her poise but it was calculated now. 'Amelia would never have allowed someone else to take control.'

'You have no idea who it could have been?'

'Of course not.'

'The three of you had no enemies?'

'No. Amelia, Angela and I – for a while we were known as the Three As. You know, like the Three Bs.'

They looked at her blankly.

'It was an old song. "Barrelhouse, Boogie And The Blues". It was a long time ago.' She detached her cigarette and tapped the ash. 'We enjoyed each other's company, especially if one of us had some gossip. We celebrated birthdays and met at Christmas to chat about the old days.'

'Did anyone else know that the three of you were friends?'

'Not to my knowledge. But if I think of anyone I'll be sure to call you.' She stubbed out her cigarette and rose to her feet. The meeting was at an end.

'The statue thing,' said Sidney.

The others turned to look at her. She pointed to the pewter model of London Bridge that stood on an occasional table. 'Mrs Hoffman had one.'

Annie dismissed it with a glance. 'Oh, the paperweight. A

colleague at GCHQ brought them back from America don-key's years ago,' she said. 'A souvenir, quite ghastly.'

'Who gave it to you?'

'I forget her name now. I never got around to throwing it out. I didn't want to hurt her feelings. Allow me to show you to the door.'

Sidney looked at the collection of artworks on display. Everything in the flat had been carefully curated. It was un-likely that Wynn-Jones had simply not got around to throwing out the ugly souvenir.

As they passed, Federico flexed his iridescent wings and screamed.

'How did you know Mrs Hoffman had a model of London Bridge?' Janice asked as they stepped out into the rain.

Sidney turned her phone towards her mother. Bryant had sent her a photograph of it, although he had managed to put his thumb over half the lens. 'She was lying. She said someone at work gave them the souvenirs but the bridge wasn't even open in Arizona until 1971, after she'd left GCHQ. She was acting like a little old lady but she was watching both of us.'

'She worked for a spy agency, what do you expect? Little old ladies are not to be messed with,' Longbright warned. 'People always underestimate how much they can eat, how far they can walk and how secretive they can be. It's not all post offices and wool shops.' She ruffled Sidney's hair. 'You have a way of seeing things very clearly.'

'I don't want to let my emotions affect my judgement.'

Janice sighed. 'Then you're definitely not my child.'

'Given the amount of time you've spent with me, I guess not.'

'That's unfair.' Janice went ahead through the side streets that led back to the unit. 'Have you spoken to your step-mother since you got here?'

'We're friends on Facebook and I follow her on Twitter. I'm

not sure you two would get on. She has a meditation yurt in her garden and bakes her own bread.'

'I could have—'

'And don't say you could have been a good mother. You took me on a stakeout. I was six.'

'There was no danger.'

'Don't worry about it.' She caught her mother's look and softened a little. 'I came back, didn't I?'

18

MISLEADING LADIES

Inside her apartment, Annie Wynn-Jones poured herself a gin and sweet vermouth. She had known that this day would come. It had been astute of the girl to work out that there were three of them. If the police were sniffing around it could only be because they believed Amelia had been killed.

Presumably the man who had prevented poor Amelia from getting help was the dunderhead who had been following her lately. She re-examined the conversation with Longbright. She had always told the others that when dealing with the police the trick was to offer plenty of information, most of it useless. What had she told them, really? Very little. It was an art she had perfected over a long career in disinformation.

She had lied, of course. There had been no letter. She had known from the moment Amelia failed to contact her that the three of them were in trouble. *If I don't send my signal on the last day of each month you'll know what's happened*, she had said. Amelia knew all about signal sites, the secret signs placed in public spaces that alerted others to danger.

Annie had walked past the back of 58 Cruikshank Street to

see if the London Bridge souvenir had been placed on the ledge of the upstairs window, but it was not there. In the event of discovery, they had all three agreed to do what they did best: mislead, misinform, misdirect.

She rang Angela's number and waited for her to pick up. She was probably looking for her phone again. Angela had to be protected at any cost. She was the weak link in their chain, an operative who could barely look after herself, hopelessly unprepared for any kind of fieldwork but as loyal as a dog and their last line of defence. They had always said that if this day ever came one of them would have to remain in the shadows, so it made sense to keep Angela in reserve. It was essential to have a fallback available.

Nobody could ever know about London Bridge.

Arthur Bryant and John May looked up at the immaculate terraced house, painted in teal and trimmed with white, tucked in the corner of Moon Street. The ground-floor curtains were open, the rooms dark. Bryant depressed the doorbell with the ferrule of his walking stick and stepped back.

'Fancy street,' said May.

'This was always one of the nicest.' Bryant swung his stick in the opposite direction. 'A V2 rocket landed over there and took out one house as neatly as if it had been picked up by a giant hand. We used to play on the bombsite as nippers because it was great for finding bullets and bits of shrapnel. We were always taking them into school.'

'Was that allowed?'

'Oh yes. I remember a very small boy nobody liked brought in a landmine. Everyone wanted to be his friend after that.' He looked up at the windows. 'Where is she?'

'Why did nobody like him before?'

Bryant's wide blue eyes swam at him. 'Who?'

'The small boy.'

'Oh, he was the ink monitor and smelled of paraffin. But his father owned the corner sweetshop and gave free aniseed balls to anyone who would let him touch them above the knee so it was swings and roundabouts.'

They waited but no one came. Bryant creaked back and forth on his boots, rubbed something from his nose and flicked it away. Finally he went next door and rang the bell. A wide-eyed young Indian man in a startling sweater opened the door.

'Your neighbour, Miss Angela Carey – do you know where she is?'

'You just missed her.' The young man was clearly wondering why these two odd-looking gentlemen were bothering him, but natural politeness took charge. 'She went out about ten minutes ago. She was going for dinner.'

'How did you . . . ?'

'My mother.' He pointed upstairs. 'She can't go out. She sits at the window and tells us where everyone's going. It drives us up the wall.'

'You wouldn't know where she went, by any chance?'

'Hang on.' He suddenly bellowed up: 'Where did she go, Mum?'

'Where she always goes, one of those Turkish places in Upper Street,' came a shrill voice from above.

'The Royaume is the best,' said the young man.

'Try the *imam bayildi*, it's delicious,' his mother called down.

The young man shrugged. 'They do have good aubergines.'

May thanked him and they headed back towards the main road. Bryant dragged a scrap of paper from his pocket and squinted at it. 'I wrote down a list of questions for her but they don't make much sense.'

'You sound surprised. It would help if I knew what we were looking for.'

'I'm starting to get an idea.'

Bryant tapped a faded photograph of a belly dancer tacked to the window and pushed open the door of the Royaume. A glance around the almost empty dining room revealed two girls photographing their starters but no elderly lady having dinner with a friend. Bryant saw trays of sizzling chicken being set down and realized that all he had eaten today was a bag of jelly babies.

John May sought out the manager and questioned her. She checked the pastel panels on her screen. 'We have Miss Carey down for dinner – just by herself tonight, table at seven thirty p.m. She's been coming here for years. Sometimes people leave messages for her. She had a starter and a glass of wine, then left.'

'What time did she leave?' asked May.

'A little before eight.' She turned to the skinniest waiter May had ever seen. 'Enrico, did you see Miss Carey leave?'

'No, she must have gone while I was in the kitchen.'

The other diners had stopped talking and were looking over at them uneasily, sensing that something was amiss. Bryant remained at the entrance, watching the street. June in London. Rain darkening the bare pavements. He could smell wet bricks and car fumes. There was malevolence in the air. Maggie had once told him that everyone became clairvoyant after a certain age. He was overdue some insight. He could tell that something bad was about to happen; his fingertips tingled. He stood listening.

May beckoned the waiter. 'I don't suppose she said where she was going?'

'No, she never says much. She's always in a hurry.'

'Has anything unusual occurred lately, anything that stands out? Have there been any calls for her, any messages?'

'A man rang here a couple of days ago.' Enrico looked as if he was betraying a confidence. 'He asked if Miss Carey had a booking, and I told him I couldn't give out information about our customers. He tried to insist, said I didn't know who I was dealing with, so I decided he would get nothing from me and hung up on him.'

'What did he sound like?'

'Very well spoken, but aggressive.'

May had one last thought. 'Does she ever come here with friends?'

The manager exchanged a look with the waiter. 'Sometimes – with two other ladies. I think they used to work together.'

May thanked them and rejoined his partner. 'Colin and Meera should be near them now. They're keeping an eye on the phone signals.'

'Two on surveillance? It's not enough.' Bryant rubbed at his nose, thinking. 'Where did Carey go?'

'I've not got anything from her phone,' said May. 'We need to retrace our steps. Something might have happened to her.'

Larry Cranston's stomach rumbled so loudly he felt sure it had been heard. He hadn't had a decent meal in days, not one with a starter. He looked out from the shadow of the doorway and released his breath very slowly.

The policeman – if that's what he was, because his enormous overcoat made him look like an unemployed Dickensian character actor – was no more than fifteen feet from him, pacing in front of the Turkish restaurant, lost in thought. He was short and old and bull-necked, with a battered homburg jammed over his ears and a silver-topped walking stick in his left fist. Although he moved with the care of a horse trying not to slip on an icy pavement, he was curiously strong-looking. Cranston's father was like that, clinging to life like a barnacle on a rock. Surely he was too old to be an under-cover agent? He couldn't be tailing anyone: he'd never be able to keep up. What if he was looking for the same woman? Could there be someone else involved that he didn't know about?

He realized he was becoming paranoid. A terrible chill crept over him. This was something to do with that CIA agent, Paige Henderson. She could have him followed, cut him out of the loop and leave him stranded here to face the British courts for causing death by dangerous driving.

He hated the old ladies. He never understood Amelia Hoffman's loyalty, clinging to ideals that had been trampled into the dust long ago. He felt sure this peculiar old man blasting out noxious fumes like a factory chimney was also involved somehow. They were leading each other in a merry dance across London.

He thought back to Mrs Hoffman. His second and third visits to the old lady in King's Cross had won her trust. She had allowed him access, just a little at first, and after she had the fall – just a small one, a trip on the bedroom rug he had carefully rumpled – he offered to stay overnight in the spare room to make sure she was fine. She had refused his help, of course, but a door had been opened.

He had no idea how to cook, couldn't even break an egg without leaving a mess. His offer to prepare her food was rejected with amused suspicion. She was trying to work him out. He took every rejection on the chin; it was one thing life had taught him to do well. He returned the next afternoon.

She invited him in. He checked her ankle, not really knowing what to look for. She talked down to him, using the kind of backhanded insults he'd grown used to in boarding school. He controlled his temper, listened with patience and answered with kindness, an entirely new experience for him.

They found a mutual interest in the *Times* crossword. She wrote in the answers almost as fast as she could read the clues. He promised to buy her a book of them, and was as good as his word. He stayed in the spare room more and more. He started to take the pens away when she fell asleep. Each night he checked everything in the room to make sure that she had not tried to leave any hidden messages. For someone of her advanced years she was as sly as a cat.

It still took a while longer for her to trust him. She was a lot stronger than he'd expected. She refused point blank to discuss her two friends in the photograph she kept in her living room. *I'll wear you down yet,* he told himself. *You'll tell me where you've been keeping your secrets all these years or I'll throttle the life out of you.*

She slept for an hour or so every afternoon at two, but awoke if he made the slightest noise. Eventually he had to crush up a sleeping pill and put it in her coffee. He searched the flat but found nothing at all, no hiding places of any kind.

She played innocent with him, pretending not to know what he was talking about. Sometimes he wondered if she was faking senility. He decided to stay by her side until she admitted the truth. Late at night he slipped out and headed back to Belgravia for clean clothes. Once or twice he risked going for a drink, paying cash. By now she had given him a key to the main door that led from the street, but expected him to ring the bell to the flat first. Her friendliness still masked suspicion. She was careful, but he was persistent.

And so it continued, until the night he made a slip.

19

THE CLOAK OF INVISIBILITY

Angela Carey, the youngest of the Three As, stepped back into the doorway of an estate agent's office as a police vehicle raced past, and caught sight of herself in the glass. She had never been called pretty: handsome perhaps, or healthy, which was worse. While the other girls smoked and joked in school break she had completed her time trials on the track. She did not feel that she had given up much for her career; it was hard to imagine the life she might have had otherwise.

Panels of blue light slid across the buildings. She caught a glimpse of the man who had been intermittently following her, an impression only – too much rich food, a double chin, hair slicked back in an old-fashioned Jermyn Street cut, pouchy eyes – and then he was gone.

She had first spotted him from the corner of her eye lurking outside a wedding dress shop. How long had he been on her tail? In her old job she would search for anomalies in every street scene, studying people from the narrow-windowed office in Leadenhall Street that was her life. She missed it still; the clatter of typewriters and the smell of cheap cigarettes, the mysterious half-whispered conversations, the warm fug in the air that blurred all edges.

Always check the street before you walk out into it, she thought, *basic training from the old days. You've become undisciplined.*

Every atom warned her that this was the man who would betray them and their country. He had gone after Amelia and now he had come for her and Annie. How had he found them? How much did he know? Amelia would never have given up their names voluntarily. He seemed an unlikely enemy, sweaty and confused, stupid even, obviously wishing he was anywhere but here, more like a middleman than—

A middleman.

Of course, she thought, *he's working for a buyer. The Russians? The Americans?*

Amelia had been easy prey, trapped in her flat. He could stay in the shadows, unseen and unsuspected. He appeared to be working alone, yet his actions made no sense unless he had a buyer for London Bridge.

She became aware that her phone was ringing. 'I do wish you'd pick up more often,' said Annie.

'I'm sorry. It was in my pocket.'

'Then turn the ring up. There's no point having a phone if you never answer it. You're absolutely hopeless. I thought you were going to leave me a sign about where to meet?'

'I couldn't. It's gone. The bollard in the middle of Camden Passage: they must have taken it out when they were digging up the road. We'll have to use the one at the end from now on. Where are you?'

'I'm nearby. Some clueless idiot has been following me.'

'You too? Oh God. Is he fat, chinless and rather stupid-looking? Early thirties?'

'That's the one. Under normal circumstances I'd say make

sure you're not followed but you needn't worry, he'll plod along behind you like a dog after a biscuit.'

'Couldn't I just call a constable and have him arrested for, I don't know, being a pervert or something? Say anything just to get him off the street.'

'He's a murderer, Angela. It won't be enough to stop him. I think we have to take care of the problem ourselves. Amelia always said we might have to do it one day. Listen, I don't want to go back to Covent Garden right now. Can you grab some overnight stuff for me?'

'Share your location with me so that I can find you on my phone. I'll be there as quick as I can.'

She rang off. *Spies*, she thought. *If we hadn't started playing spies none of this would be happening. I've had enough of this. I'm going over there to talk to him.*

She set off across the road.

'Can you help me please?' Angela asked with the broadest of smiles. Cranston looked at her as if she was about to bite him. She pulled her address book from her handbag and thrust it in front of his alarmed features. 'This is the Upper Street of Islington, yes?'

'No, I'm afraid it's not,' he said briskly. 'It's over in that direction.' He pointed back behind him, not knowing or caring if it was the right way or not.

'It is where I wish to go. I wish to find the – how you say – the *berühmtes Schuhgeschäft* – the shoe shop that is most famous in London, yes? And English people are so helpful.'

'I really don't know where that would be. I'm a stranger here. I really must be going.' Disentangling himself, he retreated as quickly as possible.

And this man is a killer? she thought, watching him flee. She had forgotten how exhilarating it was pretending to be someone else. She had always spoken German. It was why she had hired Ingrid Krause as their bookkeeper. And she liked order, which was why she detested the clumsy idiot following them.

Annie knew she would be a tougher target than Angela. Although in her seventies she had never forgotten her training, and was as alert as ever. All that mattered was carrying out their duty. That was the key; once you decided where your loyalties lay it was easy to know what to do.

Stay in the city, get lost in the crowds, she told herself. *Be proactive and keep moving. Angela is right, we need to outwit him. Only communicate by the signal sites. What we have must be protected at all costs, even if it risks lives.*

A cluster of students strolled past with their umbrellas up. Annie slipped in behind them, moving swiftly along Upper Street. The pub on the corner threw golden light over its noisy outdoor revellers.

She had a premonition that things were going to get rough from here on in. She had come out with only her credit cards, her phone and an old raincoat too short in the arms when she had suddenly realized that she might not be able to go home again. Her shoes were not made for distance. Of course it had started tipping down and she was hatless. Rain rinsed away the pedestrians, leaving the glistening pavements bare around her. At least she would see anyone approaching.

She could ask a neighbour to feed Federico. One of their trio was gone and she could not rely on the other; Angela was a stalwart but also impetuous and irrational. She grew overheated in arguments and always allowed her passion to undermine her authority.

Annie realized, with some reluctance, that everything was now down to her.

She stopped before the Union Chapel, the Gothic Revival

church near Highbury Fields. From the exterior it was just another rain-streaked brick tower surrounded by dank plane trees. Only the building's angel-filled rose window hinted at its importance. A hidden organ, one of the finest in the world, took advantage of the unusually clear acoustics. She could hear its mournful, rumbling surge from here.

She found a dry bench beneath a beech tree in the gardens and waited. Flickering light in the trees, rainswept streets, the organ pulsing an ominous track in a monochrome spy film: she looked out at this strange new world and longed to be home in Covent Garden.

A shadow stretched across the tarmac and abruptly disappeared. The organ piece ended and an even darker piece began, complete with a squall of shrieking top notes, like gulls pecking out someone's eyes.

She started to worry about Angela. People were protective of her with good reason. She was a brilliant profiler whose loyalty to the State was beyond reproach, but she did not inhabit the same world. Part of her was forever sailing above them, lost from view. As a consequence, her cover was deeper than the others'. But of course none of them were quite who they appeared to be. They were hard-edged and suspicious as Blackpool landladies but viewed across café tables, seated together with a bottle of wine, anyone younger would have written them off as three pensioners enjoying a retirement tipple.

Everyone has more than one life, she thought. Nobody stopped to consider who they had once been, only who they were now. They had acted more bravely and achieved more than most young women of today, at earlier ages and for higher stakes, but memories were short. The achievements of their youth counted for nothing. The camouflage of age served as a cloak of invisibility.

She was fairly sure there was no one else in the park,

although she had forgotten to bring her distance glasses. It was getting dark, and the persistent drizzle was chilling the air.

Pushing back against a hedge, Colin Bimsley tried to make himself inconspicuous.

'It's not working,' said Meera. 'I can still see you. You're too bloody big. Look at you, you've got shoulders like a bus.'

'That's not my fault.'

'Let me go ahead of you.'

They were in Upper Street near the Union Chapel, following Annie Wynn-Jones. She seemed not to know where she was going, or perhaps she was waiting for someone. Meera called the unit.

'I don't like it,' Bryant said, 'both of them in the same area. There's a reason for it, but I'm not sure who's manipulating whom.'

'We could do with some decent back-up,' said Colin. 'We could end up being outnumbered by old ladies.'

'Colin, the case doesn't even have official status. There's a bloke coming over from another division. Until then you'll have to make do with what you've got.'

Meera tugged his sleeve. 'Isn't that her?'

Annie Wynn-Jones was sheltering on a bench in the little park beside the chapel, looking like just another late shopper taking a breather on her way home. She was grey and floral and rather nondescript. If it was a disguise, it was perfect.

'Are you sure that's her?' Colin asked. 'They all look the same to me.'

'Well, there are two of them now.' Meera pointed into the park, where Wynn-Jones had been joined by another woman. As they crept closer, Colin set the audio on his phone to record the conversation.

*

Annie rose and followed the path, avoiding the rain that pattered into the laurel bushes around her. When Angela Carey appeared and touched her on the shoulder, she nearly had a heart attack.

'Change coats with me,' Angela said. 'Mine's waterproof. It's going to rain until the morning. Here.' She opened her backpack and handed Annie a plastic carrier bag filled with supplies. 'I threw it together. I don't know if I picked up the things you need.'

'I just hope we're wrong about this.' Annie accepted the bag. 'Everyone else seems to think Amelia died of natural causes. Imagine trying to explain that she was tortured for information. God, it's undignified, going on the run at my age. But we have to stick to her original plan.'

'I agree. London Bridge is the only thing that matters now.' Angela took her friend's arm and led her to a more sheltered pathway. 'I think the man who's following us got our names from Amelia before she died.'

'He must have done. How else could he know who we are?'

'I went over and talked to him.'

'Angela! You're supposed to be our deep cover!'

'I pretended to be Ingrid. He looked very shocked.'

'I bet he did.'

'I wanted to hear how he sounded. Did you know I used to transcribe audio files? I can pinpoint an accent to within a few streets.'

'And how did he sound?'

'Like an Old Etonian who'd spent time on the east coast of America.'

'That doesn't exactly narrow it down.'

'I recognize him. Do you remember Olivia Banks? She used to be married to him – the most frightful man. I only met him once, at a meet-and-greet thing in the US ambassador's residence in Regent's Park. His father's a peer and the family seat's in Somerset but I don't think any of them talk to him. Olivia landed him a job at the residence but he messed it up and they got divorced. I lost touch with her but it's definitely him. I ran a few searches on my phone . . . hang on.'

She dug in her bag for her phone, trying to avoid trickles from the overhead laurel leaves. 'His name is Laurence Cranston. He's on the embassy payroll but used to work in a low-level capacity for the FBI. One point in our favour is that he seems to be fairly incompetent.'

'He killed our friend.'

'Amelia was ninety-one,' Angela reminded her. 'It wasn't much of a challenge.' She turned up the collar on her coat. 'We have to find out how much he knows.'

'Amelia would never have given him any information. The money was still going into her account quarterly. He could have looked at her bank statements.'

They had always sworn that they would leave no trace of their movements, but somehow there was now a line glowing in the electronic ether between them and London Bridge. This man Cranston might know about the payments, but it wouldn't be enough to make him realize what they were for. The two of them held the future safety of the city in their hands. She still found it hard to believe that Amelia had gone.

'I know they're just tiny amounts,' Angela said, 'but I always worried that we hadn't disguised them well enough. We grew complacent. He picked on Amelia because she was the most vulnerable.'

'They're just figures on a spreadsheet,' said Annie. 'What else do you think he knows?'

'Maybe he's working with someone at the CIA. I don't have any contacts there any more. Most of them are dead. Annie, he is going to kill us if we don't give him what he wants. Somebody has to go and make sure that everything is all right.'

'It can't be you,' said Annie. 'I'll go.'

Angela looked distraught. 'You'll lead him straight there. London Bridge is insurance. It's the only thing keeping us alive.'

'It didn't help Amelia, did it?' said Annie.

Colin and Meera could go no further without revealing themselves. Having reached the nexus of fierce street lights clustered at Highbury Corner, they were forced to remain behind as the ladies crossed the road.

Checking the audio-record on his phone, Colin found he had been too far away to pick up the end of their conversation. All he heard was traffic noise and the odd word. Perhaps Dan would be able to get something more from it.

'If I didn't know better I'd say they were on to us,' said Colin.

Annie led her old friend to Canonbury Square Gardens, past high rustling elms and a glowing white gallery of Italian modern art. The rain did not bother her but Angela looked as miserable as a wet cat. 'I think he's given up following us for the night,' Annie said. 'We could both do with a drink.'

The Compton Arms had existed on the street since the middle of the sixteenth century, and was now dedicated to its local cricket legends. It looked like a country pub that had been dropped in the middle of North London. Surrounded by thick foliage, its sign swung in the rising wind. Annie shoved back the door and found the bar almost deserted.

'George Orwell used to drink here. Did you know he kept a permanently updated notebook of people who were Soviet sympathizers?'

'That's appropriate,' said Angela, taking a stool.

'Do you remember the photographs Ingrid took of us in Joe Allen's? I don't know what Amelia did with them. They're the only things that could have linked us. I keep wondering if she tried to get in touch somehow. You know what she was like about tucking away little messages. Old habits die hard.'

'Well, something will have to be done.' Angela unbuttoned her coat. 'This was never a problem before. Nobody ever knew I existed. I've always been good at dealing with last-minute changes but this – the police already know we're connected to Amelia.'

Annie recognized the tone. She was starting to fret, and whenever she did she became irrational. Angela had always been a bundle of nerves. She was younger than Annie and in excellent physical shape, but her mental health had always worried them.

'I can't protect both of us, Angela, and we can't talk to the police. You have to stay hidden.' She knew that hiding was easy when you were older.

'What are you going to do?' Angela's worried eyes searched Annie's face.

'Amelia's plan was always to make it look as if London Bridge didn't exist. Now somebody knows it does. If I can move it to a new hiding place it'll cut you out of the loop. At least you'll be safe.'

'But what about you?'

Annie smiled. 'I have experience with this kind of thing. Leave it to me. As you said, he's none too bright. I'll stay in town but I won't go home. Maybe you should find somewhere else to stay too.'

'No, I'm better off in the house than you are in your flat. You have all those communal areas. Anyone can get in through the main entrance.'

'I'll be in touch as soon as I've moved it,' Annie promised.

'Can you manage by yourself?'

'What choice do I have?'

'Isn't there someone else who can help?'

Annie stared thoughtfully into her glass. 'Do you know how naïve I used to be? When I started work I was thrilled to get away from my family. I didn't want to end up like my mother, cooking and cleaning and *waiting*. I swear she spent the last third of her life standing at the window trying to open walnuts. I was so excited to be in a position of real responsibility that I never stopped to wonder if what we were doing was good or bad.'

'It was good,' Angela assured her. 'We did it – we do it – for our country.'

Annie gave a mirthless laugh. 'Have you seen our country lately? There are no statesmen any more, only opportunists. What I did back then I wouldn't do now.'

'That's the difference between us,' said Angela. 'I would do it regardless. Times change. You have to be ready for them. Will you find a way to contact me?'

'I'll try another of the signal sites. I'll stay at the Charlotte Street Hotel tonight. If anything happens to me, you're our secret weapon. Cranston seems to be by himself. He can't go after both of us at once.'

They drank their gins in companionable silence. After, Annie saw Angela back on to the street. The last thing she felt was the grip of her friend's fingers on her shoulder before she slipped on to another pathway and vanished between the trees.

Larry Cranston watched the parting of their ways and realized what they had done. He did not know which one of them to follow. If Amelia had found a way to warn them about him before she died, they would be alert to his presence.

He was running out of time. The CIA woman from New York had sounded ominously relaxed. 'We have absolute faith in you, Larry,' Paige Henderson had told him. 'You'll figure out how to get it to us. But just to make sure that it happens soon, we need to light a fire under you. It's Wednesday, so let's say one week from today? The window will close then. We'll be pulling back our offer of extraction and turning you over to the British authorities.' Her voice grew more reassuring. 'Don't worry, we just like to keep you incentivized. I'm sure you'll manage to deliver ahead of schedule.'

It was possible, he decided. The main thing was not to panic. He would have to follow them until they could be tricked into revealing themselves. He chose to follow Angela Carey, and set off after the figure stepping nervously through the shining rain.

As he walked, he thought back to the night of the fatal mistake.

Amelia's bookshelves were lined with Trollope and Kafka, Steinbeck and Arthur C. Clarke. They had been sitting companionably in the living room, two people separated by almost sixty years. The evenings were long because there was no television, and Amelia mentioned that she had been reading Graham Greene's *The Quiet American*. She'd had a glass of Syrah and warmed to her subject, talking about betrayal and how ethical choices always came at a cost. Then it seemed they were not discussing the novel at all, but talking about her own life.

She was still guarded, of course, the habit was as deeply ingrained as checking three times before crossing the road, but he could see around the edges of the conversation. His certainty grew as she talked. She mentioned the past, her friends and her work, but he was drinking far more than her and became muddled, unable to separate truth from fiction.

She laughed and opened another bottle, topping him up, barely sipping hers, and as she talked he had a momentary glimpse of who she had been. The light of dangerous youth was in her eyes.

She spoke of toppling governments and derailing the plans of powerful men, of information being able to change the world, but was she only referring to abstract ideas? Without thinking, he asked her to clarify. Had she ever heard of something called London Bridge? Not the crossing, the concept.

It was a step too far. In an instant his true nature was confirmed. She had seen the hard glint of desperation in his eyes. Sitting back, her wine glass barely touched, she coolly assessed her foe.

And the game had taken a new dark turn.

Ingrid Krause inserted her earpods and headed along Noel Road, down the steps to the canal path. Despite treacherous puddles and a mischief of hoodies skunking under the bridge beside the oily water, it was faster getting home this way, and less depressing than walking between the blank towers of the City Road.

She passed what she thought was a black and white blanket, but saw it was a nest of moorhens tucked in against one another at the foot of a tree. Below the roads there was no sound of traffic, only the repeating plash of water as a duck took flight. The canal curved ahead, its edges lost in the shadows of unkempt bushes. The light from the nearby road illuminated rain stipples on the water.

When her sight was suddenly taken away she screamed, only to find her mouth filled with plastic. A Tesco Bag for Life had been pulled over her head, hands gathering it at her neck. She tried to pull it off but the handles were held together somehow, and without visual bearings she felt her balance tip.

As she fell forward she tried to put out her hands, fearing the concrete path, but there was no brutal slam, only the shock of brackish water. Although the canal was only five feet deep at this point she could not touch its bottom and could not stand because something was holding her down, pulling her head towards the silted bed of weeds and rubbish. She fought for breath and found none. Her lungs burned and made her vomit. As she choked, something metal scratched at her face and legs, a shopping trolley in the water. Half trapped in its cage she thrashed and tried to turn but there was nowhere to go and no way up.

Less than an hour later, a community police officer at City Road Basin saw something sprawled just below the surface of the canal water. A navy-blue coat with a waterproof lining had trapped air and fanned out in such a way that it concealed the body beneath. When the officer waded in and tried to lift it, he realized its head was caught on something and decided to wait for the emergency team, but they didn't have much more luck.

It wasn't until another officer arrived with a powerful torch that they saw the problem. The shopping bag placed over Krause's head had been joined at its handles by a plastic tie and pulled tight, and had become caught on a piece of wire.

The bookkeeper was trapped in a sunken tangle of bicycles, traffic cones and the remains of trolleys. When they finally managed to release her, the bag came free and her white face with its shocked mouth appeared, lacerated by emerald strands of weed, a phantom Ophelia hauled from the clutches of the city canal system.

20

BACKROOM GIRLS

'Where the bloody hell are they?'

Raymond Land opened his office window and looked out at the Caledonian Road. 'I asked them to share their location. Why can't my detectives obey even the simplest rules? Year in, year out, it's always the same thing. Every summer we get blown up; every winter we get shut down. Do you remember when Bryant insisted on interviewing that snake charmer here? He arrived with six snakes in a basket and left with five. Who was the muggins who found the missing one? I'll never sit on a toilet without looking again. And the performance artist who poured a bucket of pig blood over my desk? The clairvoyant who warned us we were heading for financial ruin just before she stole all our wallets? And all the rubbish Bryant brings back from his little trips. There was a harp stuck in the hallway for six months and I do *not* want to find another life-sized statue of Kali sitting in the middle of my floor with its tongue sticking out. This isn't a police unit, it's a cross between Petticoat Lane and auditions for *The Exorcist*.'

Janice stood listening politely. 'They're struggling with this just as much as you, sir. No one is telling us the truth.'

'Oh, grow up, will you?' snapped Land. 'When did anyone ever tell the police the truth? Suspects with gore-caked knives in their hands film themselves standing next to their victims and *still* insist they were never there.' He leaned on the windowsill for a better view of the street. Stumpy stepped back warily. 'I can handle the pig-thick ones. You know where you stand with them. But what do you do when smart people start lying to you? How are we supposed to cope with this?'

'We have an ID on the suspect—' Longbright began.

'I was being rhetorical, Janice. I know we know who he is, but we have the minor problem of not being able to bring him in for questioning because technically the unit no longer exists, there's no case and nobody in the Met is prepared to bloody help us.'

'Couldn't we just frighten him?'

'Oh, that would look good, wouldn't it? We couldn't arrest him, your honour, but we did manage to give him a heart attack and now he's suing us.' He wiped his forehead with the end of his tie. 'Just find out where they are, will you?'

Angela's random selection of overnight items that she thought her friend might need included leg wax and a spa mask but no toothbrush. Annie booked the room at the Charlotte Street Hotel under another name, knowing she could make up some story about a lost purse at the front desk. Subterfuge came naturally to her.

The broad wet pavements of Charlotte Street were sheened with yellow lamplight. The generous proportions of the low brick buildings set back from the wide road made her feel safe. Fitzrovia had barely changed since she was a child, visiting the toy museum up the road with her mother.

Annie's hotel room overlooked the street. She opened some snacks and poured herself a Scotch and soda, and sat on the edge of the bed in the lamplight that framed her window, rattling the amber glass between her palms, wondering how she could dig the pair of them out of this trap.

She thought back to the night they had gone to dinner and decided how to share the burden of responsibility between them. The beauty of the exercise should have lain in its inconspicuousness. They were three overlooked women with forgotten careers whose achievements could never be acknowledged. People spoke of the backroom boys but they were the backroom girls.

Restless, she went down to the bar and sat alone with another whisky.

She was joined by a woman in her early thirties, handsome, sleek, lightly oiled, in the way some wealthy American women always looked, as if they were tastefully restored boats. 'Is this seat taken?'

Annie waved a hand at the stool with a distancing smile and looked away. Her bar companion ordered a vodka that arrived in a fist-sized tumbler with a single giant block of ice. 'I never get used to it,' she said, possibly addressing her. 'It's eleven seventeen and most of London's gone to bed.'

Annie gave a slight nod but said nothing.

'I can't handle these trips any more. I don't bounce back like I used to.' She reached over and held out her hand. 'Paige Henderson.' Her grip was strong, her eye contact direct.

Annie returned the handshake hesitantly and lightly. 'Welcome to London, Ms Henderson.'

'Oh, I live here at the moment but I spend a lot of time in New York. I guess if you're staying here you're from someplace else too.' She waited, her eyes enquiring, a guileless smile held in place.

'I'm Ingrid Krause,' she said. 'Just visiting.' The lie came out smoothly and naturally. The bookkeeper's name was the first one that popped into her head.

'From Germany?'

'Yes, Nuremberg.'

'You hide your accent well. What are you in town for?'

'A sales conference on the future of European media. What line of work are you in?'

'Office furniture. Modular units and partitions.' Paige slowly turned the ice in her drink. 'I'm here for a big London convention.'

The lies tripped back and forth between them. Annie let the conversation run to a trickle and stop, sand through an hourglass. 'I have to get to bed,' she said finally, calling the barman over.

'It's been a pleasure talking to you. Why don't you let me get this.' Paige slid the bill tray towards herself with two fingers. 'I need to put *something* on my expense account.'

Annie conceded. 'That's kind of you.'

'I'm here for a few days. I hope we see each other again.'

'I hope so too.' Her smile was calibrated. There was something about this woman that set off an alarm: the severity of the black trouser suit and white shirt, the intensity of her gaze. She waited until Henderson had gone and headed for the reception desk.

'There's an odd smell in my room. I'd like to change it for another one.'

The clerk checked her records. 'We have an identical room on the floor above. I can send up a porter.'

'I'm travelling light, I can move myself.'

Don't talk to anyone else, she thought, settling into the new room and setting her alarm for 5.00 a.m., *especially when they look and sound exactly like CIA personnel*. She ran a check through the National Association of Retail

Furnishers, and failed to find any conventions scheduled for London.

When Annie rose and opened the curtains she found the streets empty and the sky a clear, fresh indigo. The distant glass towers of the Square Mile were blocks of red fire. At this time of the year the sky was nearly always clear at dawn. Soon there would be barely more than four hours' darkness a night.

Snapping the price tags from a sweatshirt and new jeans, she donned plain trainers and set off. Halfway down Charing Cross Road she realized that Cranston was following her again, still wearing yesterday's clothes. Did he really think he was being discreet, crossing the road by running out to the traffic island, then having to wait for a break in the oncoming traffic?

She couldn't lead him to London Bridge. *What does it take to lose you?* she wondered. *I'd like to show you what we old girls are made of and push you under a train.*

Suddenly the idea seemed feasible. Turning back, she headed for Leicester Square tube station. He followed her down the brass-lined steps into the ticket hall, ridiculously ducking behind a copy of the *Metro* if she ever looked in his direction. But on the Piccadilly Line platform she saw the impossibility of dispensing with him. There were cameras and passengers everywhere, as well as a guard who warned everyone to stay away from the edge of the platform.

At least the tunnels back to the surface proved useful for losing him.

Angela Carey looked out of her hall window and saw a young man with a constabulary haircut behind the wheel of a silver BMW outside her house. She checked out the extra instrumentation on the dashboard and the low-riding boot. The supposedly unmarked vehicle might as well have put a flashing neon sign on its roof.

She needed to get out and see what was going on. The officer was coming to the end of his shift and his reaction times would be slower. For the next half-hour she watched him, waiting for an opportunity. When he bent over to fish for something beneath his passenger seat she made her move.

Out on the pavement she found herself facing a broad-shouldered, thick-necked young man in a black PCU jacket. He looked up from his phone in surprise.

Colin Bimsley would have had no problem stopping her if the dozy PC they had borrowed for surveillance hadn't suddenly realized what was going on and blundered into him. He turned the officer around and shoved him out of the way but it was already too late. The street was as empty as it had been a moment ago, but she couldn't have gone more than a few yards. She had to be hiding behind one of the hedges.

'Don't stand there,' he instructed, 'check every garden on this side.'

A blur of movement flashed in the corner of his right eye. He ran across the road to a spot where the hedgerow leaves had just shivered to a stop.

'Come out,' he called. 'I'm here to help you.'

A fox shot out of the bush in a spray of leaves and dashed past his feet.

'I think she went down here,' shouted the surveillance officer.

Colin ran back. 'Where?'

In between the narrow, high brick walls of two semi-detached houses was the entrance to a ginnel that snaked through to the next street. At the centre of this brick corridor there was almost no light at all.

Colin did his best to ignore the overwhelming sensation of

claustrophobia that suddenly enveloped him and pushed on, but by the time he emerged from the other end there was no one in sight.

Sweating, he smashed at a hedge with his fist. The road ahead was utterly deserted. First Annie, now Angela – the old ladies were running rings around all of them.

21

SHOW ME THE EVIDENCE

Later that morning, at ten, the detectives hosted a briefing session in the common room, standing on either side of the whiteboard before the team. The Home Office removal crew had torn sockets from the unit's walls in their rush to remove all government-financed items, acting with all the subtlety of Lord Elgin's troops destroying the Chinese Summer Palace.

Bryant looked at the mess and tutted. Normally Dan Banbury would have been secretly pleased at the thought of having to upgrade the fittings, but this time he was distraught. Raymond Land sat moodily tapping a biro on a closed notebook like a pupil held back for detention. This was no way to run an investigation. Longbright was writing notes with a Wonder Woman pencil. Bryant had brought a very old book with him. Sidney's face was obscured by a curtain of hair that shone red in the light of her iPad. Banbury was furiously taking apart a plug adaptor with a penknife. *Our crack team of hotshots*, he thought bitterly.

'Utterly useless,' Land said again. 'The suspect was sighted on Upper Street but we've been officially instructed to stay away from him because – you'll love this – the CIA won't allow us to touch him. Apparently, they're "monitoring the situation". This was relayed to me with great relish by Mr Faraday, who suddenly thinks he's in an American film.'

'Have they said why they're involved?' asked Janice.

'Amazingly they're not in the habit of explaining themselves until some years after the bodies have been found,' said Land.

'We have an ID,' said Meera, holding up her phone. 'We recorded the conversation between Carey and Wynn-Jones in the park and had Dan clean up the sound.'

'They mention him by name,' said Dan. 'Laurence Cranston. I ran a check on every record I could think of: family, hospital, prison, employment, social media. There's nothing on him apart from a handful of biographical details about school and college.'

'How can there be nothing?' Land marvelled. 'Are you sure you got the right man?'

'It's him – the CIA has done too good a job on the redaction. He stands out precisely because there's so little information.'

'Let's concentrate on the rest of the case,' said May. He pinned up three photographs of the canalside. 'Ingrid Krause, seventy-two, resident of Islington, died in the Regent's Canal just after midnight. She'd been drinking in a restaurant with some co-workers, three minutes away from the Royaume and ten minutes' walk from the canal. She was attacked on part of the path where the lights are obscured by trees – some kids heard the splash as she went in – and she was found in the water nearest the edge of the path.'

'With a bag over her head,' Sidney added.

'Oh, so you *are* with us,' said Land. 'Perhaps when you rise from your electronic reverie to ask a question you could raise your head.'

'It's a coward's way of killing someone,' said Sidney, looking up. 'Like they had to do it but were squeamish.'

'What makes you think that?'

'Would you want to look into an old lady's eyes as you killed her? So, bag over the head and then push them in the canal. Reach out and put your foot on her head to hold her down. It wouldn't take much effort, especially as she was probably a bit drunk by that time of night and then became snagged on underwater debris. I think we should work out exactly how she died because it sounds like something this creep would do.'

Raymond threw up his hands. 'Wonders will never cease. John, will you do the honours?'

May pulled Colin out from the group. 'Working from Sidney's hypothesis and bearing in mind Ms Krause was wearing earpods – or, as my colleague here would call them, "walkie-speakers" – our attacker came up fast behind his victim and immediately bagged her. Seeing as Mr Bimsley had trouble outpacing a lady some forty years older than him, perhaps he could help us in another way. Colin, please oblige us by dying.'

Bimsley stood in as the murder victim while May attacked him in slow motion, a rugby tackle in an action replay. Raymond Land looked over at Bryant to see if he was paying attention. He was reading a book on bridges.

'Mr Bryant, I wonder if it would be possible to tear you away from your historical studies for a moment while your partner restages a tragic and senseless murder?'

Bryant could always turn an attitude of minor annoyance into a *tableau vivant*. 'It's not,' he said, laboriously closing the book and looking up.

'Not what?'

'Senseless. I asked Giles to check through her clothes for a notebook or any kind of scrap paper.'

'I'm not with you,' said Land.

'Thank heaven for that. If you ever catch up I'll know I'm going too slowly.'

'Then please explain properly.'

Bryant gave a theatrical sigh. 'Krause financially organized all three women, and it seems she organized us too. She had been out with other members of her profession for a birthday dinner that turned into late drinks. Her friends say she always carried a notebook on her. Nothing was found, so it's likely her attacker took it.'

'You don't know that,' said Land, exasperated.

'No, but her husband does. He says she rarely went out without it. I had to call him this morning to do the boring bits.'

'By which I assume you mean offering him counselling services after he'd been informed that his wife was dead.'

'And another question. The dining area of the Royaume restaurant is small and the kitchen wall is all glass. So why didn't either the waiter or the manager see Angela Carey leave?' Bryant removed his Spitfire from his waistcoat pocket and cleaned out its bowl with a clock spring. 'I'll tell you why. Because she didn't exit via the front entrance. She was meeting Wynn-Jones and needed to lose the man who was following her. There's a cocktail club in the Royaume's basement that gets busy when the restaurant closes, with a door leading out to an alley. Carey left while Cranston was still watching the restaurant.' He flicked bits of burned tobacco on the floor. 'Then he went after Krause.'

That was enough for Land. He raised his hand like a constable on point duty. 'I know where you're about to go. From a pissed bookkeeper falling into a canal to a global conspiracy that ends up involving fortune-tellers, bat-people and alien crop circles. Well, don't. Most murders come down to a simple equation. Alcohol plus stupidity times anger equals death. Anyway, there are always muggings down by the canal.'

'Raymondo, do we have to go through this every time?' Bryant asked. 'You say it's not murder, I say it is, I'm proven right and make you look like a total hinge. Can't we just skip straight to the part where you're a total hinge anyway?' He blew through the stem of his pipe and glued an eyeball over it.

'Show me the evidence.' Land folded his arms.

'Dan, tell Mr Land what you found.'

Dan tried to read his own writing. 'Angela Carey left fingerprints at the bottom of the staircase handrails that match ones on the unlocked gate at the end of the alley. Colin and Meera saw the ladies talking by the Union Chapel but there was no sign of Cranston.' He turned the page around. 'When Ingrid Krause went into the canal she hit her forehead and suffered a haemorrhage. The concrete edge tore her supra-orbital vein open. She was sick in her mouth and ingested filthy canal water full of rat urine.'

'Do you mind, I have stomach acid,' said Land.

'I thought Maggie gave you a concoction for that,' said Bryant.

Land grimaced. 'She gave me a jam jar full of vinegar with a dead eel in it. Told me to drink it twice a day. My apostle spoons went green.'

'But did it help?'

'Not at all. Could someone explain *why* she was killed?'

'No,' said Sidney, still studying her iPad.

Land's irritation found a fresh outlet. He turned to the new girl. 'No – what? Just no?'

Her eyes were unreadable grey blanks. 'You have to be very angry to kill someone. Can you remember what it's like to be my age?'

Land felt his face knotting up. 'I can't imagine what it's like to be you at all. Imagination isn't my strong point. What has that got to do with it?'

'You assume the killer has a plan. I never make plans. If someone hired me to get rid of people I'd just follow them about until they were somewhere dark and bash their faces in one by one whenever I got the chance.'

'Charming. Remind me not to get on your wrong side. You think he's just throwing this together on the fly?' Land was appalled by the idea. 'It doesn't sound very professional.'

'If someone else is controlling him he only needs to do what he's told.' Sidney turned off her screen. 'He's been watching and waiting but now he has to act.'

Land rose and drew himself to his full unimposing height, turning to Bryant. 'Happy? You've got her doing it now.'

'What?' asked Bryant, confused.

'What you always do. She's not been here long and you've already infected her with your abnormal thought patterns.'

'I want to make it clear that *I* never said the deaths were connected,' Dan told Land. 'The others have come up with this.'

'Don't be a creep, Dan.' Janice turned back to Bryant. 'Where do we go from here?'

Bryant tamped some Jolly Jack Tar Old Navy Rope Tobacco into his pipe. 'Double down on our leading ladies. Go back over their movements. Dan, I've been calling Wynn-Jones without luck. Can we get into her flat?'

'Perhaps you could try phoning her once more before asking me to climb through another broken window without a warrant.'

'I've rung several times.'

'She's not under suspicion.'

'That's not why she's avoiding us,' said May. 'She mistrusts the police.'

Dan Banbury was tired of everyone overriding his opinions and had been disappointed to discover that his Biometric Recognition Surveillance technology would not be needed. The women could be easily traced through their phones. His job was to study data from rooms, clothes and cars; there was no point in sitting around trying to second-guess their suspect. 'I agree with Raymond. There's no grand conspiracy. It's not *Three Days of the Condor*.'

'What's that?' asked Sidney.

'An old film about a government cover-up,' Longbright replied. Since being reunited with her daughter she had grown used to providing explanations for apparently obvious things. Last week she had caught herself explaining that red telephone boxes were glass booths with landlines inside. When Sidney had first come back to stay at her mother's flat, Janice had watched with amusement while she tried to operate a CD player. It was a shock to realize that she knew almost nothing about this girl. There were no mannerisms that marked Sidney out as her daughter. Time would tell if they could even stand the sight of each other.

Land pressed a hand on his combover. 'To think I gave up the Isle of Wight for this. I shall be in my office until you've all come to your senses.'

Bryant turned to the whiteboard with his Sharpie. 'Good, now we can get on with some proper work. John's going to give you assignments. It's probably best if we keep everything away from Raymondo. He won't mind; he's used to people avoiding him. He'll only get all sweaty and distraught if he thinks we've broken the rules again.'

'I'm still here,' called Land from the doorway. 'I can hear you.'

'Sorry, old ullage,* we all thought you'd gone. We normally try to avoid lying to your face. Did you know your name is derived from the Germanic root *Raginmund*, meaning "giver of sage advice"? What advice do you have for us?'

Land was perplexed. 'I don't want you to keep anything from me this time. Whenever you do I always end up in the wrong. If I thought you were right I'd admit to being wrong, but you're wrong, and I insist on being right until you're

---

* Unfilled space in a container of liquid.

proven wrong. Or I'm wrong.' He ran the sentence back in his head. 'I think that's right.'

Bryant patted him on the hand. 'You're having an attack of the vapours. Why don't you pop into your office for a camomile tea and a lie-down? John, over to you.'

May drew on the board. 'Annie Wynn-Jones checked into a hotel in Fitzrovia last night. She's now in Finsbury. Carey was at home in Islington until she managed to outmanoeuvre Colin. Mr Cranston could have been anywhere. Janice, I want you to start by talking to Wynn-Jones again.'

'Why?'

'She's wary but she might be persuaded to open up. See if you can get more out of her. Colin, Meera, Sidney: you're all on witnesses. Dan, I want to get inside Annie Wynn-Jones's flat and search it while Janice is with her. She'll fight a warrant, so let's do it while she's not around. I'll come with you.'

'Completely illegal, John, but I don't suppose that worries you,' said Dan. 'At least you won't wander around dropping orange peel all over the evidence like your partner.'

Bryant lit his pipe with relish, a cue for everyone to vacate the room. 'I think this is going to turn into something bigger than anyone expects.'

'You say that like it's a good thing. And what are *you* going to do?' Land was unable to fully leave the area until he could be sure that no one was being rude about him.

'Me? I need to talk to some unusual people about . . . certain things,' Bryant said evasively. 'I won't explain further; it would only annoy you.'

'What's got into him today?' Colin side-whispered as the meeting broke up and he headed out with Meera and Sidney.

'You know how he is after a murder,' Meera replied. 'Let's talk to the barge residents on the canal path.'

Sidney glanced back at the room they had just left. 'Mr

Bryant's up to something, isn't he? He's got that look again. I don't understand him.'

'You could try to understand him, or you could repeatedly punch yourself in the head until you're unconscious,' Meera said. 'You'll never make sense of his methods.'

'My mother managed it,' said Sidney firmly. 'If she can, I can.'

22

GENETIC BACKGROUND

Janice Longbright arrived in Finsbury, a neighbourhood which, in true London style, confused everyone, there being two Finsburys near each other, one with a park and one with a square.

She pushed through the revolving door of the Monkberry and crossed the foyer. The hotel was so blankly corporate that it was impossible to remember what it looked like seconds after passing through it. She noted that the glass-and-marble reception was dusty pink, battleship grey and the yellowy-orange of shopkeepers' acetate windows in the hot summers of the past. A clerk was staring blankly at a screen, her face lit kabuki-white, her mind offline.

Annie Wynn-Jones seated herself opposite in a vast flabby armchair, but was as upright and obstructive as a fence post. Longbright had met special-unit careerists like her before. Their loyalties were woven into their DNA.

'I know your work was sensitive, Mrs Wynn-Jones—' Janice began.

'I am not married. I believe we established that the last time we met.'

'I can see why you don't want to involve others, but this is a murder investigation.'

'That's not why I can't talk to you.'

'What concerns me is the welfare of you and Miss Carey.'

Annie picked lint from her sleeve. 'You seem to have grouped us together for the purposes of easy identification. Nothing else has happened or will happen.'

'I'm afraid it already has. Your bookkeeper, Ingrid Krause, was murdered just a few hours ago, very near to the spot where you met up with Angela Carey.'

Wynn-Jones's steadfast gaze did not alter. 'How did she die?'

'She was drowned in the canal.'

'You're sure it wasn't an accident?'

'Not unless she accidentally placed a plastic bag over her own head first.'

'I don't appreciate your tone,' said Wynn-Jones, still holding her eye. 'I have no idea where Angela is.'

The reaction caught Longbright by surprise. 'Really? We know you met yesterday; we know you're in trouble. If you're withholding information that could lead to an arrest—'

Wynn-Jones's smile lost its warmth. 'I am very aware of what you can and can't do, DI Longbright. I know everything about you and your unit. We used to be in charge of the surveillance on your team.'

Janice had always suspected that someone was watching them. The unit had accumulated too many secrets over the years. 'Then you know that if you or Miss Carey are found to be obstructing a murder investigation—'

Wynn-Jones leaned forward and tapped her gently on the knee. Her features softened. 'Formality doesn't suit you, Longbright. Let's talk woman to woman.'

'Very well.'

'Amelia recruited us a long time ago. We've carried out our

duty without ever breaching her trust. All we need is for you to stay out of our way until this has been dealt with.'

'You don't have the power to ask that,' Longbright said. 'We can bring you in as Persons of Interest and find reasons to detain you.'

'But you won't because if you do you'll only make things worse. We can handle it ourselves, Janice. We can't work with you on this. Mr Bryant will understand.'

'Amelia Hoffman warned you, didn't she? She was locked up and left to die and now someone else is dead. That leaves an assassin moving about the city, Angela trapped at home and you here, doing whatever it is you're up to. You're placing yourself and others at risk.'

'Tell me, Janice. What do you really know about the people who came out of units like ours? Trusspot was an Admiralty man brought in by Churchill. Winston admired what he called "corkscrew minds". He used them to run the kind of covert operations no one else would touch. Dirty ops, they all cried, not for us. In their heads they still lived in a world where mutually agreed artillery bombardments started after breakfast.'

'That was a long time ago,' said Janice. 'Attitudes have changed.'

'Have they? The Royal Air Force was happy to carpet-bomb German cities, murdering tens of thousands of civilians in attempts to kill a handful of important men, but when you showed the War Office an operation that could inflict maximum damage without a single casualty they claimed it wasn't cricket.' She glanced around at the foyer. 'The saboteurs had a rough war, working around the clock to save the nation, going to their graves without mentioning their work to anyone. Their strike rate was higher than that of the army, navy and air force combined and yet they were reviled, rather like the PCU. Exactly like the PCU.' She unfurled a forefinger. 'Because that's where you came from, Janice Longbright, that's your genetic background. You're the old sabotage unit, reinvented to protect and serve in peacetime.'

'No one has ever—'

'Informed you about it? Hardly surprising. The age of so-called ungentlemanly warfare ended long ago.'

'I don't understand where you fit into this.'

'Perhaps you should talk to your boss,' Wynn-Jones suggested. 'Ask him how you stay funded. Your unit's job is to protect the public at all costs but what are you protecting them from? The answer might not be one you want to hear.'

Annie rose and waved Janice back into her seat. 'Stay here until I've gone. Remember one thing. Despite what you think, we're on your side. But you need to keep out of our way. We're trying to end what you started.'

'Mr Bryant thinks that a fresh pair of eyes might do the trick.'

'Well, I guess his own are on their last legs.' Dan Banbury let himself into Annie Wynn-Jones's Covent Garden flat using Bryant's skeleton keys. They were even older than the detective but, unlike him, in decent working order. Dan stopped and breathed in. He mostly found himself entering the homes of the recently deceased. Homes that were still lived in had a different energy, as if they had souls.

As he bagged his shoes, May studied a copy of last night's *Evening Standard* on the hall dresser. 'There used to be six daily editions, so you could always tell what time someone had picked one up.'

'Well, now we can trace journeys from travel cards,' said Dan, 'so your life has been made simpler.'

'A child can trawl data. Where's the fun?'

'You're turning into your partner, you know that?' Dan sniffed the air and headed towards the kitchen. A row of hidden LEDs threw ambient light on the walls.

'A Lutron system,' said May. 'Very fancy. They're usually commercial installations. She has money.'

'It could have already been here.'

'No, this is the latest update. She's lived here for at least four years.'

'How do you know?'

May pointed at the kitchen.

The forensics officer followed his eyeline. 'What?'

'Top of the cupboard.'

'I have no idea what I'm looking for.'

'There's a tester tin of Farrow & Ball paint up there. The colour is called London Stone. It was discontinued four years ago.'

'The previous owner could have purchased it.'

'Her name's been put on the side of the tin. Farrow & Ball do that.'

Banbury was amazed. 'How do you know?'

'I used the same colour in my flat.'

'They must have dozens of shades.'

'I can tell them apart; my eyes aren't quite as old as my partner's.' He moved into the living room.

A low growl rolled from beside the fireplace. Federico the emerald parrot was shifting his weight from one black claw to the other along his perch. Dan eyed him warily. 'I hope that thing isn't a mimic. What are we looking for exactly?'

'Anything that links Wynn-Jones with the others. Correspondence, photographs, personal items. Like that.' He pointed to the ugly London Bridge paperweight on a side table. 'Dust it for me?'

Dan took prints; then he checked his phone. 'Wynn-Jones's thumb and right forefinger.'

'Matching souvenirs.'

'Sentimental value, a reminder of the time they worked together?'

'Except all three of their working careers didn't overlap.' May turned the model of London Bridge in his gloved hands. 'The Three As are more than a decade apart from each other. Carey was the last in and almost worked with Wynn-Jones, but not Hoffman. Krause came on board much later, and only to keep track of their finances.'

Dan ran a lint brush over a chair and tipped it to the light. 'You're missing a common link. You'll need your partner to find it.'

'He's doing his own thing, as usual. He's not a team player.'

'No, I imagine he'd be the last one picked by any side. Doesn't it annoy you that he goes off on his own? You are meant to be a team.'

'He'll involve me once he knows his ideas are workable,' said May, a little defensively. 'He hates the idea of losing face, even to me. Let's try the bedroom cupboards. She might have left something behind in one.'

May's phone buzzed. Longbright was calling to warn him that Annie Wynn-Jones had left the hotel. 'We have to speed it up,' he told Dan. 'She could be on her way back.'

Two steel-grey Rimowa suitcases were stored in a wardrobe. May checked the clothing rails and drawers. 'Why did she stay in a hotel? What's she up to? She can't be planning a long trip, all her stuff's still here.'

Dan wrinkled his nose. 'How do you know that? You've forgotten what it's like to be married. My wife's wardrobe is like the Tardis. I have no clue what she fits into the gigantic leather sack she drags everywhere. Maybe she carries out hits for the mafia. I once found a chopping board in her backpack.'

'If we follow either of them too closely we could place them in danger.' May knelt to examine the baseboard of the wardrobe. 'She can't use her credit cards without getting tracked. Maybe there are other places she can stay.'

'You won't know unless you call all her contacts and if you do that someone will start taking notice. You're not a government man, John. You're too honest for cloak-and-dagger stuff.'

May pulled out shoes and tapped the wardrobe floor. 'Scratches down the sides. This panel comes out.'

At the back of the board he found a groove that allowed his fingers purchase, but screws had been added along the edge. 'Have you got a Phillips screwdriver?' May asked. Dan handed over his Swiss Army knife.

The six screws were hard to loosen. The wood began to splinter and make a mess.

'You're definitely not a spy,' said Dan. 'It doesn't matter. She already knows you're here.'

May rocked back on his heels. 'How?'

'Oldest trick in the book. She left a blob of glue in the door crack, just above one of the hinges. We broke it by opening the door. I'm surprised she hasn't got cameras everywhere. What have you got there?'

May raised a small oblong box made of thick grey cardboard. 'Something to get started on.'

Dan looked over. 'Show me.'

May turned the front of the box to him. Inset on the lid were two words picked out in black felt tip: 'London Bridge'.

He wanted to stop and open it but there was no time.

23

IN HIDDEN HANDS

The terraced house ahead of him was freshly painted, although white was an optimistic choice in King's Cross. A house-proud owner, he thought. Making his way to the front door, Bryant called upon the complaining neighbour none of the Met officers had wanted to talk to. Women like Mrs Ormond were a necessary evil; every street needed a resident busybody to keep an eye on things.

Bryant remembered his childhood in Whitechapel, and how his mother used to sit with a so-called 'wise woman', someone whose role in the street had barely changed in five centuries. Old Mrs Laverstitch had been a tiny bustling thing of indeterminate years with a palsied hand and a frightening way of staring at children. She invariably turned up armed with witch hazel branches, potions and poultices, offering the neighbourhood wives advice on sexual health, colds, the healing of spots and sores. Beneath these services were diagnoses of a more dubious nature, methods of inducing abortions, folkloric cures for sexually transmitted diseases and rituals for placing a curse on a violent husband.

Such women did not fully disappear until the late 1960s, yet their spirit lived on in the neighbours who ran online community groups, reporting daily on unemptied bins, late-night parties and suspicious strangers.

When the door opened, Bryant doffed his homburg and presented his card. For years Raymond Land had been trying to get him to use an MG11, an official statement form that could temper Bryant's more florid reports, but he had used the last one to clean out his pipe; the paper was just the right thickness.

Mrs Ormond was heavily upholstered, with large, faded eyes and tortured hair, and the kind of chunky jewellery that would drag her down in a strong current.

'A quick call about your poor neighbour, Mrs Hoffman,' Bryant said before she had a chance to question him. 'Good Lord, what's that awful smell?'

This was not the best way of endearing himself, but it got her talking. 'I'm boiling an octopus,' she replied.

'Blimey, what did it ever do to you?'

'I'm preparing for a dinner party. I doubt you're here to discuss my culinary skills, Mr . . .' She squeezed her eyes together in a hopeless attempt at reading his ID. 'Is this about the old lady next door?'

Bryant jumped in fast. 'To die alone like that, so sad, with nobody looking in on her to make sure that she was safe and well, and yet you live right next door, but I suppose you had your reasons for not checking on her, what were they? Arthur Bryant, Peculiar Crimes Unit, King's Cross, official police business, a minute of your time?'

'I don't. You have no— I tried,' said Mrs Ormond, on the back foot now, trying to catch up as Bryant moved past her and bustled about inside, keeping ahead of her, picking up ornaments, pulling paperbacks from the bookcase, handling things.

'She hardly ever spoke to me – please do *not* touch

those – she always kept to herself, and obviously I respect people's privacy.'

'Even if it leads to a lonely death that could have been avoided.' He mentally priced a complete set of Ian Flemings.

'She couldn't have been alone, there are social workers and helpers for that sort of thing, and that little kebab man downstairs took food up to her.'

'Because he alone cared about her.'

'She was paying him! People don't help you for nothing.'

Bryant contemplated stealing the book in his hand (*Goldfinger*, first edition, obviously the deceased husband's) but reluctantly decided to replace it. 'Since Christmas you've lodged twelve complaints about your neighbours, eight specifically about Mrs Hoffman. Yet you never spoke to her face to face.'

'I don't see why I should have to. It's not my job.'

'You moaned a lot about her cat.'

'It kept using the garden as a toilet. And it tried to get inside.'

'Is that why you attacked it?'

A look of outrage. 'I did no such—'

'The man over the end garden was having a barbecue with his neighbours when he saw you beat it with a broom. He called the police but they were too busy to respond.'

'That's a lie. He's nothing but a troublemaker.'

'He said he saw it lying in the gutter later. A car had gone over it so there was no proof left of your mistreatment. He wanted to do right but you know how it is, things that can't be fixed get overlooked. I would have happily had you arrested. Who else called on Mrs Hoffman? Did you see any friends, any women her age or younger?'

Mrs Ormond was still inarticulate with outrage. Her mouth opened and flapped shut.

'Concentrate on my words, please. Visitors to Mrs Hoffman, how many?'

'One or two, last year. I really don't remember.'

'You never checked on Mrs Hoffman, never made sure she needed anything, even though you knew she was housebound.'

'She's not a relative. Why should I suddenly have to make friends with her? When my sheets blew over into her garden she didn't let me know. People just take advantage of you.'

Bryant thought of his mother and felt a familiar ripple of shame. Elsie had wasted away in Whitechapel while her husband was unconscious with drink. And where had he been? Lost in his work at the new Bow Street police unit.

'And she never smiled,' Mrs Ormond was saying. 'There's no point in being nice to people these days.'

As a police officer in the employ of Her Majesty's Government he was supposed to refrain from passing personal comment, an instruction he took perverse pleasure in ignoring. 'So an old lady died,' he told her, 'and you assumed someone else would take care of the problem. You should bloody well be ashamed of yourself.'

'You have no right to talk to me like that, you're a public servant,' Mrs Ormond complained, visibly shocked.

'When I was growing up these neighbourhoods were communities, and people like you have helped to destroy them.'

'I went around there,' Mrs Ormond all but shouted. 'I heard banging and went to see if she was all right but she didn't even have the common courtesy to answer the front door.'

'When was this?'

'About three weeks ago. The window going up, someone shouting—'

'Was it her or someone else?'

'A man, and then she wouldn't open the—'

'Did you see him leave?'

'I saw him come out.'

'What did he look like?'

'How would I know, with my eyes? Like any other man.'

'Young, middle-aged, old, you must have been able to tell.'

'Middle-aged.'

'He must have been wearing something, what was he wearing?'

'A suit, a smart suit.'

'What colour hair?'

'I don't know – I don't remember.'

'Presumably you were looking down at his head. Blond, black or bald?'

'Black. Something shiny.'

'Shiny – you mean hair oil. Nationality?'

'I don't know. Pale-skinned. Overweight.'

'Did he look back or keep going?'

'He kept going, as if he was pleased to get away.'

'Well, Mrs Ormond, it appears you saw quite a lot.'

He let himself out. Mrs Ormond watched him go, made herself a strong mug of tea and then rang the police to complain.

The unshaven man in the donkey jacket sitting opposite John May smelled rank. He knew it, the detective knew it, and so did most of the other customers. The man settled in his seat and smiled, entirely unconcerned.

May also knew it was his partner's fault that he was here at all. Bryant's abstract thought processes and eccentric investigation methods were part of a balancing act that had taken a lifetime to refine. But it meant that they all found themselves interviewing people they would normally go out of their way to avoid. Despite his better instincts, May had this morning agreed to meet with a London sewage worker in the Ladykillers Café, next door to the unit, not quite realizing what it would entail.

'You can smell me, can't you?' Tom Bonnamy sniffed the shoulder of his jacket. 'I'm a regular Pepe Le Pew. It never goes away. You can wash and wash, it makes no difference. I still smell of drains.'

Bonnamy's educated pronunciation was at odds with his appearance. He had been recruited to spy for MI6 while still at Oxford, but after the work pushed him into a nervous break-down he had become a fine academic, teaching history at the University of Westminster. Now he had undergone another sur-prising career change. He was a waste operative and proud of it.

'I'm finally an essential worker,' he explained, blowing his nose into a white linen handkerchief and checking the con-tents. The people on the next table thought about moving away. 'It was all very well being a history professor but I rarely had a sense of doing anything useful. When people start thinking about who they really need to be practical in a crisis, who are they going to choose: someone who can dis-sect espionage networks in bohemian London society 1750 to 1830, or the chap who unbungs their shit-pipes?'

'Tough call,' said May, watching as Bonnamy stuffed a crois-sant with marmalade.

'A colleague of mine, Nigel, is an emeritus professor of medieval theology and he's down the drains too. He swears it's strengthened his immune system, although it's done noth-ing for his sex life. We're living in an anti-intellectual world, Mr May, and only those who adapt will survive.' He tore a chunk off his croissant and chewed it thoughtfully. 'My son works for an insurance company, handling social media pro-motion for their in-house lifestyle magazine. He acts like he's curing malaria. When I told him I was going down the drains he looked at me as if I'd gone insane. It's a noble profession, sewage work. You know what they used to call us? Goldfind-ers, because we emptied the jakes to locate lost coins. It has a fascinating history.'

May sipped at his coffee, taking the opportunity to engulf himself in its roasted aroma. 'What about the health risks?'

'Of course you get the odd bout of gastroenteritis and you never get used to breathing hydrogen sulphide, but you quickly find out how the city runs. We hit full flow at lunchtime: non-degradable baby wipes, condoms, and some things you'd think it was impossible to lose down a lavatory. You should come below and see our funguses. They grow on solidified fat in total darkness. Quite extraordinary. And every neighbourhood has a different odour. I know when I'm under Knightsbridge because I can smell rich restaurant food. Vauxhall has hints of iron and engine oil. Leicester Square reeks of pizza sauce. It gets inside you. You always remember where you've been. Sometimes you break wind and think to yourself, Oh, that's Elephant & Castle.'

May pushed away his *pain aux raisins*. 'How do you know Annie Wynn-Jones and Angela Carey?'

'My mother was in the Foreign Office for forty years. Annie was her contact at Hanslope Park. Angela was introduced as a colleague.'

The Buckinghamshire country mansion housed MI6's experimental technical unit. Some of the most creative and devious minds in the country were based there. May was intrigued. 'Why did she have a contact at Hanslope Park?'

'The archives were being declassified and she needed help identifying some documents. I would never have put them together if your partner hadn't contacted me. Am I on some sort of a list?'

'Knowing Bryant, that's highly likely. He keeps details of anyone who can assist him.'

'Annie Wynn-Jones is a real piece of work. Old school, loyal to the Crown and tough as old boots. I heard she left her mother's funeral early to go back to the office. Her friend Angela is just as bad. They'll go to their graves clutching government secrets to their chests, not that they'll get any thanks for it. Of course, she must have retired years ago.'

'You say their secrets go to their graves. How do they get through their lives never speaking of what they know?'

'They have a technique. They'll tell you a lot but mix fact and fiction together until you can't separate them. Data overload is a subtler tool than holding information back. It's the original version of "fake news", a wall of nonsense built around a grain of truth. It probably stops them from going mad.'

A young woman came in to choose a sandwich. She sniffed the air and hurried back out.

'If these ladies won't help us, how do we know they're not working for the other side?' May wondered.

'They're not talking to you because it's ingrained in them not to do so. Self-protection is a powerful motivator.'

'But the work they did finished decades ago.'

'Women like my mother and Annie Wynn-Jones think at a government level but work at street level,' said Tom. 'They calculate everything and remain in contact with each other using the old ways, pre-arranged places where messages can be left. They'll work behind your back without ever telling you.'

'You're going to make me paranoid,' May warned.

'Perhaps you should be.' Tom picked up a croissant crumb and sucked his fingers. The woman behind him fanned her newspaper.

Niven, the café owner, leaned over his counter. 'John, I'm assuming that pen and ink is emanating from your mate. Next time can he have a bath before he comes in? He's scaring off the customers.'

Tom turned around in his chair. 'My wife boiled this shirt last night and sprayed me with *L'Air du Temps*.'

'Smells more like *Arôme de Merde*.'

He turned back to May. 'Wynn-Jones was one of the first female officers in the British secret service, working out of Century House on Westminster Bridge Road. Quite famous in her time. Not that the public ever knew.'

'If she and her colleagues had access to something that could prove valuable to a foreign power, what form would it take?'

Bonnamy dabbed up the last crumbs, thinking. 'It could be digitized into anything. The tech-work is left to Hanslope Park. Information is more valuable than arms, Mr May. China has already harvested a third of the world's data. If the CIA is involved you have a much bigger problem. It would be best to walk away from the whole thing.'

'Why should we when these are British citizens?' asked May.

'Because being British won't stop you from ending up tied to a chair in an Eastern European hotel room,' said Bonnamy.

'I'm trying to get my head around this, Tom. If they *are* withholding something, what physical form would it take?'

Bonnamy pushed away his plate. 'There was an argument some years ago about the size of diplomatic bags. If they cross borders, their opening by unauthorized personnel constitutes a violation of the Vienna Convention. Some European diplomats tried to push their luck by increasing the size of the bag from a holdall to a shipping container. If you don't want to attract unwanted attention, I'd suggest keeping the bag to the size of something an ordinary person can lift and carry. A physical object, not an electronic one. That way it can't be traced.'

'Then we have something to look for,' said May.

Tom smiled and waved a finger at him. 'If they have something they don't want you to find, you'll never get your hands on it.'

'Why should we have to fight our own side?'

'The sides have changed, John. People owe more allegiance to Amazon and Google than they do to their countries. The world will always have secrets but now they're in hands which are hidden from governments.'

'This is an old school secret,' said May. 'Something as abstract and dry as a safety deposit box number.'

'There are still human lives at the end of it, aren't there?'

'Yes,' May admitted.

'Then you and Mr Bryant must keep pursuing it.' He put on his orange donkey jacket and rose, instantly clearing a social space. 'I'm going back down the drains. Things are cleaner there.'

24

TOGETHER AGAIN

'Oh, *there* you are. What's that funny smell?'

Bryant had bumped into his partner on the Caledonian Road outside Achilles Heels, the Greek cobbler's.

'*Nostalgie de la Boue*,' said May, waving his hands before his face. 'Janice had an enormous bottle of it on her. A fifties classic, apparently. Does it mask the smell of drains?'

'No. I take it you handled my meeting with Tom Bonnamy. How was he?'

'Pungent but interesting. He thinks we're looking for something the size of a diplomatic bag. And there's this.' He produced the cardboard box from his pocket. 'I found it in the bottom of Wynn-Jones's wardrobe.'

'That's an old medal box, government issue. What's inside?'

'I don't know yet, I haven't looked.'

'How could you not? It must be burning a hole in your pocket. Give it here.' Bryant snatched it away and opened the lid. Something shiny slipped out between his sausage fingers.

May jumped forward and caught it just before it hit the

pavement. He raised it up to his eye. 'Why would anybody make this?'

It looked like a standard Yale door key but was made of thick glass. 'It's not ornamental,' said Bryant. 'The key to a treasure?'

'That's unlocked with *this*?' He handed it to his partner to examine.

'It was usual for document boxes to be protected with keys equally shared between those who needed access. Dan found ground glass in Hoffman's flat. What are the chances she destroyed hers so Cranston couldn't get his hands on it? She may even have tried to feed it to him and failed.'

'Three keys. Made of glass.' May tried to keep the incredulity from his voice.

'It's a matter of trust. In the event of something unfortunate happening, it would be obvious who'd used their key. If Hoffman's got smashed and we have Wynn-Jones's, it just leaves Angela Carey in possession of hers.'

They headed back into the unit together. 'That piece of paper with the symbol on it,' Bryant remembered. 'I can't afford to get it analysed in a lab. You find out where the key came from, I'll talk to someone who'll know about the symbol. No, wait – better idea.' He stopped sharply and turned to his partner, clapping him hard on the shoulder. 'This is a matter of national security. I'm completely out of my depth. You know me and politics; I was surprised to hear that Margaret Thatcher had died.'

As usual, Bryant's elliptical manner left May confused. 'What do you want me to do?' he asked.

'You know how you always tell me off for not being terribly detail-oriented in my reports?'

This was an understatement. Bryant would have forgotten to mention the Charge of the Light Brigade in despatches.

'I want you with me for this. We've been conducting

separate investigations for too long. Let's go back to how it was in the old days. You and me together, comparing notes, conducting interviews and hounding innocent passers-by. That's where our strength lies.'

'I'm glad to hear you say that,' said May. 'I've been getting nowhere by myself.'

'Good, because I have a plan.'

'What is it?'

'Where?'

'Your plan.'

'What about it?'

'You were going to tell me what it was.'

'Was I? I don't think so. You'll be on a need-to-know basis, obviously. But we'll be working together, and that's the main thing.'

'But you have to tell me what we're doing, Arthur. Heaven knows I'm a reasonable man—'

'Don't worry, I can change that. We should set off right away.'

'Don't you think we should brief the team and tell them what we're doing?'

'There's no time.' Bryant yanked his black leather Dead Diary from his pocket and checked the pages. 'I thought we should take a shufti at London Bridge itself, but first let's visit a jeweller I know.'

'Perhaps we should call in at the unit—' May glanced back at the PCU as his partner headed off down the pavement. For an old man he could certainly shift when he needed to.

Around the corner an old black cab was idling, a gleaming curvaceous Austin FX4 from the late 1950s. Behind the wheel sat a large, ghost-pale woman in a black T-shirt commemorating a Rihanna world tour with the singer's name wrongly spelled. May saw a glossy black fringe, a ponytail, hoop earrings, scary eyebrows. She was reading a volume of the *Encyclopaedia Britannica*.

Bryant held the door open for his partner.

'I'm afraid Victor lost his wings,' he explained, referring to his beloved rusty yellow Mini. 'I needed to disconnect the anti-theft device Dan installed for me because it nearly took someone's eye out. This is Rita Rondola. She does repairs, so I drove over to her garage in Romford but the door was too narrow and I knocked Victor's wing mirrors off. I've never used them but apparently they're not optional. Rita's going to fit new ones, along with a working exhaust pipe. Meanwhile we've come to an arrangement. She'll drive us around for a measly stipend. You might want to strap yourself in as she's a bit of a Stirling Moss on the arterials.'

'Hello you handsome,' said Rita, leaning out of her cab window to reveal a big strong arm, 'get in vehicle and hang on.' Her accent was Slavic but hard to pinpoint. She set aside her encyclopaedia. The second the passenger door was shut she put her foot down and roared off in the direction of Farringdon as Bryant gave directions.

'Joolery,' she shouted back through the window, 'you want to go to joolery shop? Because I have cousin from Lithuania who put his hands on anything. And I mean *anything*. From royalty. *Better* than royalty.'

'We're not fencing your cousin's stolen goods, Rita,' said Bryant. 'This is my partner, John May.'

'Please to meet you, Johnmay.' She put her hand over her shoulder. 'You are the handsome one, yes? And he is just the older one. Johnmay, where is your second half?'

May looked at Bryant. 'The last one left me.'

'Oh she like to go around with other men blah blah blah, good for her.'

'Number seventy-eight Hatton Garden, please, Rita. Why are you reading an encyclopaedia?'

'I want to learn all of the English,' she called back as if the answer was stupendously obvious. 'I am up to "Agnosia".'

'Ah, the inability to interpret sensations. Our boss has that.'

She swung around a corner, blasting her horn. 'Cyclists, hey look out your back wheel is going round! I love this joke is very funny.' She shouted out of the window. 'I hope you are signing the lease on that piece of road you own! This is funny too. Do you want me to go down Farringdon Road, Mr Bryant?'

'If that way's quicker.'

'Not at the moment it won't be seeing as it is shut. I do not use satnav it is Devil capital D. I use the Knowledge. I like knowledge.'

'I'm going to be closing the window now until we arrive.' Bryant slid the partition shut and returned to his partner. 'Rita's husband is an old mucker of mine, one of the last true cockneys. If you ever meet him I'll give you a full list of subjects to stay away from.'

May gazed through the window, feeling pleased to be part of his partner's strange world once more. Farringdon flashed past. A bit of Clerkenwell came and went. Next was the jewellery district of Hatton Garden, although just to confuse matters it was technically part of Holborn. It existed in one of those parts of London that seemed able to disappear at a late hour when one was suffering from a surfeit of alcohol.

The Hasidic diamond merchants were less visible than of old, but the street still shone with jewellers' shops as fortified as castle keeps, their windows harshly iridescent with gemstones. The detectives alighted and found a storefront called Rooks & Emeralds, where Maurice Weiss, maker and supplier of traditional tricks to the magic trade, awaited them on the street, dressed in a splendid black satin waistcoat crisscrossed with silver stitching.

'The usual Arthur, I see,' said Maurice. 'Five minutes' advance warning, no welcoming bottle, just some curt social intercourse and then gone until the next time, like a cheap West End Romeo.'

'Thank you, that was the effect I was going for. Have a sherbet fountain.' Bryant handed him a squashed yellow tube. 'This is my partner, John May. I usually leave him at home.'

'Ah, you're the one who got himself shot.' Maurice held out his hand. 'You should have talked to me first. I could have shown you how to catch a bullet in your teeth.'

'I didn't know I was going to be shot,' May pointed out.

'He showed me how to do it,' said Bryant. 'I had to put my teeth on the mantelpiece first.'

'You'd better come in. Is that cab waiting for you?'

'She's my chauffeur,' Bryant explained.

'Are you sure a taxi's not too delicate for her? She looks like she could jack-knife a forklift. Mind you, I like a big woman.' Maurice was five foot one.

He led them into the cluttered shop, through a thicket of hanging puppets and dolls. Silken banners of vermilion and teal wafted apart to reveal cabinets of Vietnamese water puppets and African silhouette figures. 'To what do I owe the pleasure this time?'

'I want to know what you think of this.' Bryant stopped before Maurice's close-up magic counter and set down the cardboard medal box, unclipping it to reveal the glass key.

'May I?' Maurice donned a single white glove.

'Please do.'

The magician flicked on a magnifying lamp and screwed an eyepiece beneath his brow. 'It looks ornamental, like a trophy for the year's best locksmith. It's thicker than a normal Yale. You couldn't use it and yet . . .'

'What?'

'This has been laser cut from a single piece of crystal. The ridges are sharp-edged and exact.'

'Is it valuable?'

'To the owner perhaps.' He bobbed his head closer to the shining key. 'There's a faint indentation running just below the shoulder – that's the broader bit beneath the head of the key. Well, well.'

'Clever,' Bryant concurred.

'What?' May looked from one to the other.

'It's a single-use key designed to break,' Maurice pronounced. 'There's a pre-cut etched into it.'

'What's the point of that?'

'It's quite unusual but not unheard of. A speciality order. This fits a special rotorless lock that doesn't have to be turned. The tumblers simply need to be kept depressed. Whoever uses it can stop anyone else from doing the same. You insert the key all the way in so that the lock opens. When you're finished you twist it hard and break off the end. It would be virtually impossible to remove from the lock.'

'Thanks for your help, Maurice. I'll see you next time.' He took back the key and slipped a twenty-pound note under one of the impecunious magician's puppets as he left.

'Like I said, it's always the same with you,' Maurice called as they left. 'In and out like a cheap West End Romeo.'

Bryant clambered back into the taxi. 'Now for London Bridge. Rita, drive like the wind.'

'It will be more like light breeze with the Blackfriars junction tailback.' Rita put down her encyclopaedia and her Terry's Chocolate Orange, took off the handbrake and crunched her gears. They tore down through backstreets towards the Thames, into the barren grey canyon of the Victoria Embankment.

In a typical act of confusion, Upper Thames Street and Lower Thames Street met underneath London Bridge, where the two signs touched each other even though the road did not change. The causeway was a storey lower than the bridge itself, cutting through the city's north side in an unparalleled act of concrete vandalism. London Bridge passed over the roadway, creating a tunnel. It had right of way, having been there first.

Rita's taxi came to a jolting stop beneath the bridge, setting off a glissando of horns from the vehicles behind. 'Am I to wait here for you to play the silly buggers?'

'That's the plan, Rita. We'll be right back.' Bryant climbed out and made his way to a rectangle of black shadow in the tunnel's granite wall. 'There has to be a staircase leading up from here, like the one for Blackfriars Bridge.'

He slipped inside the unlit tunnel. May followed hesitantly. He was starting to remember what it was like trailing Bryant around. 'Are there any spots in this city that aren't used as public toilets?' he wondered aloud.

'Yes, public toilets,' Bryant replied. 'They've all been sold off as cocktail bars. I can see stairs.' He vanished inside a doorway as small as the entrance to a pyramid. May lowered his head and followed.

They found themselves on a walkway at the base of a new office block. The tide was high and had come in beneath them to an open culvert. Bryant pressed his eye to the steel grille that covered part of the path. He could see a broad staircase leading down into the water.

'The original stairs are still there,' he said, surprised. 'But we can't get up to the bridge.'

They turned around and took another staircase, coming out on the pavement of the bridge above. Bryant shielded his eyes and searched east. 'Look at all that Wagnerian tat along the river-line. The least interesting view from any bridge in London.'

'You can see the Shard,' May pointed out.

'Is there anywhere you can't?' He blew a raspberry that rattled his false teeth. 'The idea that its form echoes London's churches is blasphemy, and I'm an atheist. It's a vulgarian power-grab, rammed into the Southwark streets like a fat man squeezed on to a bus seat. I've been up there; the urinals are set in a glass wall so it feels as if you're pissing over the city, a sensation that I imagine is already familiar to the bankers who use them. My word, it says something about modern architecture when you leave the country's tallest building remembering nothing but the toilet.'

'Arthur,' said May, gently tugging at his arm, 'why are we here?'

'The key-box lid said "London Bridge". I thought we might find something knocking about. At least Wynn-Jones can't run off with whatever it unlocks.'

Bryant stopped and donned his trifocals. Barely checking to see if the coast was clear he strode out across the road, using his walking stick to ward off traffic. May ran helplessly after him.

'And there is something,' Bryant cried. 'Can you see?'

He pointed to the wall beside elegant Adelaide House, built on the site of the old London Bridge Waterworks. Set at its base, stamped into a brass plate, was the symbol he had found inside Amelia Hoffman's flat.

25

NO MICHAEL CAINE

'The boys are just getting out of a taxi,' said Janice, pushing the meaning of 'boys' into a new dimension. 'Where have they been?' She turned down an enamel mug of tea from Dave One and came away from the window.

'Mr Land wants to be updated,' Sidney said, swinging past the doorway of the operations room. 'He's waiting in his office and is asking to see everyone.'

'We can't all fit in there,' sighed Janice. 'Come on, you lot.'

Dave One set down his tea tray. Since all work had stopped on the building he and his teammate had taken to providing refreshments, racing tips and reiki sessions.

'Not you,' said Janice, sending Dave One away. 'We know all about your ideas for the future of metropolitan policing. Amputation is never coming back.'

They arrived outside Land's office just as Bryant was hauling himself up the stairs. 'Leave this to me,' he announced to the others. 'You'd better all wait outside. It could get ugly.' He mimed pushing the non-door open with the end of his walking stick and ushered May in before him. 'Ah, Raymondo, *poleznyi durak*.'*

'I should be saying that to you,' Land snapped. 'I just had MI6 on my extension and it wasn't pleasant. Some fellow accused me of treading on his toes. I told him, how could it be me when I haven't got a clue what's going on? What on earth have you two been up to?'

'Our suspect is proving elusive,' said Bryant. 'If we could get into the CCTV system we'd have a chance of finding him. I need to use North One Watch.'

The underground surveillance centre beneath King's Cross Station was one of London's better-kept secrets. Eighty monitors provided multiple views of the concourses of three stations, King's Cross, St Pancras and Euston, mapping the route of every traveller. Unfortunately, it was expensive to access.

'Well, you can't,' said Land. 'We have no clearance and no money.'

'I can still pull in a few favours,' said Dan. 'I've placed your suspect at Hoffman's address. He was photographed coming out of the building.'

'If MI6 or the CIA are watching him without taking action it could mean he's a counter-intelligence agent,' May said.

'We *cannot* get ourselves involved in espionage,' cried Land. 'The only thing I know about spies is *The Ipcress File*, and I'm no Michael Caine. I don't want the CIA using pliers and a torch on anyone in my team. Where are the old bags now?'

'How about just calling them women?' Janice suggested. 'They already get more than their fair share of names.'

'I haven't got time to be "woke", thank you. It was bad enough when we had to stop saying "cripples". And you two can't find a murderer because a couple of dotty old dears won't help you.'

---

* 'Useful idiot'.

'There could be a simple reason for MI6's interest,' said May. 'Say, if Hoffman knew about a forthcoming terrorist attack on London Bridge.'

'Oh, why didn't I think of that? Perhaps jihadists have started recruiting from Cheltenham Ladies' College. If MI6 had knowledge of such an attack they'd swoop in and lift everyone off the street.'

'MI6 has always created aliases for its operations,' said May. '*LONDON BRIDGE* could easily be a government codename. There have been other attacks on the same spot.'

'In 2017.' Bryant thumbed through his Dead Diary. 'Three extremists crashed a van into pedestrians and began stabbing people in Borough Market, killing eight. Before that there was the attack on Westminster Bridge. And in 2019 a supposedly reformed terrorist wearing an electronic tag attended a conference on offender rehabilitation in a fake suicide vest. He ran amok with knives in Fishmongers Hall and was challenged by a bystander armed with a four-foot-long narwhal tusk he'd found on display in the hall. Look at all the links we've found between Amelia Hoffman and London Bridge. Wouldn't you be concerned?'

He let that sink in for a moment.

'Let me see if I can summarize,' said Land. 'Two women dead, two more at risk, neither of them willing to tell us the truth. One male attacker at large, apparently untouchable. No motives, or witnesses. All information redacted. Plus the possible involvement of MI6 and the CIA. And we're in this mess all because you popped over the road to check on an old lady who'd passed away.'

'You missed a bit,' said Bryant. 'According to our Sidney the killer has no plan. Then there are these.' In one hand he held up the grey cardboard box containing the glass key. In the other, the scrunched piece of paper bearing the symbol from London Bridge.

'Oh, *clues*.' Land's voice oozed sarcasm. 'It wouldn't be a Bryant and May case without a couple of ridiculous red herrings, would it? What's in the box?'

'A crystal key that can only be used once.'

'So we have a touch of Hans Christian Andersen too.'

'The Brothers Grimm, actually, but yes, and more than just two clues,' replied Bryant happily. 'What do the colours red and green signify to you?'

'That you've just taken one of your pills?'

'In colour theory red and green are opposites, yet they complement each other. Do you see?'

'No, I bloody don't,' said Land.

'Then there's the pink paint. Don't worry, all will soon be made clear.' Bryant prestidigitated his hands. 'You just have to trust me. Have I ever let you down in the past?'

'You got us shut down eleven times.' Land's features changed, chameleon-like, from taupe to mauve. 'You blew up your old unit. You set fire to the new one, twice. You got us quarantined as a chemical hazard. And had us banned from the London Policing Awards for releasing cockroaches at the dinner table.'

'That was an accident.'

'You shouldn't have had them on you!'

'I forgot the box was in the pocket of my dress jacket. It was an experiment.'

'What, to see how socially excluded you could make us? I know all about your experiments. I have to cross the road whenever I pass the dry-cleaner's. "Try adding this to your cleaning solution," you told them. Poor old Mr Johnson still has to wear gloves.'

'He couldn't read my handwriting and got the dosage wrong.'

'Now we've got keys and symbols and colours—'

'About the colours, let me explain,' said Bryant. 'I didn't find any intelligence reports or classified documents in Hoffman's flat, but there were letters between the three women full of staff gossip. Paperwork was codenamed and stored in large metal cupboards, in manila folders, in ancient safes and green government filing cabinets. Paper leaves no trace but for its physical form, so in many ways it's still the most secure medium for passing information.'

'You can encrypt information,' Dan muttered.

'Yes, and you can decipher it too,' Bryant replied. 'The letters were written in different inks. MI6 heads still write their most important communiqués in green ink, in honour of their founder. It's a practice that dates back to captains in the Royal Navy, when commanding officers wrote in red ink and flag officers in green. It makes exchanges easier to follow. If Amelia was in charge it would explain why the letters from her were green and the incoming ones were red. Annie and Angela returned all their correspondence as a security measure.'

'And what do they tell us, these precious colour-coded letters?' asked Land.

'MI6 also used green filing cabinets for key documents. It occurred to me that the women needed somewhere secure to store their most sensitive information. Hoffman used departmental acronyms, with a handful recurring. One of them was PFC, used in the way we use PCU. The FC in PFC could stand for "Filing Cabinet" and P could be the colour, say pink.'

'You have the thought processes of a small child. Do you really think it would be that obvious?' Land gave a snort of derision and then wished he hadn't.

While he was unfolding a tissue, Bryant continued. 'It has to be in the London Bridge area. We're trying to narrow down our search at the moment.'

'I've a better idea,' said Land. 'We should drag Cranston in here and scare the living daylights out of him until he tells us what he's after.'

'And set ourselves at odds with the CIA.'

'All right, then we put more officers on the street.'

'Raymond, there are six of us here in the building plus an intern and the cat, not counting you, obviously.'

'So we pass it over to Serious Crimes.' Land pushed up the window-frame and breathed deep, trying to stay calm. The pigeon backed away and warbled warily.

'We'll lose the unit,' said Bryant.

'You already lost it!' Land cried. 'If you hadn't started poking your nose into a local news story we wouldn't be in this mess now.'

'Uncovering a crime doesn't cause criminality,' said Bryant heatedly. 'It was there already. We should run towards misdeeds, not tiptoe away from them.'

'Well, I'm tiptoeing away from this,' warned Land. 'I've had enough for one night. I want a beer and a pie and at least three hours in front of the telly.'

'You raffish bohemian,' said Bryant. 'Take the next sedan chair home and rest your gout while we take care of the investigation.' He turned to find everyone in the doorway watching him. 'Head home, all of you. There's nothing more that can be done tonight.'

'I think Mr Land is right,' said Sidney out of the blue. Heads swivelled. 'We should bring Cranston in and force a confession.'

Janice stared at her. 'Did I really give birth to you?'

'I don't expect you to remember, Mother.'

Looking into her daughter's blank grey eyes she searched for some gesture or inflection she could recognize, but found nothing. There was a certain physical resemblance, but that was all. 'You don't use a scorched earth policy for something that requires delicate handling.'

Sidney shrugged. 'Then someone else will die.'

John May was thinking of his wife.

Different versions of her lived in his head. Jane running

across Oxford Street, almost getting knocked down, so excited was she to see him. Jane writing her answer in the Cornish sand when he asked her to marry him. Jane screaming and weeping at seagulls on the lawn of Broadhampton Hospital, unable to control the firestorm in her brain. No single mental image could capture her. Even added together, the whole eluded him.

She wanted so much from the world, he thought as he walked towards the tube station in spiteful rain. *What did she really get from it all?* A derailed career, an errant husband, children who could barely remain in the same room with her, the slow separation from her wits. He was sure she would not want to be remembered as grey-haired in a wheelchair, tipping her dinner tray on the floor. *We owe it to our women to do better*, he thought.

'Stop thinking about her.'

Bryant's walking stick hit the side of his leg. He turned to find Bryant behind him, catching up.

'How do you know what I'm doing?' May asked.

'Because I know you. Have you ever wondered why hardly anyone at the unit is married? It's because we're afraid we'll fail anyone we care for. We're not equipped for normal life. That's why this case feels so strange. The victims are like us. Half-hidden and overlooked.' He patted May on the back. 'We should be allies. Instead we've done nothing to earn their confidence. Why should they trust us? We'll get nothing more from Wynn-Jones or Carey now.'

'Then I hope you have something up your sleeve,' said May, 'because I'm out of ideas.'

'As it happens, I do,' said Bryant with a look of mischief. 'There are nearly nine million people in this city and I know one or two who can help us.'

PART THREE

You become aware that you are no longer noticed: nobody sees you; nobody hears you; nobody regards you; you do not even regard yourself.

Thomas de Quincey on London

26

BENEATH THE BRIDGE

Six fifteen on Friday morning in the neat red-brick housing estate on Harrison Street in Bloomsbury. Light summer rain brushing the windows, a ginger cat lurking beneath a dripping rose bush, yellow lights shining on the third floor.

'What on earth are you doing up there?'

Arthur Bryant was balanced on a wicker chair which stood on some books on his bed, the entire edifice quivering like a blancmange.

'I'm trying to reach my copy of *Anomalous Architecture* – the Balkan edition. It should be here next to my *World Almanac of Pine Cones*.' Arthur swayed alarmingly but clutched the top of the wardrobe, dislodging the book, which fell to the bedspread in a cloud of dust.

'Why would you even keep a book there?' Alma grabbed his arm and carefully guided him down from the bed.

'I didn't think I'd be needing it. Usually I only put experimental poisons out of reach. I don't know why I still keep nitroglycerine up there. It's probably degraded and unstable by now.'

'It's not the only thing around here that's degraded and unstable. You woke me up with all that banging around. What have I told you about storing explosives in your bedroom?' His landlady eyed the top of the wardrobe suspiciously. 'All those beakers and books, and whatever that thing is.'

Bryant followed her disapproving eyeline to a statue of a peacock being eviscerated by a wolf. 'That's called *Vanity Destroyed by Hunger*, a masterpiece of Hungarian art.'

'Then why is it hidden away on top of the wardrobe?'

'Look at it, it's horrible. Tell me, what do you know about London Bridge?'

'It's near the Monument and I have to cross it to get to Borough Market, which is a pain in the arse when you're coming back lugging potatoes. Dust yourself down and I'll make you some ginger tea. You shouldn't be up yet.'

'It's been light since four forty-six a.m. I'm old, I don't want to miss anything. Was there anything else?'

'Your pyjamas are on the wrong way around.'

'I mean about the bridge.'

She thought for a moment. 'It fell down, didn't it? In the song? It took ten thousand men to put back up.'

'That's "The Grand Old Duke Of York", you daft prune.'

Alma shrugged. 'It's the same thing.'

'It's not at all,' said Bryant irritably. 'My earliest memory is hearing my mother sing "London Bridge Is Falling Down" while she washed me in the tin bath. She used to add new verses of her own but I can't remember what they were now.'

'Instead of relying on your dodgy memory you should go and talk to someone. Didn't you research this stuff when you were looking for the Fruit and Vegetable Killer?'

'Oranges and Lemons. Yes, I did. I put it somewhere.' He followed her into the kitchen. 'May I present you with a hypothesis?'

Alma regarded him doubtfully. 'It's not something covered in fungus?'

'It's not a plant, it's an old lady. Her name is Amelia Hoffman and she died a few roads away from here.' As he followed her to the kitchen, he explained how Hoffman had met her end.

'Was she weak in the head?' Alma asked.

'She was physically frail but she had all her marbles.'

Alma put the kettle on. 'It's not that easy to come out of the care system. A council officer would have continued to check up on her, especially as she'd have been classed as a patient at risk.'

'She had a private doctor who told me that she was fundamentally healthy apart from the usual delightful panoply of age-related conditions,' said Bryant. 'She turned down all offers of help. She said a relative would be taking care of her.'

'She must have trusted him. My son was no good – Mr Sorrowbridge threw him out of the house on many occasions – but if he'd come back after my husband died I'd have let him in. It's Christian charity. More than that, forgiveness is in every mother's blood.' She turned the oven on. 'There'll be eggs on the table in a few minutes. I made a cabinet pudding last night. Do you want cream on it?'

'With my arteries? I don't have time for *jentaculum* today. I have to see a man about a dog. Specifically, I need to talk to some of my academic colleagues.'

'Oh, the nutters. It's too early to call on anyone yet. At least get a breakfast inside you. You haven't had enough sleep. Your eyes are very red.'

'You should see them from my side. What do you think of this?' He set down the London Bridge paperweight, sprinkling dirt on to the tablecloth.

Alma dried her hands and came over. 'That's horrible as well.'

'It was in Hoffman's back garden. She'd thrown it out of her window.'

'I used to love them though.'

'What do you mean?' Bryant turned it over in his lumpen hands.

She took it from him. 'We had these souvenirs when I was a little girl.'

'They weren't making these a hundred years ago, it came from Arizona in America.'

'I was still in Antigua then. They came off the cruise ships and got sold on the dockside along with models of red telephone boxes, Big Bens and St Paul's Cathedralses. A little bit of London, I thought. I never expected to end up here, but that's another story. My people thought London was going to be exciting. Instead nobody talked to them and they got stuck in poky little flats up the wrong end of the Edgware Road. You know the Buckingham Palace clock-ashtray in our living room?'

'Unfortunately, I do.' It was a treasured heirloom of Alma's that he had tried to destroy many times.

'My mother got that in the port back home. She said it would bring us all luck. I brought it with me when I came here.'

'Madam, like all of your stories, particularly your fanciful adventures of Jesus, it sounds like balderdash.'

'So this is balderdash?' Alma scraped at the sticker on the base of the model with a butter knife and showed him the words stamped underneath: 'Soho Square Souvenirs'. 'I don't know why you always have to overcomplicate things. Honestly, I could do your job for you.'

To Bryant it seemed like a good place to start. He left Albion House and set off up Harrison Street for his six-minute walk to the unit, so lost in thought that he walked right past his partner.

'I was just coming to get you,' May said, grabbing his arm.

'Today you're going to do what you do best. What's your thinking right now?'

'I'm trying to find the company that supplied the pewter models of London Bridge.'

'Why on earth would you want to do that?'

'Remember that film *The Lavender Hill Mob* and their counterfeit statues of the Eiffel Tower? It made me think: what if this is to do with the person who supplied the souvenirs?'

'Have you tried contacting the company?'

'Alma looked online and found the name of the owner, but he died some years ago . . .' Bryant whacked at a dandelion with his stick. It still amazed him the way weeds sprang up on backstreet pavements overnight. Bloomsbury was overwhelmed with greenery in summer.

'You see, this is where you go wrong,' said May. 'Lateral thinking is a useful tool but if it leads nowhere, let it go.'

'You're saying I shouldn't try to track down his family in the West Indies.'

'Precisely. Cross it off the list and let's move on. What's next?'

'We arrange an appointment at the British Library.'

'Let me guess, that shouty fellow Kirkpatrick.'

'Indeed, a chap to whom I owe my life.'*

From here the library was equidistant to the unit, so they diverted along Euston Road, tacking through the grey canyon of traffic.

They found Raymond Kirkpatrick supervising the restoration of an immense nineteenth-century map of Thames staircases. In his vast blue checked shirt and hoodie he looked like a lumberjack.

'That's a coincidence, we were just there,' said Bryant,

---

* See *Wild Chamber*.

tapping a digit on the London Bridge stairwell. 'It's not open to the public any more.'

'We always think of poor old Nancy being bludgeoned to death on that staircase,' said Kirkpatrick, 'although in the novel she's hideously murdered in her room and even Bill Sykes's dog gets blood on him.' He strode around the great lithograph, gesturing at it like a weatherman revealing incoming storms. 'Nancy's death was based on the real murder of one Eliza Grimwood, described as a prostitute rather than destitute. Hello, John, we don't usually have the pleasure of your company in these rarefied environs. Sorry to hear about you getting shot.' He reached across the pages spread before him to wrap a paw around May's hand and shake it vigorously. 'I'm giving a lecture about this lot in a few minutes so you'd better state your business with all celerity.'

'I thought your speciality was cryptographic semantics?' said May.

'If you want me to list my specialities we'll be here all day. Arthur, darling, that's a couple of hundred years old, please put it down before you break it.'

He removed a frosted-glass barrel from Bryant's hands and set it aside. 'That item once stood in a shop on Pickle Herring, a street by St Olaf Wharf. The thoroughfare was filled with iron bridges that the improvident clothheads of Southwark Council saw fit to demolish in the 1970s, along with Pickle Herring staircase, which I am trying to recreate on this map without interruption from excessively mature members of quasi-policing units.'

'London Bridge,' said Bryant, slapping the hand-drawn symbol down on Kirkpatrick's counter. 'There's one of these inset on the bridge wall. What is it?'

'Oh, is that all?' Kirkpatrick stroked his whiskers and peered at it. 'Every trader or householder had a pictographic design put on to a bridge tile. Most people couldn't read but they remembered symbols: that's why we have pub signs. This one's the Bridge House, a company established in the thirteenth century to maintain the bridge. Privatization was all the rage back then. All leases, rents and tolls were collected by company wardens. The bridge was stacked with houses and shops, half of them ready to tumble into the river. Bridge House used the revenue to buy property until it became one of the biggest landowners in the city. That's how the other bridges were built. They're still privately maintained without taxpayers' dosh. What are you looking for?'

'We think London Bridge is being used as a hiding place, but we've been there and found nothing.'

'You may be looking for a bridge that's not there any more.'

'What do you mean?' May asked.

'It was removed in the nineteenth century after over six hundred years of faithful service. It had been patched up for years and was literally falling down.' He traced a finger along the broken line of arches on the map. 'Some stones were used in the construction of church towers. Most were dumped in the river. Several of the alcoves are still around. There are two in Victoria Park. One's in the courtyard of Guy's Hospital with a statue of Keats sitting inside it. London loved building arches and alcoves; their remains are everywhere. When the workmen pulled down the balustrades they found the original wooden piers underneath, and those were carved into souvenirs. Snuffboxes were popular; I have one at home. There's a company that still makes jewellery containing bits of the bridge. So even though it's been demolished much of it is still in London. These days we cheerfully destroy everything old, but in past times buildings were recycled. Our finest erections lasted much longer back then. As I was apologizing to the wife.'

'Your sense of humour has always been rudimentary,' said Bryant. Kirkpatrick might have had the brain of an astronomy professor but he still laughed at *Carry On* films.

'You're not giving me enough information to work with,' Kirkpatrick complained. 'I need to know what you're looking for.'

'You're one of our trusted partners—'

'That makes me sound like a building society.'

'—but in this particular case I can't give you all the details.'

'Why not?'

'It involves matters of national security.' Bryant's eyes swam meaningfully around his spectacle lenses.

'Just because I share a Christian name with your dunderhead chief, kindly don't treat me like him. So "London Bridge" is presumably the codename of an operation.' Kirkpatrick ruffled his huge Karl Marx beard and thought for a minute. 'You have to look beneath the bridge, as it were.'

He snatched a piece of paper from one of his startled students and scribbled a phone number across it. 'Call this woman; she was an archaeologist specializing in Britain's so-called Dark Ages, but got kicked out of college for expressing some unorthodox views. She's quite a woman; a single smouldering glance from her could take the fur off your tongue. Don't tell her I sent you.'

'Why not?'

'We used to date but it ended badly.'

'How badly?'

'She tried to kill me. But she may be able to help you.'

27

GUARDED BY DRAGONS

Rita Rondola had tied her hair above her head in a gravity-defying ball and added another pair of gigantic hoop earrings. She motored along Piccadilly, across into Knightsbridge, past Harrods and the Victoria & Albert Museum, up Exhibition Road and on to the forecourt of the neo-Palladian Institute of Historic London Studies in Bayswater.

'I'm going for the breakfast,' she warned, tucking her ency-clopaedia under her arm as she waited for her passengers to alight. 'I am on "Amyotrophia: progressive wasting of muscle tissue". I want to see what happens, is very exciting. Call me when you are done.'

If Bryant seemed incapable of manoeuvring an umbrella, a walking stick and his leather satchel out of a taxi, he had even more fun with the institute's glass revolving door.

Elizabeth Montague was waiting for them in the reception area. Tall and assured, she reminded Bryant of a seventies tie-dye militant. Her copper necklace, purple glasses and crimson bandana brought a splash of joy into the antiseptic atrium. She shone.

'I thought it would be full of books,' Bryant said, looking around in disappointment.

'I'm afraid not, Mr Bryant. We store everything online. The board don't like having verminous old volumes lying around the place. Books aren't clean.'

Elizabeth led the way to the spartan glass box designated as her office. 'I feel like a museum piece in here. Those tubular things are actually chairs. Please feel free to balance on them.'

'Kirkpatrick says you were chucked out of your university,' Bryant said. 'What did you do?'

If Elizabeth was surprised at his directness she managed to hide it. 'I went against the accepted orthodoxy about London in the Dark Ages. I presented a case suggesting that London did not suffer an atavistic collapse without the Romans but remained a thriving town using many modern inventions which were lost in the four centuries that followed.'

'Heresy.' Bryant left the sculpted steel chair to his partner and opted for something with a cushion. 'I can't imagine that went down well.'

'Not when so many of my fellow academics were writing papers on the opposite hypothesis,' said Elizabeth. 'You said you need to know about London Bridge. I'm not sure I can be of much help. You probably have the key facts.'

'Don't worry about what I know,' Bryant assured her. 'Hit me.'

She set out some drawings before them. 'This first bridge was probably built in 43 CE but may have been temporary. There were several more before the permanent one was constructed with a central drawbridge. London would not have been created without the crossing, so London Bridge was, and still is, guarded by dragons. Ethelred the Unready tried to stop the Danish invasion of London by getting the King of Norway's men to tear the bridge down, so its collapse actually became associated with saving the city.'

'Hence the song?' said Bryant.

'Exactly. The Norse war chant "London Bridge is broken down, Gold is won and bright renown" became the basis for the nursery rhyme. "London Bridge Is Falling Down".'

'Every Londoner must know that tune,' said May.

'But how many of them know what it means?'

'What does it mean?'

'The repeated refrain "My fair lady" throughout the song supposedly refers to Anne Boleyn's lady-in-waiting Margaret Wyatt. She stayed beside Henry VIII's second wife right up to the scaffold. So the song may be about the rise and fall of Anne, who was hated by the general population, and how pride went before a fall. The mentions of silver and gold referred to the fancy shops that were built along London Bridge. There were around a hundred and forty buildings rising up to seven storeys. They overhung the river and weighed so heavily on its arches that the bridge began sinking into the Thames mud.'

'It doesn't explain why the bridge has such a central place in the popular imagination,' said Bryant.

'Come with me.' Elizabeth led them downstairs to a climate-controlled white room filled with plan chests. It only took her a minute to locate some elegant sketches. 'These were made for a book that was never published. The bridge was always a place of celebration and rebellion. In 1863 a triumphal arch was built across it to celebrate the marriage of Princess Alexandra of Denmark to the Prince of Wales. Crowds didn't just gather there for pageants. They lined up to watch fires, riots and disasters. It's not a spiritual spot but if I had to locate the heart of London I wouldn't choose a church or a palace. I'd pick London Bridge because it has seen two thousand years of tumultuous life. It represents humanity.'

'Humanity,' Bryant repeated thoughtfully.

He thanked the academic and prepared to take his leave. Even in midsummer this involved a gathering-up of sticks, bags and detached items of clothing. 'By the way,' he said, 'why did you try to kill Kirkpatrick?'

She answered without needing to think. 'Oh, he got ink everywhere, slept in his socks and took me to a double bill of Norman Wisdom films. I thought he wore a hearing aid, but it turned out he was listening to heavy metal bands. I lasted a month.'

As the detectives exited the institute Rita Rondola reappeared in her taxi, reversing into the forecourt. She removed a bacon roll from her mouth. 'Where is next?'

'Parsons Green. It's a bit out of the way.' To Bryant, anything beyond London Underground's zone one might as well have been in the Lake District.

'*Parsons Green?*' Rita raised a ringed hand to her mouth and sniggered. 'Is a joke name I think.'

'What's there?' asked May.

'The Library of the Esoteric,' Bryant replied. 'Many of my informants use it as a meeting place. If they've heard anything, the chief librarian will know about it.'

Angela Carey remained in the kitchen while they finished their little treasure hunt. She tried not to let her anger show. Clearly, working for the security of the nation was now judged a crime, and this jumped-up little man, so nondescript and suburban, was rifling through her belongings like a thief at a wake.

Dan Banbury had finally received a warrant approval, and Angela had no choice but to acknowledge it. A warranted search was far more disruptive than most people realized; in Carey's case it meant impounding all electronic equipment and deconstructing her home to its bare bones. Banbury was apologetic but thorough.

'I'd prefer it if you were out there arresting the man who's been following us,' Angela called to the empty doorway.

Banbury appeared in it, holding long-handled pincers in his gloved hands. 'Sorry, I'm in your cistern. What were you saying?'

She longed to tell him everything but the thought of turning traitor was unconscionable.

'Airing cupboard,' said Dan, 'all right to take your clothes horse out?'

They arranged to meet at St Christopher's Place, in the network of narrow brick alleyways behind Oxford Street. There was an Italian café in the corner, invisible from most angles.

Larry Cranston was early. He seated himself on a bench in the dark interior, hoping that she wouldn't see how badly his jacket needed dry-cleaning. The buttons would not stay done up. He wasn't sure what to expect. After five minutes he had begun to shred a paper napkin.

Paige Henderson appeared from nowhere and slipped casually into the chair opposite. She wore a white shirt under a black trouser suit that gave her the appearance of a train attendant. Her hair was tied tightly back, her skin so translucently pale that she might have been preserved in ice. Dark irises exhibited a button-eyed hardness, so that when she examined him it was as if she could see through his clothes.

'Mr Cranston, you've led us a merry dance.' She waved away a waiter.

'I had to be sure I had the right buyer.' He shifted uncomfortably on his bench.

'You understand that we don't make purchases. Our services in this case may extend as far as . . .' She searched for the appropriate word. '. . . *facilitation*.'

'I think you'll find it's worth it. Before I hand anything over, I need to get some assurances in place.'

Paige patted the air. 'Let's slow down a minute. You're jumping the gun. *We*'ll dictate the terms.'

He tried to unstick the shreds of napkin from his wet palm. 'What I can provide for you is worth a lot of money.'

'We're not interested in its monetary value. I assume you haven't brought it along.' She wiped a speck from the white linen tablecloth.

'It's in a safe place. I'm prepared to make the delivery as soon as you offer me proof that the US authorities won't accede to an extradition request from the UK.'

'That's not how it works, Mr Cranston.' She smiled almost warmly, with a hint of apology. 'The charges against you can't just be pushed under the rug. But they can be delayed. You will not be able to return here, ever. We'd provide you with a shield.'

'A shield?'

'A guarantee that prevents you from being prosecuted.'

'What form does that take? When will I get it?' He forced himself to leave the paper napkin alone.

'It will just appear. We deal in the invisible. It will be activated when you deliver.'

'How will I know it's working?'

'You won't be arrested leaving the country. So let's talk about timing for London Bridge.'

He tried not to look as if he was bluffing. The back of his neck felt wet. 'I just have to pick it up.'

'When? Today?'

'Hopefully, or if not, by close of play tomorrow. I'll need to check its authenticity.'

'You need to be more exact.' She glanced at her phone. 'Let's set a time, twenty-four hours from now. I'll meet you in the City, somewhere quiet. The roof garden in Fen Court, midday tomorrow.'

Cranston felt the first tremor of betrayal. He knew the roof garden; it was one of the most secure spots in London, open and bare, surrounded by cameras, guards and electronic pass gates. If he handed her London Bridge then – and he still had no idea what it looked like or how much room it took up – she could have him hauled away seconds later. He had known where he stood with the FBI and their stolid, workmanlike operatives, but the CIA's reputation was more complex and far less trustworthy.

'Very well,' he heard himself saying. 'Until tomorrow.'

He had already decided that, whatever happened, he would not show up. He would let her see who was really in control and make her come to him.

'We lost the battle,' said Frank Huxley, chief librarian at the Library of the Esoteric, a grandiose name for some bookcases in a lock-up. 'The council tricked my mother out of her bequest and closed down our old building. She told me she would leave behind a codicil but none of us were able to find it.'

'I was sorry to hear about that,' said Bryant, leaning on his walking stick. Behind him John May waited, politely observing.

'I have to sling a lot of this out.' He held up a mouldering volume. '*Cabalistic Symbology in the Rules of Test Match Cricket*. Want it?'

'Good Lord, no. I know the place was very dear to Dorothy. I hope the collection can stay together.'

'Not for much longer, unless we get a benefactor. I don't suppose you'd care to invest?'

Bryant patted down his waistcoat. 'I'm a police officer, Frank, and an unemployed one at that.' He took down a volume entitled *The Art of Fencing in the Weimar Republic*. 'This looks interesting.'

'That's a mistranslation,' Frank pointed out. 'It's actually about German fences.'

'I know, I have the companion volume on Austrian guttering. Mr May and I have a question for you.' Bryant flicked through a volume entitled *Tethys & Oceanus: An Anthology of Mythical Rivers.* 'Do you have the earlier edition? The one with the separate chapter on Phlegethon, the river of conflagration?'

'Is that the question?'

'No, no.' He paced between the musty stacks. 'Anything bound in human skin?'

Frank gave him a weary look. 'The technique of binding in skin is known as anthropodermic bibliopegy and no, we don't have any. Mr Bryant, have you come here just to be annoying or do you wish to make a donation?'

'Good God, no. I'm a huge fan of Dorothy's collection but there's some right old rubbish here as well.' He tossed a Lobsang Rampa paperback aside and raised his voice. 'I understand you still get a lot of academics in. How would you describe them as a group?'

'Secretive. Obsessive. Territorial.'

'Fruitcakes?'

'There are a few upstanding members of the maniac community.'

'As I thought. They can outline the nine meditational approaches to traversable wormholes but can't remember how to work a teapot. Neither can you, apparently.'

'Sorry, would you like a cup?'

'Most obliged. What about women?'

Frank brewed up. 'None lately.'

'Not you. I mean in general.'

He tried to think. 'What *do* you mean?'

'You know – women: kind, vindictive, can do two things at once, hardly ever become serial killers.'

'Possessors of sinister wisdom,' said a familiar voice from the stacks.

Bryant peered between the poorly lit shelves. Maggie Armitage hove into view like a Gothic ship, or rather, as she was shrinking, a dinghy, albeit one cheerfully bedecked with beads and chains. She had at least thirty protest badges pinned on her blue denim jacket. Her coiffure, usually the colour of a London bus, had been renovated into something purple and punky while her eye shadow had turned black. She looked as if she was about to take a ride on a haunted carousel.

'What are you doing here?' asked May, annoyed. 'What have you come as?'

'I'm looking for a rare work on the erotic subconscious,' Maggie explained.

'I told you if it pops up I'd let you have it,' said Frank. 'Which reminds me, Maggie, you damaged our only copy of *Invocations for a Satanic Mass*.'

'Yes, sorry about that.' She glanced at Bryant. 'I accidentally baked it. I didn't realize it was in the oven tray. It made everybody sick.'

'I did warn you that the green bindings on certain seventeenth-century books are coated in arsenic.'

She turned her attention back to Bryant. 'When I said that women were possessors of sinister wisdom I meant in the sense of left-handedness. Traditionally Eve is always depicted standing on the left side of Adam. She is the conveyor of knowledge but not its generator. Nice to see you out of your usual jurisdiction, Arthur.'

'Thank you. I have my own taxi now, and John is accompanying me to make sure that I—'

'—don't fall over or get lost.'

'—conduct investigations in the approved manner. Ever heard of groups of women guarding treasures? Please, feel free to impart your distaff knowledge to this mere male.'

'Women are the keepers of the hearth,' said Maggie. 'In German folklore the *Weiße Frauen* or "Sunlight Ladies" are elf women who guard treasure. The English equivalent is the White Lady, usually a ghost.'

'We're limiting our search to the living at the moment,' said Bryant.

Maggie wagged a beringed finger at him. 'Some of us are still the keepers of secrets. Remember Joanna Southcote's box.'

'I'm sorry, Maggie, your call did not go through. Try again?'

'She was one of the Seven Divine Prophets. At the end of the eighteenth century she presented a large wooden crate to her followers to be opened in the presence of twenty-four bishops. It was believed that the contents of the box would bring a thousand years of peace. For decades after, posters were put up all around London demanding the opening of the box.'

'What happened?'

'They lost it. They think it's buried in an allotment in Bedford.'

'Tell me,' May asked, 'do all women go mad when they hit fifty?'

Maggie was indignant. 'We have a women's group that meets here every month to discuss forbidden knowledge. Frank sat in on the last one.'

'I learned a lot more than I'd expected,' Frank admitted. 'Mostly about reproductive rituals and the difficulty of finding a decent plumber.'

Maggie drew them in closer, overwhelming them with the scent of patchouli oil. 'There are secrets guarded solely by women.'

'This is getting us nowhere,' said May, impatient to leave.

'What kind of secrets?' asked Bryant. 'Any to do with London Bridge?'

'The legend of the Swaffham Pedlar ends with the discovery of buried treasure under London Bridge. It's located through a Latin inscription: "Under me doth lie another much richer than I". Historically, it's the perfect spot for the burial of secrets. My clairvoyant Dame Maude told me that treasure would never be found if women lost touch with their inner Circe.'

'Dame Maude has lost touch with her inner reality,' May said. 'Arthur, really—'

Maggie would not be stopped. 'The sudden exposure to hidden knowledge can have a profound effect, like the ecstatic visions you can access from cabalistic numbers. The ladies in my Seditious Literature book club said we should specifically think about bridges.'

Frank took the book Maggie was holding and stamped it. 'Of course, they were pissed at the time.'

'There are thirty-five bridges over the Thames in London,' said Bryant. 'I don't see how this is useful.'

'Not physical bridges, silly boy.' She slapped him chidingly on the arm. 'Psychic connections.'

'Arthur, we really have to go,' said May, looking at his watch.

She jabbed his arm. 'Where men see unconnected events, women see a holistic picture. Men gather data; women connect it.'

'That's why the women did so well in GCHQ,' said Bryant as the penny dropped. 'They spotted something nobody else could see.'

'Perhaps what others saw as innocuous, they saw as dangerous.'

'Maggie, you are as ever unexpected.' He handed Frank a volume covered in dust. 'This was Dorothy's favourite book. *The Occult Roots of Science*. It was misfiled.'

Opening its gold-edged pages, he allowed a fold of grey paper to slide out before Frank's astonished eyes. 'Unless I'm very much mistaken that's the missing codicil you've been looking for. Stop dawdling, John, we've got work to do.'

28

POETRY IS NOT GOING TO HELP

Angela needed to get out of the house as soon as possible. She knew that by now Annie would have left her a message at one of their signal spots, but the idiot forensics fellow, Banbury, was still packing up his equipment. He had taken everything apart with astonishing speed and put it all back leaving no sign of disturbance. Typically, he had concentrated on the nuts and bolts of his task, never stopping to think that she might keep incriminating evidence off-site.

'I'll be out of your way in a minute,' he promised, placing swabs inside a bag. 'I usually only do this at crime scenes but it was part of the brief, I'm afraid.'

She waited impatiently as he finished clearing up. 'I hate to hurry you but I have an appointment in the West End at two p.m.'

'Not a problem, almost done,' he replied amenably. 'I must say you're very calm, considering someone might be trying to kill you and the other lady.'

'Annie.'

'That's the one. The three of you worked for the government, yes? You were like us, helping to protect the nation, holding the front line against enemies overseas.'

'I suppose so, yes,' she said, thinking, *Intrusive little man.*

'At first I thought it must be a revenge thing, you know? For someone you peached on in the past. That's the sort of thing you did, isn't it, compiling lists of people, pointing fingers?'

'I can't talk about the work I used to do, Mr Banbury, you know that.'

'Of course not, fair play to you.' He threw the last of the swabs into his box. Dan was workmanlike and dogged. It made people underestimate him. 'Only I thought to myself, why would anyone wait so long to take revenge? They wouldn't, would they? I mean, decades, no offence, it just stands to reason.'

He closed his case and snapped the locks with finality. 'So you must have something this bloke wants. Maybe even you don't know where it is, but all three of you must know *what* it is. I can understand you not wanting to breach the terms of your service but if there's a chance that it could save your lives . . .' Banbury shrugged. 'Just a thought.'

She hoped he had finished, but after donning his jacket and heading for the door he turned back. 'I mean, we know all about codenames and that this one is called London Bridge. I wish we could place twenty-four-hour security on the ground until this is over but we don't have the capability.'

'Codenames are designed to point enemies in the wrong direction,' Angela told him with impatience. 'I imagine you already went to London Bridge and realized there's nothing to be found. I'd advise you to stop looking. There are matters of national security that go far beyond the remit of the police.'

Banbury considered the point for a moment. 'Still, you chose London Bridge for a reason.'

He's like a terrier, she thought. *What* is *it about the people in this unit?*

'It was chosen for a reason only obliquely connected to bridges,' she said, remembering Annie's advice about providing just enough information to keep the police off their backs.

'It's still connected,' said Banbury, thinking aloud. 'I must say I admire your dedication to misinformation. Fair makes you one of us. Well, I've finished here so I'll leave you alone.'

She watched him leave, waited ten minutes, then donned a raincoat and set off towards Angel tube station.

The skyline was a charcoal drawing. The clouds above her had been pinched and left bruised. The air was London-strange, at once too warm and too cold. As she approached the last remaining iron bollard at the end of Camden Passage she saw that it had two pink knots of chewing gum stuck to its side. It was an indication that Annie had decided to risk everything.

Amelia, Annie and Angela – that had always been the running order, in age and responsibility. What they had done out of youthful idealism now seemed so misguided that Angela could scarcely recognize the actions of her younger self.

As the first fat raindrops splattered on the pavement, she ducked beneath the cover of the tube station entrance. *It will all be over today*, she thought. *I wonder if Annie took the gun with her.*

They went to the operations room to argue it out.

'Connection,' said Dan Banbury. 'Obviously a bridge connects, but what else?' He looked at each of the detectives in turn, expecting a fast response.

'Email,' said May.

'Telegraph poles,' said Bryant. 'Semaphore. Breadcrumbs. String.'

'The railway.' Banbury looked at each of them triumphantly. 'London Bridge Station has just been completely rebuilt.'

'Opened in 1836,' said Bryant absently. 'I think it now has

fifteen platforms. I have a book on it somewhere.' He clambered up on his library steps and checked the shelves. 'Ah, here:

'Inside the station, everything's so old,
So inconvenient, of such manifold
Perplexity, and, as a mole might see,
So strictly what a station shouldn't be.

'Davidson, 1909.'

'I don't think poetry's going to help us,' May remarked. 'Does the new station have luggage lockers?'

'They removed them to improve security,' said Banbury.

Bryant turned to a map. 'They had to tear out the old vaults underneath. What if we started there?'

May took the book and studied its diagrams. 'The code-name isn't the location, it's the name of the thing itself. "London Bridge" could be anywhere in the country.'

'Then we're marooned,' said Bryant. 'Let's go back to the beginning.'

The others groaned. 'There's no time,' warned Raymond Land. 'Faraday's coming back today. He's going to kill me.'

Bryant pulled open his hand-drawn plan of 58 Cruikshank Street and spread it across the floor, slopping tea mugs. 'We went through Hoffman's belongings and found the paper-weight, the symbol and the photograph taken in the restaurant. The symbol matched the one on London Bridge. The photo commemorates a meeting. All of us have been over to the flat except Raymondo and that was because he hadn't finished his crossword, and probably never will. Five Down is "Berliner", by the way, not "binliner". Was there anything else out of place we might have missed?'

'Carbolic,' said Sidney, slipping her phone away. 'It's this stuff—'

'Thank you, we know what carbolic is. Disinfectant soap

containing phenol. Very old-fashioned. Good for scrubbing blood out of floorboards.'

'There were tons of soap wrappers in her cupboard.'

'How many? Don't tell me you didn't count them.'

'One hundred and thirty-two.'

Bryant was almost impressed. 'Nothing written on them?'

'No.'

'How large are they?'

'I brought some back.' Sidney held up a plastic evidence bag.

Bryant took it from her and tore it open. Donning his trifocals, he minutely inspected them. 'She mailed these out and got something back in each case,' he said at last.

'You *cannot* possibly know that,' said Land. 'You're not a – what are those people called who see into the future?'

'Weather forecasters.'

'Stockbrokers.'

'Chimney sweeps.'

'Everybody shut up,' called Land.

Bryant raised one of the wrappers. 'They're made of foil and each one has a date stamp. They fit neatly inside an envelope. Whoever received one of these would know who was sending them. It was Hoffman's guarantee of authenticity, to ensure that there had been no tampering.'

'Oh, this is ludicrous,' said Land.

'Not at all,' Bryant reasoned. 'It's an old Second World War trick, arrived at by the same process we used to deduce that you left school at sixteen. But I know you're all wondering, how do soap wrappers tell us who is sending messages? Could there be a connection between London Bridge and bars of soap? Somewhere in the dim recesses of my mind a bell rings.'

'That's your tinnitus,' said Land.

'I have seen something that connects these clues.'

The unit chief poked him in the waistcoat with a finger.

'Now look here, I've gone along with some pretty outlandish ideas working with you, but this beats them all.'

'Bear with me, *ma vieille chaussette*, while I examine the question, viz: why use a bridge as a codename? While you were lost in the latest issue of *Caravan Monthly* I was carrying out some research.'

'No, no, no,' warned Land, raising his palms. 'I don't want to know.'

'From all that information I was able to distil— Oh.' Bryant froze.

'Is he having another one of his turns?' Land asked.

'We have to go.' Bryant grabbed his partner's arm. 'I know where it is.'

'Then we should come with you,' said Janice. 'You'll need back-up.'

'No, everything here must look completely normal.'

'Give me a clue as to what that looks like,' said Land helplessly.

'Get on the phones, send emails, make sure Faraday sees that the PCU is hard at work. Even you, Raymond, find your favourite book and colour in the farmyard; just make it appear that you're doing something. And don't call us, we'll call you.'

With that he and May headed down to the parking bay where Rita Rondola was waiting in her taxi.

29

WHAT MR BRYANT LEARNED

(NB. This chapter may be omitted by those in a hurry. AB)

Lian Tan: Researcher, author of *River Traffic in London*, denounced by Chinese government as a subversive, now working at University College London:
Thank you for your email, Mr Bryant. What do I know about London Bridge?

1. After Boudicca burned the wooden bridge (and the rest of the city) a new one was built linking to 'South Works', the borough of Southwark.
2. Knights used to joust on the causeway.
3. The construction of a permanent stone crossing was started as a penance by Henry II for the murder of Thomas Becket.
4. Driving on the left was invented to control the bridge's traffic.
5. Until the early eighteenth century it was the only way of crossing the river into the city without getting a ferry.

I hope this helps.

Maggie Armitage, Grand Order Grade IV White Witch of the Coven of St James the Elder, Kentish Town:
It was more than just a bridge; there was a thriving community here. The crossing-point always had a watchman to protect it. The idea of sacrificing someone and interring them in the foundations to ensure its security is fanciful but quite widespread. With a thinner, more permeable line between the living and the dead, corpses could keep watch more reliably than an old man dozing over a brazier.

In folkloric terms, men carry out a great many actions at the prompting of women, so females provide advice and knowledge. It was long thought that London was protected by the Mother of the City, not its founding fathers. The spirit of the city, always female, watches over the bridge, the ceremonial entry point into London.

Stanhope Beaufort, disbarred architectural engineer and designer, Hoxton:
It's likely the old stone bridge housed a *menhir*, a milestone, possibly the London Stone itself, from which all roads sprang. The stone is still on display in Cannon Street. Popular legend suggested it had been taken from the sacked city of Troy; a load of bollocks, sadly. But it may have formed part of the bridge's entrance, the Stonegate.

The old bridge was one of the great wonders of Europe. It lasted for over six hundred years. The entrance was topped with around thirty severed heads of traitors. Thomas More's head was boiled and displayed, then thrown into the Thames. There was a chapel in the middle that looked as if it had been built upside down, and Nonsuch House, a prefabricated red-and yellow-panelled mansion shipped over from Holland, entirely held together with wooden pegs, sort of early IKEA. But we know nothing about the people who lived inside it for the next two centuries.

Terje Pedersen, former Director of Classical Studies at the Norwegian Institute of London:
The Norwegian mercenary Olaf Haroldsson helped return King Ethelred to the throne by attaching ropes to London Bridge and tearing it down. After being made a saint, the cult of St Olaf took root around London Bridge in half a dozen churches. The Nordic influence in this part of London is still there in plain sight more than a millennium later, on flags and heraldic symbols.

Günter Vogel, author of *The German Diaspora*, Freiburg University Press:
There was not only a strong Nordic influence around London Bridge. Subsequent centuries brought a strong German presence. The confederate guilds of the Hanseatic League were based there. The Hanseatic League still has a building by the bridge, so the site has international importance.

Chasen D. Williams, Professor Emeritus, Roman Architecture, University of Chicago:
Londinium began on the north side of the Thames because it had an unbroken shoreline. It very quickly became a city of immigrants, craftworkers and merchants selling Mediterranean glass, Turkish grain, wines and oils and jewellery. Even after the Roman bridge was destroyed you could see where it had been by the glitter of fallen coins lying in the riverbed.

Barney Calman, editor of the academic magazine *Mephiticus* (currently awaiting sentencing):
The fair ladies of London still watch over the city in the form of the Three Graces or possibly Nereids, who help sailors face storms. London Bridge, the access gate to the most ancient part of Londinium, must always be guarded

by women. The monumental Stonegate on the south side of the bridge was so enduring that it survived until nine years before of the invention of photography.

Daisy Meadows, Heritage Adviser, Society for the Protection of Ancient Monuments:
There were nineteen Gothic arches below London Bridge that forced the Thames into violent torrents. As the watermen shot the rapids their boats were often smashed to matchwood, so they used to praise London Bridge before going under: 'God bless thee, London Bridge, thou never did I no harm.' Then they swore at it after passing: 'Damn and blast thee, London Bridge.'

So many waterwheels were built between the piers that around thirty people a year lost their lives in the rapids. When boats went through the narrow rushing arches they dropped more than six feet. In 1290 a ship full of expelled Jews turned over and all were drowned. It was said that their desperate cries could be heard centuries later in the turbulent waters.

The arches also held water back, which is why the Thames froze so solidly that they held frost fairs on it. When the ice broke up it often smashed away chunks of the bridge supports. During the Great Fire the surrounding houses dropped burning timbers on to the bridge, preventing fleeing residents from crossing the river to safety.

George Canning (1770–1827), British Prime Minister:
    'Shoot we the bridge!' – the venturous boatmen cry,
    'Shoot we the bridge!' – the exulting fare reply,
    Down the steep fall the headlong waters go,
    Curls the white foam, the breakers roar below.
    The veering helm the dextrous steersman stops,
    Shifts the thin oar, the fluttering canvas drops;

Then with closed eyes, clench'd hands, and quick-drawn
   breath,
Darts at the central arch, nor heeds the gulf beneath.
Full 'gainst the pier the unsteady timbers knock,
The loose planks starting own th'impetuous shock;
The shifted oar, dropp'd sail, and steadied helm,
With angry surge the closing waters whelm –
Laughs the glad Thames, and clasps each fair one's
   charms
That screams and scrambles in his oozy arms.
Drench'd each smart garb, and clogg'd each struggling
   limb,
Far o'er the stream the cockneys sink or swim;
While each badged boatman, clinging to his oar,
Bounds o'er the buoyant wave, and climbs th'applauding
   shore.

Dante August, Curator, Museum of London:
More than anything it's a symbol, a representation of per-
manence, like the Tower of London and now, I suppose, Big
Ben. But it also embodies the spirit of the populace that
swarmed around it – men and women young and old, birth-
ing and dying, angry, screaming, fornicating, fighting,
laughing, forever feeding the voracious maw of London
trade. That spirit of rebellion and free thought is still in all
of us.

**Emiline Carter-Thompson, author of *A Social History of
Engineering*:**
Bridges have a significance that goes beyond their physical
purpose. Lobbyists block the construction of new crossings
in order to keep areas undeveloped, the better to protect
their own commercialized properties. When London Bridge
became too congested to use, proposals for a new bridge at

Westminster were quickly buried. The merchants in the City didn't want to direct more traffic towards the politicians of Westminster. So a bridge can be used both as an opener of the way and as a blockade.

30

THE CRYSTAL KEY

Caught in mid-mouthful, Rita Rondola lowered her bag of crisps and warily opened the cab door. 'What now?'

'The south side of Blackfriars Bridge,' Bryant told her. 'Leave your lunch, we're in a hurry.'

'No lunch, is breakfast. I cannot eat lunch while driving, is soup.'

'I must introduce you to our Colin. You share the same epicurean proclivities.'

Rita put her foot down, pressing them back into their seats. She clipped the lights on King's Cross Road and narrowly missed a troupe of students from Rome, who were at least used to being run over.

The encyclopaedia at Bryant's feet slid about. 'Where are you up to?'

'The first book in English written by a woman.'

'Julian of Norwich? Oh, "Anchorite". Still on the As then.' He turned to May. 'You see the connections making themselves visible now, don't you?'

'To be honest, Arthur, I'm not sure I do,' May admitted.

'These seemingly random points of curiosity are all leading to the same place.'

'But you have so many of them,' May replied.

'I need to make sense of the world.'

'The world does not make sense. You can't construct an equation to represent it.'

'History equals People plus Time.' Bryant slid about in his seat as the taxi swung around the Aldwych and over Waterloo Bridge. He then closed his eyes and fell into a coma until they arrived on Blackfriars Bridge.

May studied his partner. Sometimes it seemed as if he was from another age. May could imagine him scurrying across Paternoster Square with an armful of psalters, lost in abstruse calculations. Perhaps he had always existed in the city, weaving his way through history in multiple guises.

'We're here,' said May. 'Wake up.'

'I'm trying to. My backside's still asleep.'

'Yes, I heard it snoring.'

'Sorry. Alma's pudding.' Bryant extracted himself from Rita's cab and set off for the bridge staircase. They climbed down a floor, up a floor and found themselves at the entrance to a peculiarly angled public house wedged almost under the bridge.

'Doggett's Coat and Badge,' said Bryant as they entered. 'Thomas Doggett was a Hanoverian comic actor. He inaugurated the Thames boat race that takes place at the start of August. It's the only event I can think of that's still connected with London Bridge. The winner gets a red coat and a silver badge.'

'It makes no sense,' said May. 'Why hide something here, inside a busy pub with only a tenuous connection to the bridge?'

'Do you have a better idea? This pub is easily accessible and right in the heart of the city.'

They found the landlord and carried out a search, but

uncovered nothing. Bryant pushed his homburg back on his head and scratched his ear. 'I feel more and more that I understand Amelia's thought processes. I'm sure she would have chosen a spot like this.'

'There's no direct link,' said May. 'It's not like you can find something that came from the actual bridge here.'

Bryant gave him a searching look. 'I'm an idiot,' he said with confidence.

'Why?'

'Something from the bridge. We're in the wrong place. Let's get back to the taxi. There's no time to lose.'

Rita was just about to head into her bag of crisps when the detectives made her jump, grabbing at her doors.

'Get us to Borough High Street as fast as you can,' Bryant instructed.

'I am not breaking law.' Rita brushed crisps from her blouse.

'We are the law,' Bryant reminded her.

'Now you are in a haste?' she asked. 'Life is short, why you want to make it shorter?'

'Because I should have thought of it earlier. The soap wrappers. Carbolic. It's been in front of me all the time.' He strapped himself in. 'Put your foot down, Rita.'

Larry Cranston stepped back off the pavement into the shadows. He felt cursed with bad luck. It had started long before the girl on the crossing. His father had always said he would come to a nasty end. Refused a position in the old man's export firm, he had been forced to make his own way and that hadn't worked out so well. Now he had placed himself in the hands of strangers. What was to stop Paige Henderson and her team from throwing him to the wolves?

He remembered his final days at Hoffman's flat in King's Cross, knowing that they would stay with him forever. On one of the evenings they passed in the living room with books in their laps, before everything went bad, Amelia, a little befuddled by wine, had allowed herself to reminisce a little, telling him about the exhausting months she had spent cracking a diplomatic code. When she entered her office the next morning the men had risen and stood beside their desks, applauding her as she walked between them.

She spoke of being greeted in the Pall Mall Club by Sir Anthony Browne, Winston's private secretary, who congratulated her. 'Our nation is indebted to you,' he said, handing her a glass of Pol Roger. She had worn a dress sewn with black rhinestones at the collar, and her first pair of high-heeled shoes. Heads had turned as she passed. People wanted to know who she was, but she could never tell them. She was an anchoress, sealed in a cell and declared dead. It was the price of loyalty.

He remembered more.

On her third day without food Amelia had reached out a hand to him as if in supplication, only to turn it into a slowly wagging finger that said, *You'll get nothing from me*. She had been an anchoress all her life.

He remembered her dry cracked lips on the glass of water that got smashed. The hem of her dress snagged and tearing. A weak fist batting him away. Tiny sharp diamonds on the floor. The glass had broken into neat helices, a sign of its fine quality. Water dripped from the side table. The sound of the slap resounding in the silent room.

A lady of her years and dignity should not have had to crawl painfully across the floor on her hands and knees. He wanted to lift her and set her upright but she would not let him comfort her. She was folded up in pain, then foetal on the sofa, barely alive, translucent skin stretched tight over her skull, her eyes clouded, hair dry, breathing shallow and rank. There had been no dignity in her death.

He had not expected her to die so quickly. He remembered

the moment the light flickered out in her eyes. By this time she weighed nothing. He carried her back to the sofa and set her down, carefully arranging her as she had always sat. She did not look peaceful. She seemed to be grinning at him.

He hated her.

After he was sure she was dead, he was possessed with the feeling that something was missing from the living room, something he was used to seeing that he could not now place. What had she done with it?

He was pulled back into the present by an errant, optimistic thought. What if Paige Henderson turned out to be as good as her word?

Why, then it would be plain sailing. He still operated from a position of authority. He was part of the establishment, someone to be listened to. When he spoke, shouldn't he expect deference? After the delivery had been made he would put the last of his affairs in order and board his CIA-sponsored flight to New York, ordering large gins all the way. He would be charged *in absentia* by the British Crown Prosecution Service, but the extradition request would be refused.

He contacted Henderson by sending a message to the secure address she had given him. The exchange would take place later at a different venue, one of his choosing. He would call her. It was important to take control of the situation. Then he could put the mistakes of the past behind him and start his new life.

Stepping into the stone recess of the building at his back, he glimpsed Annie Wynn-Jones moving between the parked cars. She had proven harder to keep up with than he'd expected. So far she had travelled from Chancery Lane to Notting Hill Gate and across to Vauxhall. Now she was heading for the south side of London Bridge.

She was wearing a hoodie with the top up, and was using the tube to get around, swiping in with what was presumably an unregistered Oyster card. If the police were watching her they were staying well hidden. Cranston knew very little about spycraft but he could tell that her methods for losing him were something from a Cold War playbook.

She was hurrying past the tower of Guy's Hospital. The sudden rainstorm had reduced visibility on the street. It was hard to keep track of her because there were delivery vans lining the kerb. She was careful to pass behind them.

Then suddenly she was gone.

He struggled to catch his breath, and darted across the road in her direction. She had turned right into Newcomen Street but when he reached the turning it appeared to be a dead end of concrete bollards and discarded rubbish.

No – he could see now that it continued on but became too narrow for vehicles, a fragment of a pre-war street cut off by a tide of rebuilding.

She did not stop and look around. She wasn't expecting him to follow her in daylight. His timing had to be exact. He would not be able to delay his meeting with Paige Henderson again.

When Annie disappeared into the shadows ahead, he broke into a run.

'Do you feel like explaining where we're going on this next wild goose chase?' asked May as they passed under the railway arches from Southwark Bridge Road to Union Street.

'Not wild geese, Winchester Geese.' Bryant pointed out Crossbones Garden, the graveyard of fallen women, its railings bedecked with coloured ribbons. 'Named by the Bishop of Winchester and buried on unconsecrated ground. Now they represent female solidarity. It's as if they're pointing the way.'

'So that's not where we're going.' May looked back, confused.

'No, no. We're looking for the tollgate – the Stonegate as it was called.'

'Why? Surely it can't still exist.'

'It was demolished in 1760 but not all of it was lost. Below the severed heads on spikes was the grand shield, a lion and a unicorn, the heraldic symbols of the nation's coat of arms. The lion stands for England and the unicorn for Scotland. It was preserved for posterity.'

'But we're in – actually, where *are* we?' May asked, puzzled.

'In Southwark,' said Bryant. 'The shield was built into the wall of a public house, the King's Arms in Newcomen Street, right around the corner.'

'It still doesn't link to Amelia Hoffman,' said May.

'Oh, my dear fellow, that's the beauty of it. It does. If it were not for the bibulous pastimes that require me to remain inside boozers on many a winter's night, I would never have heard of it. The King's Arms may have been spiffed up with a fine coat of green paint but it once had a reputation. Being so close to the Thames it was the haunt of press gangers, those rough naval gentlemen who persuaded strapping lads to take the king's shilling. Unfortunately, they used rather too much force to get them out of the pub and on to the gangplank. So many fights took place in the public bar that the floorboards had to be regularly scrubbed clean of blood. As a result the pub gained a nickname which is still in use today. It was known by all who used it as *The Carbolic*.'

They turned the corner and there it was, a handsome building with curved glass and gold lettering. 'Amelia's little spy tricks were already outdated when she was taught them. I can see how her mind worked even if she couldn't; a direct line from the codename to its hiding place. She folded her requests in foil carbolic soap wrappers and sent them out through the post because you couldn't read them by shining a light through the envelope. I wonder how many she mailed out over the years.'

May felt increasingly lost. 'But who did she send them to? What did she expect to get back?'

'I think you're about to find out,' said Bryant, pressing ahead.

Annie could not guarantee that she had been followed, but hoped very much that it was the case. At Notting Hill Gate she had briefly glimpsed a shifty-looking individual who might have been Cranston, but already her memory of the moment had altered. Perhaps he was having trouble keeping up with her. As murderous opportunists went, he really was quite useless. She couldn't wait for him any longer. Lowering the hood of her sweatshirt, she set off across the road.

It was the end of lunchtime, and the King's Arms was roughly still a third full. Standing back from the regular bar-flies were flush-faced laughing men, a sea of grey and navy suits. They might even have looked up at her if she had been young.

The pub's landlady was seated at the bar filling in paper-work and gave no acknowledgement of knowing her. Annie handed her a slip of paper with the symbol of the Bridge House on it. Without speaking, the landlady rose and went into the back room behind the bar.

Annie used her key to the cellar door and made her way down damp steps, through a chill odour of hops and brackish water. The floor was slippery with river dew. She turned on the lights and unlocked the door at the rear of the pump room.

There against the wall was the filing cabinet, a tall steel thing left over from the War Office. Once it had stood in a serried rank with a dozen such cabinets, before being singled out by two changes. It had been painted bright pink, the 'PFC' of Amelia Hoffman's coded notes, and it had been fitted with a most unusual lock that could only be opened once.

Annie withdrew the case containing the last crystal key. They'd intended to have one each, but she hadn't felt comfortable entrusting Angela with one. The Yale's cuts slid smoothly into their corresponding tumblers. For a moment she thought it would not open, but a tug of the handle screeched the drawer out.

She had brought a large black nylon bag with her, but wondered now if she would be able to lift it once it was filled. The landlady would keep her mouth shut, whatever happened. She had known Annie since the old days.

Removing the cabinet's contents, she quickly loaded the holdall. She understood the risk she was taking; there were no surviving copies. Once her cargo was out in the world there would be no stopping it.

Her legs ached from kneeling on the wet floor. She consoled herself by thinking that this was the last time she would ever have to do such a thing.

The holdall was awkward to lift. She thought about leaving some of it behind, but did not dare to now that the cabinet could not be relocked. She was still struggling to close the zip when the cellar door creaked open behind her.

31

NOT *THE MALTESE FALCON*

Larry Cranston kept walking south along Tennis Street towards Long Lane, choosing side streets, keeping close to the walls. The traffic hid him from view. He couldn't stop crying. Tears streamed down his face. His breath came in sore gasps. His forehead was smeared with blood, but he was able to wipe most of it off with tissues.

His mind was a seething chaos. He felt as if he was having a heart attack. Forcing himself on, he placed one foot in front of the other, swearing under his breath. He needed to lose himself in the side streets and calm down. He breathed deeply, feeling the sweat dry on his back.

A teenaged boy stopped and stared at him as he passed.

'What the hell are you looking at?' he barked at the boy. A woman also turned to look at him.

Great, he thought, *strangers will remember me now*.

A windowless room beneath a pub: it was an ignominious place to die. Annie Wynn-Jones had fallen on her side with her jacket rucked and twisted, one trainer half-off. Her face was partly hidden by the hood.

Annie's life had leaked out on to the wet stone floor and mixed with the ebon run-off from the Thames. It looked as if she might simply sink into the silted riverbed and disappear, absorbed by the primeval waters. Beads from a broken bracelet lay on the floor's black mirror like surrendered pearls.

'No one should end their life like this.' Bryant raised one of the beads between his thumb and forefinger. 'Why kill her? Why not simply push her to the ground and leave?'

He studied the body, getting blood on the knees of his suit trousers. Checking her pockets, he removed a red card from her purse and flipped it over. 'That explains the amount of blood.' He held up the card. 'A twenty-four-hour hospital emergency number. She's on anti-coagulants. She bled out in no time at all.'

May typed on his phone. 'It says users must avoid getting cuts. I guess that includes bullet wounds.'

'How did you find that so quickly?'

'Why are you so perpetually amazed by any sort of technology?'

'Because when I was a child I played with a hoop and stick.'

He turned her over. The pistol lay beside her right hand. 'A Glock 9mm handgun. He didn't try very hard to make it look like suicide. People don't shoot themselves in the stomach. He followed her through a crowd of plods from Southwark cop shop—'

'Are you telling me they're all police officers upstairs?' asked May.

'Couldn't you tell? They smell of beer and gherkins and have size eleven boots. Then there's the small matter of the door, and the fact that we had to get the spare key from the landlady to open it. Wynn-Jones came in, locked the door behind her and went to the filing cabinet. She opened it with her special key, snapping the shaft in the lock, and pulled out the drawer.'

The pink filing cabinet stood open and empty. The broken end of the key lay on the floor.

'The door back to the pump room is still shut.' Bryant leaned on his stick and rose unsteadily. 'How could he get through a roomful of coppers unseen and enter a cellar locked from the inside? The cellar door key is still in her pocket.'

'We need to close the pub.' May headed for the stairs. 'And make sure someone is keeping watch on Moon Street. He'll be heading for Angela Carey next.'

'Why? He's got what he wanted.'

'She knows who he is. He can't afford to leave anyone behind. The bookkeeper, remember? If Dan can get a drone to cover her—'

'Your belief in the infallibility of electronic gizmos is touching,' said Bryant, joining him. 'Can you stop staring at your phone all the time?'

'It's Raymond,' said May as they reached street level. 'He says if we don't get back to the unit within the half-hour he's going to set fire to your books.'

An incandescent Raymond Land paced across the complaining floorboards. Bryant was twitching with impatience, May keen to placate. They had failed to inform the chief of their whereabouts and now Land was wasting more angry heat than an unserviced boiler. The proceedings were overseen by Stumpy, who took a keen interest in conflict situations, especially if they ended with food being abandoned.

'I just had a call from a DI at Southwark,' he informed them. 'He nipped out for a quick jar and a sausage roll with his mates and now finds himself shut in the pub.'

'We have to interview all the customers,' said May. 'They

saw Cranston skulking outside before heading in the direction of Borough High Street.'

'Unfortunately, several of the witnesses are unreliable,' Bryant pointed out, 'owing to the extravagant amount of Guinness they consumed.'

'Didn't any of them see him go downstairs to the cellar?'

'Not so far but we've only just started interviewing.'

'You must have an idea of what they kept in that bloody filing cabinet,' said Land. 'It can't be that hard to figure out. This isn't *The Maltese* sodding *Falcon.*'

'Please don't Billingsgate* about it,' said Bryant. 'We want this solved just as much as you.'

'Is that blood on your trousers?'

'It's Annie Wynn-Jones's blood. There was nothing I could do for her.' Bryant shook his head sadly. 'What worries me more is that vein in your forehead, throbbing like a pressure gauge swinging into the red zone.'

'It's not me you should be worrying about,' said Land vehemently.

'Cranston is being protected until he delivers. He can't leave the country without help.'

'And what if this gormless diplomat decides to sell his haul on to the Russian Federal Security Service? Or just to the highest bidder? You have to stop him before he can make contact.' Land dropped his head into his hands. 'We cannot let this go international. I can't deal with Interpol; it would mean talking French. Can't you try Angela Carey one more time?'

'She and the others were trained to lie,' said May. 'She's not on our side, even though Wynn-Jones's death places her in the firing line. I have a feeling her loyalty to the Crown will take precedence no matter what happens.'

---

* To show blind rage at the slightest provocation. Nineteenth century.

'The Crown? Are royals involved? What's wrong with these people? What am I supposed to tell the Home Office?'

Bryant waved the idea aside. 'Don't worry about it, Raymondo. They're not going to fire you even if they have to pay you a year's wages. You hardly cost them anything.'

'They already fired us – they can't do it again.' Land clutched dramatically at his skull-veins. 'Three dead plus the loss of whatever-it-is they're all after: we're going to be crucified. This will follow us all to our graves.'

'You should have taken an easier job in an ordinary police unit full of blue jokes and latent sexual tension but no, you came here,' Bryant said. 'Try to imagine a pastel-blue aura of pure calm. Don't let stress get to you.'

'Will you stop saying that!'

'One day there will be a great social upheaval in which everyone will kill everyone else and it will make no difference whether you stayed in your job or not. There you are: I bet you're less stressed already.' A rising off-kilter hum sounded beneath his words.

'I. Am. Not. Stressed,' said Land through gritted teeth.

'Yes, you are, you're all clenched.' The humming rose by half an octave and became more grating.

'I know what you're doing,' Land warned. 'You're gaslighting me.'

'I'm sure I don't know what you mean.' Bryant leaned closer. 'It's all in your mind.' The hum grew even louder.

'Oh, for God's sake stop torturing him and answer that,' said May.

'Hello?' Bryant placed his hand over his phone. 'That's my special ring for Alma. Sultanas, yes, I'll pick some up. She's making a bread pudding.' He turned back to Land. 'I hope you're feeling better now.'

32

A FUNNY LITTLE THING

'Twenty-four hours? I'm not sure you should have promised him that,' said Bryant as the detectives headed back along the passage to their office.

'Why not?' asked May. 'It's what you would have done.'

'Yes, but I lie all the time because people believe me.'

May gave up and went to his room. Bryant picked a Japanese umbrella from the stand in the hall and climbed up to the roof.

Several of the tea chests were still sitting in the warm, light rain. Propping the red lacquered umbrella in the top of an orange chimney pot, he set to work.

He carefully removed the contents of the oldest chest layer by layer, trying not to get everything too wet. At the bottom were neatly tied packets of correspondence and inter-office memos. *Before emails we only wrote to each other when something was important*, he thought, unwrapping one of the bundles beneath the umbrella.

As water started dripping down his neck, he decided to take the rest of the correspondence down to his office. Loading his arms, he blundered back to the roof door.

May jumped when a dozen bundles of soggy paper cas-caded all over their connected desks. 'Arthur, do you think it's the right time to be doing this?'

'It may have relevance.' Bryant tore open a packet and emp-tied it out. 'I was thinking: Hoffman came up with this plan of hers a long time ago. Some of these materials date back to her time at the unit.'

May gave him a hand unfolding documents, newspaper clip-pings and memos. Within the foolscap sheets they found bulletin-board notices, staff announcements and notes detailing long-forgotten office quarrels. One bundle contained mostly illegible carbons from Hoffman to a colleague.

'This one's handwritten,' said Bryant. 'Listen: "He's been in the office several times to see Bentley, and is certainly strange enough to fit in here. I think he is going to be offered a job. He's a funny little thing. His clothes don't fit and he wears a homburg indoors and smokes a horrid old pipe but I've rather taken a fancy to him."'

'It could be someone else,' said May doubtfully.

' "Of course eligible bachelors are thin on the ground here so if things get desperate I may have to set my cap at him. Although I don't suppose he'd even notice me. His sort never do. They're in love with their slide rules."'

'The dates fit,' said Bryant. 'I don't remember meeting her. I don't really remember anything about my time there. I was a rabbit trapped in the headlights of Bentley Trusspot's intel-lectual daring. I should have paid more attention.'

'Here's something.' May unfolded a newspaper article. 'From the *Daily Sketch*, "Women's Liberation Campaigner Eleanor Hamilton chains herself to the door of Soho's Sunset Strip Club". Isn't she one of your crackpot academic friends?'

Bryant pinned on his trifocals and examined the photograph of a sparrow-like woman jammed against a pair of glass doors, surrounded by posing strippers. The Bridge House symbol had been drawn in a corner of the article in red ink.

'I wouldn't say "crackpot", but if you put in an ad for a wild-haired lesbian bargee who once tried to bomb an arms conference she would be overqualified to answer it. Let's look for other articles marked with the same symbol.'

The next clipping featured Herbert Constantine, captioned beneath his photograph as 'Biochemist and radical thinker faces jail after "act of terrorism"'.

'Herbert and Eleanor used to share a squat on the Cromwell Road,' said Bryant. 'There were others in their group.'

They found further articles marked with the same London Bridge logo and one piece on 'the Dagenham Three', Eleanor, Herbert and their friend Oscar, when they had all been hippies together and had liberated caged animals from laboratories testing beauty products. They considered themselves anarchists. The press branded them terrorists.

'What are all those?' May pointed to a pile of scraps held together with bulldog clips. Some had an amount followed by a name, scribbled out on pieces of paper bags and torn-off corners of envelopes.

'A hundred and fifty pounds to Oliver Golifer, seventy-five pounds to Harry Prayer, thirty-seven guineas to Daphne and Andrew Brockenhurst – these are all payments to your informants, Arthur. Whatever they were supplying, they didn't get very much for it.'

'London Bridge.' Bryant spread the items before him. 'It's not a thing at all.'

'What do you mean?'

'It's a concept. A collective term.'

'For what?'

'For every academic we've secretly hired. Don't you see? All those communist schoolteachers and outlaw scientists, the rebel politicians, the analysts and whistle-blowers. They couldn't legally go through the books so they mailed Hoffman invoices for their advice. London Bridge isn't a thing, John, it's a group. A unique repository of information. Collectively, it could be as important in its own way as the NSA cascade released by Ed Snowden.'

'You mean the women simply wrote to them?'

'Look at this: doctors, scientists, politicians, prisoners, housewives, artists, teachers. We have a long history of sharing information. The Mass Observation project ran from 1937 using untrained volunteers to record daily life here. And they came from all professions.'

'Didn't you keep copies of all these names?' May asked.

'Their *names*, yes, but they run into hundreds. We couldn't keep a record of what they all knew. It was far too dangerous.'

'We have to get to Cranston before he meets his buyer.' May picked up his phone. 'Janice, you said Cranston's record is clean. Are you sure about that?'

'I'm only next door, I can hear you through the wall,' said Longbright. 'Hang on.'

She came in. 'I've been badgering West End Central for days. It seems Cranston was stopped by the police a few weeks ago, but we only know that because one of your sources was cycling past and saw his Daimler at the side of the road. There's no record of why he was pulled over.'

'Where was this?' Bryant asked.

'Somewhere in Regent's Park.'

'On the Outer Circle?'

'I assume so. It's the only cut-through.'

'Get me the Superintendent at the CoL Serious Crimes Command, would you?'

'Link?' asked May in surprise. Darren 'Missing' Link was a disliked but grudgingly respected officer, with the proportions of a street bollard and an unnerving split left eye. He was feared because of his zealous morality and his preference for punishment over rehabilitation.

'He has his good points,' said Bryant. 'One of them is his inability to tell a lie.'

He took the call out to the corridor. There was a part of Bryant that preferred to keep his cards close to his chest, if only out of fear that others might sometimes realize he had a weak hand. When he returned, his mood had darkened.

'Well?'

'His case is *sub judice*,' he said at last. 'We're not allowed to see any part of it.'

'His case,' May repeated.

'Exactly. Mr Link just gave away more than he intended. If the police wanted to interview Cranston why would they pull him over in the middle of the afternoon in Regent's Park?'

'Because it wasn't an interview,' said May.

'A long lunch. A wobble at the wheel. Drink driving.'

'A Daimler. CD plates. He has diplomatic immunity. He could have got off.'

'Not if it was something serious. Janice, find out if anyone else was in the area around that time, will you? Does central London still have any local journalists? Try the *Camden Gazette* and *New Journal*, the *Metro* and the *Westminster Extra*.'

Janice took the request back to the team. It didn't take long for her to find 22-year-old Sammi Jansome, a Latvian national, admitted to University College Hospital on the same afternoon, deceased. The absence of details surrounding her admittance suggested redaction. It would have been smarter to leave a little untidy data out there. *Typical Home Office*, she thought.

'Her landlord says she had a kid stashed in her room but someone came to collect her at around five p.m. that day,' she told them. 'No mention of any other family in the country. That's all the information there is.'

May traced a line from Jansome's room in Bayswater to Baker Street tube station and her place of employment. The journey placed her in the park at the exact time Larry Cranston was passing.

'If he's responsible for the girl's death, someone's getting him off the hook in return for delivering the information.' Bryant knocked out his Spitfire on the windowsill. 'Let's start with Jansome's parents.'

Further north-east, in Islington, one of the two Met constables who had been spared for surveillance duty was outside Angela Carey's house, barely awake.

Nothing had happened there; no one had come or gone. He stared from the passenger window, waiting for his shift change, a pit bull asleep with its eyes open. He told himself he could snap to attention in a heartbeat. His partner was eating a Mars bar and reading an out-of-date issue of *Emu Farmer*.

Something like a candle flame was silently dancing in the corner of the windscreen. An orange light flickered in an upstairs window. It shot suddenly upwards. A roller blind glowed and turned black. Something popped.

Before either of them could get out of the car one of the bedroom panes split in half and fell out. There was a muffled explosion from within.

Later it was said that the scandal of the London Bridge papers truly began with the torching of 72 Moon Street.

PART FOUR

So thy dark arches, London Bridge, bestride
Indignant Thames, and part his angry tide.

George Canning

33

LIKE RATCATCHERS

Blaize Carter's day had got off to a bad start. That was before she looked down and noticed that her oversized rubber boots were on the wrong feet.

'Oh, for—' She sat down on the kerb and pulled them off. The fire was out now. The house had black eyes. Scorch-marks blurred the upstairs windows. The shreds of curtains that hung dripping on either side of the frames were encrusted with rhinestones of broken glass. The front garden, so tidily pruned, had been flattened and flooded out with hose run-off. A neighbour stood by, conscientiously taking photos on his phone.

As the last of the fire officers finished clearing debris from the front hall, Carter looked up from the kerb and found John May standing beside her.

'You've got soot on your nose.'

'What do you want, John?' She rested her elbow on her knee, her chin in her palm. 'I just finished a double shift.'

'I'm sorry. She's my case. The woman you brought out from that house.' He waved a hand back at the ruined front hall.

'What has she done, apart from make enemies?'

'What do you mean?'

'Someone lobbed a petrol bomb through her rear bedroom window. A milk bottle, actually. Who still has bottles? It was primitive but effective. Not the sort of thing you expect in this neighbourhood.'

'Where was she?'

'She'd taken a sleeping tablet and was in her bed at the front of the house. She would have died. Luckily, she has a smoke alarm and it woke her. The firefighters were answering a call nearby and got here quickly.' Blaize wondered how he always managed to appear so immaculate in his spotless navy-blue suit and white shirt. He probably even looked good in his passport photo. *Old history*, she thought, *put it out of your mind*.

'Is she going to be all right?'

'Honestly, I don't know. She's suffering from smoke inhalation and shock, and it looks as if she fell down the stairs. It'll depend on the condition of her lungs. They took her to UCH.'

'Can I take a look around?'

She gave him a look: *You should know better.* 'No, you cannot. It's off limits until it's been safety checked. You might want to see the back garden.'

May knew what she meant. It had rained since dawn and the grass was wet enough to hold prints. When he passed down the alley to the rear of the house he found his partner.

Bryant was hitting a drainpipe with his malacca stick and listening to it. 'Look at that. Victorian workmanship. Clear as a bell. Do you want to hear?'

'Not right now,' said May. 'How is Miss Carey?'

'Janice called the duty nurse. Weak but stable. We can't talk to her yet. At least the inclement weather saved the roof. I imagine the neighbours will be thinking about their property prices.'

'I imagine they'll be wondering why somebody firebombed their terrace.'

'He threw it from here.' The ferrule of Bryant's stick tapped at an indentation in the lawn. 'Size ten brogues. We may not be able to bring him in but at least we know what his shoes look like.'

'The organization that's protecting him can wave a killer through immigration and customs,' said May. 'You think they care that we know how big his feet are?'

'Well, he's finished the job now.' Bryant scraped mud from his cane. 'Wynn-Jones and Hoffman in the morgue, Carey in hospital and the secret papers on board. Now he'll get as far away from the British legal system as possible.'

'So we check all exit points.'

'Even if we could it wouldn't do us any good. As you said, he's counting on immunity. How do you catch a murderer who can't be brought to justice?' Bryant looked up at the sky. 'I couldn't even talk to my friends at the Met about this, if I had any.'

'Did Raymond tell you? Faraday's formally taken receipt of the last investigation files. I'm not sure why he hasn't kicked us out of the building.'

'Nothing else in the garden,' said Bryant, thrashing some weeds. 'Conservatories.'

'I'm sorry?'

He indicated the surrounding houses. 'Quite a few of them. Lots of glass.' He saw he would have to spell it out. 'People might have seen something.'

'Got you,' said May. 'We'll start asking.'

'Obviously there are anomalies.'

'There are?'

'Let's get back to the unit.' He set off towards the street and Rita's waiting taxi. 'We need to see Raymondo.'

'I don't want to get dragged in there again,' said Colin Bimsley, hovering outside Raymond Land's office. 'He's as mad as a baboon's bum and when he gets upset his hair-lid starts flapping about and he looks like he's having a heart attack.'

'Colin, someone has to tell him our only witness is in hospital,' said Meera.

'Suffering Prometheus, let me do it.' Arthur Bryant shook out his umbrella, sending Strangeways hurtling off along the corridor. 'You'll only upset him. I have tact. Remember how I told that little boy his auntie had died?'

'Unfortunately, yes,' said Janice. 'The puppet show didn't go down well.'

'It was cathartic. Leave Raymondo to me. I know he's as useless as a eunuch's runnion but it makes him easy to manipulate.'

'I can hear everything you're saying,' called Land. 'There's still no door on my office.'

'Jolly good, you're awake. Can my friends come in?'

'I've told you before,' said Land. 'There's no room.'

'We can push your desk back; you're not using it.' He waved Colin and Meera forward. Together they shoved Land's desk so that he was pinned against the rear wall. Land was forced to open the window. Stumpy stared at each of them in turn, mystified by the behaviour of the Uprights.

'Miss Carey is under observation in hospital after our chap threw a petrol bomb into her home,' said Bryant, offering round jelly babies.

Land looked horrified. 'My God, is she going to be all right?'

'We don't know yet.'

'I thought you put two officers on watch at the house. How the hell did he get past them?'

'Nobody saw anything. To get to the rear he had to go down the side alley and through the gate.'

'Why was it unlocked?'

'It wouldn't have made much difference. You could have

reached over and opened it even without those lifts in your shoes.'

'So first he walks through a locked cellar door in a pub full of police officers and then goes down a guarded alleyway without being seen. I've had Faraday on my extension giving me what for. The Home Office doesn't want you to do anything else ever.'

'Ah, but have you asked yourself why?' said Bryant.

'Of course not. I don't "ask myself" things. It's obvious. The unit is redundant, the building has been sold and we are history. You only wanted the case so you could wave two fingers at your enemies one last time, and then you couldn't bloody crack it. I should never have allowed you to take it on. Codes and ciphers and dead old ladies all over the place. This chap's got what he wanted and *you* failed to stop him.'

'When you've finished monopolizing the office acoustics, let me explain something to you, old thing,' said Bryant. 'He would have acted whether we'd got involved or not. We couldn't stop Cranston because everything about him has vanished under a cloak of secrecy.' Bryant mimed the cloak of secrecy.

'Then let it go! Faraday gave the investigation to the SCC. If you go anywhere within a hundred yards of Cranston you will be arrested for obstruction. You had your chance. You had his name and address, his financial records, his work history and his shoe size and you still couldn't bloody sort it.'

'Because the person he was no longer exists,' said May.

'Which is why MI5 will probably have to take over,' Land reasoned. 'They have the resources.'

'But what if they're involved?'

'You're suggesting our own side is aiding a killer?'

'It wouldn't be the first time. The ladies withheld information right from the start. There's more to this than any of us realized.'

'There you go,' said Land, 'complicating things again. Nothing's ever simple with you, is it?'

'We failed the others,' said Bryant indignantly. 'Even if they don't want us to help them, it's our duty.'

'Why do you always go on about *duty*? We were just doing a job.'

'Because if there is one thing Queen Elizabeth the Second has taught us, it's the meaning of duty in public service,' Bryant replied heatedly.

'You're not a monarchist but you admire the Queen. You're not religious but you like old churches. What are you?'

'I often ask myself the same thing,' said Bryant sadly.

There was a crackle on the windowsill and everyone turned. Stumpy's singed feathers were sticking up. He stepped off the electrified plate and fell over.

'At least one thing around here works,' said Land.

'We've no warrant to search Cranston's flat,' Bryant muttered as he stormed back to his office, 'so we'll burgle it. Please note my correct use of the verb.'

'I can't be a part of that,' Dan protested.

Bryant laid a friendly paw on his shoulder. 'Dan, you know John and I can't do it by ourselves.' He did his trembly voice. 'I'm a weak, frail old senior citizen. Won't somebody help me?'

'Give it a rest, Mr B. Get one of your dodgy friends to do it. Edwardian Fred or Coatsleeve Charlie.'

'They're both inside.'

'I've got no job and two kids to support. I can't afford to end up in jail.'

'If you go down I promise we'll visit you regularly at first. Allow me to lure you to the common room for a moment. I have something that might change your mind.'

He led the CSM by his shirt-cuff. Sidney was there drawing on the whiteboard. She wore a shaggy orange tunic and shorts over black tights, looking more like an art student at Central St Martins than a special unit officer.

'Sidney here may appear to be an unemployed trapeze artist but it turns out she's rather good at connecting data. Sidney, before you double-somersault off would you kindly reveal what you've got for us?'

She pointed to a list printed down the board. 'I've timelined Larry Cranston's career from school to the present day using the available information. These holes are left by the security redactions. He didn't follow a career path so much as fall off a cliff. Kicked out of every job, bailed out again and again, probably by his father, until he went to New York. During his tenure at the FBI he made the kind of mistake that got him transferred to London as a penance. Then he hit the girl on the crossing. And then came this.' She pointed to a scribble of black Pentel.

'What's that supposed to be?'

'Literally nothing. An information blackout from the afternoon of the accident. Cranston didn't have the power to create that by himself. The ambassador walked away from him. The embassy is technically foreign territory but he couldn't count on its protection. Someone removed the information retrospectively. The FBI doesn't have an office here but the CIA does. That's where Cranston went for help.'

'And you want our little unit – now legally defunct, by the way – to take on the CIA,' said May, marvelling at the idea.

Bryant stared at the board as if hoping to find the answer there. 'The second Cranston hands over the papers, we've lost him for good.'

'In case you're interested.' Janice turned to the others, phone in hand. 'Miss Carey is awake.'

The detectives reached the entrance of University College Hospital in eight minutes, and would have got there quicker if Bryant hadn't managed to thread the taxi's seat belt through his waistcoat.

Angela Carey was sitting up looking battered and a little dazed, but pink of cheek. 'The doctor says I can go home,' she told them.

'There's not much of a home to go to from what I hear,' said Bryant, looking around for something to drink. He thought, *You might not be able to get an appointment in a British hospital but you can always find a cup of tea.* 'Although I've been informed that some of the rooms still have windows.' He played that back. 'OK, it's raining so maybe not such a good idea. Why don't you stay at Miss Wynn-Jones's flat? The parrot probably needs to have his *Daily Express* changed.'

To his amazement Angela burst into tears. May gave him a stare.

'Just an idea,' said Bryant with a shrug.

It turned out to be a good idea, as Angela already had the keys. Hoping to catch her off guard, Bryant tried his luck. 'I sincerely believe you have no desire to obstruct the police. It would be an enormous help if you could tell us everything you know before somebody else gets knocked off.'

She had been going through her handbag, but paused. 'Everything we saw and did at GCHQ was subject to government scrutiny. It still is. Do you see, I can't tell you without committing an act of treason.' She raised her hand horizontally. 'The law is here.' She raised her hand much higher. 'The State is here.'

'Are you afraid of what they might do if you spoke out?'

'What, to me, if I became a whistle-blower?' She gave a mirthless laugh. 'You still don't understand. My loyalty to the State is beyond question. But is yours, Mr Bryant? In September 1968 you renounced your membership of the Communist Party, and subsequently joined the Labour Party. For a brief time during the Thatcher years you voted Tory, but her privatization blitz and lack of empathy quickly pushed you back to Labour. After Tony Blair lied about WMD you became an independent, then renounced all political affiliations and started exploring different belief systems. As a detective you are unique but you have your weaknesses, including a willingness to give credibility to dangerous ideas. Most damaging of all, you've a need to apply academic principles to crime detection when a more straightforward approach would bring faster results. Most damaging of all, you've a need to prove theories you know to be wrong. You've been looking all your life for something to believe in. But I have always had something to believe in. The State. Whether it's right or wrong is irrelevant.'

'Where did you get all that information about me?' Bryant asked, horrified.

'Didn't you ever wonder how you stayed funded all those years?'

Bryant pouted, thinking. 'I suppose we perform a necessary service, like ratcatchers.'

'No, Mr Bryant, it was a reciprocal arrangement. We fed you cases. You put away the people we couldn't reach. Our jobs were basically the same: to protect the nation. But ours was to do it at any cost.' She pressed her head back to the pillow. 'Your man has got away. He wasn't a criminal mastermind or a double agent. He was just another public school idiot whose expensive education was wasted on an undisciplined brain. But in today's world a feral instinct for survival is more useful than a genius-level IQ. Cranston searched for a way out and found it by stealing a national repository.'

'And there's no way of knowing whose hands it's fallen into?' Bryant asked.

'There is one way to find out.' Her voice was almost lost. 'You just have to wait and do nothing.'

34

HERALDIC BUGLE

Malcolm Woolley was a colourist specializing in the pigment restoration of illuminated manuscripts. Pigments suspended particles in coloured liquid and were particularly susceptible to damage. They lost their tint and refused to stick to parchment, flaking off instead of being absorbed into the weave, and they reacted badly against other colours like lead white and copper verdigris. They decayed in damp and rotted bindings, but with care and patience they could be restored to their full glory.

On Monday morning he began working on a letter T entwined around an angelic herald. He regilded the herald's wings with orpiment, an arsenic sulphide found in volcanic fumaroles that could be made into a fiery orange-yellow paint.

Malcolm worked alone because it was delicate, taxing work and because nobody liked him. He, in turn, had no idea how to deal with his fellow workers, who were demanding and nosy, forever asking each other if they wanted cups of tea, when all he wanted was to be left alone with his manuscript.

The worst of the bunch on his floor was Raymond Kirkpatrick, a great messy bearded bear of a man whose headphones hissed and thumped all day. He had no voice below a bellow and was forever smacking interns around the back of the head, which got him into constant trouble with the British Library thought police.

As Malcolm lined up his paintbrushes so that the tips of the wooden handles were all exactly six centimetres from the edge of his work-board, he tried to keep Kirkpatrick's red check lumberjack shirt from his vision and imagined that he could not hear the hiss-thump screaming of his horrible death metal music.

Kirkpatrick glanced over at Malcolm and gave a faint but audible groan. He knew the guy was OCD but really, what a wanker. If anyone came near him he shrank away. God forbid anyone did what he had done when the colourist first arrived, going over there and picking up a paintbrush to try it against his palm; the guy looked as if he'd just shat himself.

Malcolm came in every day wearing something from his limited range of single-man shirts, mumbled 'Morning' and scuttled to his work-board, careful to keep his coffee cup on the floor where Kirkpatrick was liable to kick it over. Come to think of it, though, almost everyone in the department was socially defective. Hardly any of them could hold a normal conversation. At least his mates on the floor below were fun.

Kirkpatrick was by far the most sociable member of the second-floor staff. Every Friday evening he went to the Skinner's Arms with other misfits from downstairs and argued about history, art, map restoration, heavy metal, astronomy and football, in that order. He loved his wife and children but preferred to spend his time working in the British Library. Whenever Shirley called to tell him that their son needed to be taken to the dentist or that the washing machine was leaking he pretended to be going into a meeting. He was so impractical that she still packed his lunches in a Tupperware tub every morning. The woman was a saint. He wondered what he was going to eat when she moved out.

The British Library was a sanctuary, a sepulchral chalk-white chapel of antiquities where Kirkpatrick could discuss his seditious ideas without horrifying anyone. And because it housed a copy of every single publication in the British Isles, his own modest works were stored here too, just a few pamphlets, but it meant a lot to know that they were nearby. It was Arthur who had saved him from prosecution after his last publication contravened the libel laws. Which reminded him, he needed to call the old fellow with a few useful ideas for his investigation.

Kirkpatrick did not carry his great girth lightly. Malcolm jumped when he went thudding past his counter and turned to boom, 'I'm going to the café, do you want anything?'

He gave his head a brisk little shake, loosening dandruff, and thought, *There's nothing I want from you except to go far away.* Unfortunately, Kirkpatrick was a workaholic who was there before he arrived and stayed long after he left.

Malcolm stirred the reconstituted orpiment with a toothpick and tested its consistency. There was something about the colour that still wasn't right.

When the door bashed open once more he saw that Kirkpatrick had brought sandwiches for half the department. Laden, he distributed his haul and stopped for a bellowing laugh with one of the interns. So annoying.

For the next hour or so, the herald's heavenly bugle monopolized Malcolm's attention. The golden pigment seemed determined not to stick. The colour was wrong somehow. It technically matched but *felt* wrong. Not enough depth.

'God's bollocks!' Kirkpatrick tore off his headphones and threw them down beside the map he was working on. What on earth was wrong with the man? Everything he did had a violence about it. When he chewed his food he crunched it to a pulp. When he sharpened a pencil he ground it down to shavings.

Now he was shaking his head violently and wiggling a finger into one hairy ear, then the other. 'Bloody noise,' he said aloud to no one in particular. One of the interns looked over.

When Malcolm raised his head again it was because the unthinkable had happened. Kirkpatrick had opened the door to their narrow balcony. The room was temperature controlled, remaining within a tight range of acceptable humidity. The outside air was acidic and lethal to painted parchment.

Malcolm turned to yell at him but the words dried in his mouth. Kirkpatrick had stepped out on to the balcony and was leaning over the edge of the black iron railing.

The rain was falling in sabres. It was already starting to blow into the room. As Malcolm tried to understand what was going on, Kirkpatrick turned to him with a pitiful look.

'Malcolm, you really are a total and utter salad.'

And with that he levered himself over the railing and disappeared.

From below came a screech and a crash, like an effect stored in a studio for a comedy show. But when Malcolm went to the window and looked down at the rainy road, he saw nothing to laugh about. Only Kirkpatrick's left leg was visible. The rest of him was underneath an 88 bus heading towards Parliament Hill Fields.

Malcolm studied the scene. A woman had dropped her shopping in shock. The yolks of several smashed eggs mingled with a pool of cola, gleaming with the exact shade of burnished gold he had been seeking for his heraldic bugle.

35

SARGASSO MARINERS

The detectives, if that's what they were because one of them looked like he'd been rejected by the Home Guard for being too old, stood in the middle of the map restoration room looking about themselves.

Malcolm Woolley sat at his board paralysed with fear. Why were the police back, and why didn't these ones look like proper police? What if they thought it had been his fault? Everyone knew he and Kirkpatrick had not been the best of friends.

The older one was taking it personally. 'The poor fellow,' he kept saying. 'Why did he do it?'

The more smartly dressed one had to keep consoling him with little pats on the back. 'We don't know the pressure he was under. He could have had money problems, family trouble.'

'His wife was leaving him for someone else,' Malcolm piped up. 'He didn't seem that upset about it. Although I heard he broke the boyfriend's nose.'

'I suppose that in such circumstances a punch up the

bracket can be forgiven.' The older one came and peered over his shoulder, examining the manuscript. He had eyes like poached eggs and glasses that didn't fit properly. 'And you are Mr . . . ?'

'Woolley, Malcolm Woolley.' He did not offer to shake hands.

'DCI Arthur Bryant; this is my colleague DCI John May. I read your statement. Mr Kirkpatrick was an old, old friend of mine. The police don't usually tell you what they're thinking, but I think you should know I'm treating this with suspicion. Suicide is completely out of character.'

'I hardly think it could have been anything else,' Malcolm said with a certain indignation.

'What happened the last time you saw him?'

'Well, it was yesterday morning, as you know. He came in late, at around ten fifteen a.m., and we all worked through until shortly before lunchtime.'

'He didn't speak to you?'

'We don't talk much. You need a lot of concentration for this job. Mr Kirkpatrick liked to listen to this awful screaming music on his headphones—'

'Death metal,' said Bryant. 'I know, ghastly. It helped to mask his tinnitus, having probably caused it in the first place.'

'He was going off to get coffees and teas for everyone. He came back and had his lunch – he brings it every day.'

'So the lunch box is still here.' Bryant went over to Kirkpatrick's counter and looked underneath it, withdrawing a Tupperware container and handing it to his partner. Malcolm had been expecting him to examine everything on Kirkpatrick's workspace, but instead he wandered back and continued peering at the angel with the bugle.

'How long does it take to restore something like that?'

'It depends,' said Malcolm, somewhat thrown. 'If there's damage from damp or acidity any loose paint flakes have to be removed first. This one has discoloured owing to exposure and instability in the original pigment. It will take about a week to return to its former condition.'

'And this is what you use?' The old boy had picked up his pigment pot and was peering into it as if expecting to see a goldfish.

'I'd much rather you didn't do that,' he said testily. 'It's been mixed to a very specific consistency.'

'Because being a pigment the particles in it would settle otherwise.' He set the pot down without apology. It bothered Malcolm that a mere layman would know anything about manuscript restoration. His next comment was even more alarming.

'It contains arsenic, doesn't it?'

'Arsenic is a carcinogen that occurs in many minerals, Inspector—'

'Detective Chief Inspector. I do think it's important to get the details right.'

'It's also present in shrimps and rice. It's in sulphur, which is why it's present in the pigment.'

'Arsenicosis could conceivably cause enough confusion to make someone step off a balcony. If ingested, it works very quickly. Any other chemicals I should know about in that pot?'

'Cyanide can be extracted from Prussian blue. There are a number of other components, most of them toxic,' Malcolm said. 'If you're suggesting—'

'Did anyone else go near your toxic chemicals yesterday morning?'

'I don't like what you're implying. We all work with poisons. The ink in a pen is enough to kill you. I don't see why I should be singled out in this fashion—'

'All right, keep your jumper on, we need to consider all possibilities.' He picked up a paintbrush and gave the end an experimental lick. 'I read the statement you gave. Did you leave these paint pots unattended at any time?'

'Well, of course I did. As nobody unauthorized enters here.'

'So you know everyone who comes in and out?'

'I didn't say that. Plenty of people come in throughout the day but no one can enter without a pass.'

'Show me one.'

Malcolm raised the plastic card around his neck. Bryant grunted, unimpressed. 'A barcode but no photograph. Issued by the counter staff on the ground floor?'

'Only the day passes. The rest must be applied for online.'

'Excuse me?' One of the juniors raised her hand. 'We pass the cards around because of the lanyards. They aren't long enough to reach the entry pads so we have to take them off, then people put them in their pockets and forget them.'

Typical, thought Malcolm. *She's been nothing but trouble since the day she got here.*

'We'll have to check this room for contaminants,' said the more smartly dressed detective. 'To see if there's a way Mr Kirkpatrick could have accidentally ingested a harmful substance.'

'I hope this isn't going to impede our work,' Malcolm complained.

'Here's the problem, Mr Woolley.' Bryant loomed towards him and smiled, revealing a set of dentures that were too big for his head. The effect was less comforting than sinister. 'Our forensic examiner has already found four types of toxin in Mr Kirkpatrick's body, one of which is arsenic. As my old friend was in the habit of chewing tobacco and eating Szechuan noodles for lunch there's a strong likelihood that he didn't taste the difference.'

'But who would know that sort of thing about him?'

'Good point. Someone who worked with him, I suppose.'

Malcolm felt a wave of panicky nausea sweep through him. 'His wife,' he said, 'she's leaving him, she prepares his lunches, I hear them on the phone, he didn't want to give her a divorce, she could have poisoned him.'

'I can't fault your reasoning, old bean, but we're barking

up the wrong tree there. Shirley Kirkpatrick gave her husband the rest of the previous day's prepared meal, and he wasn't sick after eating that. Anyone in the room could be a suspect, of course, except that—' Bryant stopped.

'Except what?' asked Malcolm.

Bryant indicated the pots. 'You'd have noticed if anyone else had moved any of the pots by so much as a millimetre.'

'Good call on the OCD part,' said John May as they left the library.

'The problem is it's not him,' said Bryant disappointedly.

'How do you know?'

'One, no motive. Two, no inclination. Four, wrong personality type. Just look at him, for God's sake.'

'What about three?'

'Which three?'

'Never mind. You don't think he did it because Kirkpatrick messed with his stuff?'

'I'm not sure that being OCD makes you homicidal. Giles warned me that the arsenic trace wasn't large enough to harm Kirkpatrick and could have got into his system in any number of different ways. The man never stopped eating. He ate so much seafood you could have used him as a thermometer.'

'What?'

'Mercury. Stay with me. And he always bought snacks on the way into work. They give away product samples outside the tube stations, for God's sake. He could have been slipped something by almost anyone—'

'I think you have to accept that Kirkpatrick took his own life and may have had a good reason for doing so.'

'Did you read Malcolm Woolley's statement? Kirkpatrick called him a salad before stepping off the balcony. Sorry, a "total and utter salad". Is that the last thing you'd say before killing yourself?'

'If I wasn't in a healthy state of mind, very possibly,' said May.

'He did not mean to do it, John. I knew his marriage was in trouble but he didn't have a suicidal temperament. Giles didn't find anything else apart from a slightly raised toxicity level, and part of that was from the illegal chewing tobacco. It doesn't make sense.'

May put his arm around his partner's shoulder. 'My dear friend, what in the world does any more? You may have to accept the fact.' He summoned Rita's taxi. 'Let's get you home. I need you in good form for our appointment tomorrow morning.'

But the next day's appointment did not happen. The London office of the CIA called to rearrange the date, and rearranged it a second time. They said they needed to meet with senior representatives of the investigation, then suddenly withdrew the offer. Presumably they had been told to deal only with those currently in charge of the case.

Two weeks after Leslie Faraday had tried to throw the unit out on to the street its staff remained in place, stranded like Sargasso mariners, unable to move on and find safe harbour.

A few days later they heard that the London Bridge case had been officially closed, and just after that someone from the CIA capriciously summoned them to a meeting.

36

A QUESTION OF MORALITY

The park was an emerald paradise. White plaster terraces shone between the lushly foliated trees. In the last few days rain showers had brought summer to full flourishment. Soon would come a humid deadness, when even the leaves stayed postcard-still and dogs stretched out in long grass on long days.

Arthur Bryant hated summer. It was a time when portly men unwisely removed their tops and large ladies went sleeveless. *The English should keep their clothes on*, he thought. *We like cold rooms, strong tea and good books, not blazing sun, Martinis and budgie smugglers. We're not Continental, for God's sake, although I sometimes wish we were.*

John May breathed deep. 'There's nowhere in the world that has grass as green as England's. You can almost taste it.'

His partner grunted. 'That's because it's damp. You always have to check before you sit down on it.'

'You old misery. You've got a multiple murder case spiralling out of control, most likely leading to total entropic collapse, you should be at your happiest.'

The day would soon be hot, but at this time in the morning the parklands were still laced with traces of mist. The detectives entered by the golden gates near the circular rose garden and made their way around the perimeter to the café.

'Why are we even bothering with this?' asked May. 'The CIA keep cancelling our meetings and when it's too late to do anything they summon us at short notice. That's how much they think of us.'

'You remember what Angela said? Government here' – Bryant raised a hand – 'law enforcement here. We can't leak what we know to the press without implicating ourselves. Keep an open mind. Let's hear what she has to say.'

It was not hard to spot Paige Henderson. Black suit, white shirt, sport socks, white trainers, black hair tied back, a little dark lipstick. A certain kind of East Coast law enforcement look that was out of place among the café's pastel cardigans and baggy floral skirts. She rose to greet them with a stiff handshake.

'I ordered English breakfast tea for both of you,' she said. 'I hope that's OK.'

'Not bags,' said Bryant, affronted. 'I brought my own loose.' He dragged a leaking plastic sack of tea from his overcoat, cascading leaves over the table. 'I won't be a tick.'

May seated himself awkwardly. Henderson stirred her green tea in its glass, waiting for Bryant to return and settle. She looked uncomfortable in a park filled with children and Labradors.

'I've read a lot about you,' she told Bryant as he returned with a tray and a selection of biscuits.

'I didn't know there was a lot to read.' Although Bryant had been publishing his unreliable memoirs for years they were generally regarded as fantasy fiction or, at a push, second-rate comic crime novels. 'I know we attracted attention when the unit burned down, and then when it nearly burned down again. And then when we were quarantined with some kind of pox—'

'I don't think Ms Henderson wants to hear about the past,' said May hastily.

Henderson's face betrayed no emotion. Bryant's, on the other hand, remained as readable as a bus-side advert. 'Did you hire Larry Cranston to work for you?' he asked.

Henderson waited just long enough before she replied. 'We did not, although we do have a file on him. You may not believe me but we have to follow the protocols set by your Home Office.'

'I'm glad to hear your days of marauding are over.'

'Mr Cranston contacted us through a former work colleague in the FBI. When the DUI incident occurred he was working at the ambassador's residence in the kind of position that's usually taken by interns, mailing out invitations. So it came as a surprise to us when he tried to cut an extraction deal.'

'You didn't think he could bring anything to the table,' Bryant said.

'The FBI didn't want to deal with him, so we agreed to listen to his request.'

'But you wouldn't give him an escape plan until you could establish the value of what he had to trade. Didn't this at the very least strike you as immoral?'

'We're not concerned with issues of morality, Mr Bryant. If Cranston had private access to a sensitive cache of information, someone needed to know about it. You can understand why we were sceptical. This is a guy who looked like he needed a nanny to help him dress. A classic product of your country's private education system. No offence.'

'None taken,' said Bryant, who had left school at fourteen and had only set foot inside a college once, to solve a murder. 'Did Cranston tell you how he stumbled upon this miraculous treasure?'

'He traced it through an accounting anomaly. His story was just boring enough to be true.'

'Did he understand what was so valuable about it, or was it just something he could sell to save himself?' asked May.

'Knowing what you know about Cranston, what do you think? I spoke with him but it was clear to me that he was exaggerating the importance of his trading stock. It was perhaps of interest to some of your people, but not to ours.'

'You say it was clear *to you*. You decided whether it had any value.'

'I made that call.'

'Then we can also judge whether the information is useful?'

'That would be up to the Home Office.'

'And because of this you didn't strike a deal to get him out.'

'He is still here.'

'You could have lifted him off the street at any time but instead you left us with a murderer at large.'

'We had no grounds on which to take him, Mr Bryant. This is your territory.'

May inwardly winced. He could see that his partner was about to express an opinion.

'Come on,' Bryant said, 'the CIA's entire history has involved supporting corrupt dictators in the ludicrous cause of halting socialism. You invented brainwashing and waterboarding.'

Henderson twisted her glass teacup in its saucer. She had decided to address May rather than his partner. 'We informed MI5 of Cranston's whereabouts. It's a matter for your security services, not ours.'

'But we were in charge of the case.'

'And you're not any more. The important thing is to make sure he's deactivated.' Henderson looked at each of them in turn, an advocate of compassion. 'Mr Cranston has nothing else to sell. At some point he'll face a charge of causing death by dangerous driving. Putting him under lock and key is the responsibility of your government.'

Bryant thought it over for a moment, clicking his false teeth. 'So they sent you to take his information, backtrack on your deal with him and leave us with the clearing up. The CIA is living up to its reputation.'

She smiled pleasantly. 'Mr Bryant, who do you think we learned it from? Churchill's teams spent the war years putting British operatives through intensive training in and out of the field only to have your Admiralty ditch them the moment hostilities ceased. When the old saboteur units were disbanded we bought out your staff contracts. These people were highly skilled and suddenly had nowhere else to go; they were glad of the jobs. Roosevelt told everyone that the Brain Drain was a collaboration but it was a goddamn fire sale. We were happy to take your scientific expertise, including your nuclear research, and left your cupboards bare. We're still using the techniques and systems you taught us, including the training of assassins, now in the service of cybersecurity. And you know why? Because you are our parents. We're on the same side. We just evolved more aggressively.'

'You'll need to keep evolving if you want to keep China in check,' said May. 'We can't help you. Our days of power are over. Thank you for meeting us, Ms Henderson.'

He sent his partner a look that he hoped would be understood. They rose and left the agent still inside the café. She was already having an intense conversation on her phone. She did not bother to look up as they passed the window.

'We were never even in the running to deal with this,' said May. 'When Cranston doesn't turn up he'll be dragged from the Thames after suffering a drunken "accident". That would suit everyone, wouldn't it?'

Bryant led the way back through the scarlet rose garden.

'How do you think I feel? My mentor and his bosses sold off their own staff.'

'There was no more work for them in this country,' said May.

'The Home Office will never bring Cranston to justice. You know who his father is. An investigation would cause untold damage.'

'Arthur, we have no resources and no authorization.'

Bryant tapped the side of his head. 'We still have our brains.'

'If we go back to the unit now we'll have to answer to everyone.'

'Then let's not go to the unit.' He waved at Rita and she drove the taxi over. 'Besides, I won't feel comfortable until I understand poor old Kirkpatrick's state of mind. His wife won't talk to me, but his stepbrother will. Rita, take us to Marylebone.'

Rita looked at him as if he'd made a joke. 'Is only over road, you can walk down. In my country I walked to school each day, six miles.'

'Well, in my country I don't.'

'English people so lazy and entitled, is why so piggy-fat.' With a sigh she took her encyclopaedia down from the steering wheel.

'Where are you up to?'

' "Aqueducts". I have not been paid yet. I go no further.'

Bryant did his Uriah Heep face. 'Rita, I'm old and tired.'

'We all are. My daughter is only seven and even she does not look so fresh. Is this city turns everyone grey.'

'I'll write you out an IOU,' Bryant promised. 'I'll give you some of my Ernie Bonds.'

'Arthur, nobody knows what they are any more,' said May.

'Is Electronic Random Number Indicator Equipment,' said Rita. 'Government bonds, yes? Acronym. Always you English with acronym this that.'

Bryant scrunched his features. 'How do you know such a word?'

'I look ahead to letter E in encyclopaedia. I want to see what happens.'

'Please, Rita, take us.'

'I never heard you say please like this before, is good. Go on then, get in.' She unlocked the door for him.

Peregrine Summerfield was every bit as large, loud and abrasive as his stepbrother, and of no more benign a temperament. The former art history teacher was now managing an art gallery just off Marylebone High Street. For several decades after the war Marylebone had been an overlooked backwater consisting of shoe shops, pubs and seniors' tea rooms, the flats above them rented out to window dressers and retired colonels.

The area's name derived from the church of St Mary-at-the-Bourne, referring to the River Tyburn, the French definite article slipping into place because the aristocracy preferred the Gallic language. Britain's Norman occupation was another reason to find the French annoying. On its journey to respectability, Marylebone gave up its bear-baiting and bare-knuckle fights to become a desirable neighbourhood. The overpaid bean-counters who now lived there could imagine they were in an expensive little Cotswolds village in the middle of the city.

'John, Mr Bryant, my dear *senem homines*! It's nice of you to venture over this way. And it only took my brother's death to bring you here.'

Summerfield clasped their hands violently and dragged them in off the street. 'If you want to buy a stack of hexagonal nuts painted purple you've come to the right place, although it'll set you back forty thousand of your English smackers. Or a cheerful painting? This one's called *The Death of All Hope* and can brighten any room just by being covered with a tea towel.' He pointed to a scratchy black painting of a scream-ing ostrich with breasts.

'My tastes are rather more classical,' Bryant admitted.

'Quite wise. The Maryleboneheads lap up this sort of stuff. It's utter shit, of course, the art market these days being one big hilarious confidence trick, but it keeps me in readies. This place used to be a pub called the Rose & Crown. It had saw-dust on the floor and an upright joanna in the corner. Now it flogs flightless birds with tits to dead-eyed Russians who stay at the sort of hotels that have tasselled curtains.'

'I thought you'd be more upset about your brother,' said Bryant, taking an exploratory prod at a knitted sculpture of a dead walrus.

'Stepbrother, and you know we were never close. Obvi-ously I'm sad, I just don't feel the need for gnashing teeth and rending garments. I just got off the phone from his wife. She'd always expected something bad to happen.'

'Why?'

'He'd been suffering from depression for years. He'd tried to kill himself twice before.'

'I didn't know that.'

'He took a lot of acid in the nineties and had terrible flash-backs. Contrary to what art critics believe, imaginative people should never do drugs. Coleridge might have been able to knock out *Kubla Khan* after a skinful of opium but most of us would have been throwing up on our shoes.'

'Do you think the hallucinations had something to do with his death?' asked Bryant. 'It sounds as if he didn't know what he was doing when he died. Was he suffering from some kind of neurological condition?'

The art dealer cleared a space on his desk and perched. 'He'd always had mental health problems. He was very good at covering them up. He wanted to be seen as strong, someone on whom we could all depend. The poor sod was almost completely deaf. That's why he listened to that bloody awful heavy metal all the time. It made his condition worse but also gave him a sort of peace.'

'His previous suicide attempts. Did he conduct them in public?'

'No, he took pills at home. He didn't want anyone knowing about his problems. That's why this was so out of character.' A look of regret crossed Peregrine's features. 'He called and said he wasn't feeling great. I didn't have time to talk to him. Nobody feels great in Stokey. You can't go up the high street without breathing in skunk.'

Bryant remembered that Peregrine lived in Stoke Newington, a leafy North London village full of ageing Labour voters with second homes, Dalston's older stoner brother. Edgar Allan Poe had gone to school there, which seemed about right.

'Not feeling great? You mean mentally? Physically?'

'Mentally, I assumed.' Summerfield scratched about in his great ginger beard. 'He'd been a bit vague and off form lately. The last time he was here he left his jacket behind.' He pointed to a leather jerkin that lay crumpled in the corner. 'I nearly had a Chinese buyer for it.'

'I should take that in as evidence,' said Bryant.

'Be my guest, squire. He was a good bloke and I'll miss him. But I won't miss covering up for him.'

Bryant's ears pricked up. 'Covering up how?'

'You know, you had to bail him out over those dodgy pamphlets he used to print up. Of course when social media came along he was just another shouty mad bloke, but before then the Home Office marked him down on a list.'

'How do you know that?'

'He told me,' Peregrine said simply. 'He was convinced they kept a secret file on him.'

37

THE DAGENHAM THREE

Larry Cranston knew he was behaving recklessly but he needed to be outside, where he could breathe and think.

He had walked across Vinegar Yard and was now seated on a long wooden bench at a coffee house in Maltby Street Market, the narrow snaking alleyway known as Rope Walk that ran between Bermondsey and London Bridge Stations. It was raining lightly but no one around him cared. Beneath the opposite arch a bearded young man in a striped blue apron stood slicing maroon tranches of roasted beef like a caricature from a pack of cards, Mr Bones the Butcher. The smell was making his mouth water. Cranston was running out of cash and doubted they took it anyway, but he didn't dare use his credit cards.

He wondered if the Home Office was tracking him. The police had not issued a warrant for his arrest but he could not go anywhere safely. He was in limbo. He knew he should have headed for the anonymous suburbs, where no one would notice him. The countryside was off limits; new arrivals were talked about too much. Country people *pried*. His father's house in

Somerset was out of the question. He had no friends he could call in an emergency.

Paige Henderson had behaved like a Russian gangster, quite beyond the pale, lying to him, cheating him, telling him not to get in touch with her again. He had been taken for a ride. How could he have been so stupid as to trust her?

He gingerly touched the gash above his left eye, knowing that he needed stitches. A dark blue bruise ran down to his swollen jawline. Coupled with the cut, it made his face too memorable. He had to get off the street and lie low while working on his plan.

He would never have thought of stealing a wallet if the braying idiot sitting next to him had not dug about in his coat pocket and left the thing agape. As a child he had been good at magic tricks and misdirection, and his old skills came back into play as he palmed the wallet without disturbing the material.

Unhurried, Cranston finished his coffee and rose from the bench, catching a reflection of the man next to him, a banker type telling some long-winded story to impress a girl. He ducked away, turning beneath a railway arch and slipping into the shadows, moving between crates of vegetables and piled bric-a-brac. It would be best to head into the side streets that ran towards the river, through Jacob's Island, once London's most notorious slum, now the home of millionaires.

When the coast was clear he checked the wallet. Forty pounds and some loyalty cards. *You can still get your own back and get out*, he told himself angrily, regretting the day he had ever set eyes on Mrs Amelia Hoffman.

He bought a black sweatshirt and threw away his Turnbull & Asser shirt, adding the kind of woollen cap he had seen others wearing in the market. He needed to pick up some stuff from the tiny mews house in Belgravia, the only part of his inheritance that he had not been allowed to sell off. His father had made sure of that. For years it had been the old man's London bolthole, lent to his mistress and visited whenever an urgent tumescence drove him up from Somerset.

Belgravia was only a couple of hundred years old, a former swamp connecting Westminster to Chelsea. The suburb had attracted embassies and money launderers, although there had always been pockets of working-class resistance in pubs like the Bag O' Nails, a corruption of 'Bacchanals'. He had left his passport inside the house, not that it would be of any use right now, but he felt naked without it.

He stood against the wall of the house opposite, watching as a stocky middle-aged man and a skinny young girl in an orange fur top let themselves into his property. They didn't look like police but the man was carrying a cumbersome grey box. Forensics people were trying to get into his home, as if he was a common criminal.

He waited. He needed to see them pass the windows so he could remember their faces. Dropping into shadow he waited and watched, anger slicing into him like a razor. He wanted revenge, to go after Angela Carey and destroy her, to hurt them all, and above all escape the grip of this damned city—

A police patrol car drifted in shark-like silence around the corner. He pressed himself further back into the dark. When he looked up again he saw it was gliding in his direction. He held his breath and waited. It was slowing down. He couldn't bear to look. When he opened his eyes it had slid past and turned off.

He had to accept that he was a prisoner. He would learn to adapt. It was one of the few real talents he had, but it could save his life.

Dan Banbury took out the lock on Cranston's front door with a circular drill bit because now that the unit was operating beyond the law he was complicit whatever happened. Besides, he had been dying to try out his new kit.

'Mr Bryant got very excited at the thought of dealing with spies,' he said. 'He asked me for some espionage equipment so I gave him a recording pen, but he drew so much attention to himself trying to get the cap off that I took it away from him.'

The mews house was a country cottage in miniature, fake-rustic and tastefully tasteless. On the windowsill stood a marble bust of the Duke of Wellington. The dried lavender hanging from the mock-Tudor beam in the kitchen was still marked with a price sticker.

'What are the key qualities again?' Dan asked as they stood at the bottom of Cranston's narrow staircase.

Sidney looked up from her phone. 'Observe, communicate, study, persist and keep a sense of humour.'

'If you could put that thing down for a moment . . .' Dan opened his kit. 'What we've got today is a mix of standard tools: laser measurer, disposable scalpels, ethanol, a photograph scaler, a swab dryer, a haemostat, biohazard precautions, paintbrushes and lift cards, chain-of-custody labels, a trace-evidence collector and presumptive blood IDs. I'd normally have a cyanoacrylate stick in here but my daughter used it to glue her school-play costume together and it's still stuck to the dog. Is this boring for you, Sid? Let me know if it is and I'll find some way to pep things up.'

'I saw more of this crime on TV than I did on my course,' she replied. 'People shed stuff as they move about. You examine and categorize it.'

'And you think that's all there is to it? There's another element, young lady: intuition. Awareness born from experience. What do you know about gait analysis?'

'It's the way someone walks.'

'The dynamics of bodies in crowds, especially the movement of the lower limbs. Every walk can be broken down into different stages of stance and swing. We're affected by our muscular weaknesses, our weight, age, hearing and eyesight. We can't change the way we move. It's how we spot friends from a distance.'

Bryant had asked an expert in gait analysis to recreate Cranston's way of walking so they could watch for him at stations. But what was the point if they weren't allowed to lay a finger on him?

'The old man's out there talking to vicars and magicians when he should spend more time studying ordinary people,' said Dan. 'He might find his enemies nearer than he realizes.'

'What are we doing here? Cranston's not coming back.'

Dan wiped the window. 'Then why is someone just like him standing across the street? Oh God. *He's actually standing across the street*.' He leaped back and ran for the stairs, calling into his shoulder transmitter.

Sidney could not believe her luck. Her first chance to excel. She could get this. She had always been a powerful runner.

Dan held her back. 'Wait, wait, you're not going anywhere. He could be armed. Your mother would kill me.'

'It's better if there are two of us.' Sidney opened the front door. As they set off across the road Cranston spotted them and turned away.

From around the next corner came the patrol car that had cruised past earlier. The officer braked, blocking the road. Sidney seized her chance and ran, keeping her eyes trained on Cranston's back, noting the way he moved and reacted.

Cranston had clearly never run any serious distance in his life. His right leg was already failing. He held one arm further away from his body. His posture was bad. Dan was right; she would be able to pick him out in a crowd.

Meanwhile, in a livelier but less elegant part of town, a car had stopped in the middle of Avenell Road, Highbury, and was holding up the vehicles behind it.

'Why is she never ready?' asked Eleanor Hamilton. The sparrow-like veteran campaigner leaned from the window of her ancient blue Nissan and hit the horn again. The driver behind her had been about to say something rude but stopped when he realized how old she was.

Herbert, Eleanor's co-driver and co-conspirator, pulled her hand away from the steering wheel. 'Don't, you'll make her jump. You know what happens if you do.'

'I'll see what's holding her up. Park the car for a minute, would you?'

Eleanor could drive so long as she didn't have to park. Herbert knew it but neither of them acknowledged the fact. A lifetime of protest had finally begun to sap her energy. At eighty it was not entirely surprising.

She and Herbert were on their way to a public meeting about the UK's biological warfare programme and had invited Maggie Armitage to come along, much as one would invite a friend to see the new *Star Wars* film. It was a decision they now regretted because the white witch regarded time, or 'non-linear temporality' as she called it, to be infinitely malleable, especially when she was getting ready to go out.

Eleanor looked over at number 17 and decided to phone first. The little terraced house had been painted purple and covered in geraniums. If she went inside she would be caught up in a hunt for spectacles or keys that would send both of them down the rabbit hole of lost things for half an hour. Even from here she could see a key on a scarlet ribbon hanging from one of the geranium baskets.

'Maggie, are you ready?' she bellowed into her mobile. 'Darling, we have to get a move on, the meeting starts in twenty minutes.'

Maggie answered but it sounded as if she was speaking from inside a tumble dryer, so Eleanor gave up and let herself into number 17. Herbert had managed to grab a newly vacated space right outside and followed her into the gloomy hall, heading for the back of the house.

The effect of the first shot preceded its sound. The hall window disintegrated and dropped, sending shards of glass everywhere. A second bullet bounced off an iron frying pan with a clang. Eleanor was saving the battery in her hearing aid for the meeting, and failed to notice that anything was wrong until Herbert grabbed her sleeve.

There was another shot, but no sign of the bullet's trajectory. The sudden noise in the quiet street was shocking enough to send next door's cat into a dustbin.

Maggie arrived at her front door at the same time as her neighbour.

'I only went out for a minute,' she said, amazed. 'Eleanor, what on earth are you doing behind the sofa?'

'It wasn't my fault,' Maggie said. 'Not this time.' She was seated in her next-door neighbour's living room with a strong cup of tea and appeared outwardly calm, but Bryant knew her well enough to tell that she was shaken. The neighbour, a ginger-headed Rastafarian named Richard, had not quite grasped what these people were doing in his house but was enjoying the drama.

'When I heard that something had happened, I thought you might have left the gas on again.' Bryant sat beside her, patting her as if she was a dog. 'It wouldn't have been the first time. Tell me again, and this time try to concentrate.'

'As I've already explained, I was grilling some bacon for a sandwich and realized I'd run out of fags, so I nipped down to the tobacconist's shop.'

'You left the grill unattended?'

'I like my bacon well done. My kitchen is protected against fire.'

'A sprinkler system?'

'A spell. I consecrated a sacred hearth-witch protection zone around the cooker so there couldn't be any more accidents. Perhaps I didn't use enough rock salt. When I returned the back door was wide open, my sideboard had bullet holes in it and my Clarice Cliff sandwich set was blown to smithereens. Eleanor was behind the sofa. She looked very calm.'

'That's because she'd passed out,' said Bryant unhelpfully.

Eleanor accepted tea. 'I was placing my mind elsewhere.'

'It would have been better to place your body elsewhere,' said Herbert. 'Those bullets were meant for *her*.' He pointed at Maggie. 'She must have really upset someone.'

'Wow.' Richard instinctively started to roll a joint before he remembered he was hosting a police officer.

'You mean the bullet had my name on it?' Maggie grasped Bryant's arm.

'You sound like a crime novel,' said Bryant. 'You could have been killed.'

'Death is not the end, Arthur.'

'I don't know, it slows you down a bit. How could someone get into your garden?'

He already knew the answer. Even though she lived in a street with a high crime rate Maggie was unable to keep any door, gate or window shut for long. Half the neighbourhood children let themselves in to raid her fridge.

'Well, this has been most exciting but I've lived through worse,' said Eleanor, rising. 'I'm annoyed that we missed the meeting. Maggie, you should go and stay at Dame Maude's, then call a glazier. And possibly change your window treatment. I hate that material.'

A local investigating officer tested the 9mm bullet case that had been found in the yard and consulted his superior, who consulted the Home Office, who concluded that local gangs had once more been active in the neighbourhood. The shooter had entered and left through the back garden, which opened into an alley. And that, although not without several questionable aspects, would have been the end of it.

But a few days later an elderly man called Oscar Daventry fell down seven steps in his shared garden in Highbury Barn and broke his neck. The police report noted that his back gate had been left open and that size ten shoe prints had been found on the grass.

This Oscar was the same Oscar who had once shared a squat with Eleanor and Herbert, the other members of the group of animal rights activists once known as 'the Dagenham Three'. It seemed that the disparate strands of a grand conspiracy were drawing themselves together.

38

IN THE HANDS OF BRITISH JUSTICE

Still the unit remained in limbo. No workmen arrived to tear out the interior of 231 Caledonian Road and no order was issued to seal its doors, so the staff began using it as an informal drop-in centre.

Days dawned bright and hot. Londoners fell apart in clement weather. Not knowing how to make the best of the clear blue skies, they donned clothes they had last worn in Majorca and bared their flesh in every sliver of sunlight that made it to ground level.

Even Arthur Bryant was forced to leave off one of his vests. As the detectives took a shortcut from the St Pancras Coroner's Office to the unit, May thought about the fractured elements of the case and tried to make sense of it all.

'Cranston used the same MO in his attacks on Angela Carey and Oscar Daventry, entering and exiting through back gardens, taking care not to be seen. But he mistook Eleanor for Maggie, and tried to use a gun. Perhaps the London Bridge papers didn't give him as much information as we thought. I really don't understand what he hopes to gain.'

'He's not doing it for himself,' said Bryant. 'He's earning his passage out, which narrows it down to three suspects: the Home Office, MI5 and the CIA, none of whom we can touch. I don't like this; I prefer lone killers.'

'Maybe you'd like to ask Leslie Faraday what he thinks about that,' May suggested. 'He's coming into the unit soon to discuss our severance pay.'

Leslie Faraday arrived for a walkabout and was led through the first floor like Prince Philip being shown around an exhibition of Masai shields. Raymond Land hurried along beside him, anxious to explain why the staff members were all still in the building even though he had yet to come up with a plausible reason for them being there.

'I understand Serious Crimes officially closed the Hoffman case and passed everything on to MI5,' Faraday said, peering into the detectives' room. 'A huge relief for us, as you can imagine. All that paperwork.'

'The staff have been asking me about their redundancy packages.' Land slid Bryant's marijuana plant out of the way with his foot.

'I'm still waiting for clearance from head office,' said Faraday.

'I thought you were head office.'

'Oh no, it has to be approved from the very top. It should be sorted out before the end of next week.'

'But I can't just send them off without any news of when they'll be paid. We're both department heads. Can't we talk to each other as equals?'

'Good Lord, no. My dear fellow, try to understand the position you're in.' He carefully skirted a lethal-looking mains cable lying across the floor. 'The man who killed those women is only being allowed to stay on the street until the Serious Crimes Command receives assurances from other involved parties. There's a lot of internal politics on this one. I have some old opponents over at the SCC and it's really got under their skin.' Faraday couldn't have looked happier if he'd discovered the face of God on a slice of toast. 'Of course there will have to be an inquiry, possibly several. They say the investigation should have been handed to them at the outset.'

'But you agreed with us,' said Land, flabbergasted. 'I specifically asked you if we should involve them.'

It was too late. He could see how the game had been played. Others made the decisions, just as they always had. In any important conversation he was politely allowed a space in which to speak before everyone ignored him.

Faraday did it now, acting as if Land hadn't opened his mouth. 'I've been assured that Cranston can't leave the country. Sooner or later someone above us will decide to bring him in. There are forces at work that we mere civil servants will never understand.'

'But—'

'Don't worry about it any more.' Faraday patted him on the shoulder. 'You take everything far too seriously. The delay has been at our end, not yours. As soon as we've got the final sign-off you'll be out of here. I bet you can't wait to get back to the Isle of Wight. It must be very . . .' He was unable to think of a suitable word and gave up.

Land had to ask. 'Does anyone at Serious Crimes know what really happened?'

Faraday barely bothered to consider the question. 'It seems the women had some kind of private falling-out with Cranston over some stolen papers and he took revenge on them.'

It would be convenient for you to think that, thought Land bitterly. *You shovelled it over to someone else's department and washed your hands of the problem.*

'You have to look at the big picture, Land. More than a quarter of all homicide investigations in London remain unsolved. I don't suppose we'll ever know all the ins and outs.'

Faraday's air of finality suggested that the meeting was at an end. 'I'd better be heading back. Lots to do.'

'Has he gone yet?' asked Bryant, strolling in with his walking stick in one hand and freezing. 'Bugger.'

'Ah, Mr Bryant, we were just talking about you.'

'Mr Faraday, have you come to gloat?'

'Not at all. I just thought I'd pay my respects.'

'You'll forgive me for not reciprocating the goodwill. *Derideo te*, as the Romans say, *et caballum tuum.*'*

'Quite, quite,' said Faraday unsurely. 'I was just telling your superior that it's our fault.'

'We always assume that,' said Bryant.

'I mean that you're still here. Regulations to observe, expediting protocol issues and so on.'

'Ah yes, jargon. Don't worry yourself, Leslie, or may I call you *cet horrible petit homme*? We're taking care of things.' He gave a crooked smile.

'Good, that's what I like to hear. Because I can't guarantee that any of you will be paid. I mean after all that's happened. It was as much as I could do to stop you from being prosecuted. If I send the formal termination order you can make sure everything's signed and sealed.'

'Yup, I'll happily stick a stamp on it and shove it in your slot.'

'Jolly good.' Faraday looked as if he'd achieved something. 'Even if we've had the odd *contretemps* in the past, I'm sure that to you at least it's all been worthwhile.'

'Oh goodness, yes,' Bryant agreed. 'You've been an absolute hindrance. It's wonderful to know that behind that wall of official indifference there's a human face, caring, vulnerable, easily injurable.'

'Well, I'm sure you're looking forward to a well-earned rest.'

---

* Loosely, 'I laugh at you and the horse you rode in on.'

'Don't worry about me, I have all sorts of hobbies. There's my tatting, my edible moss collection and I'm thinking of taking up the tightrope.'

Faraday glanced around, saw that there was no tea going and made the sort of stretching movement an Englishman makes when he feels it is time to leave but cannot bring himself to say so.

Bryant rubbed his hands unctuously. 'You'd better be off, sir. I haven't finished the dusting and the porter is waiting for our valises and hat boxes. Mr Land, sir, we'll be out of the last remaining strands of your hair before six.' Bryant grinned so broadly that there was a very real danger of his teeth falling out.

'Is he all right, do you think?' Faraday asked discreetly.

'He seems perfectly normal to me,' said Land.

Bryant held the door wide and ushered out the bewildered civil servant. 'Thank you so very much for honouring us with your delightful presence. Please note that the third stair down is missing so do try to fall in it.'

'What was all that about?' asked Land after Faraday had gone. 'I thought you'd be much ruder to him. I didn't know you spoke Latin.'

'Oh yes, *Caesar adsum jam forte*. Right, we've got work to do.'

'What do you mean, you've got work?' Land narrowed his eyes. The effect was not menacing. 'Don't tell me you're going on with this?'

'Very well, but I am,' Bryant replied.

'How can you say that?'

'I move my lips and the words come out.' He mouthed at Land like a drag queen. '*The investigation continues*.'

Land searched the ceiling and walls for an answer. 'You're out of your mind.'

'And let me tell you why,' said Bryant.

ONE HOUR EARLIER:

'Mr Bryant, please don't creep up on someone holding a scalpel.' Giles Kershaw stood up suddenly. 'I didn't hear Rosa let you in.'

'I decided to avoid Mrs Danvers by coming in through your cadaver entrance,' Bryant said. 'My colleague caught your call. I missed it, having mislaid my phone somewhere.'

'Ah yes. You left it on my dissection table. I heard it ringing under a lung. Don't worry, I've given it a swab down.' He handed Bryant back his phone; then he headed over to a body drawer and pulled it out. 'You're here about Mr Kirkpatrick.'

May turned to his partner. 'Arthur, maybe you shouldn't look. He was an old friend of yours, after all.'

'Nonsense, most of my friends already look dead. Let the dog see the rabbit.' He peered into the drawer. 'Why didn't you tell me about your depression, you ratbag?' he asked the corpse. He looked up at Kershaw. 'You found something, didn't you?'

'I told you the arsenic was only a trace and could have come from a number of sources,' Giles began. 'There was something else. I found lysergic acid diethylamide in his system.'

'LSD?'

'It's not usually cut with anything because it's so cheap to produce, and it's very dangerous if mixed with other chemicals. Like arsenic, for instance, or components of the deadly nightshade family. And here's the oddest part. I found it in both his ear canals.'

'He was deaf,' said Bryant, digging into his coat. 'These were in his jacket.'

He produced a slim plastic box and handed it to the coroner.

'Gel plugs.' Kershaw opened the lid and checked inside. 'There are meant to be three pairs here, but there's a set missing.'

'Can you test the other two pairs?' asked Bryant. 'Dan can't do it.'

'You think somebody killed him,' said May.

'Of course, don't you?'

'Why would they go to such elaborate lengths?'

'No prints or particle evidence. And it's hardly elaborate. Leave a box of these on his desk, mail them as a free gift or hand them to him at the tube station, job done.'

'Oh, this is very neat.' Giles was already picking apart one of the ear plugs with the end of his scalpel blade. 'It's a gel sac filled with some kind of viscous liquid. As it warms up whatever's inside seeps out.'

'Think it's poison?'

'I've never heard of a medication doing this.'

'Shades of Claudius in the garden,' said Bryant. 'I wonder who came up with it?'

May raised an eyebrow at him. 'Someone in the secret service, wouldn't you say?'

AND BACK IN RAYMOND LAND'S OFFICE:

'I cannot listen to these ridiculous conspiracy theories any more.' Land shook himself like a dog shedding water.

'It's not a conspiracy theory,' said Bryant, 'it's pattern recognition. The attacks will continue until someone decides to make Cranston disappear.'

'Pattern recognition?' Land snapped, surprising both of them. 'Where's the pattern in all this? It's the sort of idea that only exists in the bat cave of your imagination.'

'It's not, and I'll prove it. Bat cave? How dare you.'

'I don't want you to prove it. The facts have to speak for themselves. Otherwise, all you'll give me is another textbook case of cognitive bias.'

May tried to be the voice of reason. 'Arthur, I can understand that you're distraught, given all that's happened—'

'If you want I'll go by the book and build a traditional case that will show you this is part of a larger pattern.'

'How?' Land was yelling now. 'You don't have a unit any more!'

'If one more person tells me that,' Bryant began through gritted dentures. 'Listen to me. I will continue the investigation from my living room if necessary.'

Land tried again, looking to May for help. 'Tell him he has to accept that the PCU has gone.'

'No,' said Bryant, 'it's the building that has gone. The bricks and mortar belong to London, not to us. We only ever borrow these structures to pass them on. The unit itself is a living thing. *We* are the PCU, not this place.'

'Don't we count?' The two Daves were looking in on either side of where Land's door was supposed to be.

'No, you're builders,' said Land. 'Bugger off.'

'Most certainly you count,' said Bryant. 'Both Daves, you're just as much a part of this. You may be better at mortise and tenon joints than modern policing but your opinions are still valid. It's all about the people, that's what the PCU stands for, a codeword for everyone who thinks differently. Like—'

He suddenly stopped. 'John, we're going to have to tell Raymondo that we know what it is.'

'What what is?' asked Land.

'This, London Bridge.' He waved a grubby piece of paper he had pulled from one of his tea chests. 'It's not a thing, Raymondo, it's a collective noun, a group of people. An acronym. Longform Ontological Non-partisan Documentation Ordered Non-officially By Restricted Information Dispersal Group Expeditors. **L-O-N-D-O-N-B-R-I-D-G-E.** My crazy game-playing informants.'

'Who'd come up with an acronym like that?'

'Any academic working in government.'

'That red-haired woman who hangs around in here isn't an academic, she's a witch.'

'True, the only skill she's got that's likely to get her killed is her cooking,' Bryant agreed, 'but she has degrees in British folklore and Wiccan history. She can play the zither and stuff a koala and gives a damn good foot massage.'

'That's no reason to take pot shots at her.' Land tried again: 'I admit your informants have very unusual approaches to life but how are their talents worth anything? You think Cranston bought his freedom by giving Paige Henderson this London Bridge stuff and now they're picking off undesirables? I know you've never trusted security organizations but surprisingly the CIA has a reputation for working with us, not against us.'

'I want to believe you.' Bryant didn't look as if he did. 'I must talk to my informants. Not all of them, obviously: that would be disastrous. I remember the last time they got together. Two of them decided to test out a quantum mechanics theory in an Indian restaurant and ended up in hospital.'

'They need a neutral meeting zone, a park perhaps,' May suggested.

'Difficult,' Bryant remarked. 'They're not very comfortable in public spaces. Some of them have exclusion orders, several are agoraphobic, one is anthophobic—'

'What is that?'

'Afraid of flowers. And one of our art lecturers isn't allowed near children.'

'Upstairs in a public house, then.'

'Alcohol. Risky.'

'I'm listening to this in amazement,' said Land. 'You cannot just go on as if nothing's happened.'

'Very well, but we are,' said Bryant. 'Fear stops people from acting. It's time to be fearless. If we don't do something right now many more could die.'

'Every time some old codger falls down the stairs you think there's a seditious plot afoot.'

'There usually is. My friends are being picked off.'

'They're being picked off by Death because they are all incredibly old,' said Land unnecessarily.

'Kirkpatrick was poisoned, Eleanor and Herbert were shot at and poor old Oscar managed to catch a broken neck.'

'Obviously if you look at them together like that it seems odd,' Land admitted, 'but taken separately—'

'You have to see the overall picture. Everything's connected.'

'Anti-vaxxers think that,' said Land. 'People will assume you've got dementia.'

'People assume that now,' Bryant replied. 'We have nothing to lose by continuing. If we can prove that the CIA is behind this, I'm prepared to put our fate in the hands of British justice.' He beckoned May to his side. 'John, do you trust me?'

'Of course I trust you, Arthur. It's the British justice part that worries me.'

'We have to act before anyone realizes what we're up to.' He slapped May on the chest. 'We start with Angela Carey. There's no need to wince like that.'

'Bullet wound,' said May. 'Lead on.'

Eleanor Hamilton looked out to see if it might rain, but the sky was Wedgwood blue. She still took a cardigan, though, just in case. Herbert Constantine was waiting for her on the pavement.

'Where on earth did you find that jacket?' she asked, taking his arm. 'It looks like the type bus conductors used to wear in summer.'

'I think it is,' he replied. 'Arthur gave it to me years ago. I can't imagine he's ever bought anything new.' They headed off along the pavement. Ahead lay the hill rising towards Alexandra Palace, the grandiose exhibition hall that had never found its purpose in London life.

'Poor Arthur.' She shook her head sadly. 'He never got over his wife's death, you know. He could never bring himself to believe it was an accident. He would sit in the pub with me going over every tiny decision that had led him to walk her across that bridge, as though he was looking for a way to make it his fault.'

They came to a gap between two cars and started to cross the road. Herbert enclosed her hand tightly in his. 'One must shed the past in order to grow,' he agreed. 'I'm not the same young firebrand I used to be but there are some things—'

The car hit him square on, killing him instantly and dragging Eleanor to the tarmac. While she was struggling to stand the vehicle suddenly reversed and came forward again, driving over her skull. This time it did not stop.

39

COMMON CAUTION

Cranston took the IKEA lamp from its table and smashed it against the bed, slashing open the padded headboard. He hurled a chair across the room. Swept his whisky bottle to the floor. Cut his hand on a water tumbler as he slammed it against the bathroom wall. Squeezed the ragged edges of flesh together until scarlet drops spattered the white tiles.

In that blind crimson moment he renounced the world. He no longer cared who came after him.

He was in the basement flat he had bought with his own money, the one he had never told his father about. A lifetime of failure rose up before him. Even in this moment he knew that his rage was insignificant, the tearful anger of an ignored and thwarted child. He was barely a participant in his own life, of interest to others only when he was worth something. A walk-on, a background filler. His efforts had all been for nothing. He had been too slow-witted to see that the CIA would strand him here.

There was no longer any point in trying to save himself. *It's better to be remembered for a death than for nothing at all.*

He sat before the bathroom mirror and studied the jowling of his cheeks, his greying hair, the way his stomach flab pushed itself on to the tops of his thighs. He had inherited the debauched look of his father twenty years too early, with none of the old man's business acumen. And now he had failed again, on this final throw of the dice.

He thought of the tangled body beneath his car and how little her death had meant to him, yet it was her face he saw before him all the time. She had a daughter; she had grieving parents. If only he had done the right thing he would not have reached this bitter end.

He finally knew what to do. In his dreams he had seen the place where he would meet his death.

Rita Rondola lived in Peckham and her taxi dashed in that direction like a dog answering a whistle. She cut through Westminster and crossed Lambeth Bridge, past Archbishop's Park to the Imperial War Museum, around the everlasting disaster of the Elephant & Castle roundabout to Walworth Road. The detectives were being swung about on the passenger seat as if they were on a fairground ride.

'At least it was over quickly for them,' said Bryant. 'And they went together, which is what they'd always intended. Eleanor told me that she and Herbert had a suicide pact, that if one got sick they would both take poison. Maggie tells me she didn't have long to live. Eleanor had already planned her own funeral. I'm sorry her time was brought forward.'

'How has no one been able to trace the car?' asked May.

'The road at the side of Alexandra Palace has no working CCTV and you know what the area's like, there's no one around except at the weekends.'

'The vehicle must be in a state. Someone will have seen it.'

'How would I know? There's no favour I can pull in this time, no one I can ask.'

'Raymond Kirkpatrick, Eleanor Hamilton, Herbert Constantine, Oscar Daventry. This is an epidemic. Did they all know each other?'

'They're all on my list of informants.'

'And you've used all of them in the past?'

'Several times.'

'You realize it makes you the link between them. You're at the centre of your own investigation.'

'And *that's* why I need to keep going,' said Bryant firmly.

'Please, exercise some common caution.'

'Two words which are entirely unknown to me. Three if you count "exercise".' Bryant sat back and watched South London speed past.

Janice Longbright had found an Airbnb flat for Angela Carey to stay in. She had paid in advance using her boss's old Home Office expense account, and after careful thought had chosen an area where few would think of looking for her.

Walworth, just off the Old Kent Road, was not a neighbourhood visited by tourists. It had existed for more than a thousand years and had enjoyed a fleeting moment of respectability in Victorian times, but had been bombed out and filled with impoverished tenants, mixed with the odd future celebrity: Michael Caine and Charlie Chaplin had both ascended from its scrap-happy streets.

The name of East Street's local pub summed it up – the Good Intent – and Angela Carey was trepidatious about finding herself staying a few doors along from it. At weekends the street transformed itself into a market, not for fine antiques or even bric-a-brac but baby clothes and phone covers. It had been known as the Lane for as long as anyone alive could remember.

'I have not been here since my cousin is arrested for selling tickets to Paradise,' said Rita, ducking to look through her windscreen.

'He's a nightclub promoter?' asked May.

'No, he is priest. Police say he cannot charge people for enter Kingdom of Heaven.'

'Could you put a cushion back here next time?' asked Bryant. 'Your driving is playing havoc with my Chalfonts.'

'What is Chalfonts?'

'It's rhyming slang.' Bryant proceeded to explain in rather too much detail. Rita had a laugh like someone trying to start a petrol mower.

'I find myself in a state of grand decay,' Bryant said. 'Unlike my partner here I don't care how the world perceives me, but I am comfortable in my collapse.'

'We are all collapsing like when my school fell down.'

Bryant nodded sagely. 'Earthquake?'

'Mortar bomb.'

'You must tell me your story sometime.'

'Is not pretty I'm telling you. I'll be here when you need me.' She hoisted her encyclopaedia back on to her lap.

Even though they had phoned ahead first, Angela Carey took some luring to the door. Her face was still bruised and she winced as she walked, but she refused their help on the stairs.

'I hope you've been into the pub,' said Bryant as they settled themselves in the kitchen. 'The landlady's one of our allies. She'll keep an eye on you.'

'Just how many of these people do you have?' Angela asked.

'As many as you do, I imagine,' said Bryant.

Angela looked about herself, still surprised to be here. 'I feel like a counter-intelligence agent tucked away in a safe house. Is someone also keeping an eye on Moon Street?'

'We've put a security door across your hall. Our builders have made the place safe for now.' He wedged a cushion under his buttocks, removed a notepad from his waistcoat and uncapped a silver and tortoiseshell fountain pen. 'Do you mind if I take notes?'

'Please go ahead. Nice pen.'

'It was given to me by the great W. S. Gilbert,' said Bryant proudly. He caught Angela's disbelieving look. 'Well, it was in a sort of dream,' he explained without properly explaining.* 'I must find out where it came from one day.'

'We need information from you,' said May, bringing what was meant to be an interrogation back on track. 'You won't be safe until he's arrested.'

'I don't think Mr Cranston will find me here,' said Angela. 'He's a low-pay-grade pawn caught up in a game that has outsmarted him.'

'But until he's brought in you're not safe.'

'You obviously have some kind of suspicion as to what's going on, so why don't you tell me?'

'We think MI5 is helping him.'

She gave a mirthless laugh. 'No, I really don't think so, Mr Bryant. MI5 is not in the business of "helping" people.'

'There's a lot you can still tell us without contravening the Official Secrets Act,' said Bryant. 'Amelia Hoffman was barely out of her teens then. The work she did for my predecessor must have been very basic, making tea and emptying ashtrays.'

'Only at first,' said Angela. 'In the experimental units, women who showed initiative could reach positions of power very quickly. Amelia was charged with providing protection to informants, so she made a list. We were always doing that sort of thing. Half the time we couldn't remember where we put the stuff we saved. It's hardly surprising given the amount of paper we generated: reams of it in boxes and folders, stacked on trolleys and alphabetized in cabinets. People forget

---

* See *Wild Chamber*.

that modern security systems have only been in place since the new century.'

'Did she attach details of their activities?'

'I honestly can't tell you,' Carey said. 'She kept the case notes long after everyone forgot about her. When she left, she kept everything back.'

'How come?'

'She didn't trust anyone else to look after them – at that time there were leaks all over the police network. Soon no one even remembered the list's existence. To keep the papers safe she put them in her pink filing cabinet. She moved it from Baker Street to Snow Hill to Bow Street, then up to Mornington Crescent. Annie and I were recruited as administrators. We made sure the bills were paid and the cabinet stayed secure. We even repainted the damned thing. There were new names added right up until the events of 9/11. After that the CIA became more active in British affairs and the papers were sealed. Amelia had a set of special keys made for the cabinet so that it could only be opened once.'

Angela hobbled to the window and looked down into the street. Two West Indian women were patiently waiting for custom beside a stall of rainbow-coloured socks. They eyed a dog-walker passing them with four prissy schnoodles on leads, different worlds overlapping.

'I imagine Cranston started looking for something that could advance him within the service long before his accident,' said Bryant, joining her at the window. 'He traced the payments to Amelia, who pretended she didn't know what he was talking about. What I don't understand is how a man everyone agrees is an idiot has managed to get this far.'

'He's out of his depth and panicking. I'm not scared of him.'

'That's brave of you,' said Bryant, 'but Cranston's fate rests on factors beyond his control. That makes him dangerous. The US State Department and the Home Office were already at war with one another before this happened. We don't know what the state of play is between them now.'

'What about the family of the girl on the crossing? Do you know if they met with anyone from the embassy?'

'I understand the victim's father is planning to pursue a civil claim against Cranston in North America. I'd like to know whether the CIA passed the papers to another buyer. We met an agent who told us they'd turned Cranston down.'

'You got a standard denial,' said Angela. 'The CIA rarely admits to anything. Sometimes you see a crack in their armour, but when you look into it – absolute darkness. Perhaps they made a deal with the Russians or the Chinese: payback in an arrangement we will never know anything about.'

'Angela, we can get no further unless we find out why anyone would be interested in the papers. The decades-old opinions of a few self-published academics are not going to excite a world power.'

'Then I can't help you,' said Angela. 'Amelia thought it would be safer if only she was aware of the content. Annie and I just knew that the papers had to be protected.'

40

FULL CIRCLE

The meeting was official insofar as there were wooden folding chairs and people to park on them, but it looked more like someone had rounded up visitors to an antiques roadshow and put them in a holding cell while they sorted out who'd stolen a Georgian tea service. The room was a sea of khaki quilted jackets and elasticated fawn slacks, and everyone was arguing defensively.

'You must think of this as a council of war,' said Bryant, optimistically holding his arms wide for hush.

'Well, that's not going to work, is it?' said a shaggy-haired old man in the front row. 'Seeing as we're all pacifists.'

'I'm not,' called a woman from the Contradiction Society, more as a matter of habit.

An argument broke out between two elderly scientists as one tried to claim his chair by sitting on the other. 'Schrödinger!' he kept shouting at the man beneath him.

Arthur Bryant looked around the fuggy upstairs bar of the Wheatsheaf, a mock-Tudor horror in the backstreets of Fitzrovia, and wondered if this had been such a good idea after all.

At least the room contained nothing breakable. Some of tonight's attendees had been lured out with promises of free alcohol and sausage rolls and, in one case, a copy of *Gas Chromatography for Beginners*. After assuring them that there would be no secret cameras or asbestos in the walls, he had booked the room above the pub.

Glancing about himself he could see Jackson Ubeda, the Egyptian artefact broker who had recently lost an eye at a stress management conference; Audrey Beardsley, the misanthropic historian and numerologist who had taken over as leader of the Semantics Club, not to be confused with the Semantics Group; several puzzle-solving Friends of the British Library who were mourning the loss of Raymond Kirkpatrick; the writer Darcy Sarto, holding court even though no one was listening; Rachel Ling, the Jewish-Chinese head of the London River Society; Precious Moonbeam, the transgender psychogeographer; and the arsonist Henry Steppe, currently on day release from the Manderfield Healthcare Centre. All had stratospheric IQs, hidden talents and secret afflictions. Most were shockingly inarticulate and unsociable. Few were employable in the traditional sense of the term.

Yet the outsiders shared a common bond: they recognized patterns in life's random chaos, bringing sense to disorder and sometimes the reverse. They were united by other commonalities: all were fabulously indiscreet and hopeless judges of character, hyper-intelligent babies at the mercy of wolves. Whoever was in possession of the London Bridge papers now had a road map leading them to some of the nation's most radical thinkers.

'Each of you has a speciality that has proven useful to the unit in the past,' said Bryant. 'I need to know if the information you hold is likely to put you or others at risk.'

'I can knot a shoelace with my tongue,' said Arbuthnot Green, a homicide-evidence interpreter who had been thrown out of MI5 for repeatedly exposing himself in the orchid room at Kew Gardens.

'Anyone else?' asked Bryant.

Audrey Beardsley raised her hand. 'I have absolute proof of the identities of Lee Harvey Oswald's co-conspirators.'

'We all have that,' someone shouted. There were cries of 'Boring' and 'Old news'.

'I headed an inquiry into the death of the Speaker of the House of Commons,' said Mary-Sacred-Heart Gomez, astronomer and UFOlogist. 'For you and Mr May, in fact. I never showed you my findings but I submitted them.'

'What do you mean, you submitted them?' asked May.

'To the London Bridge papers,' she replied. A murmur of assent ran around the stuffy room.

'Wait, have others submitted work? Just a show of hands, please.'

Every hand went up. A mad-looking old lady at the back raised both hands.

'How? Where did you send it?'

'To the same address my father used,' replied Gomez. 'Box 750, the London Bridge Vaults.' She dug into her coat and produced a crumpled envelope. 'I was about to post one today about Cliff Richard inventing the perpetual motion engine.'

'You all did this? Who started it?'

'It wasn't me!' cried a man with a persecution complex at the back.

'Actually, Mr Bryant, I think it might have been you,' said an elegantly attired Jamaican gentleman just in front of him. 'It was back when the unit was still at Bow Street. You don't remember me, do you?'

Harrington Shamwell was one of the great thinkers of his time, a polymath philosopher, logician, political activist and former Black Panther. He had been briefly seconded to the unit in between jail terms.

'I seem to remember, and I surely do because I suffer from hyperthymesia, that you complained the unit wasn't doing enough to protect its sources. Of course you were even more annoyingly sure of yourself at the time so nobody listened to you.'

'What did I do?' asked Bryant, fascinated.

'You asked us to note the names of anyone who might be at risk from exposure,' said Shamwell. 'You wrote a memo and handed it to everyone, don't you remember?'

'Harrington, I don't remember putting my trousers on each morning. They just seem to appear on my legs.'

'I might still have the memo,' replied the polymath. 'I'm the kind of person who keeps everything. There are doors in my house it's not wise to open.'

'You wouldn't happen to know what I did with the original?' asked Bryant hopefully.

'You probably put it somewhere safe,' said Harrington. 'You were obsessed with secrecy in those days.'

He thanked them for coming and watched them all for a while. They bickered and snubbed and sulked, but were thoroughly enjoying themselves. They were his people. He needed to make sure they stayed alive and active.

'Useless,' said May as Rita's taxi swept them past the Monument, down to London Bridge and across the burnished pewter plain of the Thames. 'Your loonies, dutifully posting their mad theories to vaults that were closed down. God knows where all their mail ended up. In the Thames, most probably. It's incredible. Handwritten envelopes. She gave them all soap-wrapper envelopes and forms to fill in based on your bloody memo. Of all the things to have forgotten!'

'There was no technology involved, nothing to be traced back,' said Bryant. 'Why do you think I prefer my reservoir pen? Anything I write is the only copy.'

Rita's taxi nudged its way along Tooley Street. The going was slow.

'Why didn't you take Tower Bridge, it would have been quicker,' Bryant complained.

'When you've done the Knowledge and have your own taxi that you paid for with your dirty British money you can take the route you prefer but until then please stick to catching murderers,' said Rita.

Bryant dropped scraps of paper everywhere while May collected and organized them. 'Kirkpatrick published a book about banned chemicals which was in turn banned,' he said. 'Eleanor Hamilton had files on every jailed journalist in Europe. Herbert Constantine was a virologist who built a bio-chemical company in the Democratic Republic of Congo. By keeping each death different no one connects them and you can quietly pick them off one by one. It works for Putin's Russia, so why shouldn't it work here?'

'Because this is Great Britain, a democracy—'

'—which hides an oligarchy,' said Bryant. 'We have political parties with private organizations hidden inside them.' As they passed through Bermondsey Square he looked about, lost. 'I don't recognize any of this. We used to get here at six on a Friday morning to buy stolen jewellery.'

'Why would you do that?'

'To check its provenance and return it. Bermondsey Market was a *marché ouvert*. A seven-hundred-year-old law stated that if an item was sold between sunset and sunrise its provenance couldn't be questioned. It only changed its status in 1995.'

'You are a mine of useless information,' said May.

'So are my sources, but they shouldn't have to be murdered for it,' Bryant replied. 'Rita, it's the warehouse on the left.'

'You are sure of this?' she asked, looking up through the windscreen doubtfully. 'It looks like the place where my poor uncle was stabbed through the heart by a thief.'

'Did they catch him?' Bryant asked.

'The thief was his wife, may she rot in hell.'

'Lovely story, Rita, thanks for sharing.' Bryant hopped out and unlocked the great wooden door but couldn't budge the bolt. It took a few swift kicks from May's brogue to loosen it.

The cavernous building was the last of its kind in an area that had until recently been one of the most atmospheric spots in London. The detectives stepped around fake brass ships' lanterns and chronometers, through gloomy canyons of rat-chewed tarpaulins which had once covered rare paintings and Venetian statues.

'Colin put most of the tea chests up there with a few of his mates from the gym.' Bryant's Valiant torch picked up an incline of broken stairs. 'There was never any electricity in these places. Mind yourself on the staircase. You don't want to fall into the basement because it's full of river water and things.'

'*Things*,' May repeated, looking down at the cracked planks.

Bryant used his walking stick to prod at some rotten wood. 'This is all going in a couple of months' time. My old man used to keep stuff in here that he didn't want my mother to find at home. One time I helped him carry a suit of armour, and I remember glancing down – just about where you're standing right now – and looking through the crack in the stairs, and seeing someone staring back up at me.'

May hastily hopped over the staircase crack.

They made their way across the tilting, filthy attic space to the chests Colin and his mates had stacked in the middle of the floor. The ammoniac stench of pigeon droppings burned May's nostrils.

'I dated the contents of each box on its side,' said Bryant. 'If it's here, it shouldn't be too hard to find.'

As they dug deep into the oldest, the files became browner

and more brittle. Bryant brushed away fat grey spiders and dragged out a wrinkled folder from the bottom of the crushed paperwork. He tipped it to the torchlight.

'The address is Bow Street so we're in the right area.' A pair of moths tickled his face. 'No names on the correspondence. We must have saved all this for a reason.' He lowered himself to the floorboards and wiped mouse droppings from the sheets. 'A lot of the more important documents went into court briefs or were stored by the Home Office. Here we go, internal memos only.'

As he flipped through the pages, some broke free and fell out. One sheet had been laminated on to thick white card. Bryant read it in silence, then passed it to his partner.

MEMO – EYES ONLY – PRIVATE & CONFIDENTIAL

From the first of the month, details of all informants should be placed in File 33#20 and handed to Miss Gerwitz. These details should include:

Name and Address
Credentials
Area of Expertise
Dates of Use by Unit

Please add the appropriate red and green stickers if your informant has any of the following criteria for inclusion:

Information protected by the Official Secrets Act of 1939 or other Commonwealth government security laws
Sensitive state knowledge deemed unsuitable for publication
Police record or involvement in any kind of illegal activity

Views of a nature currently considered unacceptable i.e.
  anarchism, communism, pacifism, homosexuality, freedom of abortion, et cetera
History of mental instability
Physical risk to self or the public at large

'There you have it,' said May, rocking back on his heels.
'The brief for the London Bridge papers, lost and forgotten.
Which means that any important information they hold is
now long out of date. What was sensitive then would have no
relevance now.'

'You don't know that,' Bryant insisted. 'What if one of
them had covert knowledge of cold fusion, say, or genetic
testing?'

'You're missing the point, Arthur. The CIA saw that Cranston's bargaining chip was worthless.'

Bryant's lower lip rose. 'We still have to find him. Remember
the Lord Lucan case? He had friends in high places who helped
smuggle him out of the country. Cranston must still have
people who could help him. We have to get to him first. We
owe it to those who died and the ones who are still alive. You
saw them, John, you know how vulnerable they are.'

May climbed to his feet and dusted himself down. 'You
can't save an entire generation of free thinkers, Arthur.'

Bryant pulled a splinter out of his sleeve. 'I don't have a
choice. It's my fault all this happened in the first place. We've
come full circle. If I don't find a way to protect them, who will?'

PART FIVE

1305 William Wallace
1408 Henry Percy
1450 Jack Cade and his captains
1500s The Lollards
1535 Sir Thomas More
1540 Thomas Cromwell
1606 Father Garnet, Gunpowder Plotter

– Partial list of those rebels whose severed heads
were spiked on London Bridge

41

THE ZOMBIE UNIT

Lying in bed, hovering between sleep and wakefulness, Arthur Bryant had a lucid dream. He used moments like this to reassemble events and allow everything to fall into place. The patchwork quilt of his memory was coloured in block by block.

He dreamed of three old ladies. Mentally alert and physically in good shape, they camouflaged themselves by appearing old and frail. *When people don't see you they keep their distance.* He knew this from his own experience of the ageing process. Amelia had not been grey then but auburn, her hair tied back, her face make-up free. It would probably take several hypnosis sessions with Maggie to fully recall her. He remembered a woman who had stridden into the office of the PCU as if sizing it up and finding it wanting.

By focusing very hard he could remember the way she looked at him. How once her hand brushed his shoulder when she passed his desk. She would never have invited him to her secretarial hostel because there were no male visitors allowed after nine. Then he had met Nathalie, whom he was soon to marry, and lost sight of his colleague.

Somebody knocked on his bedroom door.

'Who is it?'

Raymond Land stuck his head in. His hair had reared up on one side like an open pedal bin. He was not happy to find himself camped out in Bryant's flat.

'I can't stay here,' he complained. 'There's a hen under your TV set and a cereal bowl on your toilet cistern.'

'The hen is stuffed and I forgot to bring the bowl out,' said Bryant. 'You couldn't have gone back to the Isle of Wight last night, it's at least three decades away. You'll have to stay here. It pains me to say it but we need you. We're using this flat as a base of operations.'

'Despite the fact that the PCU has ceased to exist,' Land pointed out.

'Raymondo, you worry too much about proof of existence. Life is but a dream. One evening I'll explain my parallel universe theory to you. For now, consider us a zombie unit.' Bryant swung his pyjamaed legs out of bed. 'I keep telling everyone to trust me, that our future is all in hand and going according to plan, but they still don't believe me. On the downside, it's the end of things as they are.'

'And on the upside?'

'Oh, is there an upside? Well, I suppose if we can catch Cranston we'll save many lives. How was the couch?'

'The couch? Oh, er, very comfortable.'

'You'd never know anyone died on it. Alma will be making tea by now – is builder's all right?'

Land winced and pressed a hand on his stomach. 'All this is making me very nervous.'

'First things first,' said Bryant. 'You need something to unknot your guts. Do you like puddings with mangoes and rum in them? There'll be a bucket of something on top of the cooker by now.'

He headed for the kitchen, crashed about in it and produced

a bowl. 'What are you going to do for clothes? You can't wear what you've got on.'

'Why not?'

'They make you look like an accountant supervising the receivership of a small engineering firm just outside Crawley.'

'That's very specific.' Land held out his arms and looked down. 'This is what I always wear to the unit.'

'Which is one of the reasons why we always laugh at you. I should get you an eye-patch.'

'Why?'

'We're pirates now. Operating beyond the limits of the law. These are unconventional times and we must rise to the challenge. Raise the gangplank and hoist the Jolly Roger.'

Land attempted to pull the creases out of his slept-in shirt. 'You're enjoying this, aren't you?'

'I'm happier working outside the system.' Bryant picked lint off Land's collar. 'You don't have to join me if you don't want to.'

'Assuming I did, how could we pay for any technical services we need? The unit charged everything back to the Home Office.'

'Don't worry: I have the company float; Alma has a printer. They discontinued the ink but we know where we can steal some. And Giles is going to give us credit at his mortuary. We have to move fast because Cranston has become expendable.'

The awfulness of the implication settled on Land like a funeral crow. 'You can't seriously be suggesting that the CIA will bump him off on the streets of London.'

'Very well, but I am.'

'Where does that leave us?' asked Land forlornly.

'David beat Goliath.'

'David had a slingshot. You don't even have any printer ink.'

Someone was pounding at the front door. It sounded as if

they had a licence to operate a battering ram. 'That'll be for me,' said Bryant. 'Perhaps you could come with me for safety.'

He opened the door to reveal a stubble-chinned man in a Budweiser vest with his huge tattooed fists clenched.

'Ah, Mr Pitt, how lovely to see you again.' Bryant turned to his house guest. 'Raymondo, this is Brad Pitt. He is beneath me.'

His neighbour scowled like a pit bull with a liver complaint.

'I mean he lives downstairs. He's in motion pictures.'

'I'm not Brad Pitt,' said Joe, who could not have been mistaken for Brad Pitt by a partially sighted person in a heavy denim veil standing in the densest of twilight fogs. 'My name's Joe and I operate heavy machinery. Which I shall be bringing up here and dropping on him if he doesn't stop his bathwater from leaking into my flat.'

'Bathwater?' Bryant repeated. 'Is it clear and sweet-smelling?'

'Well, it's clear. I haven't smelled it.'

'Try not to. It's not bathwater, it's acid. Don't inhale it or it'll turn your urine green. I made too much and some went in the overflow. I was experimenting.'

'The next time it happens I'll experiment by stuffing you down the overflow.'

'Fair enough,' Bryant cheerfully agreed to the terms. 'This is Mr Land. He'll be staying for a few days.'

Joe held out a hand the size of a cement shovel. 'Perhaps you can keep him from killing us all.'

'Probably not,' said Land. 'He blew up my building.'

'Aristotle said friendship is a slow-ripening fruit,' said Bryant. 'Thank you for your fruit.' He shut the door in Joe's mystified face and turned to Land. 'I suppose I'd better tell Alma we'll be three for dinner.'

*

Colin Bimsley was not by nature prone to depression, but he thought that if he was, today he'd be really downbeat. *You're about to become homeless*, he thought, *you've lost your job, you have no savings and you think you can somehow get married.*

He tore up the apologetic letter from his landlord and had just got his key in the door when his landline rang. No one ever used that except his mother.

'Do you remember me?' asked a vaguely familiar voice. 'It's Lajita, your mum's old next-door neighbour. How are you, Marlin?'

Marlin was Colin's middle name. Many years ago his mother had introduced him to the neighbour, who was deaf in one ear, and Mrs Goswami had got the wrong end of the stick and the name had stuck.

'Good, Mrs Goswami, how are you? How's your leg?'

'Much better, thank you. I took the liberty of calling because a lady just died near our shop. I talked to the ambulance driver. They've been trying to call your unit but there's no answer. I told them I had your home number. Can you come?'

'I'm going to the gym and it's on the way, Mrs Goswami, no problem.' Colin rang off and grabbed his kit.

A series of cries had been heard coming from a basement bar near Russell Square tube station in Bloomsbury and a woman had been found dead. When Colin arrived he was taken to a door of black-painted plywood set in the concrete wall of the Brunswick Shopping Centre. The nameplate on the buzzer beside it had been left blank. An illegal drinking den, he thought, surprised that there were any left in a neighbourhood once rife with them.

'Was this door locked?' he asked a member of the EMT crew waiting outside.

'Wide open, no lights on,' she said. 'This is the one who

called you – she says she thinks someone pushed the lady inside and down the stairs.'

'I didn't see,' said Mrs Goswami firmly. 'I said I *thought* that was what happened.' Mrs Goswami ran the patisserie opposite with her son.

'You be all right here for a minute?' asked the EMT woman. 'We're just bringing the ambulance round.'

Colin stepped inside. There was a musty smell of flat beer and something earthier: old vegetables. A strip light in a stained plastic case turned the scene sepia. The body was lying sideways across the bottom of the stairs, one leg badly twisted. Colin sat down beside her. He knew he was not supposed to move her body but it was wrong to leave it like that. She moved easily; there was a lightness of bone, an absence of weight. She was already cooling, becoming less a person than a thing.

He looked down at her chest. The entry wound was positioned to inflict maximum damage. An oval brooch of blood had blossomed on her cardigan, two or three dark drops falling to the tiled floor.

Her purse identified her as Lina Symanski. He studied Symanski's face. There were seven decades of life in her features. She was dressed in someone else's hand-me-downs. He checked for other signs of homelessness: dirt under the nails, damaged feet, unwashed hair, tanned hands.

The people who passed through the emergency services were encountered for a brief moment in time, in stressful and confusing circumstances. A report would note down 'female Caucasian, 66', with no indication as to who this person might have been: an engineer or artist, a pilot or physician. There was no time to find out how their circumstances had changed with the passing years. As far as police reports were concerned the victims were stopped clocks, frozen in time by the circumstances of their death.

He rose and looked around. The darkened bar disturbed

him. Without its night lighting it felt dead and vaguely sinister, like an abandoned fairground. It reminded him of the
clubs his uncle Charlie used to drag him along to, East End
drinking holes stale and gloomy at noon, where they always
had to meet a man about something that was never explained.

He thought he heard a noise, the shift of a shoe, a rearrange-
ment of material, but when he looked up into the darkness
nothing moved. The deep red walls receded into pixelated
blackness. He became aware that he was alone with a dead
body.

He heard a chair scraping back somewhere. There was a
small, sharp-edged noise, a glass briefly tipping before right-
ing itself. As his eyes adjusted he could make out a second
staircase topped with a brass handrail on the other side of the
room – the main entrance. He had come in through the fire-
escape exit.

Suspicious, Colin walked towards the curtains at the base
of the stairs.

Was it the air from the open fire door that made them
sway? The fingers of his right hand brushed a dusty fold of
fabric.

There was a live body behind them.

A leg kicked out. Colin was caught in the solar plexus and
fell backwards, his spatial disorientation swarming in and
turning the room about itself. As he struggled to stand he saw
a figure retreat to the top of the staircase and vanish.

When he finally reached the street he caught a glimpse of
his quarry moving at the edge of his vision, rounding a corner
and barging their way through a door that opened on to a
building site.

Colin charged across the road, throwing himself between
two buses and bringing down an imam and a Greek Orthodox
priest who were chatting outside a bookmaker's.

With his suspect gone and two flattened religious leaders

yelling at him outside Paddy Power, Bimsley made his way back to the medical team. His gut reaction had been to call for patrol cars in the area, but he no longer had a shoulder mic. He had damaged his shin and his dignity.

He went with the team in the ambulance, which drew into the forecourt of University College Hospital with its lights and siren turned off. There was no rush now, just paperwork to be filled out.

On his way back to the unit he ran a search for Lina Symanski. Instinct told him that she was likely to be on Bryant's list, and so it proved; she had once been an epidemiologist with a highly unorthodox reputation, working at the Francis Crick Biomedical Institute.

In his confused state he returned to 231 Caledonian Road, only to realize that the building had been sealed, the windows darkened, the locks changed. He sat on the low wall outside the supermarket and made a phone call. It was spitting with rain. A homeless man offered him a cigarette.

'I think we've lost another one,' he told Meera. 'An expert on viruses. That brings the total to six or maybe seven, I'm starting to lose track.'

'You're still going out on the street then.'

'Do you have somewhere better to be?'

'Actually, yeah. I've gone to my mum's. My sister's playing up again. I'll probably have to stay overnight.'

'I'm supposed to be looking at a flat first thing in the morning, if you want to come with me.'

'Colin, neither of us have jobs.'

'I've got enough for a month's rent.'

He decided not to tell Meera that he had earned the cash by knocking an opponent unconscious at an illegal boxing match in Bethnal Green last year, or that it wouldn't cover the cost of moving in.

'Send me the address. I'm not trusting you to choose a

place without me. Especially if I'm going to be spending a lot of time there.'

'OK, and afterwards we'll face your mother together. And then we'll get married.'

'We have to talk about that, now that we don't have any work.'

Colin's heart sank. It had taken him years to get this far with Meera. *Now your girlfriend is backing out*, he thought. *It's time to give up chasing phantoms and pay some attention to your own problems.*

Except.

He thought of sitting on the steps in the darkened bar waiting for the ambulance, beside the small body of an old woman once famed for her scientific brilliance, her spirit rendered to inert flesh in a reeking basement.

Lost, he called John May for advice.

'Arthur wants to keep going,' said May, who was just letting himself into his flat in Shad Thames. 'He says we owe it to those who are most vulnerable.'

'Meera's upset with me. I don't blame her, but what can I do? Where could we work?'

'He's found a place where we can meet. Maggie Armitage has a hall in Somers Town that she uses for her spiritualist meetings.'

'I was afraid you'd say something like that.' Colin did not want to let his bosses down but could feel himself wavering. 'I don't know where any of us stand any more. I don't know what the hell I'm doing. I should bow out and leave this to you . . .'

'Colin, we need you but you must do what you think best. You know Arthur has always come through for us. Admittedly he's often left it to the last minute and given everyone heart attacks but I'm prepared to trust him one last time. I'd like to think that you do too. Talk to the others. I'm going to send you the address of Maggie's hall anyway.

Follow your conscience, but if you decide you're with us, be there at nine tomorrow morning.'

Colin had the sense of an ending now, a final shining moment before blackness descended. Their last stand. He was fairly certain that he had to be there for it.

PC Isla Wentworth was bored out of her mind. *A chihuahua of below-average intelligence could do this job*, she decided.

She'd been seconded to surveillance for the past three months thanks to the Met's everlasting staffing problems. A month of sitting in windowless basements staring at furry-edged CCTV images of idiot street vermin slipping each other packets in public corners, somehow thinking they were invisible, had done her brain in, and she was glad to get back on the streets. She should have been more careful about what she wished for, because now she was posted outside a flat in East Street next to a pub called the Good Intent, making sure nobody tried to break in and brain some old dear.

Wentworth had caught a few glimpses of the woman she was guarding, passing behind the rain-stained front-room windows, so she knew she was all right. There was only one way in or out, and no one even vaguely dodgy had passed by her. Her shift ended in twenty minutes, and she was going to be through that pub door like a rat up a drainpipe the moment another officer arrived.

She had been asked to sign off her shift by confirming that the surveillance target was in rude health and that no one had entered the flat, so she rang the doorbell and waited to be let in. When the buzzer sounded she stepped inside and found the inner door ajar.

'Miss Carey?' She walked into the living room and looked around. An opened magazine lay on the hideous red leather sofa, as if someone had just walked away from it.

The flat was silent but for a tap dripping in the kitchen. She checked the bedrooms upstairs and found them both empty. It occurred to her that the old bag might have fallen down and got wedged somewhere, so she headed back downstairs and looked inside all the cupboards, then behind the television screen and the armchairs.

It began to dawn on PC Isla Wentworth that her charge was not in the flat and that her own neck had suddenly been placed on a chopping block. It didn't make sense. The TV was still warm.

'Impossible,' she said aloud. 'She must be here.' She called again, half expecting an answer from a cupboard.

She was alone with the sound of her own voice.

She checked all the rooms a second and third time, reluctant to call in the mishap, but then her replacement turned up outside. Now there was no way of hiding the fact that although she had admitted no one to a first-floor maisonette, which had only one narrow door and no other way out apart from the windows, someone had managed to spirit Miss Carey away.

42

A WINDOW TO HEAVEN

The sign above the door read:

St Æthelwulf the Pious Temperance Hall
for Recidivist Bibulists
Founded 1832

Beneath this was taped an A4 sheet of paper that read: 'Needle Exchange Closed Mondays'.

'It looks abandoned.' Sidney wrinkled her nose. 'The guttering's hanging off. Can you even go inside without a hard hat?'

'Come in, lovey,' said Maggie, appearing suddenly at a gap in the door. She was eating an onion ring. 'Mind the floor, it's not all there.'

Janice followed her daughter inside, stepping over broken parquet blocks. At a refectory table they found a tall grey-haired woman with chained half-moon glasses frying eggs over a Bunsen burner.

'This is Dame Maude Hackshaw,' Maggie said. 'She helps out when we're short-staffed.'

'I say, could you pass me those?' Dame Maude pointed behind Sidney to a stack of tinned beans. 'Do carry on with your meeting, chums, I'll bring you brekker in a few.'

'Can she be trusted?' asked Janice.

'She's helped Arthur out in the past,' Maggie said. 'She caught the Cricklewood Axeman. Not on purpose. She just happened to be there at the time.'

Meera was here. Colin gave her a hug. 'I knew you'd come,' he said. 'I *knew* it.'

They arranged the chairs in a circle and prepared for a council of war. Janice noted that Raymond Land arrived with the detectives and was wearing a purple sweatshirt with the price label still on the back. What was going on?

'It seems we have a full complement,' said Bryant. 'Thank you all for being here. I wish I could pay you. Raymondo is sleeping on my sofa at the moment so he certainly can't. I can only tell you that if we find a way to crack this, everything will be all right. Have I ever let you down in the past?' He moved hurriedly on before hands went up. 'So where are we? What's the first thing you notice about the victims?'

'They're all old,' said Sidney.

'They divide into two groups,' Janice added. 'The early deaths involved the curators of the London Bridge papers, and the others are named in them.'

'Exactly,' said Bryant. 'Cause and effect. But we haven't correctly apportioned the blame, because now we have two different motives. Imagine you have a state secret that must be buried forever. All who are aware of it must be rendered mute and the secret itself must be destroyed. Let's take another look at Cranston.'

He pinned up an enlarged photograph of Cranston's face. 'Academically undistinguished, physically unprepossessing, "thick lineaments in a spacious visage", as Charlotte Brontë so eloquently put it, unseen and unknown in diplomatic circles. A bean-counter, and when some of the beans he counted didn't add up he followed their trail to a hoard of information nobody remembered. He added it to the mental file of things he could save for a rainy day and continued serving time at the embassy until one day a drunken accident placed his future in jeopardy.

'Cranston's no intellectual but he's a survivor. He goes after his rainy-day nest egg and starves an old lady to death trying to get his hands on it. That's when he discovers that although she knows where it is, she doesn't have the key any more. She's ground it to nothing in the kitchen and flushed it down the sink. Maybe she also tried to feed it to him; we'll never know. Furious, he takes out his anger on the bookkeeper and goes after Mrs Hoffman's allies. After making off with the papers, he sells them to gain his freedom. So why is he still here?'

Janice raised a hand. 'His buyer demands that he carries out the killings before they get him out of the country.'

'Excellent, Janice. Let someone else do the dirty work. We've seen the Russians pull a similar trick in the UK before. But there are hundreds of names in the papers; why pick out a handful of victims?'

'They all have something in common,' said Sidney, looking up at Bryant.

Everyone stared at her. The silence stretched.

'Well, what?' cried Land finally.

'I don't know,' Sidney admitted, 'but it would make sense, wouldn't it?'

Everyone groaned. The silence became a babble of argument.

'Arthur, you know these people better than anyone,' said May, ever the voice of reason. 'Do you see any common factors?'

'They're all disrupters,' Bryant said. 'Natural loners. If they continue to die we may be the only ones who notice. They are my friends and allies.'

'Thank you, but not helpful.'

'I can get hold of them,' said Maggie, pulling something from a knot of crimson hair.

'What's that?' asked Meera.

'My divining rod.'

'It's a biro.'

'But it will divine the names of all those in danger if I allow myself access to the spirit world.'

'Perhaps you could allow yourself access to the real world,' Meera suggested.

Bryant was staring at his phone, not an activity that usually engaged him. He looked up at the others. 'Stanley Purbrick's dead. His wife wants to know if I can do something about it. I used to tease him that one day he'd become a victim of his own conspiracy theories.'

May vaguely recalled a wild-haired man in his mid-fifties in a pub chewing his ear off about Spanish flu. 'What happened?'

'Stabbed outside a tobacconist's shop in Hounslow. Dan, can you liaise on this? Find something – anything – that connects him to the others.'

'You can't assume his death is connected,' said Land.

'He was on my list, a total lunatic and an excellent debunker of social panics. He impressed the government so much that they offered him the position of communications director in the cabinet office.'

'Did he take the job?'

'I believe his exact words were "Stick it up your arse". Lovely chap. He was essentially harmless but what he knew could have brought down a hundred politicians.'

'Then let's add him to the list because Mr Bryant here liked him, shall we?' said Land.

Bryant drew himself up to his full unimposing height. 'Let me tell you something about Stanley Purbrick, then you might understand why the names in the papers are so important. The influenza pandemic of 1918 to 1919 killed an estimated fifty million people worldwide. In 2005 CDC researchers re-created the Spanish flu virus. They wanted to understand its exceptional virulence. Specifically, they were studying anti-viral compounds like the new polymerase inhibitors. Eleanor Hamilton was one of the team heads. She was worried that unscrupulous traders would try to copyright their findings, so she hired Stanley Purbrick to release information prior to peer review. Doing so damaged both their careers. It didn't help that they were promoters of FreshStart.'

'What's that?' asked May.

Bryant waved his hands about airily in an effort to explain. 'An apocalypse group. They believed Armageddon should be brought about as soon as possible to spare humanity a gradual decline into barbarity and ignorance.'

'They should have started earlier,' said Colin. 'I bet they were fun at parties.'

'What is their combined knowledge worth? Are they heroes or enemies of the State? That depends on your point of view.'

'This is too bloody abstract for me,' Land complained. 'The way I see it, we're being led around by a nutter with a grudge.'

'The CIA and their multi-million-dollar resources are oblit-erating Cranston's tracks,' said Bryant. 'If you don't believe they're capable of doing such a thing, may I remind you that they once tried to kill the Congolese leader with a tube of poisoned toothpaste? Anything you can imagine them doing, no matter how outlandish, they've probably done.'

'You should be on that list,' said Land. 'Polymath law enforcement officer, conspiracy theorist and accidental origin-ator of the London Bridge papers. Needs assassinating.'

Larry Cranston's flat was no longer a hideout but a prison. After his drunken tantrum it had taken a fistful of cash to shut up the concierge. He had built himself a trap from which he could not escape.

For years Cranston had assumed himself to be the victim of atrocious luck. Despite having been born with every advantage, he had spent the whole of his adult life stumbling from one disaster to the next. It had led him here to an arctic-white basement jail in the East End, surrounded by the ghosts of all he had failed.

For the first time he saw his trajectory clearly. It hadn't been bad luck at all. It was him. He was damaged beyond repair. He thought of the old lady dying in front of him and felt sick.

There was a way he could gain the upper hand and take control. He still had the old cut-throat razor with the ivory handle that his father had given to him on his eighteenth birthday. How appropriate it would be to take his own life with it. He opened the wooden case now and removed it, watching it spread in welcome.

It was probably best to lie down on the sofa and put a towel down on the cushion. Perhaps he should remove his shirt. It took him a while to find the best position. He couldn't get comfortable. He held the gleaming blade over his thick white throat.

And so, like H. G. Wells's Mr Polly, who had tried to kill himself with a razor but found that it stung like a nettle, he hesitated, terrified, failing even in this final cowardly act.

It did not take long for the vodka to kick in but he felt no effect from the sleeping pills, perhaps because he only had over-the-counter ones from Boots and couldn't guarantee their strength.

It seemed that H. G. Wells had got the details right. The blade hovered motionless above his Adam's apple, its light like a window to heaven.

He touched it to his neck, closed his eyes and pushed. His face drained moon white.

The hot cascade of scarlet over his fingers made it hard to grip the handle. He thought of the shame he would cause his father and used both hands to push deeper.

43

THE FOURTH VISIT

'Is he to stay for tea?' asked Alma in an intrusive stage whisper. She glanced back at Raymond Land, who was sitting at the dining table trying to work out whether the china ostrich centrepiece did anything. 'Only I can pop some cloves in a ham. He looks like he wants feeding.'

'That poor ultracrepidarian* has had a rough decade,' Bryant explained in an equally theatrical whisper. 'His wife left him and there was trouble with his prostate, which amounted to the same thing. He'll be here for a couple more nights.'

'On that sofa? Its springs are coming through.'

'Well, we don't want him too comfortable. You know what they say about guests and . . . ducks, is it? Something aquatic. He hasn't complained so far. Or possibly he has, I've had my earplugs in. In fact I've still got one in.' He rummaged around for a pastry fork.

---

* Someone who holds forth on a subject on which they have absolutely no expertise.

'My ladies are coming round for choir practice tonight,' Alma pointed out. 'I hope he doesn't mind.'

'Mind? Who doesn't love "Guide Me, O Thou Great Redeemer" being bellowed in their ear just before bedtime? You might tempt them to have a bash at something a bit more upbeat.'

'We're not doing *Fiddler on the Roof* again, not after the last time, on my dining table.'

Luckily, Bryant had no recollection of last time. 'I may have to requisition the living room for a meeting,' he warned. 'My informants are in terrible danger. John, there you are. You look like you're about to present an award.'

May had appeared in the doorway. He had a tendency to overdress when he was tense. His grey silk tie was a step too far. 'I'm sorry, Arthur, she accosted me in the street. She says she has something very important to tell you.'

He stepped aside to reveal Maggie Armitage, lost inside a bright red duffel coat that made her look like the murderer in *Don't Look Now*. She set down her bin bag, shucked her hood and buffed her hair. 'Hello, Alma, I didn't know I'd be dropping in, otherwise I'd have brought your ring spanners back. Arthur, I came to return your notes. You left them in St Æthelwulf.'

'I'm sorry?'

'Our temperance hall. I took the liberty of perusing them. I've decided your investigation needs a bit of a rethink.'

'Please do tell,' said Bryant. 'I'd love to know where we're going wrong.'

'You know how much I admire your methods, but you don't look *inside* people.' She dug in her bin bag and produced a deceitful-looking stoat standing on its back legs. 'Salteena is one of my spirit familiars. She used to be a laundry maid up the Holloway Road in 1845. Her employer left her with a baby girl. She died in the workhouse, poor thing.'

Maggie set the stoat on the kitchen table and arranged Bryant in the chair opposite. She listened intently to Salteena, and then nodded. 'She says you don't see people like her. You just see pieces in a puzzle.'

'Of course I see them.' He cleared his throat and looked to Alma and John for support.

She listened to the stoat again. 'She says you don't see their souls.'

'I don't believe in the soul.'

'Why not?'

'If I acknowledge that the soul exists I can no longer be an atheist, can I? And I am not going to take advice from a stuffed stoat, so kindly stop listening to it.'

'Then we'll try something else. Remember when you first went into Mrs Hoffman's home.' She reached across the table to place a cool palm on his forehead. 'What did you feel there? What did you see?'

John tapped his foot impatiently. 'Really, Arthur?'

Bryant took the moment seriously and thought hard. 'I saw my childhood. Steamed-up windows, the smell of boiled washing and hot gravy, the women hushed in the front parlour, a clock ticking.'

'Why?'

'Amelia – I suppose she was like the old aunties of my past.'

'Forget who she was when she died. Who had she been?'

He struggled to think. 'She was dedicated to her work, a wife and a mother. Apparently she liked me.'

'Why do you think she liked you?'

'I was young and adorable.'

'She recognized a similar mind,' said Maggie. 'You said she rose quickly through the ranks. Her husband hated her working in an office, knowing she might achieve more than him. He didn't want competition from his wife. That's why he left.'

Bryant was confounded. 'It doesn't say that in my notes.'

'Amelia chose a life of abstract study over one of domesticity and made sacrifices to do it. Loyalty is a demanding master.'

'Maggie, I have no idea what either you or your stoat are on about.'

'Touch the things she touched; see the things she saw. You looked for clues to her killer. Now look for clues to her.'

'How do I do that?' he asked. 'We have nothing left to work with. We can't go anywhere, do anything, talk to anyone. Our hands are tied behind our backs.'

Maggie looked puzzled. 'You still have the keys to her flat, don't you? Why do you think she keeps drawing you back there? It's because that's where the answers lie. Look harder.'

Bryant walked back towards 58 Cruikshank Street, past the Iranian grocery store with its display of mottled bananas like boxers' fists. Past the African shop whose owner spent an hour each morning meticulously arranging plastic bins and baskets outside, only to stack them neatly at the end of each day unsold. Past the barber shop with four empty chairs, its Greek owner pushing his broom across the blue linoleum through a harvest of black hair. He bought a tea in the bright yellow café where everyone was just passing through, their backpacks beneath tables like well-behaved dogs.

He headed up the darkened staircase to the front door, into the hall where lavender spray had failed to disguise the air's staleness. Seated in the armchair beside the sofa where Amelia Hoffman had been placed, he sipped his tea, thinking.

The hand-drawn symbol of the Bridge House had been used as shorthand to mark out papers for inclusion. A sigil that hid its meaning from others.

What else had Hoffman hidden?

She was a polymath: an analyst, a linguist, an artist, a theatre-lover with framed programmes in the bathroom.

She could not let her unwanted house guest find anything, so what could she do to snare the attention of the crime unit where she had started her career? Had she followed their cases?

He examined the shelves again, taking out books and riffling through their pages. Between volumes of bland English landscapes – my God, the British were terrible painters – he spotted a ragged page and found himself looking at a portrait of a startled young man in Tudor dress with his right hand outstretched.

It looked as if Hoffman had torn out the print complete with its overlay.

I know this, he thought. *It's by Hogarth. Richard III waking from his nightmare at the Battle of Bosworth.*

The unit had once investigated a murder at Sir John Soane's Museum, where some of Hogarth's paintings were displayed. Bryant had written about them in an early volume of his memoirs. What if she had read them? Was that why she had torn a page out of an expensive art book? Because she had intended him to find it?

He looked harder.

It was a famous scene: 'A horse! A horse! My kingdom for a horse!' Richard had just seen the ghosts of all his victims and was frankly bricking it.

Bryant peered at the page until his pug nose almost touched it. There was something more. He racked his brain. *You know this*, he told himself. The painting was a trick. It wasn't Richard III at all but David Garrick playing the role. Instead of painting the greatest actor of his day on stage performing, Hogarth had dropped him into the real location of the battle. But Garrick wouldn't have been there at Bosworth. He'd have been in . . . Nothing came up.

He called his partner.

'Where did Garrick perform *Richard III*?'

May took the question in his stride. 'I don't know, maybe the Garrick Theatre? Are you at Hoffman's flat?'

'I can't talk now. I need to see the professor.'

Bryant rang off and fled the apartment with the picture in his hand. As much as he wanted to stay and see if there was anything else Amelia had left for him, he needed to talk to Professor Emilia Cortez.

The professor was as beautiful as only a Spanish woman can be. At this time of the day she could be found helping out in the Science & Biology Bookshop on Euston Road, where she brightened lives just by walking through the anatomy section.

'Yes, of course I know this picture,' she said, stepping out from behind the counter with the colour plate in her hands.

She seated herself on a rattan sofa and patted the seat beside her. 'Please, I have to sit, we've had children in all day. It's Bacteria Week.' She took a closer look at the plate. 'Señor Garrick was very handsome then, no? Twelve years later Hogarth painted him again, still a kind face but getting fat. Too much good living. But Richard III, *muy importante*, the date is the nineteenth of October, 1741. Garrick had never appeared on the stage before, so the theatre said. He took the city by storm.'

'But where is it?' asked Bryant.

'The Hogarth paintings are scattered all around. This one is in Liverpool.'

'What about the theatre? Where did he perform the role?'

'Ah, that was in Goodman's Fields, *muy famoso*, where Dick Turpin shot the man whose horse he stole and renamed Black Bess. It was on a spot where the whores were said to be dog-cheap, half a dozen for half a crown. Long gone. It's a new building now, apartments for the rich, you know, pool, gym, concierge, super secure. Hard little boxes of glass and steel, not my taste, like somewhere to hide, not to live.'

John May collected him on the way. Rita's taxi sped the detectives through Pentonville and Clerkenwell, Shoreditch and the lower part of Hackney, finally arriving in Leman Street. A severe modernist apartment block had been built on the site of the old theatre that had once been considered too remote for the London cognoscenti to visit.

May led the way, smoothing a path through security guards where his partner would only have made them angry. 'There are fourteen flats here,' the concierge explained. 'Who are you looking for?'

Bryant flashed an embassy ID photograph of Larry Cranston and was directed to the rear lower-ground floor. 'We've had trouble with him,' said the concierge, 'smashing things up, drunken shouting after midnight.'

When ringing the doorbell produced no result, the concierge brought out a pass key.

Bryant fancied that Cranston's body would lay sprawled across the sofa with the fingers of his right hand brushing the carpet, looking a little like Henry Wallis's painting of the death of Chatterton. The cushions had absorbed the spills of scarlet, but although a cut-throat razor lay on the floor there was no sign of the man himself.

'Garrick would have injected greater drama into it,' said Bryant, disappointed. 'Where has he gone?'

May followed the blood splashes across the room. There were smears on the door handle; nothing outside in the hall.

'Everything's just been left here. It's like the *Marie Celeste*. His keys are on the counter.' Bryant picked up Cranston's phone. 'Who leaves their walkie-phone behind? It's as if he's been press-ganged.'

'With this level of blood loss he can't have got far,' said May. 'How did he escape again? Maybe we'll never know now.'

'What are you talking about? We can't let them get away with this! Murders, abductions, arson . . . let's see, what else? Stabbings, shootings, hit-and-run – have I left anything out? Do you want to just walk away?'

'What can we do, Arthur? I mean, realistically? We have nothing. They made sure of that.'

'Then that's the end of it.' He threw himself down on the nearest seat. Slumped on the sofa like a deflating lilo, he suddenly looked more tired than May had ever seen him.

'In all the years I've known you, I have never heard the slightest suggestion pass your lips that you might be willing to give in,' he said.

'You're right, times have changed,' said Bryant with steel in his voice. 'We should have bowed out at our peak. I joined the service to help preserve the balance. I thought it was about right and wrong. But it's not. It's all about money.'

'What is?'

'Everything. Information. Loyalty. Principle.'

'Then you and I must prove that it's not,' said May.

44

THE FINAL VISIT

Without unit status, neither Bryant nor May (nor indeed Raymond Land) had any luck in securing further funding. They had no cards left to play.

A second meeting with Paige Henderson was cancelled without being rescheduled. Bryant lodged a formal complaint with the National Crime Agency, who warned him not to interfere but refused to say if they had made any progress. Leslie Faraday no longer returned their calls. The SCC refused to share details of their own investigation. It was death by doing nothing. The British way.

Cranston was thoughtless enough not to have left a signed confession; he might have told them how he had crawled off to die and what he had done with the remains of Angela Carey.

Land had a theory about that: Cranston had not had time to kill her, so he had bundled her off to some deserted spot – there were plenty of building sites at the back of the Elephant & Castle – and had left her there to pass away unnoticed. Searches were presumably ongoing, but the SCC told them nothing.

It seemed to be the tragic fate of these indentured public servants that their loyalty should be so shamefully repaid. Bryant mourned them and blamed himself. It affected him more than any case in recent memory.

John May went to Somerset to interview Cranston's father, adding to the collective humiliation of their family. He went because he now had time on his hands and had not been instructed to stay away. He longed for someone to have the guts to confront him.

The taxi dropped him at the edge of a field. The house, when he found it, was sunken in a sunless vale, set in parkland that distanced it from the world. It was wet of brick and small of window, with mean gables and ginger lichen quilting its grey slate roof: a house to escape from. There was a tang of cow in the air.

Edmund Cranston allowed him no further than an unused damp-smelling room that had been set aside for meetings with lawyers. The old man's most notable feature, apart from his corpulence, was his mouth, loose and wet, vaguely obscene, like a turned-over mollusc. He shared information parsimoniously, as if he was handing out wages to a worker he regretted employing.

'Sir, I'm aware that you were briefed by the Serious Crimes Command,' May began. 'Were they able to provide you with a satisfactory explanation for your son's actions?'

His face was always ready to take offence. 'Satisfactory? What on earth could be satisfactory about anything now?'

'I thought they might have been able to give you some closure.'

'I don't need "closure". One of those ridiculous words with which the young try to protect themselves. You came all this way for nothing.'

'But didn't they—'

'They tried to tell me that Laurence suffered a nervous

breakdown after his accident in Regent's Park, that it caused him to run amok and then commit suicide. If he truly went mad it was because he was naturally weak, just as some children are born deformed.'

'We've been working on the idea that an outside agency was involved.'

'I can't imagine why. My son was given ample opportunity to succeed in life and repeatedly failed. It comes as no surprise to me that he chose the coward's way out.'

'We haven't found his body.'

He gave a grunt. 'And you never will.'

'I don't understand.'

'Of course you don't,' he said tonelessly. 'It was the one thing I taught him. If you fail, don't let anyone see you fall. Die cleanly alone and spare the family. I even showed him how to do it. Why do you think I gave him the razor?'

The door behind them banged open and a pair of golden retrievers galloped in, hurling themselves at the old man. 'Wilberforce, Clive, where have you been?' he cried, finally showing some emotion. 'Look at you, you scallywags, all covered in mud!'

With the arrival of the dogs the meeting came to an end.

Back in town later that day, May passed the former home of the Peculiar Crimes Unit and peered in through the darkened windows. There were no workmen on site. The few sticks of furniture left in the bare rooms were blanching with dust. On the table nearest the window he could see one of Bryant's more trying junk-shop purchases: a South American statue of a child being squeezed to death by a python. Saddened in ways he was not qualified to explain, he quickly moved on.

He sat outside the Ladykillers Café with a coffee, watching Londoners attempting to adjust to the sunny weather. There was no Parisian café atmosphere on the Caledonian Road.

He wondered if things could have gone differently. As a young man he had imagined being old. In his mind's eye he was seated in a wicker chair in the Spanish countryside, nodding beneath the drone of bees. A pipe dream perhaps, but he had never thought he might end up watching homeless people going through bins, just a short distance from where he had been born and worked all his life.

Over the days a routine shaped itself. On Wednesdays and Fridays all unit members met at Bryant's flat in Harrison Street except Raymond Land, who had reluctantly headed back to the Isle of Wight. On Tuesdays they travelled over to May's immaculate minimalist apartment in Shad Thames. Any extracurricular meetings took place at Janice's flat up in Highgate. The gatherings were falsely hopeful and very little was achieved.

When news reached Arthur Bryant's ears that Mrs Hoffman's flat was to be cleared and sold, he decided to go back one last time before they changed the locks.

Sidney had become frustrated and depressed by recent events. Her promising new career in her mother's unit had been terminated by forces she could not comprehend. In their meetings she made a point of studying her mentor. She could see furious clouds behind Bryant's vacant blue eyes, but it was impossible to tell what he was thinking. He was as easily distracted as a five-year-old. His mind was fragmented, yet occasionally he surfaced with some simple thought that stopped her in her tracks. She suspected he was barely listening to the others.

Then, out of the blue, he invited her to accompany him back to 58 Cruikshank Street.

As she walked beside him, she tried not to inhale the exotically perfumed pipe smoke that he had seemingly trained to settle over non-smokers.

The café with the unpronounceable name on the ground

floor had closed its shutters. There was no indication of where its owner, Constantin Yavuz, had gone. The cashier in the newsagent's next door thought he might have been taken ill, because the place had suddenly closed the previous week and no one had been to collect their post, which was piling up behind the glass door.

Struggling to release the keys from his pocket, Bryant scattered sweet wrappers, Post-it notes, a theatre handbill, some string and a lump of plasticine on to the pavement before he managed to get the door open.

The power was off in the flat, so Sidney led the way.

'Feel free to slap your mitts around,' said Bryant. 'The next people to come in here will be estate agents. I suppose we could leave a bear trap in the hall. I have one somewhere.'

'Has Dan made an inventory?' she asked, standing in the centre of the kitchen and turning slowly about herself.

'That's Mr Banbury to you. Yes, I believe he's done so.' Bryant picked some pinned pages from the counter and handed them to her.

One entry immediately caught her eye. 'Paint and paintbrush (wet)'. She looked under the sink, then in the cupboards.

She pulled out the can of pink pint. 'Odd.'

'What?'

'He says there's a wet brush but the can is glued shut.'

'Perhaps it means artist's brushes,' said Bryant. 'Dan said there were some around. She was a polymath.'

They found the box beneath a pile of paperbacks in the hall cupboard. Inside it were half a dozen fine brushes and twenty small tubes of acrylic paint. Sidney opened a tube of Cyan Blue and examined its lid, then checked it against the brushes and the mixing palette.

'They've been used in the last couple of months. Plastic paints dry out fast. These haven't had time to go hard and crack. And one of the brushes is slightly wet at the roots.'

'There are no new paintings.' Bryant returned to the living room. 'She was being watched by Cranston all the time so we know she resorted to leaving clues, like the bridge and the Hogarth. What if there's still something else to be found?'

'Like what?'

'I don't know – something so obvious that I'm overlooking it.'

They searched for over an hour and found nothing. When Bryant finished unsticking some sherbet lemons from their paper bag, he looked up and saw Sidney transfixed in front of the painting of London Bridge.

'Mr Bryant, I see it. It's right here.'

Bryant threw the sweet bag aside and rose. 'What is it?'

Raymond Land came in. 'You're not answering your sodding phone,' he complained. 'Why do I always have to come to you?'

'We're right in the middle of something, Raymondo, you can't just come wandering in here without a pass.'

'I don't have a pass.'

'Then you'll just have to wait outside. Hang on a minute, Sidney.' Bryant eyed his boss in disapproval. 'Why are you here? Is life on the Isle of Wight proving too wildly hedonistic for you? You look like you've been dug up, are you ill?'

'I haven't been sleeping well.' Land scratched the strands of his combover back in place. 'It's the investigation – I hated the way we had to leave it.'

'Ah, good, you do have a conscience. I always said that underneath that thick skin was something more substantial than clogged arteries.'

'Janice told me you were coming here with – hello again, young lady.'

Sidney rolled her eyes. 'I'm non-binary.'

'I've never been good at maths either. How are you getting along?'

She stood beside the epic painting of London Bridge that

covered the chimney breast. 'Mr Land, what do you see?' she asked.

Land took a minute to get over the shock of being consulted. He leaned close and examined the picture minutely. 'Waterloo Bridge,' he announced with certainty.

'It's London Bridge, you josser,'* said Bryant. 'I suppose I can't blame you for getting it wrong. Type "London Bridge" into the Google and all you get are photographs of the more photogenic but utterly bogus Tower Bridge. Mind you, if you google my name you get a picture of Arthur Bryant's BBQ restaurant in Kansas. Don't tell me technology's the future when it can't tell my face from that of a barbecued cow.'

'Have a really good look,' said Sidney with impatience.

Land tried to draw together all of his analytical skills. It made him appear constipated. 'Well, it was painted more than ten years ago because there's no sign of the Shard being built yet.'

'Did you know the Shard was accidentally named by English Heritage?' said Bryant. 'They objected to the design by calling it "a shard of glass through the heart of London" and to their horror the name stuck.'

'What else can you see?' asked Sidney.

'There are some figures on the pavement,' Land said.

'Here, try these.' Bryant handed Raymond his trifocals. The unit chief looped the wire frames around his lugs.

'Good Lord, how can you see anything out of them?'

'Oh, that's just some egg mayonnaise.'

'The lenses are so *thick*. Where did you get them, Jodrell Bank? I don't know what else I'm supposed to be seeing. Can we enlarge it?'

'No, Raymondo, it's a *painting*.'

'But the figures are just blobs.'

'You're not *looking*,' said Sidney. 'Try it from an angle.'

---

* A person in a circus who does not perform.

'Nope,' said Land, 'still not with you.'

'Amelia Hoffman painted something while Cranston was here with her. She added a new detail. Take another look.'

Land squinted again, tilting his head. 'OK. Well, it's London Bridge seen from the north side looking south. It's early morning – the light's coming from the east.'

'Good.'

'There are eleven people on the bridge, indistinct figures.'

'Not exactly T. S. Eliot's hellish vision of enslaved workers,' Bryant pointed out.

'I don't know who that is,' she told him.

Bryant shrugged. 'It's good to be frank about what you don't know. In *The Waste Land*, Eliot wrote: "A crowd flowed over London Bridge . . . each man fixed his eyes before his feet." I have always thought of myself as Eliot's Sybil, who was granted immortality by Apollo but forgot to ask for eternal youth. The Sybil's advice was still sound but when she shrank and grew old everyone stopped listening to her.'

'I literally have no idea what you're talking about,' said Sidney flatly.

'Few people do,' Bryant replied. 'Unnecessary addition of the word "literally" in that sentence, by the way.'

'Do I keep going?' asked Land.

'Yes, for pity's sake,' said Sidney, now exasperated.

He turned his attention back to the picture. 'It's quite a jolly scene. That's about it.'

'Mr Bryant, you tell him.'

'Well, it's set in the past, recent to me, ancient history to you. Look at the bus on the bridge. The adverts on the back are for Heal's furniture store, from sometime around 1968, so she must have painted this from memory. Except . . .'

Readjusting his spectacles, he got closer.

'That can't be right.' He poked his forefinger at a small white streak of paint. 'That thing.'

'What's it meant to be?' asked Land.

'It's a sculpture of some kind, leaning and rather monumental. It certainly wasn't there in 1968.'

Sidney stood to one side and studied the brushwork. 'It's new. It's sitting on top of the existing paint.'

'Why would she add that?' asked Land.

Sidney checked her phone and found a Google Street View of the sculpture. She showed them a tall, tilted spear of stone, blackened by weather at the top. 'The spike was constructed in 1999. It is sixteen metres high and made of light grey Portland stone,' she read out. 'Its official name is the Southwark Gateway Needle. It's a marker tilted at south-west 19.5 degrees. It doesn't say why.'

'Amelia had plenty of time on her hands but no way of communicating her predicament,' said Bryant. 'She was a GCHQ girl to the core. She tried everything she could think of to alert us without drawing Cranston's attention.' He called his taxi service, placing a hand over the phone. 'No sense in wasting time. You'd better go back.'

'I want to come. I can help you,' she insisted.

'If there are any more nasty surprises ahead and you get involved, your mother would make Giles perform an autopsy on me and then kill me, then dig me up and kill me again, only better. You have far too much to lose.' He stopped and studied her. 'Your turn will come. My time is almost past. "Once my world was orderly, now it's chaos, soon my fate will be decided by those too young to understand me" – the Austrian author Stefan Zweig said that. Haven't you read him? Oh, you should. You'll realize that none of this is new, just the ever-turning cycle of the world. We always think we're the last until we hear a baby cry.'

And then he was gone.

Once more she was shut outside the main event, left to watch as John May collected his partner in a taxi and they sped off, into an adventure she could not share. She knew Bryant was right, that she could afford to bide her time. She would prove her worth whatever the cost. Her mother and her grandmother had both done the same.

Soon it would be her turn.

'I'll walk you back to the tube,' said Raymond Land. 'They never take me either.'

45

ARTHUR ON THE BRIDGE

It was one of those overheated afternoons when London's traffic turns into a still life.

Without any work from the PCU, Rita Rondola had been taking run-of-the-mill customers. She had spent the day giving a Chinese family a sightseeing tour around Buckingham Palace, along Birdcage Walk into Belgravia and through the Portland stone corridors of Westminster. When the call came in from Bryant she kicked them out and hurtled back to King's Cross.

'London Bridge was rebuilt in 1971 because its arches were dropping,' Bryant explained, hanging on to the taxi's interior strap as they coasted a corner in Holborn. 'The remains of the medieval structure were left underneath it. There used to be wide stone staircases going down to the water's edge. It must have looked rather Egyptian.'

May barely heard. His partner's interest in the city's history was equalled only by his fascination for murderers. 'What is the point of going to look at this sculpture?' he asked.

'It's the only remaining link to Amelia Hoffman,' Bryant replied. 'I should have realized she was on to Cranston's game.

You don't spend all that time working on official secrets without learning how to protect yourself, especially from an idiot. I've been looking at the problem from the wrong angle. They were all so much stronger than they appeared. They used the assumptions of others about their age as weapons against them.'

'Really, Arthur, I don't see how.' May found something to hang on to as Rita drove over a kerb. A young woman darted across the road and was nearly flattened.

'Bloody sod streetwalkers!' Rita shouted, turning back to Bryant. 'I am learning to swear like British cabbie, yes?'

'I'm closing the partition now,' said Bryant. 'People don't change, John. Hoffman was just as feisty in her later years. Wynn-Jones, devious, secretive and defensive. Carey, patriotic and devoid of sympathy.'

'You got all that from them?'

Bryant looked surprised. 'Didn't you? I'm going to attempt a tortuous analogy. When London Bridge still had houses it looked less like a bridge than a shopping street. By the time you walked down Fish Street Hill and reached Wren's clock tower at the bottom you were already crossing the Thames. It's all about appearances, don't you see? A bridge that doesn't look like a bridge.'

No, thought May, *I don't see at all but I'm not about to tell you that.*

They alighted at the southern end of London Bridge, beside the tall stone spike that should have been aggressively thrusting itself into the sky. Only it wasn't. Four workmen in yellow safety vests were standing around with pickaxes and two-thirds of the spike had been dismantled, leaving only the base.

'Hairline cracks,' said one of the workmen. 'From heavy traffic. Don't worry, squire, the bits are numbered. They're going back up tomorrow.'

Bryant ducked back into the taxi. 'I thought the spike

commemorated the spot where executed traitors' heads were displayed,' he told May, 'but the base line points across the river to the building next to the bridge. Amelia couldn't indicate it in the picture because it had been painted from the other bank.'

'Don't tell me you looked that up online,' said May.

'Don't be ridiculous.' Bryant pulled a tattered blue book from his pocket. '*Jackson's Pocket Guide to London Sculptures*, the revised edition, obviously.'

'Get in,' said Rita. 'There is a car in my bottom.'

She ran them back to the north side and dropped them in a dark corner of Lower Thames Street. 'A bad area, this,' she said disapprovingly. 'Dark alleys like at home, full of ghosts. I'll wait for you up the road in the light.'

'It's perfectly safe,' said Bryant. 'There's no one around.'

'The spirits from the river,' Rita told him. 'Many people died under this bridge. There was nowhere for their souls to go.'

'Has she met Maggie Armitage?' asked May.

'No, I don't believe so,' Bryant answered.

'Good, let's keep it that way,' May decided. 'Rita, how do you know this?'

'Saw it in a documentary,' she intoned very seriously. 'Also, scary one on penguins.' She roared away, leaving them on the pavement.

The detectives found themselves in a cleft between buildings. The tall iron gate before them was so narrowly propped open that they had to hold their breath to get inside.

They made their way across a deeply shaded flagstone courtyard lined with mature plane trees, almost invisible between two grey stone edifices.

On one side was a granite partition that stood at the foot of London Bridge. On the other was the church of St Magnus the Martyr, its entrance barely discernible. The few who passed the churchyard gates rarely thought to look inside.

The church door stood ajar. Bryant pushed it further open with his walking stick. They stepped into deep shadows, making their way across the nave. The temperature fell by several degrees. The walls beneath the stained-glass roundels were lined with colourful plaques, epitaphs and decorative bas-reliefs, but a sensation of settling melancholy was palpable.

Bryant recognized the elegant woman behind the postcard counter. She was far too radiant to be subdued by a deserted city church. Elizabeth Montague, last seen at the Institute of Historic London Studies, greeted him with delight.

'Mr Bryant, how nice to see you again. Did you know I'd be here? I help them out once a week, not that there's much to do. I haven't had a single customer this afternoon. How did your investigation go?'

'It's led us to this church. Perhaps we could enlist your services.'

She came round from behind the counter. 'I can try. This is my favourite London church.'

'What's so special about it?'

'It has endured despite being in the way of everything.' Elizabeth led them between the pews. 'They still hold an annual fire sermon here. St Magnus was destroyed in the Great Fire of 1666 – it's only three hundred yards from where the conflagration started. It was rebuilt by Sir Christopher Wren.'

'So the lives of the bridge and the church are intertwined,' Bryant said, stopping to study an epitaph.

'It was always at the centre of things, a gathering place where proclamations were read out and wrongdoers were punished. People had a habit of falling off the bridge or being crushed by horses, and when they did they were always brought here. It's one of London's better-kept secrets. We don't get many visitors.'

'I'm not surprised. It's bloody dark in here, as if we're dug into the ground.'

She pointed up into the shadowed eaves. 'The only part that can be seen from outside is the great tower. When people couldn't pass they dug a walkway underneath it, and to stifle the noise and stink of the fish market they blocked up the windows. It's been attached to the bridge for a thousand years. There's a chunk of the original Roman bridge out in the courtyard that's dated 75 CE. You could write a dozen books on this little corner's turbulent history.'

May bit his tongue, determined to show patience. Every element of the case had been eradicated, yet Arthur was still digging around the edges of it, as if it was a long-term archaeological project he could take up as a hobby. They passed an immense, incongruous statue of a Viking, his axe resting by his boots.

'Many Norsemen arrived here and raised families,' Elizabeth explained. 'St Clement Danes was the centre of the Danish settlement.'

May walked further down the apse. His partner's attention was forever being diverted. He could hear Elizabeth reciting bits of history as Bryant listened eagerly. *I am trapped*, he thought. *While Arthur potters about, everything has gone to hell.*

It was hard to avoid listening to Elizabeth. Her voice was soft and mellifluous.

'It's an oasis of calm in here now, but St Magnus was never a peaceful church for long. It's too deeply embedded in the heart of city life. And there were darker tales told.'

'What sort of tales?' asked Bryant, brightening. More irritated than ever, May carried on circling the aisles of the church.

Elizabeth raised her hand to the river-facing wall and let her palm rest on the cool stones. 'Women were drowned here. In the year 963 a witch was weighted down and thrown into the river for possessing a nail-studded effigy. It's said that the nursery rhyme refers to the burial alive of children in the foundations of the bridge. The structure would fall unless a living soul was interred in its foundations.'

'I take it there's no archaeological evidence for that?'

'On the contrary. In 2009 they dug out the network of tunnels underneath and found many bodies of plague victims. They don't know what else is down there.'

May's walk had brought him to a lengthy plexiglass case set up on wooden trestles in the apse. 'What's this?' he called back to the others.

The scale model showed London Bridge as it would have appeared in 1400. It was around fifteen feet long and incredibly detailed, a personal labour of love.

'We're rather proud of that,' said Elizabeth. She leaned over the model, tapping the plastic cover. 'It was created by a liveryman of the Worshipful Company of Plumbers. He hand-painted over nine hundred figures following King Henry V's horse.'

'There's one figure in modern dress,' said Bryant, pointing to a tiny male figurine. 'I think he's a paraffin.' Elizabeth's blank look pulled him up. 'A paraffin lamp. A tramp. What's he doing in there?'

'I've never noticed him before.'

'Look at the way he's standing,' said May. 'He's guarding the bridge. And he's in modern dress because he's still guarding it.'

'There's something . . .' Bryant tapped the air. 'Can we open it and have a look?'

'Before you go smashing up an antique,' said Elizabeth, 'the Cardinal Rector told me that the case has remained closed for over twenty years.'

'I won't damage anything, I assure you,' said Bryant unconvincingly. 'I have my Swiss Army knife.' Producing it, he selected an appropriate blade and unscrewed the aluminium rivets holding sections of the lid in place. Elizabeth winced and looked around guiltily.

'Here, hold this.' He handed May the lid and studied the tiny squat figure in its long scarf and baggy raincoat more closely. 'Keep a lookout.'

Bryant reached inside the case. The figurine came away with a crack. Turning it over in his fat little fingers, he held it in the ruby shaft of light that fell from the stained-glass windows.

He was looking at a miniature version of himself, perfectly detailed, right down to the homburg.

'It's me,' he said softly as the truth dawned. 'Of course it's me. Now it all makes sense.'

46

SHOOTING AT THE RAPIDS

Bryant grabbed at his partner's lapel. As May was somewhat taller than him, this was an awkward move. 'You are teamed with a dunderhead. I should have listened to you from the outset. Understand people's character and you understand the crime. Maggie told me as well, but did I listen?'

'Can you explain yourself a little more clearly?' May asked.

'We've walked into a trap,' said Bryant. 'Elizabeth, may I ask you to stay inside until you're sure we've gone? For your own safety, you understand.'

He pulled May out of the church and into the sheltered courtyard. The blackened stanchion of the Roman bridge had been tethered upright against a wall, its ancient timber stranded in the present like an unexorcized ghost. At its base was an iron drainage cover, recessed into the surrounding stonework without bolts or screws to hold it in place.

Bryant reached down and stuck his fingers through the spaces in the drain lid, and pulled.

Beneath was a stone culvert tall enough for a young boy to

stand in. 'John, would you do the honours?' he asked. 'My back.'

May lay flat on his stomach and lowered his arm into the hole. He shone his phone beneath the drain. 'I can see five, no, six folders in plastic bags – there are more further on.'

Bryant helped May up. 'Leave everything where it is. We're not safe here,' he warned. 'I fell for it, every last bit of it.'

As they were watching, a piece of the Roman piling chipped off and lazily dropped on to the flagstones. The detectives looked at one another in puzzlement.

Nearby, a blue-tiled wall plaque read: 'This Churchyard formed part of the roadway approach to Old London Bridge 1176–1831'. Suddenly a diagonal crack appeared in the ceramic. A circular section the size of an old penny fell out of it.

As May tried to understand what was happening, he saw puffs of grey grit appear across the floor of the yard, one, two, three in a row.

Someone was shooting at his partner. Bryant's left boot burst open at the toecap.

May pulled him down as carefully as he could.

'Mind my knees,' Bryant cried.

'It's coming from there.' May pointed through the foliage of the courtyard trees. 'There's someone on the lower level of the bridge.'

'Thank goodness, a silencer, I thought I was going deaf.' Bryant watched in amazement as the paving stone at his feet sparkled and a splinter flew away from his walking stick. 'Not that anyone can hear anything down here with the traffic on the bridge. Nobody else can see us. The offices are all empty.' He glanced down at his partially exploded boot. 'Bugger, I've just had these resoled.'

May tried to follow the dark form but the branches of plane trees blocked his view.

'The security camera network must have been tapped into

all this time,' Bryant muttered. 'That's the only way it's possible. We were watched right from the start.'

'Arthur, did you have any idea about this?'

'I had my suspicions.'

'It would have helped if you'd told me. At least I would have been able to warn someone.'

Bryant peered around the side of a tree, then quickly withdrew. 'I sent the others a little marker-thingy from my telephone telling them where we were going. That's if it worked. I'm not really sure I pressed the right button. We need a decoy, someone to take the flak. If only we'd brought Raymondo with us.'

Another shot took a neat triangular chunk out of the church wall. 'This is a venerable church. For God's sake, show a little respect! Somebody needs target practice. Probably can't see very well through the trees, or needs new glasses. At least I know it's over now.'

'What are you talking about?'

Bryant turned to study his partner. 'I'm the last one, you see. The top of the list. It would be a good idea to make sure I remain alive because nobody else knows what really happened.'

May could think of a few more reasons to keep his partner alive, but right now he was more interested in getting Arthur out without being fired upon again.

'Wait, is that what I think it is?'

Bryant pointed to a bright red dot that travelled across the stonework until it reached his sleeve. May snatched his arm away as another brick exploded.

'That's more accurate. Although a laser sight seems like cheating.'

The church door had swung shut behind them. May could hardly head back there to stand exposed while he fumbled with the latch. Nor could they make for the archway that led back to the bridge. It would mean running twenty yards across the courtyard without cover, and Bryant was slow at the best of times.

'Go back inside the church,' May instructed. 'You'll be safe in there.'

'And leave you out here?' said Bryant. 'That's not how we do things. We're a team.' Another round bit a chunk of bark from a plane tree just in front of him.

'I just don't want us to be a team like Butch Cassidy and the Sundance Kid.' May raised his arm and ducked low.

'I don't know,' Bryant mused, 'I've always thought of myself as the Robert Redford type.'

Through the archway May saw Rita pull up in her taxi. She looked over at them and called May's number. 'Are you two going to be all day?'

'Rita, stay back, you're not safe here,' he whispered into his phone as a branch came down in a spray of leaves.

'How many bullets are in that thing?' asked Bryant. 'Are we supposed to know? Aren't you meant to count them or something?'

'I have seen guns,' said Rita. 'Is no big deal, just men being bad. You want me to come over?'

'No!' said May. 'You need to find Colin. He should be near by now.'

They heard the sound of a rifle reloading.

Colin Bimsley had never harboured any illusions about himself. He would never win Brain of Britain but he was stout-hearted, decisive, intuitive and . . . he couldn't remember the other thing. Good at running, that was it.

So when Mr Bryant's marker had pinged on his phone and he realized he could easily reach London Bridge on foot from the cop shop in Snow Hill, where he had been collecting interview notes from a colleague, he'd taken off like a firework, fizzing along High Holborn, maintaining a powerful pace past St Paul's, over Ludgate Hill, down the stairs and through the stalled traffic on Cannon Street, around the Monument into Lower Thames Street.

Instead of entering through the courtyard to the church as the detectives would have done, he hurled himself up the staircase to London Bridge and looked down.

There he saw an extraordinary sight.

The detectives were caught in what appeared to be an extremely one-sided gun battle with a sniper taking aim from behind the courtyard wall. Judging by the pocked flagstones around the kneeling body of Mr Bryant, his boss was in imminent danger of being ventilated. Colin looked around for anything he could use as a weapon, but the bridge had no debris of any kind.

'Hello, I say are you Mr Blimey or not?' Rita called from her cab window.

Bryant's description of him proved unenlightening: 'He's roughly the size and shape of the Wicker Man, but with a squarer head.' Luckily Rita had seen him before, in the café next to the unit.

'Bimsley,' Colin corrected. She waved him over.

'You don't happen to have a gun on you, by any chance?' asked Bryant. Although he had illegally tested out weapons in the office, nobody at the PCU had ever been cleared to carry firearms. 'There could be an entire arsenal aimed at us. The CIA probably hand assault rifles out like chocolates.'

He dared to raise his head through the leaves once more but could see nothing.

'I can't believe you're taking this so calmly.' The red dot reappeared and a fresh volley peppered the wall above May's head. 'You should be in fear of your life.'

'Why? I've had my life and it was pretty good except for the bad bits. When I leave this world I should remember to add a tip.' He squinted through the leaves to the source of the gunfire. 'I can see something. A balaclava. In summer? Wait, I have an idea.'

Bryant dragged over a piece of branch, took off his homburg and dropped it on the end. Reaching out as far as he dared, he waved the branch at arm's length. Nothing happened. 'That's odd. No response.'

'Of course not,' said May. 'Anyone can see it's you waving a hat on a stick.'

'So let's think. How do we get out of this?' Bryant examined the bullet hole in his overcoat. 'Sooner or later our luck will run out.'

'We just have to cross the courtyard,' said May.

'How are we going to do that?'

'I'll buy you the time to make it to the other side. If I get taken down, you can have my Francis Bacon sketch.'

'I'd rather not, if you don't mind.'

May braced himself. Another round spaffed the concrete inches from his right foot. A branch came down in a spray of wood splinters, giving the shooter a clearer view of the target.

'I really don't think you should try to make a run for it,' said Bryant. 'You've never been able to move well at speed. I remember the first time I saw you run, 1968, Camden Town. You went after the thief who snatched your man-bag. It was embarrassing.'

'I was wearing wood-soled sandals. They were fashionable then. It's now or never.'

May decided to ignore his partner's entreaties and set off at a sprint, but his speed was not as great as he'd hoped. An errant muscle in his right thigh refused to unbunch itself.

From behind a projection in the churchyard wall came a clatter as a rifle was thrown aside and replaced with some other metallic-sounding firearm.

'What else do they have back there?' asked Bryant. 'A ground-to-air missile launcher?'

Something that looked like a matt grey can of Coke rolled across the flagstones and began to leak smoke. Bryant covered his mouth and nose with his scarf. The tree trunk behind him exploded in a shower of bark shards and shredded leaves.

'It feels like the unit's last stand, doesn't it?' he said. 'We've spent our lives fighting state control. History is not on our side.'

May saw the figure on the wall taking aim and knew that he had to get ahead of the next blast. When he tried to shift himself his right leg seized up.

This is it, he thought, *the end of a beautiful career. At least I've been shot before, so I know what to expect.*

He was caught halfway between Bryant and the archway, unable to move in either direction.

He recognized the warning vibration in his thigh. His leg gave way and he fell sprawling on to the flagstones. A shot passed so close to his skull that it lifted his silver hair. There was no way of reaching the archway now. Rita had not returned. They were alone.

Ten seconds turned to twenty. He glanced back at Arthur, on all fours and surrounded by debris. He squeezed his eyes shut and prepared for the worst.

Instead of a discharged round, there was an odd chunking noise followed by complete silence.

He tried clambering to his feet but a painful tingle zig-zagged through his thigh. He was still squirming on the stones when a hand reached down. Rita's formative years had been spent lifting sacks of coal on to a cart. She grabbed May and lifted him up, dragging him to her idling taxi.

A few moments later Bryant dropped in beside him. 'You're still with us, then. Next time will you follow my instructions?'

'What happened?' May asked, wincing as Rita lifted his leg inside the cab.

'Colin acted entirely without our authority,' said Bryant. 'There's hope for him yet.'

Rita drove them on to the bridge, where Bimsley was now surrounded by half a dozen anti-terrorist officers who had pinned him on to the kerb. A few more were standing at the back touching their guns, trying to look as though they were also involved. Two squad cars and an immense ARV had sealed off the bridge. Overhead a helicopter arrived. The first camera crews were no doubt scampering towards the scene.

'He's with us,' Bryant shouted, holding up his bus pass. 'Colin, what did you do?' He reached the wall and leaned over. The figure below them had been felled with a geometric chunk of Portland stone.

'I dropped a bit of London Bridge on him,' Colin grunted up from the pavement.

The sniper lay unconscious on the flagstones below. In a black sweater, trainers and jeans it looked like a child's action figure cast aside now that playtime was over.

One of the officers pulled at the balaclava until it came loose.

The stone pinnacle of the dismantled spike had caught Amelia Hoffman on the shoulder and knocked her from the wall.

No report of the shoot-out made it to the national press. In the stunned silence that followed the event, the detectives vanished. Even Niven at the Ladykillers Café proved unbribable.

Two days after, Raymond Land was summoned to the Home Office, where he was kept waiting for an hour and a half in a small glass holding pen before Fatima Hamadani hurried in to find him.

'I'm sorry about the delay,' she said, beckoning him. 'Things are very busy at the moment and Mr Faraday is in a terrible mood.'

'How can you tell?' Land asked.

'Oh, trust me, you'll know.' She opened the door to Faraday's office and ushered him into a room of unremitting drabness. On the sideboard, police awards and generic golf trophies were arrayed beneath three prints (*Harbour Boats*, *Thanet at Sunset* and *Seagulls, Broadstairs*).

The police liaison officer was waiting behind a pine-veneered desk and clearly meant business; there were teacups but no biscuits. He affected an attitude of nonchalance, tipping his chair back and balancing his feet on the edge of his waste-paper basket. Land noticed that his soles were of shiny yellow leather, unsullied by toil.

'Raymond, I just want to know where they are,' he told the ceiling nonchalantly.

'It's not my business to keep tabs on my detectives any more, Leslie. They're not on the payroll.'

'Somebody told me they've left the country. Is that true?'

'I'm sure you can find out. I couldn't.' Land was through listening to Faraday. He had no reason to be polite any more.

Faraday turned to his assistant. 'Fatima, I thought you said you spoke to them about this.'

'They've gone away for a couple of days,' Land said. 'It's private business.'

Faraday unwrapped a mint-flavoured antacid and crunched it. 'I heard several of your former staff members have been seen in the Caledonian Road. What does it take to keep you all away from the unit? The building is no longer leased to you.'

'It's a free country; they can walk where they please,' said Land. 'You took everything from us – what more do you want? My staff are still waiting to find out whether they've been assigned new positions.'

'Fatima, you were supposed to tell them.'

'You didn't ask me—' Fatima began.

'They're not being reassigned,' said Faraday, wincing as he dug out another tablet. 'There are no positions currently available.'

'What, for *any* of them?'

'Letters should have gone out. The lease has been sold. The Met doesn't want you. All I need to make life easier for all of us is for you to sign this. Fatima, do you have the letter?'

'I sent it to you, Leslie. It can be signed online.'

'You know I don't like that. You can never tell where it might end up.'

Fully prepared for this, Fatima brought forth a single typed page and a pen. Faraday cringed as she came close. 'I do wish you wouldn't wear that sari thing. What's wrong with a nice British-made blouse? Can I have a fresh cup of tea?'

He pushed the page towards Land. 'It's just a formality but you should read it first.'

Land scanned the paragraphs before him. No amount of baroque legal terminology could disguise the letter's demand; it was a cease-and-desist order. ' "If the above conditions are met no further action will be taken against you," ' Land read out. 'So, provided we don't seek re-employment in any part of the national police service, the Home Office won't pursue us in court for – what are these "reparations"?'

'The cost of fixing legal irregularities.' Faraday looked in vain for a teaspoon. 'I'd say you got off lightly.'

'Incredible. I've spent the last few years putting up with the pure hell of Bryant and May.' Land shook his head at the wonder of it all. 'And I was only able to do it because I was working with you.'

'That's very reassuring to hear.' Faraday was forced to stir his tea with his pencil.

'You see, working with you made me realize how much I actually enjoyed working with them.' He tried to keep the emotional quaver from his voice. 'They're opinionated and impossible, but you . . . Mr Faraday, you represent everything about this nation that's mediocre. You're a modern office block, a salad in a cardboard box. My detectives make bad decisions and admittedly do a fair amount of damage along the way but they're a force for good.'

Faraday gave a laugh of disbelief. 'How can you say that after the way they humiliated you?'

Raymond felt his face heating. 'They're allowed to make fun of me. They've earned the right. If it wasn't for them I'd have wasted away in a dead-end job, hating everyone in that special English way where you pretend to like them while they're in the room. I used to try and make sense of your ridiculous briefs and mission statements. I told myself you should never write off a fellow just because he's never had a sensible idea before. But you never think about the men and women who've abandoned their normal lives to keep you protected. The idea is as alien to you as being Egyptian. It must be awful waking up every day and realizing you're you.'

'Look here, steady on,' said Faraday, his half-visible smile of triumph fading. 'I know things can't have been easy lately.'

'Easy? You sit there behind your laminated pine play-fort while the frontline services collapse about you and every disastrous government decision mires the country deeper and deeper in the *merde* and you can't even decide which biscuit to have with your tea. You couldn't be more useless if you were coated in treacle.'

The whites of Faraday's knuckles showed. 'I will not be spoken to like this,' he snapped. 'You seem to forget that we pay your wages.'

'Not any more you don't. I'm free of you.'

'The meeting's over,' said Faraday. 'I have far more important matters to attend to. I'm due at a photocall in a children's ward.'

'I hope you get measles.' Land rose to his feet and found his calves quivering with anger.

As he walked from the room, Fatima followed him out and shyly touched his arm. 'Do you have a minute?' she asked quietly. 'Thank you for what you said. I am Egyptian.'

47

THE ZIPPO

It was raining bullets in New York City.

The taxi driver misunderstood their instructions and took them to a completely different part of town. He was Indian and from the Bronx and they were British and jet-lagged, and as communication between them disintegrated over the pronunciation of a hotel name he finally pulled the cab over on Riverside Drive, half an hour from where they were supposed to be, and jumped out, storming around and shouting at the electric sky, punching at a wire fence that quivered and zinged before he climbed back in and took them to the right hotel.

When they disembarked he leaned over and apologized. 'My family is living in a roach-infested dump and I'm not making enough money in this job no matter how many hours I pull down. I'm drowning, man. This city is killing me. Killing me! Hey, do I still get a tip?'

After the bad start things got better.

'The last time I came to Manhattan was in 1974 or thereabouts. There were still empty lots downtown where homeless people gathered around burning oil drums. When they tore down the projects there were parts of the city that looked like they'd been bombed out by the Luftwaffe.'

This was Arthur Bryant at the corner of Mulberry Street near Broome Street, where a blue neon sign welcomed visitors to Little Italy, even though there were no Italians to be seen. It was just before seven in the evening and diners had settled beneath narrow green awnings for plates of spaghetti.

'There were ten thousand Italians living here in 1910.' Bryant waved his arm at the bright red buildings opposite.

'I didn't know New York was one of your subjects,' said May, looking for the address they needed.

'Everything interesting is worthy of being a subject. It was the ground-level detail that fascinated me at first. The colours of old Manhattan: faded reds and browns, interiors painted a dingy shade of ochre peculiar to the city. Those little iron hoops that bordered all the trees. Racks of vegetables sprayed with water. Basketball courts on the street. Smelly subway gratings through which you could hear the distant thunder of trains. Vending machines chained to the ground, but trusting you enough to take just one newspaper. When I first came here as a young man I thought it was the grandest city of the twentieth century. Now it looks like America's *Vieux Carré*, frozen at some point after the Chrysler and the Empire State Buildings were erected. A living Astaire and Rogers film. It's finally grown into its future. We can't afford to live here but at least we can come and see. I like the rogue elements best. I remember buying a suitcase in Times Square from a shop that sold guns, ammunition and statues of the Virgin Mary.'

They skirted around two Slavic taxi drivers shouting at each other. Bryant failed to notice them. 'I ask you, what other city could have a shore called "Dead Horse Bay", named after all the bones that washed up on it from horse-rendering plants?' He was fairly exploding with enthusiasm.

May knew that his partner's passion was not just for

London. He was curious about everything he ever encountered. Most people found it too exhausting to maintain such a level of enthusiasm, but it was the motor that kept Bryant alive.

'Did you know they used to have firefighter shows at Coney Island? One hundred and fifty firefighters racing up a fake six-storey building while the residents jumped out of windows. Can you imagine? Such showmanship! Of course, later the artifice was mirrored in appalling real-life tragedies. In a way, New York lost every bit as much as London. But look at it! It's still here, still strong, and it thrills my hard old heart.'

May patiently waited for his partner to get it out of his system, but Bryant's excitement was not dimmed. He stood in the middle of the road looking up at the buildings and shouting back historical facts while drivers swore and swerved around him.

'You know what I'd like to have seen? The elevated trains, the Hippodrome, the Astor Hotel, the Vanderbilt mansion. Automats, trolleybuses, pushcart markets, the naval yards – all gone! So much lost. A ghost city imprinted over the corporeal one, rising to the stars.'

'Come to the pavement, old chap, let's get you inside,' said May, taking his arm.

Tony's was not the kind of restaurant that made the press. No celebrities dined there and the food was not special enough to warrant critic approval, but its survival was to be celebrated. The floor was laid with black and white tiles, the walls lined with dark wood. Tables were set in crimson leather booths and had red and white checked cloths and low brass lamps with green glass shades.

Bryant clapped his hands together joyfully. 'It's like a Martin Scorsese film. I adore it.'

'You're not meant to be adoring it,' said May, bringing him back to earth. 'We're here on very serious business.'

The CIA man, Benjamin Alvarez, had chosen the restaurant. He was already seated in a corner booth with an old-fashioned bottle of Coca-Cola and looked up as they approached. When he saw Bryant he tried to avoid a spit take. The guy looked like a testicle in a hat.

He shook their hands with grave formality. To speed things up, he ordered for them. The meeting would not take long.

'I was kind of surprised when you called,' Alvarez admitted. 'I don't think any of us knew how far this thing would go.'

'It was very decent of you to pay for our flights,' said Bryant amiably.

'We don't keep our country safe by being decent, Mr Bryant. We want something from you. This whole thing's in the crapper and we need a way out. We know you no longer have authority but you have knowledge.'

The waitress brought mountains of food. Alvarez rolled pasta around his fork, then disconcertingly took a swig of cola. Of all the evening's revelations, the one that disturbed Bryant most was seeing the CIA agent drink Coke with spaghetti.

'Which brings us to the London Bridge papers.' Bryant tapped the side of his pug nose. 'It's a pity you never got to see them. I understand Paige Henderson decided they were worthless to you.'

'That wasn't her call to make. She will face disciplinary action.'

'At least we managed to remember to bring the papers with us, unlike Sir Arthur Sullivan.' His chuckle stalled when he saw Alvarez staring at him peculiarly.

The agent talked with his mouth full. 'Is he someone on your team?'

'Gosh no, he died in 1900. He was bringing *The Pirates of Penzance* to New York when he realized he'd left the music for the first act back in England. It was a jocular comparison. A joke.'

'I forgot. You British think ancient history is recent.'

'It can't be helped. My local pub is several centuries older than your nation.' Bryant flicked tomato sauce over his shirt and partway up a framed photograph of Al Capone.

'You say that like it's a good thing.' Alvarez speared a meatball.

'It is, isn't it? The deeper the foundations, the stronger the building.'

'You sold off your building to the highest bidder a long time ago.'

May could see that any minute now his partner would achieve the impossible and offend a CIA agent. He tried to head the conversation off.

'We spoke to Paige Henderson, Mr Alvarez, but she stopped communicating with us.'

'If she's not talking to you it's because she doesn't want to,' Alvarez replied. 'You have no status any more. Her report is restricted and has been sealed. It touches on some contentious issues that could damage what's left of the relationship between our two countries.'

'That's a pity,' said May. 'We were hoping for a bit of quid pro quo: our report for yours.'

'We already know what's in yours.' Alvarez bit the meatball in two and let the other half drop back into his spaghetti. He looked like an alligator chewing a baby chick.

'Then perhaps you can help us with information on public record. Did you know about the papers?'

'We knew they existed. We didn't know how to get to them.'

'So you let us lead the way.'

Alvarez dabbed bloody sauce from his lips and leaned close. 'You know how a Zippo works? You use your thumb to open the top, then to strike the flint wheel and light the wick. It's not easy. If you give a Zippo to a baby it might be able to get the top open, but it wouldn't have the strength to strike the flint. Yet there's always a chance, one in a million, that the baby might manage it. That's why we've been concerned about you guys. You had a highly incendiary object in your hands and we wanted to trust you with it, we really did, but there was always a chance you would burn everyone's asses.'

'You think I didn't know what I was dealing with?' asked Bryant hotly. 'Why, the whole thing was our—'

May hastily cut him off with the sudden pressure of a hand on his shoulder. 'I think what we're both wondering is, would you have allowed Larry Cranston to be extradited?'

Alvarez gave a mirthless chuckle. 'Never in a million years. You don't blackmail the CIA.'

'Nine British citizens died in the course of your investigation.'

'Mr Bryant, we had no hand in the postulated causation of their deaths, as you well know.'

'*Postulated causation.* Perhaps you could have *burglarized* us for the papers, like Watergate.' Bryant left four-fifths of his spaghetti and turned helplessly to his partner. 'It's no use, we don't speak the same language.'

'How you fellas doing here?' asked a delightful waitress in a white apron and tennis shoes.

'How are we doing what?' asked Bryant.

'I'm guessing you're gonna want the apple pie.'

'Wouldn't it be easier just to ask us?' The woman was clearly mad.

'It's the best apple pie in the city.'

'Madam, I have just tried to consume a portion of spaghetti clearly intended to feed a family of six. What on earth makes you think I could eat a pie?'

She waved a friendly finger at him. 'Are you British? Would you like me to get you some tea?'

'Not if it comes in a glass with the string hanging over the side of it like a tampon, no thank you.'

'Let me make this simple for you,' said Alvarez as soon as

the waitress had beaten a retreat. 'Henderson's report is incomplete. I need to fill in the blanks.'

Bryant caught May's eye. He could tell that May did not want him to speak. He decided to speak.

'If you want I can tell you the whole story.'

Alvarez studied each of them in turn, then called to the waitress. 'Get us all some pie,' he said.

'First I want you to bear in mind two irrefutable facts,' Bryant said. 'Larry Cranston was not a murderer. And Amelia Hoffman is not a sweet little old lady.'

'OK.' Alvarez checked his watch. He was prepared to suspend his disbelief while the crazy old Brit spun him a fairy tale.

Bryant set before him salt, ketchup and mustard sachets. 'Once upon a time there were three women united by the old-fashioned concept of duty. They worked in something we now call . . . I've forgotten it.'

'Diplomatic cryptosystems,' May prompted.

'Yes, that. Angela Carey was the most senior member of the group. After she retired she remained loyal to the Crown and continued to protect the details of vulnerable informants: the ones who knew too much and could be compromised. It seems it was my idea to hire them.'

'What do you mean, it *seems* it was your idea?'

'I really don't remember how it started. Back then we were coming up with fresh ideas every day. If it didn't cost much and got results, it was implemented. Amelia obeyed her boss's orders and later shared the task with other loyal women who put the safety of the nation above their own wellbeing.'

He moved the condiments about, adding a sachet of sweetener. 'Let's start here, when Amelia came up with the idea of swapping identities with Angela.'

The morning was blue-skied and luminous. Blinding sunlight flooded through the windows, so that even the dust looked exotic. Amelia Hoffman sat with her hands folded in her lap, legs crossed at the ankle, her greying hair neatly brushed, a picture of composure. She had been kept in hospital overnight and had only been released into their care because no one else had a handle on the case. She was still dressed in the scruffy black jeans and sweatshirt she had worn at St Magnus the Martyr.

'A blend of truth and lies,' Bryant had warned his partner, 'that's all she'll give us. Add fiction to the facts, stir them together and form an alternative narrative. It's what they were taught to do.'

Amelia barely acknowledged their presence. She spoke with such clarity and sincerity that it was hard to imagine any of it was false.

'Angela was the oldest, of course. She briefly worked for you at the unit, Mr Bryant, not that you could accurately recall her. It was her idea to switch identities with me. It helped to protect the London Bridge papers and suited us both to do so. In our old jobs codenames, subterfuge and identity changes were such an everyday occurrence that we thought very little of them. There was no such thing as electronic tracing, so it was easy. She just had to retype our files. Neither of us had stayed in contact with our families or had any close friends from the past. My poor lost grandson Edgar was the only person who visited, and he hadn't seen me in years. He thought all old people look the same. When he saw Angela he accepted her as me.

'In 2001 the London Bridge papers were locked away for good. We celebrated the successful discharge of our duties to the State. Nobody remembered who we had been. Then Larry Cranston paid a visit to the flat in King's Cross.

'By this time Angela was older and more infirm than either Annie or I properly realized. Cranston made himself useful and probed her about the files. She saw right through him – how could she not? At first she thought he would be easy to get rid of, but as the days passed I think she came to understand just how determined he was. She didn't know that he planned to use her as his way of escaping the country. But she did know he was going through her things. She couldn't let him locate the papers. It frightened her to think where they might eventually end up. Cranston watched her all the time. I wanted to help but she was determined to handle it on her own.'

Amelia Hoffman barely moved a muscle. There was nothing about her that gave Bryant any clue to her emotional state. He wondered if perhaps she had always had her own agenda. In the course of a lifetime she had learned to close herself off so completely that no one would ever truly know the truth about her.

Hoffman sipped a glass of water. 'Angela fought back against him, of course, but covertly. She left clues that she knew he was too stupid to spot. Then she simply stopped eating. It was an act of supreme willpower. She'd done living. She took her information to the grave.'

'Your apple pie,' the waitress announced, toting three vast beige segments. Bryant harrumphed but allowed one to be set before him. 'And how about a slice of our famous key lime pie, on the house?' She set before him a quivering slab of emerald jelly topped with meringue.

'Where did you get this, Roswell?' asked Bryant. 'It looks radioactive.' He gave it a tentative taste, winced at the sweetness and turned back to Alvarez. 'Angela Carey allowed herself to waste away, thinking she had left Cranston with nothing. She carried out her duty to the end. The papers could be forgotten and left to become irrelevant.

'But I think her younger friend Amelia changed in the interim years. We know that GCHQ sent her out as a security consultant, first to the Middle East, then to Africa. When she returned to England her attitude had altered. We have proof of this because she was required to undergo an annual psych evaluation. It's virtually the only document we've been able to locate on her. She came to regard those named in the London Bridge papers as enemies of the Crown.

'We never fully learn what changes agents' minds about their roles in the world. We only know that they do change. History is littered with the names of disillusioned defectors. Amelia set about wiping away all trace of the papers' existence. She knew she would become a suspect if she wasn't also targeted, so she made herself a Molotov cocktail and took a calculated tumble that went a bit over the top, landing her in hospital.

'Nobody saw Cranston in the King's Arms pub in Southwark because *he never went inside it*. He waited for Annie to come out. Amelia needed Annie to unlock the filing cabinet. She was a regular in the pub, unnoticed, invisible. When she left, she pepper-sprayed Cranston.

'To get out of the safe house Amelia tried another ruse from the secret service playbook. She answered the doorbell and hid inside the box sofa. She clumsily tried to implicate Cranston by leaving shoe prints, but found us receptive to almost anything that added to his guilt.

'The biggest subversives could now be removed, including, apparently, me. Our *Who's Who* of every dissident in the country became an assassination list. Ingrid Krause got caught up in the purge; she was just a bookkeeper but she linked everyone and had to go. Fear of betrayal is always accompanied by paranoia.'

Alvarez had not touched his dessert. 'Explain something I don't get,' he said. 'What made these contacts so high risk?'

'Tell me, Mr Alvarez, what do you know about the Spanish flu virus?'

Alvarez cast around for an answer. 'What everyone knows, I guess. It infected a third of the world's population.'

'Several of our informants were on the team that successfully recreated it in 2005. Mathematicians and scientists don't always consider human consequences. In the process of helping mankind they became dangerous, so in Amelia's eyes they had to be removed. And there are plenty of others on that list who represent a threat.'

'Which is why we need the papers from you,' said Alvarez.

'I had someone put it on a dongle-thing.' Bryant unlocked his briefcase and lifted out a black plastic stick. 'It's encrypted but you'll be sent the key.'

Alvarez held out his hand.

Bryant hesitated. 'There are many good people on these files. Only a very few pose any risk. I need your guarantee that they won't be pursued.'

The agent took the flash drive and slipped it smoothly into his jacket. 'You knew who they were but did nothing to stop them.'

'Nothing has happened yet.'

'That's not a good enough reason for not acting, not in today's world.' Alvarez rose from the table, looking like a man who was tired of dealing with idiots. 'Mr Bryant, Mr May, stay and enjoy the rest of the meal. There's no need to ask for the cheque. This is our company restaurant.'

Looking around, the detectives realized they were entirely surrounded by CIA agents. They were all enjoying the key lime pie.

48

BACK TO THE BRIDGE

Like most of the world's expensive thoroughfares, 5th Avenue was less interesting on foot, especially in its endless Central Park section, but Bryant insisted on strolling back to their hotel. They were leaving for London at seven the following morning and he wanted to enjoy his brief time in the city.

The night was warm and humid. Dog-walkers were wearing shorts. Bryant was wrapped in his favourite green scarf. He cracked pistachios in his false teeth. 'Do you think we can trust that fellow?'

'We don't have a choice,' May replied. 'Do you think Alvarez's people are going to start trawling through hundreds of names, trying to figure out which ones might become a liability?'

'You've met some of the informants. They're old and indiscreet and liable to say something they shouldn't. Amelia must always have been aware of that.' A shameless squirrel darted over Bryant's feet to snatch a fallen pistachio. 'I think she planned all of this a long time ago. They became a thorn in her side.'

As they walked, Bryant tapped his stick along the low stone wall of the park, thinking aloud. 'Eleanor Hamilton and Herbert Constantine. Scientists and anarchists, working together for decades. They co-authored a paper in *Nature* on population control. Herbert in particular felt the planet was too crowded to survive for much longer.'

'A lot of people feel that way,' said May.

'The difference is that he wanted to do something about it.'

'Like what?'

'He talked of culling the weak in order to strengthen the herd. You know, let the hyenas pick off the sick and the elderly. Eugenics reared its head and that was pretty much the end of both their careers. And then they died together. Herbert is being cremated the day after tomorrow. I dare say someone from the Serious Crime Command will be there watching the crowd. I'd like to go but I'm supposed to be meeting the editor of my memoirs. I suppose I could invite him along. You should come too. It'll be a nice day out.'

'I still remember that DIY funeral you invited me to where the coffin came apart on the pallbearers' shoulders. I'd never heard so many people scream in unison.'

'Come on, it'll take your mind off the fact that you're retired now, with nothing to do and nowhere to go except stay home and fall asleep watching Netflix, longing for the release that death will bring.'

'When you put it like that, how could I resist?' answered May.

And so Arthur Bryant found himself in Golders Green Crematorium, a North London building that had more than a touch of the Spanish hacienda about it, on an unfortunately sunsoaked afternoon with just a handful of the old familiar faces in attendance. Choosing to kill two birds with one stone, as it were, he had invited along the reluctant editor of his memoirs.

John May had mercifully managed to miss the service.

'How was it?' he asked as Bryant came stumping through the garden of remembrance towards him.

'Oh, maudlin, as per. An obscure Old Testament speech about laying waste to the wicked that Herbert would have hated, what with him being an atheist, and "My Heart Will Go On" played in the wrong key on some kind of electronic kazoo. I don't think you've met my editor.'

Simon Sartorius came over and shook May's hand heartily. 'I feel as if I know you. Your partner's descriptions are extremely vivid.'

'Oh dear.'

Simon looked about uncertainly. 'It's – ah – a rather unorthodox place to meet.'

'Yes,' May agreed. 'Welcome to my world.'

'Herbert's widow just remarried,' Bryant said. 'She organized his wake, a case of the marriage baked-meats coldly furnishing forth the funeral tables.' He laughed at his own joke. 'Do you want to go?'

'About as much as I want kidney dialysis,' said May.

'Oh, don't be a grump. It's at a house on Temple Fortune Lane. A fancy neighbourhood. We can walk there from here. This may be your last chance to poke fun at the Serious Crime Command. They'll be easy enough to spot, hovering around the sausage rolls. You up for a bit of nosh, Simon? Celebrate our new deal?'

'Gosh, not at the wake of someone I didn't know but thanks awfully. Perhaps another time.' He glanced ostentatiously at his watch. 'I think I should be getting . . . um.' He gave an awkward farewell wave and headed off across the lawn.

'Delightful chap,' said Bryant, watching him trip over a headstone.

The white-painted villa was set back from the road in a graceful horseshoe of mature elms. Cars had jammed the driveway so that the guests were forced to climb between bumpers. Inside the living room, incongruously upbeat nineties pop was playing through immense speakers. The wallpaper had vertical silver stripes, like prison bars. Four red leather sofas had been pushed back against the walls so that the wobblier mourners had somewhere to collapse.

'There they are,' said Bryant, pointing across the laden tables, 'the only two not togged up in funeral bling.'

The SCC undercover officers had not made much of an effort. Both were wearing standard-issue police shirts. The male was indeed stuffing his face with sausage rolls. The female was listening intently to one of the drunken old lags holding court in a corner. She held her phone low in her left hand.

'She's recording the conversation,' said May.

'Unfortunately, she's listening to the wrong one,' Bryant pointed out. 'I can pick up everything on this.' He touched the tiny flesh-coloured hearing aid behind his ear and nodded at three large sweating men on the patio. 'She should try those Congolese gentlemen, for example. And him in the corner, Herbert's oldest friend.'

He indicated a ravaged-looking bald man who looked like a heavy metal drummer who had finished his absolutely last world tour. 'That's Tony "Bones" Mahoney, his former accomplice and co-worker. I do believe he's on the pull.'

They watched as Mahoney breathed over his rather brassy lady friend. 'I'll save you a seat next to me on the coach, Evie, 'cause you're lovely,' he was telling her. 'You and I can have a little ride together.'

Bryant edged in, trying to look inconspicuous. If an elephant had joined the line-up in *Swan Lake*'s 'Danse des petits cygnes' it would have looked less conspicuous than Bryant did right now, but in the testosterone-powered heat of the moment, Mahoney only had eyes for the lovely Evie.

'It's only gonna take a few minutes, and we can go up the

Dog. It's a little boozer I know where we can celebrate Herbert's passing over a game of bar billiards, yeah?'

'Yeah, awright,' said the lovely Evie.

A few minutes later someone came into the living room and shrieked, 'The coach is here! It's here!' The mourners reluctantly began to search around for their belongings, disappointed to be leaving their drinks.

'Where are we going?' Bryant found the lovely Evie adjusting her fascinator in the hall mirror. As she jutted her jaw to reapply lipstick she reminded him of a deep-sea angler fish.

'We're gonna scatter Herbert's ashes,' she said. 'From London Bridge. It's what he wanted. He and Eleanor made their funeral plans ages ago.'

'How odd. Why would they have done that?'

'He was reeeeally specific,' said the lovely Evie, pouting in the mirror and pushing her breasts about. 'They were gonna share the urn.'

'Which urn?'

'I dunno, a special one. Herbert's widow, Freda, she's all upset because of the urn.'

'Oh really? Why?' Bryant lounged with one hand in his jacket pocket, insouciant.

'She didn't get to choose it. Herbert left it for her with strict instructions. She thinks it's hideous.'

'I thought all urns were the same.'

'No, he had this one made. You're not supposed to chuck ashes from London Bridge any more. Pollution, and passing boats. We're just going to cast a handful of him on to the waters, sort of symbolic. There's too much of him to throw over the side, anyway. You wouldn't wanna give a boatload of tourists a shovelful of his mortal remains.'

The coach was a shade of medical pink that reminded Bryant of Amelia Hoffman's filing cabinet. The detectives sat at the back of the vehicle as it set off and nosed down from

Golders Green to Finchley Road, listening to the mourners' memories.

'Eleanor and Herbert remained good friends even after they went to prison,' said Bryant.

'Why did they go to prison?' asked May.

'It started as a libel case but got out of hand. They were almost married in a circus once but their best man was arrested during the wedding rehearsal for inappropriately touching a clown. It turned out he had a history of coulrophilia.'

'Your informants lead unusual lives,' said May.

'They tend to choose paths that get them into trouble. There's a thin line between a Nobel Prize and a jail sentence.' He tapped the shoulder of the woman sitting in front of him and chatted amiably for a few minutes, returning with information. 'The widow says Herbert had his own urn specially made six years ago. Why would he have done that?'

'Some people like to plan ahead. I guess we'll find out in a few minutes.'

The coach sped on beneath a darkening sky, through the squared-off eloquence of St John's Wood, down to Lisson Grove and Baker Street. It was forced to park in a bay some way off from London Bridge, which was a nuisance as rain was announcing itself.

The group disembarked furtively. Smiles and jokes had evaporated. The ritual upon which they were about to embark had an atmosphere of illegality, as did several of its participants.

Freda, Herbert's newly married widow, her hair frosted golden for both occasions, stood by as the little group congregated around the railing of the bridge. Tony 'Bones' Mahoney managed to complete a few sentences without swearing, then read out a terrible poem written by his daughter.

Freda stepped from the protection of an umbrella and produced the urn, ready to whack a fistful of cinders over the side of the bridge in the direction of St Magnus the Martyr.

'Herbert, we release your soul to Old Father Thames and on to every one of the seven seas,' she cried, clearly unfamiliar with oceanography.

For the past minute or so Bryant had been shaking his head and muttering to himself. Now he stepped forward and pushed his way through the crowd. As everyone started to protest he showed what he hoped was his badge. Nobody paid him any attention.

'Don't open it,' he shouted.

Too late. Freda had unscrewed the lid, ready to reach into the urn and grab a palmful of ashes.

'Put the lid back on it, Freda.'

'No one's gonna know, just a handful.' She dared him to defy her.

'Put the lid on right now. Whatever you do, don't breathe it in.'

She was about to argue but the look in his eyes warned her off. She carefully closed the urn, then raised her right hand and examined it. It looked as if she had touched the contents.

Bryant was always cold, even on a summer's day. He was wearing gloves. He seized the moment and seized the urn.

Unfortunately it surprised him by being incredibly heavy and slipped out of his hands. For a moment it hung suspended over the side of the bridge. Bryant watched in horror as it fell.

At school, John May had always been teased about his long arms. Now his reach extended far enough that he was able to grab the urn and hold on tight, even if it meant going over the rail. Hands pulled at his coat and trousers but were too late to stop him from slipping away and falling.

Compared to its baroque counterparts along the Thames, the new London Bridge appears to be featureless concrete. Not entirely so, though, for if you look carefully you'll see a pair of tall stone pillars jutting from either side of the bridge's starlings.

May landed squarely on top of one, and only his quick reflexes prevented him from rolling off it and hitting the water. There was no way back up, so he hung on to the top of the pillar, clutching the urn to his chest, and waited.

Bryant turned to find himself facing an angry mob. The congregation, few of whom one would ever wish to meet on a dark night, were advancing on him. Even the lovely Evie looked less lovely and more like a predator of the deep. The Gentleman in Charge of Stealing Things from the Department of the Congolese Interior stepped forward and prepared for a scuffle.

'It's burning,' yelled Freda. She darted towards the others for help, only to find them backing away from her.

'Mrs Constantine, please remain still and keep your hands in the air,' Bryant called.

'Give the urn back, Arthur,' said Tony Mahoney.

'I don't have it.' Bryant raised his walking stick and backed up against the railing. 'It went over the side.'

The kleptocrat lunged forward and snatched at Bryant's voluminous coat, only to find himself holding a detached lapel.

Freda was in terrible pain. 'It's inside me,' she cried, trying to grab Evie.

'Don't touch her!' Bryant cried. 'Keep your hands away from everyone, don't touch anything.'

But Freda had touched the faces and arms of two other mourners, and now they were crying out in alarm.

'Do any of you have bottles of water?' asked Bryant. 'You must rinse every surface she's touched.'

Tony 'Bones' Mahoney threw Evian over Freda. Bryant emptied another bottle over her hands.

Bryant stole a glance over the side of the bridge and was gratified to see his partner crouched on top of the pillar with the urn still in his arms. 'John, you mustn't let the top come off.' He turned to the others. 'I'll explain everything if you just help me to get my partner up.'

The coach driver came through with a tow rope, which May was able to knot around himself. The funeral congregation turned out to be as strong as any tug-of-war team and hauled him over the railing.

Once May had been landed back on the bridge he disappointed the assembly by following his partner's lead and refusing to hand over the urn.

From behind them came a familiar double honk. Rita's taxi awaited just beyond the bridge barriers. May grabbed his partner's arm and virtually flew him to the safety of its passenger seat. Rita took off just as the mob started to surround the cab.

'Always you are making trouble and now sacrilegious with a funeral, why you do this?' Rita was staring angrily in the rear-view mirror at them.

'Arthur, she's right, what have you done? My chest hurts. It's hard to breathe.'

'Let's hope it's from your fall and not the toxin,' said Bryant. 'We'll get you checked out, just hang on for a few minutes more.'

His partner sat back as the urn rolled between them and the taxi raced away, scattering the funeral party.

'You want me to take you to a doctor?' Rita asked.

'No, get us to the Francis Crick Institute in St Pancras.' He carefully lifted the urn and handed it to May. 'Take a look at it, but whatever you do don't open it.'

'I thought it was a bomb.'

'In a way, it is,' said Bryant. While he made a call they headed up to the biomedical research centre behind St Pancras Station.

'When you examine this, make sure you follow the highest protection protocols,' Bryant instructed the biologist Jamel

Letheeto. 'I think whatever's in there is pathogenically transmissible.'

'Let's get your partner into isolation first,' said Jamel. He was an epidemiologist who had specialized in toxicity therapies before his nervous breakdown, and was a trusted friend of Bryant's. 'Do you want this kept off the books?'

Bryant saw that it would be a good idea to continue protecting his resources. 'Perhaps you could make the file non-electronic,' he suggested, handing Jamel his notepad, which had a stub of pencil attached to it on a length of string.

The biochemist subjected the urn to close scrutiny. It was steel and ceramic, hand-painted around the rim with Piranesian scenes of collapse and chaos. He turned it over. Bryant saw now that Eleanor Hamilton had signed the base. No wonder Herbert's widow had taken such a dislike to it.

Bryant watched from the other side of the glass as Letheeto headed to the testing apparatus in a white protective hazmat suit and slowly removed the urn's lid. It took him three-quarters of an hour to inspect the contents. He left the urn behind, sealed in heavy-duty sterile plastic, and emerged from his cocoon.

'Well, I didn't find anyone's remains. It contains a toxin I'm fairly certain will turn out to be a derivative of VX, the same nerve agent that was used to kill Kim Jong-nam in Kuala Lumpur Airport. It's fast and often fatal, but it's not a respiratory pathogen.'

'Why didn't it kill the woman who opened it?' asked Bryant.

'Probably because it takes longer to work through the palms of the hands,' Jamel replied. 'The skin is thickest there and the nerves are deep. We don't know what properties it has yet, or how hard it is to counteract.'

'It was what the CIA feared most,' said Bryant, 'that someone on the list would go rogue and do something utterly mad. It seemed like just the kind of operation Eleanor and Herbert would carry out. I was sure of it as soon as I heard he'd commissioned a special urn.' Bryant regarded the urn thoughtfully. 'Knowing the pair who designed this, I'm willing to bet it's already burned itself out. Eleanor and Herbert would have been more interested in firing off a warning shot than causing mass extinction.'

'Let's hope you're right,' said Jamel.

It took more than a week for Letheeto's team to uncover the true nature of the toxin, which was related to smallpox, something of a speciality area for Herbert Constantine. It contained a 'closed gate' reagent that prevented air transmission after exposure – but might easily not have done so.

'Quite a cocktail,' May remarked. 'I guess if they had intended to cause serious loss of life they would have got it to a more heavily populated city.'

'Herbert needed a foolproof delivery system that would make their warning public,' Bryant replied. 'Where better than at his own funeral? He managed to outwit the old ladies.'

'What made you so sure it was in there?'

Bryant gave a rueful smile. 'I always knew that the benefit of using my informants came with its own in-built threat. When you employ a loose cannon it's always a good idea to see what ammunition it can use.'

49

THE INNER CIRCLE

They met in Regent's Park.

Lately each day had been more glorious than the last. If the herbaceous borders were exuberant, the grand flowerbeds were positively overwrought. The detectives made their way through the riot of fuchsia, canary and indigo to the Inner Circle and waited for Paige Henderson to arrive.

'Why does she need two cars?' asked Bryant as he watched a pair of gleaming black Mercedes saloons draw up beside the kerb. A third car was discreetly idling outside a white pillared embassy opposite.

The pair of suited secret service men who emerged from the lead Mercedes had every reason to wear shades on such a bright day, but were transformed into Hollywood clichés in the process. Paige Henderson slid from the back seat but was still wearing her usual work clothes, which Bryant felt lacked a sense of occasion.

'Do you want to do this or shall I?' he asked May.

'I think you should, seeing as you're the one who unravelled Angela Carey's clues,' said May.

415

Bryant lifted the satchel from his partner's hand. 'Are you absolutely sure we took everything out of that drain?'

'Yes, and I followed your instructions.'

Bryant had asked him to remove twenty names from the London Bridge papers: the informants with whom he was still most in contact.

'And you have the key for the dongle-thing?'

'It's a flash drive, Arthur. Yes.'

'Wish me luck.'

He walked forward across the corner of the lawn and out on to the scorching pavement.

Henderson greeted the ambulatory jumble sale moving towards her without a flinch. 'Mr Bryant. A pleasure to see you again.'

'You'll be more pleased to see this, I suspect,' he said, raising his satchel. The pair of clichés slipped in on either side of him and lifted the bag. Bryant marvelled at them. 'Where do you find such people? Is there a special shop one goes to?'

'I don't suppose we'll be meeting again,' said Paige. 'I'm heading back to New York for good next week.'

Bryant made an attempt to look saddened. 'Oh well, one up for London.'

He stood politely waiting while she returned to the Mercedes. She carried on past it to the second vehicle as its blacked-out passenger window rolled down.

Inside sat someone whose face he had only seen in a newspaper: Sammi Jansome, the toastmistress from the ambassador's residence.

Jansome spoke briefly with Paige, then stared straight ahead. Just past her, against the far window, was Larry Cranston, sour-faced and sweating. The window slid shut and the vehicles slowly moved off.

'Did you see that?' cried Bryant as he rejoined May at the edge of the park. 'The dead girl! The CIA knew Cranston was on to something and needed to force him into action, so Henderson tricked him into thinking he'd killed someone.'

'How did they pull it off?' asked May, watching the cars go in amazement.

'They had to have switched her with an operative just before she got to the crossing. A fancy little field exercise, putting their own EMT on it.'

Bryant mentally slapped himself. He wondered what the toastmistress had been promised. A work permit? Somewhere to live? Protection for her daughter? Or just the threat of deportation?

He turned around on himself, furious. 'I missed a trick: the CCTV at Baker Street Station showed her in black pumps but the body under the Daimler was wearing trainers. The CIA couldn't have known she would change her footwear.' He followed the thought back. 'They got to Cranston before he could die. That's why there was no blood outside the room.'

'Then it looks like everyone got what they wanted,' said May.

'That depends. Cranston's at the mercy of the CIA now. He's being taken into the lion's den. They'll use him, then they'll lose him. There's no one who can help him get out of this one.'

May watched as a familiar portly figure clambered from a third car that had been idling outside the embassy. 'Well, well. Look who's here.'

Leslie Faraday glanced about himself uneasily, checking the scene one last time before hopping up the steps and disappearing inside the building. A minute later he was seen skulking at a first-floor window before ducking behind a curtain.

'Someone had to get the charges dropped in the UK and make sure the prosecution was delayed,' said May.

'What a turn-out.' Bryant thrashed at the grass with his stick. 'Every single one of them. How could I have been such a fool? We never stood a chance. We were set up right from the start, possibly from the birth of the unit.'

'You shouldn't be surprised, old chap,' said May. 'We always knew we were fighting the establishment.'

'Was somebody watching decades ago when we first began using informants? We're the only ones left on the outside looking in.' He pointed to the street sign with his walking stick. 'No wonder the whole charade began and ended here.'

It read: 'The Inner Circle'.

50

MR BRYANT AND MR MAY SAY GOODBYE

As Charles II once pointed out, the British summer consists of three fine days and a thunderstorm, and so it proved again this year.

A week after the toxin was identified at the Francis Crick Institute, the PCU members assembled outside their old building's boarded entrance in a state of mystification. Rain lightly sheened the Caledonian Road, turning the Caithness flagstones of its pavements a deep glittering grey. Unconcerned, the patrons of the bar opposite stood outside in floral Bermuda shorts and flip-flops, their hands protecting their beers from being watered down. They watched in bemusement as Raymond Land raised his hands to get everyone's attention and was ignored.

'You're probably wondering why I've asked you all here,' he began.

'You're going to pay us.' This was from Dan, who found himself laughing alone.

'There's been a rather surprising development,' said Land.

'Mr Bryant's swung it and we're back?' Meera asked.

'I'm afraid not. The Home Office has washed its hands of us. We rather burned our bridges there.' Everyone started talking again. 'BUT – but there is a way we can still operate. However, you would have to all agree to it.'

'Well – what?' asked Dan. 'Stop dragging it out.'

'We become a private unit,' said John May, stepping forward. 'A self-funding outsource. It's a project my partner has been working on for some time. The government seems quite enthusiastic about the idea. They like not having to pay for public services. It seems they'd much rather hand over twice as much to the private sector.'

'How would we self-fund?' asked Meera. 'Who would pay us?'

'We bill the government a flat fee for each successful inves-´ tigation,' said Bryant, joining his partner in front of them. 'The cases will be assigned by a senior liaison officer from the Met, with an annual amount raised from private subscription, set aside for wages.'

'Why should we do that?' asked Colin.

'It would take us back to our roots.'

'It would still be us and them, with someone like Darren Link lording it over us.'

'No, because this time our go-between would be someone we know and trust' – Bryant held out his hand – 'and love.'

Janice Longbright stepped forward.

She had saved her Max Factor Bowanga Rouge lipstick (discontinued 1958) for just such a moment. 'I'll be your liaison officer,' she said. 'It's time for another member of the family to start pounding the streets. My feet are big enough as it is. I'll still be there, but this time I'll be controlling you all, and it's about time.'

She shot Sidney a smile. 'If my daughter gets too big for her boots, you can remind her that she wasn't named after the actress Sylvia Sidney. She was named after Sid James.'

'Oh, cheers for that,' said Sidney. 'The ugly comedian with the dirty laugh.'

'I was a big fan of his at the time,' said Janice with a shrug of apology.

'We still wouldn't have a home,' Meera said, ever the pragmatist. 'We can't all keep coming round to your flat to work.'

There was a crash and a small tsunami of dust as the chipboard cover to the building's entrance fell down. Arthur Bryant stepped forward, batting dirt from his coat sleeves.

'You wouldn't have to,' he said. 'It seems we have a benefactor to thank.' From behind him stepped Fatima Hamadani. 'Fatima found working for Mr Faraday a not entirely fulfilling experience.'

'You all know what he's like.' She looked around uncertainly. 'I put up with his . . . can I say "shit"?'

'Oh yes,' said Bryant. 'We're all terribly fond of swearing as creatively as possible.'

'I put up with – it – for seven years,' she told them. 'I thought I was moving towards promotion, but all Mr Faraday ever did was insult me. He is an ignorant man. So I want to help you.'

'Fatima, tell them what *you* did,' Bryant coaxed.

'I bought your building.'

She became aware that they were all staring at her. 'Strictly speaking my father did, but I persuaded him that it was a good investment. The freehold was less than we thought because too many people know what's wrong with the place.'

They guessed that she was probably referring to the fires, collapses, detonations, corpses, contagious diseases and rumours of ghosts that had all at some time afflicted the building's wonky rooms, but in fact Fatima was alluding to the impractical shape that made it unsuitable for turning into flats. It was the newly gentrified neighbourhood's only truly undesirable property.

'A certain amount of investment money has been set aside to make it habitable again,' said Fatima, 'so there's no reason why you shouldn't start work within the month. It's important that none of this gets back to Mr Faraday.'

'You can count on us to be souls of discretion,' said May.

'It seems an old book can still have new chapters,' said Bryant, who knew a thing or two about old books.

'Just give me one straight answer,' Colin begged. 'Is this for real or, like, a dream or something?'

'It could be a dream,' said Bryant. 'Reality is overrated.'

Over the last three generations the Mangeshkar family had risen in the world but Rasika Mangeshkar was far from happy. Her first daughter and her son had disappointed her with bad marriages and weak characters and her husband merely wanted to be left alone with the cricket scores.

Her hopes had been pinned on her youngest, Meera, but she had let them all down by joining the police force, which was an immoral profession, like nursing. Rasika knew it was a rather old-fashioned viewpoint these days but she felt it was wrong that a young woman should be out in male company all hours of the night. Nurses were worse because they often did not come home until dawn and even though they were working, what were respectable bachelors supposed to think?

Now Meera was bringing a colleague to tea. Since Rasika fancied that she knew her daughter's every thought, she was sure this young man was being presented to her as a prospective husband. Being from a proudly traditional background she would smile graciously and use her best cake stand, and serve masala chai and lassi with *vada pav* or Mumbai sandwiches and perhaps some fig and goat cheese parathas. Best not to be too extravagant, though, because she did not want him thinking he had the upper hand and could be a lazy fellow letting the parents do all the work.

When she saw him she wished she had not used her best china.

He was enormous, a great blond fleshy lump of a man with hands like boxing gloves and feet like a circus clown's.

'Cheers for having me,' he told her, pumping her hand vigorously and seating himself in a chair that might possibly not hold his weight. He took up too much space in the living room. She should have moved the tea to the conservatory.

Rasika addressed her daughter, keeping the conversation as light as possible, but could not resist asking how long they had known each other and whether they enjoyed their work and – and—

'Why don't you just come out with it and ask him?' Meera snapped finally. 'You know you're dying to.'

'Meera, please remember we have a guest.' She turned to Colin. 'But since the subject has been raised . . .'

For the next twenty-two minutes she outlined her vision for her daughter's future, which involved leaving the police, marrying a doctor, learning to cook and being a good wife and mother, for which Meera would need a minimum of four children and a large home in which to house them all, for Rasika planned on coming to live with them one day when her husband finally visited the great cricket pavilion in the sky.

Finally Colin had had enough.

'I appreciate your concern, Mrs Mangeshkar, but it's my job to decide with my wife how we will choose to lead our lives.'

Rasika attempted to turn Colin to stone with her stare, but the young officer held his ground. 'A mother has every right to stop her daughter from making mistakes she will regret,' she said firmly.

'Then we have different views of mothers,' said Colin.

'Why don't you tell me about your mother, Mr Bimsley.' Rasika sat back, folded her arms and waited.

Colin cleared his throat nervously. 'When I was nine, my mother came to my room all dressed up. She announced that she was leaving us. She stood before me and took my hand, and said she would probably never see me again because she was going far away with someone she'd met. And just as I was trying to understand this, she looked at me with her head on one side and beckoned me close and whispered so that my father couldn't hear. May I tell you what she said?'

Rasika could only nod.

'My mother said to the nine-year-old me, "I wish I'd never had you, because you took away my best years." For a long time after I felt ashamed for making her so unhappy. But then I realized I had nothing to be ashamed about. I discovered that there was another kind of mother who is capable of feeling nothing but love and gratitude for her child. I can see that you're the other kind and I hope in time you will come to think of me as your son.'

There, he thought, like one of the two Daves fixing a shelf in place with a couple of dodgy screws, *that should hold it for a while*. Meera glared at him but behind her scowl was relief.

As it was his day for helping out at the local hospital, he left Meera with her family to talk things over. He was walking towards the tube when he found the card in his pocket. There was no envelope. On the front was a gloomy painting of a wreath. The word 'Condolences' had been crossed out and replaced with 'Congratulations'.

He recognized the Babylonian scratches inside: the boss's handwriting. It said: 'May I be the first to wish you both every happiness in the world, even before you are conjugally matrimonified. Mr Bryant.'

How could the old man have known? There was a PS.

' "Matrimonified" is not a made-up word. W. S. Gilbert uses it in *The Pirates of Penzance*.'

Laughing, he put the card back into his pocket and headed down the tube station steps.

*

Bryant and May walked together without feeling the need to speak of a destination, down through the city from King's Cross to the ironically named Mount Pleasant, across the lawns of Spa Fields heading south.

They stopped before a busy restaurant called Swan & Edgar, tastefully painted in grey and cream, and studied the menu.

'Courgette, butternut and thyme cannelloni under a tahini and lemon glaze with kimchi and Japanese radish,' Bryant read out. 'Eighteen pounds.'

Cupping his hands around his eyes, he pressed his face against the window, giving the diners inside a fright. 'There's nobody in there over thirty. This one's not for the likes of us, even if we could afford it. Pretty rooms though. I don't suppose any of them realize it's named after a grand Piccadilly Circus department store founded in 1812.'

'They don't need to,' said May with a smile. 'Only you need to know that.'

'If I had been born in York or Liverpool or Manchester I would do the same thing,' he replied, 'dig into the past to increase my understanding of the present. I'm not sure if it's a gift or a curse.'

May stepped back a little, the better to observe the specimen before him. 'How do you do it?' he asked.

Bryant's aqueous eyes widened. 'Do what?'

'That thing. You never try to be something you're not. In any situation you have the same social ease. Why is that?'

Bryant pulled a face. 'What brought this on?'

'All the people you dealt with on this case. You don't care what they think of you.'

'I don't.'

'Why not?'

'If they like me they'll say what I want to hear. They won't tell me the truth.'

'And the truth is important.'

'Only for the case. In the lives of Londoners there are no absolute truths.'

The parts of the city they loved best were all walkable if you knew the shortcuts. As the sun began to sink they headed across Waterloo Bridge, past the busking musicians and pavement artists, past the man in the Edwardian tailcoat and top hat who played a flaming tuba, through the raucous fairground crowds of the South Bank. The sky was burnished copper, trimmed with clouds like crushed roses.

Arthur found himself thinking, for the first time in a very long while, about the future. 'I'm thrilled to know that the unit will survive, not for me but for all those who rely on it. I want people to know the truth about Angela Carey. When I go to St Martin's Lane and look at the statue of Dame Edith Cavell, I think of the words she spoke before her execution. "Patriotism is not enough. I must have no hatred or bitterness for anyone." It's London's watch-cry. Angela's duty is ours now; we must guard our kindred spirits and make sure they're not badly used.'

They bought coffees and wandered back on to Waterloo Bridge.

John stopped when they reached the centre and stuck his hands in his pockets, looking out at the ruffling umber waters. 'We may have to take on the kind of cases you hate. It won't be like it was. At least now we'll have some control over the process, with Janice feeding us leads and Fatima controlling our cash flow.'

He talked on with growing enthusiasm for the new arrangement, describing how they could set everything up to suit their needs, but as Charles II's storm moved in above them May's voice gradually grew fainter and city sounds crowded the electric air – not the muted low roar of today but the voices of yesterday and the day before, and the years before that.

Bryant rubbed at his temple. The city overwhelmed him.

He had been ready to make a resigned peace with the world but the worst possible thing had happened: he had been offered a sliver of hope for the future.

A group of smartly attired millennials drifted past them, shiny faces anticipating the pleasures of a summer night. Such people saved the city from itself, the majority being predisposed to kindness and willing, after some initial wariness, to offer anyone a helping hand. He watched them with curiosity and appreciation.

When the feeling of temporal disorder returned this time it felt much more intense than before, an escalation of the sensory disconnection he had grown to fear. Around him swam imperfectly remembered faces, names, streets, buildings. He closed his eyes and they crowded in. His first meeting with an absurdly fresh-faced John May in Bow Street.

'*Panic in the streets is an image that scares the hell out of them. We're to be more of a propaganda unit than a detective squad.*'

A jump through the decades to his healing stay in Wimbledon Buddhist Temple.

'*I've had a great time and I adored the food. Nobody ever gets fed up with pad thai.*'

In the carcass chambers beneath Smithfield Market, talking down a murderer by discussing bicycle death statistics and Shakespeare, Colin holding a pig's grinning head by one huge ear.

John May being shot and left for dead on the floor of his office. A sense of all things ending.

A rivulet of rainwater weighing down a single hornbeam leaf, the perfect teardrop falling on to the pale upturned face beneath it, death sudden and shocking in a London park.

Erroneously projecting a police safety film entitled *Autopsies: What Can Go Wrong?* to a darkened classroom full of terrified toddlers.

A particular smell, brackish and complex but not unpleasant, like moss, mud and wet bricks. The tide of the Thames, gently flopping, a woman chained to a post, the water blooming around her free arm, momentarily restoring it to life.

A phrase: *We go on.*

Incendiary riots outside the Bank of England, police battened down beneath the burning buildings like a phalanx of tensed wasps. He and May in the middle of it all, looking for a firebrand murderer.

We go on to the end because it's what we do.

St Bride's Church bathed in lunchtime sunlight, a young woman lying on the polished marble floor. Schoolchildren thinking they'd killed a witch.

Dr Gillespie telling him to act his age. '*If I did that, I'd be dead.*'

A dead child, a Mr Punch puppet lying on a nursery floor, the only suspect in an impossible murder. Tragedy and grotesquery always hand in glove.

'*I do not wish to choose a "type" of coffee, madam, I don't care if it's been boiled through an aardvark's entrails, I want a cup of plain tea, leaves not bags, whole milk, no sugar, as strong as a priest's breath.*' He had always been difficult.

Walking dank tunnels on a hunt for a maniac. Searching through the maze of alleys and backstreets in Soho, Southwark, Bermondsey and Bow. Secret societies, underground rivers, forgotten music halls, hidden pubs and clubs, crafty old London hiding itself behind veils of class and wealth. The rich protected, the poor exposed.

John having the audacity to date a Frenchwoman. Bryant trying to congratulate him. '*She's very nice for a divorced bottle-blonde alcoholic.*'

Colin charging after an offender like a centre forward, Meera on her Kawasaki, Dan rewiring his drone, Janice with a house brick in her handbag and ever-hopeful Raymond just looking for a little respect.

Gladys to Janice to Sidney, the mothers to the children, vocations and habits passed down through the years.

The endless arguments about taxidermy and necromancy with Maggie Armitage as she sorted through her mummified pets. '*You'd be amazed how much gas a cat can hold.*'

Reversing all the way to Mornington Crescent, where the unit made its home behind the glossy maroon tiles of the tube station, and to Bow Street, once an elegant magistrates' court, now sold to Qatari developers.

Fighting authority, fighting the government, fighting everyone all the time, his stubbornness sticking up like a rock in a stream.

Back to Camden Town in the sixties, May dressed in a Regency collar and flared loons, girls in shimmering mini-skirts, the streets painted red and blue and sunflower yellow.

Down through the years of grimy austerity, all the way to the Palace Theatre, where a friendship was forged to last a lifetime.

And to his childhood in Whitechapel, the years scattering like dead leaves. The clatter of horses' hooves seeking purchase on wet roads. The cries of rag-and-bone men. His father on the street corner, always one eye out for the law, bringing home a monkey he bought from a sailor who warned him, 'It's a bit of a biter.' His mother sweating in the steam of the washing, wringing out her neighbours' laundry. His poor bewildered brother hiding in the rusting Anderson shelter.

Did it all really happen the way he remembered? How much had been real, how much fantasy?

The past receded, the rocking ground steadied itself, the city returned to sharp focus, the last of the saffron sunlight suffused beneath a bar of indigo cloud.

'Mxcvw qrasdk jnpisq?' asked May.

'I'm sorry?'

'I said you've had a bit of a turn, old fellow, are you all right?'

'Thank God for that, I thought for a minute we were using code.' He looked down and patted himself. 'I have a button missing.'

'You're looking awfully pale. I think I should get you home.'

He held May's arm. Suddenly it was very important not to leave.

'I didn't hand them the names,' he said.

'What are you talking about?' asked May.

'The London Bridge papers. The so-called originals I gave the CIA. I got them from the bottom of one of my crates. I had to age up a few of them with cold tea and cat litter.'

'What on earth did you give them?'

'A complete list of Marylebone Cricket Club members for the year 1823, plus a full account of their various hobbies. They'll have quite a bit of trouble tracking everyone down. The dongle-thingy has several old episodes of *The Avengers* on it. The Emma Peel episodes, obviously.'

May's mouth closed and opened. 'I don't know what to say. I don't know if what you've done is a good or a bad thing.' He tried to think and gave up.

'The price of freedom is eternal vigilance,' said Bryant. 'Generally ascribed to Thomas Jefferson but first coined in 1770 by the Lord Mayor of Dublin. It's our duty, John. Someone must always keep watch over London.'

May decided to hail a passing cab for them, but it was best to do so at the foot of the bridge. He left Bryant alone at the railing.

Bryant studied the living diorama before him with an intensity that would have made anyone think he was taking it in for the very last time. Waterloo Bridge at twilight on the span of the Thames. Everything was laid out neatly, as if built in a shoebox.

The river was high and bronze. The setting sun had turned the city's towers to gold leaf. The residents flooded across, around, over and under the bridge in a never-ending tide. They arrived on foot, on boats and buses, as indifferent as the wind, unstoppable and unrepentant.

And just as his thoughts took a troubled turn, here before him once more was John May, as neat and reliable as an undertaker in his elegant black raincoat. 'The taxi's waiting for us back there when you're ready,' he said.

Bryant sat on the edge of the railing and rested for a moment. Suddenly feeling very tired, he gently set his walking stick to one side, placed his hands on his knees and breathed in the river air.

The wind made his eyes water. He looked up and smiled. He was surrounded by wonderful dreams, and they were all it took to make his little life complete.

'I was thinking,' said May. 'Before we start our new venture we should take a little time off. We've never done that, either of us. Go somewhere utterly different from London, some-where with minarets and souks. Or Liverpool. I've never been. The time was never right, but perhaps it is now. Although I'm not getting back in your car. It's time Victor was retired. We could get Rita to take us. What do you think?'

The dusk had not quite shaded into night, but suddenly the bridge lights flickered and came on. Looking towards the South Bank, he saw white necklaces racing between the dol-phin lamp-posts, all along the river's edge, until the city shores were entirely illuminated.

May's smile faded. 'Arthur?'

When he failed to receive a reply he tapped his partner on the shoulder. There was no response. He looked down and saw that Bryant's homburg had settled over his eyes.

'Are you all right?'

Dropping to one knee, he pressed a hand inside Arthur's

coat but felt nothing. A piece of paper with a single fold protruded from his shirt pocket. He took it out and unfolded it.

It read: 'GNOM.'

Commuters on their phones hurried past, failing to notice either of them.

'No,' said John. 'You can't do this now. We still have work to do.'

The taxi waited patiently. The crowds flooded past. The detectives might have been entirely alone.

He rose to his feet, a hand still resting on Arthur's shoulder. 'What was it all for?' he asked.

The answer was right in front of him. The people of London weaved their way across the bridge like shoals of fish in a never-ending stream.

He turned back to the slumped figure and carefully straightened his homburg. 'Oh, Arthur,' he said softly. 'Good Night, Old Man.'

It looked as if, in the perfect contentment of the summer evening, Arthur Bryant had simply fallen asleep, tiptoeing away without fuss or fanfare to search for his place among the stars. The city was too bright to reveal them, but everyone knew they would always be there.

Bryant and May for ever

ACKNOWLEDGEMENTS

When my mother finished reading the third Bryant & May novel, I asked her for her opinion. Closing the cover with finality she said, 'I think you've mined out that particular seam, dear.' For her, a crime novel was a sealed room and some suspects. She didn't appreciate that through them you could reflect the whole of life. On one level they must provide a satisfying mystery, but on another they're a Trojan horse in which to smuggle all kinds of peculiar and wonderful notions. I hadn't imagined that two elderly detectives would continue to unravel London's mysteries for two full decades – more if you count their non-canonical appearances in novels like *Rune* and *Soho Black*, or in their graphic novel *The Casebook of Bryant & May*.

With me from the beginning, shepherding Bryant & May into public view and keeping their wayward author on track, Simon Taylor has gone far beyond his editorial brief, becoming their mentor, archivist and ever-patient minder. I'd be lost without Anne Speyer, Kate Samano and Richenda Todd, who accepted the challenge of making this patchwork quilt appear smooth and seamless, improving the text in every way. Every writer should understand just how much a good editorial team can bring to a book. My agent James Wills also goes further; I've lost count of the long conversations we've had about structure and balance in novels. My perspicacious New York agent Howard Morhaim is someone I wish I'd met much earlier in my career. Over the years, Mandy Little has shown extraordinary kindness and patience with me. The whole experience has been driven by passionate, artistic people, not marketeers or number-crunchers. Each of them has proven to me that publishing is more than a business.

I had always known that the Bryant & May storyline would eventually bring me full circle, right back to the start. So, is it truly over? Not quite. I may still have a surprise up my sleeve.

Find me on Twitter @peculiar or on www.christopherfowler. co.uk

Christopher Fowler is the multiple-award-winning author of almost fifty novels and short-story collections, including the Bryant & May mysteries. His other novels include *Roofworld*, *Spanky*, *The Sand Men* and *Little Boy Found*. He has also written two acclaimed memoirs, *Paperboy* (winner of the Green Carnation Prize) and *Film Freak*, plus *The Book of Forgotten Authors*. In 2015 he won the CWA Dagger in the Library for his body of work. He lives in London and Barcelona, and blogs at www.christopherfowler.co.uk. Twitter: @Peculiar

 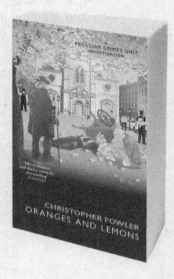

From *Full Dark House* to *Oranges and Lemons*, there are nineteen not-to-be-missed Bryant & May books to discover. All are available in paperback and digital editions.

www.christopherfowler.co.uk
Twitter: @Peculiar

Discover Christopher Fowler's gloriously entertaining memoirs

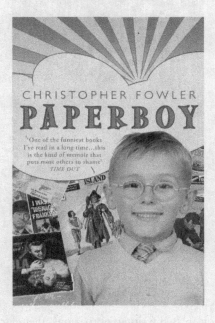

PAPERBOY

'One of the funniest books I've read in a long time . . . this is the kind of memoir that puts most others to shame'
Time Out

'Anyone who remembers Mivvis, jamboree bags, streets with no cars, Sid James and vast old Odeons will love this Sixties retro-fest'
Independent on Sunday

'The book is fabulous, and I hope it sells forever'
Joanne Harris

'Paper-dry wit, natural charm, brutally funny anecdotes – Fowler's likeable memoir unearths the trail that led the schoolboy to become a writer'
Evening Standard

'Entrancing, funny, deeply moving and wonderfully written. Please read it'
Elizabeth Buchan

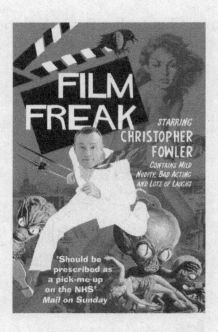

FILM FREAK

'Gold-plated writing: uproarious, then dark,
and surprisingly moving' *****
Mail on Sunday

'An homage to pre-digital cinema, an elegy for a
vanishing London . . . a tribute to friendship, gonzo-style.
Two thumbs up for this triple billing'
Financial Times

'Charming, funny, perceptive . . . I found myself laughing loudly
and lengthily. Above all, though, I was moved'
Daily Mail

'Brisk, chatty . . . trenchantly funny . . . he's so entertaining'
Daily Telegraph

'A master storyteller . . . a beautifully written and
often hilarious book'
Sunday Express

Both titles are available in paperback and ebook

Watch out for Bryant and May's guide to the city that lies at the heart of their twenty-book career: London (as you've very likely never seen it before) . . .

BRYANT & MAY'S PECULIAR LONDON

As the nation's oldest serving detectives, we know more about London than almost anyone. After all, we've been walking its streets and impulsively arresting its citizens for decades. Who better to take you through its less savoury side?

We'll be chatting about odd buildings, odder characters, lost venues, forgotten disasters, confusing routes, dubious gossip, illicit pleasures and hidden pubs. We'll be making all sorts of odd connections and showing you why it's almost impossible to separate fact from fiction in London.

With the help of some of our most disreputable friends, each an argumentative and unreliable expert in his or her own dodgy field, we'll explain why some streets have genders, why only two Londoners got to meet Dracula, how a department store and a prison both played tricks on your mind, when a theatre got stranded in the past, how a building vanished in plain sight, where the devils hide in London, and what excited Charlotte Brontë about the city.

We hope to capture something of the city's restless spirit by shamelessly and wilfully wandering off course. It goes without saying that we'll bluff and bamboozle you along the way but that's all part of the fun. History is what you remember. London is what you forget (and we've forgotten a lot). So please do join us on our magical mystery tour of our city. Who knows where we'll end up?